The
Green Man's
Quarry

The Green Man's Quarry
Juliet E. McKenna

WIZARD'S TOWER

Wizard's Tower Press

Rhydaman, Cymru

The Green Man's Quarry

First edition, published in the UK October 2023
by Wizard's Tower Press

Paperback ISBN: 978-1-913892-64-7

Cover illustration and design by Ben Baldwin
Editing by Toby Selwyn
Design by Cheryl Morgan
Consultants: Shona Kinsella & Liz Williams

No AI tools were used in the creation of the text or cover art
of this book.

http://wizardstowerpress.com/
http://www.julietemckenna.com/

Contents

For Ben

Praise for the Green Man Series

I'm here to be your good bookfriend and express my own quiet but fervent enthusiasm for this contemporary folkloric fantasy series. You should take the plunge, the water is fine if full of terrifying naiads and nixes. — Imyril on *There's Always Room for One More*

The series of Green Man novels goes from strength to strength, bringing a modern fantastical sensibility to traditional folk tales and things that go bump in the night. — Ben Jeapes on Goodreads

Praise for The Green Man's Heir

Finalist for The Robert Holdstock Award for Best Fantasy Novel, the British Fantasy Awards 2019

"... any way you look at it, the book is a delight from start to finish. [...] It's one of my favorite books so far this year." — Charles de Lint in *Fantasy and Science Fiction*

"I read this last night and thoroughly enjoyed it, more please!" — Garth Nix on Twitter

"I really enjoyed this novel!" — Kate Elliott on Twitter

JULIET E. MCKENNA

"Juliet McKenna captures the nuances of life as a stranger in a small town in much the same way as Paul Cornell does in his splendid Lychford series, with the local gossips, the hard-pressed police, the rampaging boggarts and rural legends come to disturbing life. Thoroughly enjoyable; a UK fantasy author branching out (oh god, sorry for the inadvertent and terrible pun!) and clearly having a great time doing it. Highly recommended." — Joanne Hall

"So far up my street it could be my house." — K.J. Charles on Goodreads

"*The Green Man's Heir* is a thoroughly engaging, at times almost impossible to put down, tale which, despite besides its titular character, is peopled with an impressive array of interesting and intriguing women." — *The Monday Review*

"After a stumbling start, I found myself unable to put down *The Green Man's Heir*. If you're looking for a book to read on your summer holiday, then this is it." — Charlotte Bond via The British Fantasy Society

The Green Man's Heir is a straightforward fantasy story, with a lively pace and characters who wonderfully come alive. It starts as *Midsomer Murders* set in the Peak District but with added supernatural element and turns out to be the book you won't put down because you enjoy it too much." — *The Middle Shelf*

"I hope this turns into a series. I'd love to read more about Daniel's adventures." — N.W. Moors in *The Antrim Cycle*

"And she has absolutely nailed it. This is a complete and utter joy." — S.J. Higbee in *Brainfluff*

"I'm certainly on board for reading more such novels." — Paul Weimer in *Skiffy and Fanty*

"Brilliant concept, compellingly told" — Virginia Bergin on Twitter

Praise for The Green Man's Foe

Finalist for Best Novel,
the British Science Fiction Awards 2020

"I loved *The Green Man's Heir*, and while I expected to thoroughly enjoy *The Green Man's Foe*, I did not expect it to be even more satisfying than its forerunner. Which was foolish of me, I admit – I should know by now that McKenna is more capable of outdoing her previous tales in a series." – *The Monday Review*

"If you've read the first book then I'm pretty confident you're going to love this one, and if you haven't read the first one then you need to remedy that straight away." – Naomi Scott

"This is one of my outstanding reads of the year." – S.J. Higbee in *Brainfluff*

"*The Green Man's Foe* is a great addition to what is becoming a great series. I was entirely caught up in it for a couple of days. It is a must read if you have enjoyed the first one, and a great reason to start on this series if you have missed it." – *The Middle Shelf*

JULIET E. MCKENNA

"*The Green Man's Foe* is a tasty serve of mystery and myth that has done quite enough to cement this series as one I'll be reading and cheerleading for from now on." – Imyril at *There's Always Room for One More*.

"What I loved reading this tale is how genuinely real McKenna makes the story feel." — Matt at *Runalong the Shelves*

Praise for The Green Man's Silence

"These Green Man books provide a wonderful blend of British folklore and ordinary people trying their best to make the world — or at least their corner of it — a better place. The characters are likeable, while the mythical creatures are earthy, dangerous, and full of that Sense of Wonder that makes fantasy such a pleasure to read. Recommended." — Charles de Lint, *Fantasy & Science Fiction*

"Highly recommended for fantasy fans who are looking for well-written fae adventures with a difference." — S J Higbee in *Brainfluff*

"This is undoubtedly one of the best books I've read this year and I thoroughly enjoyed it. I can hardly wait for the next book!" — *The Monday Review*

Praise for The Green Man's Challenge

Finalist for Best Novel,
the British Science Fiction Awards 2022

"I don't usually review every book in a series, but I'm so taken by this one by McKenna that I want to keep touting its

virtues so that people will, I hope, buy each one of them." —
Charles de Lint in *Fantasy & Science Fiction*

"Wowee! That was one hell of a ride. A fantastic ride, both
the main tale and the bonus short story at the end." — Pers at
Goodreads

"It is also a delight to read a novel written by someone who
knows her genre so well and works at finding different ways
to exploit its tropes. The threat in *The Green Man's Challenge* is
a giant: the hero doesn't have the strength to match the foe,
so other ways must be found, ancient knowledge must be
discovered again. By doing so, McKenna consciously subverts
the expectations of a certain kind of fantasy: no lone hero,
no unbelievable physical prowesses, no amazing powers (po-
litical or supernatural)." — *The Middle Shelf*

"Ms McKenna has a glorious sense of place" — Jacey Bedford

McKenna has brilliantly utilised the likes of the giant figures
cut into chalk hillsides and some of the numerous folk stories around hares to add to her intriguing Brit rural fantasy
tale. — S.J. Higbee in *Brainfluff*

Praise for The Green Man's Gift

"If you've enjoyed the previous Green Man books, then
you'll enjoy this one without a doubt. If you haven't read
them yet... What are you waiting for?" — *The Middle Shelf*

"The Green Man's Gift [...] is another excellent tale in one of the most interesting contemporary fantasy series around." — *Runalong the Shelves*

"As ever, McKenna writes an absorbing, utterly compelling tale." — *The Monday Review*

Highly recommended. You could start here, but I recommend you do yourself a favour and read the whole lot in order. — Jacey Bedford

Author's Note

Towards the end of this story, Dan encounters a language he doesn't speak. Rather than break the flow adding footnotes with translations, these can be found after the final page.

Chapter One

Folk tales have some things in common with uncanny creatures. Local legends can tell the truth, but that won't necessarily be the full story. Even so, things I learn from folklore can come in handy when I come across something going bump in the night. I can see the eerie creatures and supernatural folk who live unsuspected alongside ordinary people, in remote woods and in narrow valleys cut by tumbling rivers, in caves and hollow hills. I can see them because my mother is a dryad who fell in love with my ordinary, human dad.

So I didn't have a typical childhood. We lived in a solitary cottage beside a Warwickshire nature reserve, a mile or so from the nearest village. This wasn't a problem as far as I was concerned. Kids accept that what they grow up with is normal. I knew my mum was different, but mostly that meant I knew she would never tell me lies. Some of my school friends had parents who told them all sorts of rubbish. Father Christmas and his elves making toys in Lapland? Seriously?

I trusted Mum when she told me not to talk about the boggarts and sprites and the other creatures we could see. By the time I was six or seven, I realised that most people wouldn't understand. Not everyone who couldn't see these things was as understanding as my dad.

By the time I was a teenager, I started listening out for what Mum *didn't* say when I asked her an awkward question. I've met a few more dryads since then. I've discovered they're experts at dodging straight answers as well.

So I hadn't bothered asking anyone for advice after an old Welsh woman called Annis Wynne said something unnerving to me last summer. I hadn't even given it much thought. All right, to be absolutely honest, I had decided I wasn't going to think about it. That had been easy enough to do as long as I had plenty of tasks to keep my hands and my thoughts occupied.

Blithehurst House, where I live and work, is a small, privately owned Tudor manor run as a visitor attraction in the countryside where Staffordshire blends into the Peak District. It's the ancestral home of the Beauchene family. They've owned the land since it was given to a Norman knight as his reward for following William the Conqueror over to beat up Harold and the Saxons at Hastings. Over the centuries, local pronunciation has turned their name into Beechen, but it's still spelled the same.

When I'd got back from Wales last summer, the tourist season had been at its height, so I'd been busy. I helped out directing traffic when the car park filled up. I took my turn keeping an eye on visitors wandering around the gardens and exploring the medieval ruins by the river. You'd be sur- prised how often some tourist does something dangerous or destructive. They seem to think warning signs don't apply to them. I politely tell them different. I'm six foot four. Eleanor, my boss and the Beauchene who runs the business these days, has to order my Blithehurst House staff sweatshirts in XXL. People get the idea pretty fast, especially when I'm not smiling.

As summer turned to autumn, visitor numbers eased off. I filled my time making wooden trinkets for the gift shop. I like to carve birds and animals and other decorative pieces from offcuts and fallen wood I find around the estate. I make larger pieces for the garden centre, which stays open all year round. I'm a carpenter and joiner by trade. My cut of those sales is a useful bonus on top of my basic pay for managing the estate's woodlands.

Then there were the weekend craft fairs at Blithehurst in the run-up to Christmas. By then, the house was closed to visitors, but there was routine maintenance to be done around the manor, and in the old ruins. I look after other estate buildings that the public never get to see. I found jobs to do at the Dower House, where Eleanor's parents live now.

I also had plenty to do out in the woods as the trees sank into their winter sleep. I've spent the last couple of years bringing the coppices back into productive use. I started a Christmas tree plantation as well.

When I wasn't busy with work, I would meet up with my girlfriend, Finele, or visit my dad and my mum. Sometimes Fin came up to Blithehurst, or I went down to her flat near Bristol, if her work commitments made that easier. A couple of times, we met up at my dad's cottage in Warwickshire. We'd headed over to East Anglia to visit Fin's family. Like I say, I'd had plenty of other things to think about.

But now January had turned into February. I'd done pretty much every possible job I could find. The manor house would stay closed to visitors until the school half term holiday hit us in a few weeks' time. Even the garden centre and the cafe up by the car park off the main road were only open from Wednesday to Sunday at this time of year. This particular Monday morning I had the day off like every other member of staff, theoretically at least.

There was no point staying in my cottage tucked away in the estate's woods. I'd finished my book, so I had nothing else to read until I made a trip out to the library or the nearest bookshop. There's no broadband out there, so streaming something on my laptop wasn't an option. I had come up to my workshop in what was still called the Dairy Yard, though no one had made butter or cheese in these outbuildings for decades. I hadn't found a carving project I wanted to pick up. Forcing these things never works. I'd end up in a bad temper with some unwanted firewood.

So I walked around the outside of the manor house looking for anything that needed repairing or sorting out. Everything seemed fine. I followed the path down the gently sloping side of the valley, through the ornamental gardens that overlook the moated ruins of the medieval buildings beside the river. I couldn't help remembering what Annis Wynne had said.

'You could do a lot more than you realise, forest boy, if you stirred yourself. You shouldn't need me to tell you that.'

She wasn't the first person to say something like that. A couple of teachers at secondary school had been set on convincing me to go to university to study IT or economics or something else I had zero interest in doing. I have no idea why. I got some decent A levels, and I started an earth sciences degree, but I ditched that after a year. I didn't know what I wanted to do. I just knew that wasn't for me. I remember my tutor's frustration.

'You have got potential, Daniel, if you'd only apply yourself.'

That had been easy to ignore. None of those people knew the truth about me or my family. Annis Wynne had been different. She hadn't been talking about my future prospects for a good job or anything else. Old Annis knew what I was and who my mother must be. She was as human as I was, but her ties to the unseen and uncanny were far more complex than mine. She soon realised that the Green Man takes an interest in me too.

Who is he? I honestly don't know. I don't think anyone does. Dryads like my mother are as deeply rooted in the woods where they live as the trees they care for. The Green Man comes and goes through the countryside wherever and whenever he wants. All I can say for sure is he's ancient and powerful, and over the past few years, he's expected me to solve problems for him.

That doesn't happen very often, and that's a relief. These are the problems that crop up when people who have no idea what they're dealing with find out the hard way. People should really remember that originally, folk tales were a lot closer to horror movies than to fairy stories for kids. Annis Wynne knew that from personal experience.

I stood by the moat for a bit. Archaeologists who have done various surveys call the Beauchenes' original residence a fortified manor. As far as everyone else is concerned, it's a little castle. The battlemented gatehouse has two solid towers and visitors cross the moat on the footbridge to go through a stone arch and wander around the cobbled courtyard. On the other side, the ruins of the medieval great hall are raised up above an undercroft. It's a little castle.

This morning the gatehouse was firmly locked and I couldn't come up with any reason to open it. I followed the path that led to the footbridge over the river instead.

Since I'd woken up, I'd been thinking about what Annis had said. That wasn't all. Frai, the older of the two dryads who still live on the Blithehurst estate, had dropped a few hints that she expected more of me too.

All right, I'll admit it. I had some idea what Annis Wynne might be talking about. Maybe a couple of ideas. Thanks to one memorable encounter I have scars on my forearm that itch when something unpleasant is heading my way. Not exactly 'by the pricking of my thumbs something evil this way comes', but close enough. I reckon Shakespeare knew a lot more about the supernatural than most people realise. My mum's woodland used to be part of the Forest of Arden.

But I still hadn't decided if I wanted the Blithehurst dryads' advice. It would cost me, for a start. That's something else that folklore gets right. You need to be very careful if you make any sort of deal with someone who's been around for centuries.

THE GREEN MAN'S QUARRY

I went through the kissing gate and crossed the footbridge over the shallow river that runs through the valley bottom. The path heads up the far side of the valley through an ancient wooded pasture. It takes visitors to an eighteenth-century ornamental temple on the skyline. Asca, the younger dryad, had been the model for the statue of Venus in the temple. So it's a good place for me to go, to let them know I want to talk. I glanced up at the clouds, but it didn't look like rain. So that wasn't an excuse for not walking up there.

What did I think these women thought I could do? Well, Annis Wynne could summon up two of the Cŵn Annwn. According to Welsh legends, they're hounds of the underworld, or possibly the otherworld. I didn't think those red-eared white dogs would take any orders from me, but spectral black dogs with blazing red eyes crop up in stories all over Britain, and I've come across them in various places over the past few years.

I was starting to wonder if a shuck might come when I called. If I could work out how to call one. If I could decide what I was going to do if one did turn up. I didn't think a fearsome spirit of shadow and night would be very impressed if I whistled it up for nothing.

The other thing I'd been wondering about was even harder to explain. I knew the Green Man had hidden me from unfriendly eyes a few times, when I was dealing with some crisis for him. Could I possibly do that myself, when I didn't want people to see me? I had absolutely no idea how to go about finding out. I was pretty sure this theoretical ability wouldn't work on dryads and anyone else who can see the unseen.

I could hardly experiment with Blithehurst's everyday visitors. Stand in the gardens and try to disappear from view? How would I know they weren't just politely ignoring me? Would they suddenly see me when I decided I wanted them to? Startling someone by reappearing wasn't a good idea.

People don't generally react well when a man my size catches them unawares. It was a safe bet they wouldn't suspect anything uncanny, but I didn't want Eleanor getting complaints about a member of staff lurking and stalking visitors.

Besides... kids accept what they grow up with as normal. The only thing I had grown up with was the ability to see unseen creatures and supernatural folk. This was... different. I hadn't decided if I wanted to go down this path.

Staring up towards the temple, I saw something else. A dog walker in a red padded jacket and jeans was strolling down the path to the bridge. His rough-coated brown dog was on a lead, only that was an endlessly extendable leash. The animal was ranging all over the pasture. The creamy cattle on the hillside didn't like it coming so close.

Blithehurst Estate raises organic, rare-breed beef. I have nothing to do with the farming business, but I knew those cows were a month or so from calving. Matthew the stockman had warned me they weren't in any mood to be messed about. He wouldn't normally turn them out to graze anywhere near this early in the year. Their sharp hooves would churn the soft, wet earth into a quagmire. But he had some sort of crisis with the flooring in the barn where these animals spent the winter. The ancient wooded pasture was the best field available, and the cows would be out here for a couple of weeks.

I moved as fast as I could. One of the bigger, older cows lowered her head with a warning shake as the dog got much too close. The daft creature seemed to think this was a game. It pounced and waited, belly low to the ground, tail wagging excitedly.

The other cows bunched up behind the big one. The herd would follow their matriarch's lead. Most of them were her daughters. The dog had no clue how much danger it was in, and its owner was oblivious, looking at his phone. I was surprised he had a signal out here. When I got close enough, I saw his wireless earbuds.

Whatever he was listening to must have been fascinating. He didn't look up from his phone until I snatched the dog leash out of his hand. He dropped his phone, but that wasn't my problem. I was reeling in the idiot dog. Thankfully it was wearing a harness instead of a collar around its neck. I didn't want to save it from being trampled into a bloody smear to end up strangling it.

The dog walker snatched his phone up off the grass. He swiped out his earbuds and dropped them into a pocket as he stared at me, indignant. At least his dog had stopped fighting the shortening leash. Once I had the curly-coated spaniel-cross close enough, I flicked the switch to lock the lead and offered the plastic handle to the owner.

'Didn't you see your dog was bothering those cows?'

'Excuse me?' He stared at the herd as if he'd never seen cattle before.

The big white matriarch shook her head and warned us off with an ominous moo, deep in her chest. The dog walker took a pace backwards. I watched for any sign that the cows were going to come closer. It's not only dogs that end up injured or dead when they get on the wrong side of big livestock. To my relief, the matriarch decided to head for the fodder Matthew had brought out earlier. The rest of the herd followed her.

'Those cows could easily have killed your dog. Didn't you see the signs?'

'He was on a lead.'

I guessed he was at least five years older than me. Closer to forty than thirty anyway, and somewhere around six feet tall. Not a man used to being told what to do. Not a man who would react well to being sworn at, so I chose my words carefully.

'Please keep your dog on a short leash and under your control at all times. That's what the signs say.'

The dog walker wasn't going to back down. 'This is a public footpath.'

'No, it isn't.' I might not be able to swear at him, but I have a special smile for certain members of the public. A smile that might suggest I could rip their arm off and smack some sense into them with the soggy end. I pointed towards the ornamental temple. 'The public right of way goes along the top of the valley. Blithehurst House is closed at the moment. The signs say that as well.'

He sniffed. 'These paths all look the same.'

I carried on talking as if he hadn't spoken. 'There's a map next to the sign which shows the right of way very clearly.'

I hoped so anyway. Eleanor had printed and laminated the signs in the estate office. I'd put up the notice board by the stile and Matthew had used twice as many drawing pins as I would. Even so, things go missing.

The dog walker narrowed his eyes. 'Do you work here?'

I thought about saying no. It wasn't a particularly cold day for the time of year, but I'd put my army-surplus coat on before I left the cottage. I wasn't wearing anything with a Blithehurst logo. On the other hand, I could tell he was looking for any excuse to ignore what I was telling him.

'Yes, I do.' And if he was expecting me to call him 'sir', he was going to be disappointed.

He looked down at his dog. It looked up, tongue lolling and feathery tail wagging. It was a nice dog.

'It's time I was getting home.' He turned and walked back up the hillside.

I noticed that he kept his dog's lead short and locked. He was looking sideways at the cows as well. Thankfully, they weren't interested in him or his dog any longer.

I stayed where I was. If I went up to the temple, he would think I was following him. No point in risking another confrontation. I could talk to the dryads another day. I'd go back to the house and find something to read in the library. Eleanor keeps her recent paperbacks hidden behind the tall leather-bound tomes in the bookcase by the door.

I turned around and saw two women watching me from the footbridge over the river. They both wore dark trousers and trainers, with floral padded waistcoats over creamy polo-necked sweaters. They looked like an advert from an expensive mail-order clothing company.

The one with long, light brown hair was the reason I'd come to Blithehurst in the first place. The one I didn't know had slightly darker, shorter hair. She blinked, and for a second I saw her eyes turn solid blue without any white, iris or pupil. Strictly speaking, neither of them were women, which explained why the dog walker hadn't seen them. Naiads can go unseen whenever they like, and river spirits can take on whatever form they want. I wondered how long they'd been watching me.

'Hi, Dan.' Kalei waved as I walked towards them. 'Still making friends, I see.'

'You know me.' I smiled as I reached the footbridge. 'It's been a while. Is this a social call?' Somehow I didn't think so.

She shook her head. 'You know me. This is Vatne.'

The second naiad nodded with a friendly smile. 'How do.'

Her broad Yorkshire accent took me completely by surprise. I know that sounds stupid, but after I had been born, Mum kept up with the news and current turns of phrase by listening to BBC radio. She knew no one must ever suspect she was anything other than an ordinary woman, and she mimicked the voices she heard.

The Blithehurst dryads have lived alongside the Beauchene family for centuries. I assume that's why they sound like people who take expensive schools and private incomes for granted. As for Kalei, whatever she's doing, the way she speaks blends in as effectively as the appearance she's chosen.

'Hello.' I nodded at the Yorkshire naiad.

'Let's find somewhere to sit and talk.' Kalei led the way through the manor gardens.

She knew where she was going. I sometimes wonder how long she's been coming to Blithehurst. Right now, I wondered what she wanted. When we first met, I'd helped Kalei with a problem in return for her promise to tell me where I could find some dryads. She'd kept her word, but I'd been bloody lucky not to end up in hospital or in handcuffs.

Chapter Two

I followed the two naiads past the castle ruins and across the smoothly mown lawn. A stretch of untended grass on the far side of the gardens is dotted with trees grown from seeds or saplings brought home by Victorian plant-hunter Beauchenes. The guidebook calls this the Wilderness Garden. At the moment, it offered pale, dry tussocks and dark drifts of last autumn's leaves. It would be prettier once the spring wildflowers bloomed. Visitors could sit and admire those on a wooden bench I had made. If they wanted one for their own garden, they could buy one in the garden centre.

Kalei sat down and stroked one curved and smoothed wooden arm with long, delicate fingers. 'Beautiful work, Dan. Still, I know how good you are with your hands.'

Folk tales about naiads and dryads entrancing mortal men are definitely true. I'm more resistant than most, thanks to my greenwood blood, but the first time I met Kalei, she caught me unawares. She had proved how easily she could get me thinking with my cock instead of my brain. She still amuses herself by trying to distract me, though I have no idea what she'd do if I took her flirting seriously. I have no intention of finding out, for a whole lot of reasons.

'Thanks.' I sat on the other end of the bench. I had been about to ask how I could help them, but I caught myself just in time. That would have been a serious tactical error. 'What do you want to talk about? There's nothing I can do about water companies and sewage discharges, if that's the problem.'

They would know I was telling the truth. Since dryads and naiads can't tell lies, they always hear when someone's lying to them. Thanks to my mother's blood, I can almost always tell when someone's bullshitting me.

'It's nowt like that.' Vatne sat down between us. She was all business. 'I've seen summat odd, and Kalei said you'd want to hear about it.'

'Okay,' I said cautiously.

'A few days since, I was passing through a stretch of river in some woods where no one much goes. I saw a man trying to get to the water. He was desperate. Dying of thirst. Really dying, I mean. He was on his hands and knees at first and crawling on his belly by the end. A black cat kept stopping him getting to the river. Not someone's moggy,' she said, exasperated, as I opened my mouth. 'A big cat. Big as summat in a wildlife park.'

I shut my mouth. I couldn't say offhand how many zoos have rivers running through them, but Vatne clearly knew what she was talking about.

'Stopping him how?' I asked instead.

'Getting between him and the water.' She looked at me as if that should be obvious. 'Snarling and growling and chasing him off. Every time he came back, so did the cat. It wouldn't let him drink, not once.'

'He was an ordinary man? Not a wose or anything like that?' I'd learned the hard way that not everything that looks human in remote woodland really is.

'Of course,' she said, impatient.

'What happened?'

'He died.' Vatne was clearly wondering why she'd come all this way to talk to an idiot.

'I mean, what happened to the body? Did the cat drag it off or did it eat him there?'

Where the hell had some man-killing big cat come from? I don't read much beyond the headlines online, but I usually listen to the evening bulletin on the radio. I was sure there hadn't been anything in the news about a black panther on the loose in Yorkshire.

Kalei answered. 'A dryad took the man's carcass away.'

I met her gaze. She knew I wanted to find more dryads. To be precise, I wanted to find other dryads' sons, to see what they could tell me about our strange, shared heritage. She smiled, and her sparkling turquoise eyes gave nothing away.

I looked at Vatne. 'Do you know her, the dryad? Do you think she knows what was going on?'

She shrugged. 'She doesn't talk to the likes of me. Maybe you'll have more luck.'

I could think of other reasons why Kalei had brought this to me. For all their uncanny powers, naiads and dryads can't handle metal. Things like tranquilliser guns, animal traps and cages. I hadn't got a clue how to get hold of that sort of equipment, but I had valid ID and an address and a job that the coppers could verify with a phone call. I could report seeing a dangerous animal on the loose and the police would contact whoever could catch or shoot it. If I could find a cop shop still open in rural Yorkshire.

If they believed me. I'd need evidence. Photos on my phone, with something recognisable in the background to give some scale. Proof I hadn't mistaken a feral moggy for something bigger because I was an idiot. Proof I wasn't wasting police time, trying to fake an Internet sensation.

I'd have to track the bloody thing down. I recalled seeing a documentary about a wildlife sanctuary where a keeper had been attacked by a leopard. He had survived but his scars had been horrific. Getting close to an animal with teeth and claws that big really didn't appeal. Still, Kalei and Vatne could help. I was sure two naiads could drown even a lion or a tiger if they wanted to. As long as they didn't drown me as well.

'Do you know where the cat is now?'

Vatne shook her head. 'It disappeared once the man was dead.'

'Disappeared? Into thin air? It was something like a shuck?'

Vatne was annoyed with herself this time. 'No, it was flesh and bone, right enough. I mean the bloody thing legged it and I didn't see where it went.'

Where had the sodding thing come from? Keeping big cats is illegal. Of course, some people never think rules apply to them. As long as they don't get caught. Maybe the dead man could still give us some answers.

'Do you know what the dryad did with the body?'

'Dropped him down a swallow hole. Without so much as a by your leave.' Vatne was offended. Clearly she considered the caverns under that bit of Yorkshire were her domain.

'Are you going to get him out of there?' I really, really hoped they didn't expect me to do that. I still wake up with my pulse racing when I dream about Kalei sweeping me through the dark voids and passages carved by underground rivers flowing beneath the Peak District for aeons.

Vatne shrugged. 'No point. He'll be nowt but bones soon enough.'

'Okay.' I didn't know how long it takes for a body to decompose and I wasn't about to ask. 'But if we can find out who he was, we might get some clue to explain what's going on.'

Kalei was way ahead of me. 'I went to take a look, but his pockets were empty. He was only wearing old tracksuit trousers and a filthy sweatshirt.'

That was odd. Or perhaps, on second thoughts, it wasn't. Someone might grab the nearest clothes and not bother with a wallet if they realised their illegal black panther had got out in the middle of the night.

'Where did this happen? Is there anywhere nearby where someone could keep a wild animal without the neighbours noticing?' Someone who would be desperate to catch it before daylight.

'Nether Cullen's the closest village.' Vatne answered my first question. 'It's a fair walk for your kind to the river where he died.'

I thought about that. If the dead man hadn't walked there, had he driven? Surely he'd need a vehicle to take his cat home once he caught it? 'Have you seen a van or car parked up? One that hasn't moved for a few days?' Leaving your keys in the wheel arch on the top of a tyre would be a lot safer than risking them falling out of a loose, stretchy pocket in the dark.

Vatne shrugged again. 'Not that I've seen.'

'Fair enough.' I guessed a dryad would be more likely to know, especially if the vehicle had been parked well away from the river.

Kalei had a different question. 'If this creature was his pet, why would it stop him getting to the river to drink?'

Now it was my turn to shrug. 'There are plenty of stories about people who keep wild animals and think they're perfectly tame, but who still end up getting eaten.'

'Except the cat didn't eat him,' Vatne pointed out.

'True.' That was odd. According to those wildlife documentaries, a predator staking out a water source would be waiting for a chance to grab lunch. 'That doesn't mean it won't eat the next hiker it stumbles across.'

'It's more likely to go for the sheep,' Vatne retorted. 'Lambing'll start any day now.'

That was a horrible thought. An out-of-control dog can cause mayhem in a flock. A top predator with razor-sharp claws and massive fangs would mean absolute carnage.

Granted, that would prove something was out there, but how long would it take a vet to convince the coppers that something worse than a big dog was on the loose? Local zoos would do a headcount and confirm all their animals were present and correct. How many sheep or hikers could end up dead? The naiads were right. This situation couldn't wait.

I nodded. 'If this dryad can give us some clue where this dead man might have come from, or where we might find his car, I can call the cops with an anonymous tip. As soon as they realise what they're dealing with, they should bring in whatever they need and hunt the cat down.'

I really hoped for clear evidence at this missing man's house or in his vehicle that he was illegally keeping a big cat. I'd be much happier if I could keep my name out of this. Any copper who looks me up on his computer will learn I've had less than happy encounters with a couple of police forces.

If there wasn't any evidence? We'd have to think again. We wouldn't know either way until I talked to this dryad. I stood up.

'I don't see any problem with me getting a few days off work. It'll be a three-hour drive, maybe three and a half. If I get a move on, I should be there before dark. Can you get back by then? If you can, where shall we meet?'

'By the bridge in Nether Cullen. We'll see you at sunset.' Vatne dissolved into a cloud of mist that swirled away towards the river. I guessed that was her saying yes, she could get back there fast enough.

'I'll see you later.' Before I could ask her anything else, Kalei disappeared as well.

I walked back to the manor house and let myself in through the 'Staff Only' side door. The stone-flagged corridor ran past what had once been assorted rooms for servants and the big old-fashioned kitchen. Passing the door to the library that overlooked the valley, I reached what had been the Tudor great hall. Later Beauchenes divided that into this elegant room for receiving guests and the separate dining room beyond. Now the house was closed, the antique furniture and display cases holding ornaments and fine china were shrouded with dust sheets.

I went through the dining room to the smaller sitting room and took the stairs to the upper floor. Fewer of these rooms are open to the public. The stairs arrive in the morning room where the ladies of the house used to do their embroidery or read novels to each other. The historical suite of guest rooms is straight ahead, overlooking the knot garden at the front of the house. There's a bed Charles II supposedly slept in, and other antique furniture. On the other side of the house, over the kitchen and the servants' hall, the long gallery displays the family portraits.

The doors in between are kept locked. There's nothing of any interest in bedrooms used occasionally for guests. I knocked on the door just before I reached the gallery. A second suite of rooms directly above the library had been converted into a sitting room and a bedroom with a modern bathroom.

'Come in.'

I opened the door and saw Eleanor was on the landline phone, leaning back in her office chair beside the table she uses as a desk in the bay window. She's the only Beauchene who still lives at Blithehurst, when she's not doing research for a doctorate at Durham University. I raised my hands, to show her I could come back later. She shook her head and beckoned me in. I closed the door behind me and sat on the two-seater sofa to wait.

'Because we're not licensed as a wedding venue.'

While Eleanor was listening to a lengthy reply to that, I took out my mobile. Using the broadband and Wi-Fi in the main house, I could look up Nether Cullen. I found it in

North Yorkshire, on the north-eastern edge of the Yorkshire Dales National Park. The digital map showed a scatter of houses on either side of a small river.

There was a pub offering accommodation. Apparently the Buck in the Dale did bed and breakfast and their website made a point of saying they were open for guests all year round. I don't imagine many people go hiking in February, but no hospitality business can afford to turn customers away these days.

'Because it doesn't make financial sense.' Eleanor finally spoke over whoever was on the other end of her call. 'We'd have to close the house for three days. No, listen. One day to move the furniture to set up the chairs, which we'd have to hire by the way, and I don't know where you think everything we'd need to move is supposed to go. Then there's the day for the wedding itself, and a day after that to put everything straight. Three days.'

She paused briefly for the other person to say something before she went on. 'Peak season for weddings is peak season for visitors. No one looking for a wedding venue would pay what we'd have to ask to make up the money we'd lose on sales of tickets for the house. Plus getting a licence would cost at least fifteen hundred quid, and I hate to think what we'd have to add to the insurances.'

Whoever was on the phone was persistent. While Eleanor listened, I checked North Yorkshire newspaper websites for reports of slaughtered lambs or anything else that might be linked to a big cat. Nothing. I was about to check another website when Eleanor's voice made me look up.

'Do you want to see my spreadsheets?'

Whoever was on the other end of the call clearly knew when they were beaten. No one argues with the spreadsheets.

'Yes, I'll talk to you soon,' Eleanor went on after a moment. 'Listen, I really am delighted. This is wonderful news, and give my best to David. Yes, take care.'

She put the handset in its charging cradle with a grimace. 'That was Sophie. She's just got engaged.'

'Congratulations?' I've met Eleanor's sister a few times, but I can't say I know her. She's a solicitor who lives in Manchester. Whatever the Blithehurst family trust pays out to the relatives who hold shares in it, they need a day job or a pension as well. Eleanor takes a salary for running the house and the estate since her parents retired, and her brother Ben is an architect in London.

Eleanor rubbed the back of her neck. 'It's lovely news, but she had her heart set on a romantic wedding in the ancestral family home. Ceremony in the library followed by a reception in the great hall.'

That made some sense. The library had been quietly used as a chapel in the centuries when the Beauchenes had stayed stubbornly Catholic despite various laws against it. The ceiling was made from carved panels salvaged from the old chapel down in the castle. That had been stripped when the Tudor Beauchenes were pretending to go along with the Reformation.

Eleanor glanced out of the window. These south-facing rooms overlook the valley, and I knew she'd be able to see the ornamental temple. 'They'll be pleased, at least.'

Eleanor didn't only give me this job because I'm handy with a chisel. She can see dryads and naiads and the like as well as I can. Asca's mortal son Francis had been fathered by Edmund Beauchene, who inherited the estate back in the seventeen-whenevers. His human wife gave birth to daughters, which meant some cousin would get the house and the lands as soon as he died.

Asca gave Edmund an heir, which solved that problem. The dryads are just as determined to keep the property in the family these days. Unfortunately for them, Eleanor's the last Beauchene who can see them. Greenwood blood runs thin after six or seven generations.

She stared out of the window. 'I don't know what she's thinking. Where would guests who need to stay over sleep, for a start? With the spare rooms here and at the Dower House, we could probably put up family, but Soph has hundreds of friends.'

That might not be much of an exaggeration. Greenwood blood might be running thin in the Beauchenes, but they still have a lot more than their fair share of charm.

'Sorry.' Eleanor looked at me. 'What did you want?'

'I've had a visit from a couple of naiads.' I grinned as she looked startled.

I told her what Kalei and Vatne had told me.

Eleanor didn't even bother discussing what I might do. When I'd first come to Blithehurst, we'd defeated a murderous threat together, and she knew about the other situations I'd tackled elsewhere. 'You're heading off now?'

'If that's okay with you.'

She nodded. 'It's quiet enough for you to book a few days' leave.'

'There's a pub in the village which does bed and breakfast. I've checked and they're open, so I'll stay there tonight and see what I can find out tomorrow.'

'Just don't get eaten.' Eleanor broke off as a thought struck her. 'Have you spoken to Hazel about this?'

I shook my head. 'I was about to check her website.'

Eleanor opened up her laptop. 'Let's see.'

She hit the keys and clicked her mouse. A few moments later, she shook her head. 'No sightings of some Beast of –

wherever's the closest place with a name that starts with "B" around there. I'll email her all the same. Not everything she hears about goes up online.'

'Thanks.' I got up from the little sofa. 'Tell her to give me a ring if she's heard anything that might come in useful.'

Hazel Spinner is a cryptozoologist. People post sightings of strange and supernatural creatures on her website – or figments of their imagination after they've had too much to drink or experimented unwisely with drugs, depending on your point of view.

Eleanor nodded. 'Give me a call when you get there.'

'Will do.' I left her to get back to whatever she was doing and went downstairs. I used the broadband to make a VoIP call to Fin. She didn't answer. That wasn't much of a surprise. She's a freelance freshwater ecologist, and when she's doing fieldwork, she leaves her phone locked safely in her car. I left a message letting her know where I'd be for a few days.

Then I rang the pub in Nether Cullen to check the place really was open. You can't always trust what you read on the Net. This time, the website was accurate, so I told the nice lady to expect me later today. I booked for one night to begin with, but said I might stay on for a day or so longer. Would it be okay if I let her know tomorrow? She assured me that would be fine.

I made a quick stop in the library to raid Eleanor's dad's complete collection of UK Ordnance Survey maps. I'd look at that later, to see how far a 'fair walk' might be, according to a naiad. I had one more thing to do before I packed an overnight bag.

I went out through the side door and crossed the foot-bridge over the river. The cows ignored me and there was no one else around as I walked up to the ornamental temple.

The white marble circle of pillars on a plinth has a dome on top to shelter the statue of Venus. Curving marble benches offer visitors somewhere to sit, to catch their breath and tell each other that path through the pasture is quite deceptive. It doesn't look steep, but it's more of a climb than you realise.

I waited to see if one of the dryads would appear. That didn't take long. Since I was on my own, they didn't bother passing for human in modern clothes as they sat beside me. Dryads have been wearing long loose draperies since before the Greeks and Romans started putting them on vases.

Asca looks like an elegant woman in her late forties who makes good use of a gym. Her deep green eyes remind me of late-summer foliage. Her mother, Frai, looks like a harmless, white-haired old lady, and anyone who believes that is in for a surprise. The old dryad remembers when the medieval castle was built. Her penetrating gaze is the vivid autumn colour of copper beech leaves.

'What did those river daughters want with you?' she demanded.

'My help.' I explained about the big cat and waited for Frai to say this was nothing to do with us.

Asca spoke first, unexpectedly concerned. 'Something so dangerous cannot be allowed to roam free.'

'Hopefully I can report it to the police. Then it'll be captured or shot pretty quickly.'

Frai snorted. 'Don't get yourself eaten.'

I was starting to wish people would stop saying that. I reminded myself why I had come up here. I knew Frai would want to know why the naiads had wanted talk to me. Since I'd told her that, she owed me some answers.

'I need to find this dryad who dumped the dead man's body. How can I let her know that I want to speak to her, if she won't talk to Vatne?'

I didn't fancy randomly wandering around a wood where a lethally big cat might be lurking. This unknown dryad hadn't done anything to help the poor bastard who had already died there.

Asca glanced at Frai. The old dryad pursed her withered lips and shrugged.

'Come with me.' Asca rose from the marble bench in one graceful, flowing movement.

She walked to the closest of the oak trees scattered across the pasture. The trunk was bare of branches until it reached a height that browsing cattle couldn't reach. The crown of the tree spread out above that, offering the cows shelter from sun or rain, as well as a supply of wood and foliage for all sorts of purposes. Capability Brown's ornamental trees make posh parks look nice, but people who made land work for them have been tending wooded pastures for centuries.

Asca laid her hand on the rough bark. 'Ask the trees to help you. Like this.'

I reached up to take hold of a sturdy branch, feeling extremely self-conscious. In the next breath, I knew where every living creature was in the Blithehurst woods. Birds and wildlife were a low-level background blur. Frai and Asca were powerful and unmistakable presences close by. I could tell where every cow was grazing in the pasture, and I sensed which one was the matriarch. Further away, a couple of dog walkers who could read signs were following the public footpath. Most distant of all, way beyond the estate's ruined watermill, I could feel a black shuck. I knew that all in the time it took to lift my hand off the tree.

'Fucking hell.'

Asca smiled serenely. 'As you see, it's simple enough.'

'It's taken you long enough,' Frai commented waspishly.

Before I could ask what she meant by that, the dryads vanished.

Chapter Three

It took me nearly four hours to reach Nether Cullen. Online maps are hopelessly optimistic about routes that include narrow, winding roads. Though I let the BMWs and Audis tempt fate and the speed cameras by doing ninety-plus in the fast lane on the motorway. My Land Rover is more suited to keeping pace with HGVs, and I get better miles per gallon that way.

I took the M6 north. The satnav reckoned cutting across country to Derby and the M1 would be marginally quicker, or taking the M62 later on, but either way meant navigating a tangle of busy motorways with every chance of traffic jams. I stayed on the motorway until Tebay, where I stopped for a late lunch. The farming business that owns this service station offers freshly sourced local food which you can eat while you enjoy the view of the northern Lakes' fells. I resisted the temptation to sit down for a meal in the restaurant and got a snack from the quick kitchen counter instead. Still, I'd go home the same way, I decided, and stock up with a few treats from the farm shop.

That did mean a bit of detour before I got on the A66 cutting across the North Pennines. Turning off the main road, I had to rely on the satnav, though when countryside is quite literally up hill and down dale, there aren't many places for roads to go. People must have followed these routes for thousands of years.

I passed a farmhouse flanked by modern barns, and Nether Cullen wasn't much further. Before I reached the bridge, cottages in short terraces on either side of the road had front doors opening off the narrow pavement. As I drove over the river, houses on the other side were bigger and set back from the road that led out of the village.

If the Buck in the Dale hadn't always been the village pub, the long building had been here for centuries. Built from local stone and well maintained, the ground floor had two big, well-spaced windows on either side of a central door. The upper storey had five windows to match. A sign told me the car park was around the back. I pulled in beside an estate car so covered in mud I had to look twice to see it was a Subaru. A Suzuki four-wheel-drive was parked beside a Toyota Land Cruiser that had done plenty of miles. No one would give my old Landy a second glance around here.

I'd seen the lights were on in the bar, even though it was an hour or so until sunset. I grabbed my overnight bag and my waterproof jacket off the passenger seat and locked up. Instead of trying to decide which of the three doors I could see was the back entrance, I walked around to the front. A polite notice by the door asked walkers to use the scraper to clean mud off their boots before entering. I checked my feet. They were fine, I went in.

In front of the bar in the middle of the ground floor, drinkers could sit on stools around small round tables. Wood and glass partitions had replaced the original internal walls on either side, with oak dining tables and chairs for people who'd come here to eat beyond them. The floor was pale flagstones and the wooden panelling halfway up the walls was painted light green. The wallpaper above that was rich cream and the ceiling was white-painted plaster.

A handful of people on bar stools were chatting to the middle-aged barman. He was frothing milk at a gleaming espresso machine. They stopped talking and looked at me. I recalled a horror film Fin and I had seen on the telly late one night. Two American students who got lost on the North York Moors found a less than warm welcome in a remote pub. I smiled and tried to look as if I wasn't going to be any trouble.

'Afternoon,' the barman said cheerfully. 'Are you Daniel Mackmain?'

'That's right. I rang earlier to book a room?'

'I'll get Anne.' He went out through the back of the bar.

The men on the bar stools were looking at me. They wore overalls or old jeans and battered waterproof coats, so I guess they worked on local farms. I had no idea why they were in the pub at this time in the afternoon and I wasn't about to ask.

One of them put down his coffee cup. His weathered face was wrinkled, though his mottled bald head was as smooth as an egg. 'Here to do some walking, are you?'

'That's right.'

'Not planning on using one of them apps?' The dour white-haired man beside him asked a definitely loaded question.

'Not likely. I've got an Ordnance Survey map.'

'Mountain Rescue will be glad to hear that.' A younger man drinking Coke looked meaningfully at his mates.

I guessed some halfwit had gone into the hills without thinking they might lose their signal or their phone battery could run out. I waited for one of the men to explain whatever had happened, or maybe warn me some animal was out there eating sheep. No one said a word.

A middle-aged woman in a long grey cardigan came through another door with a sign saying this was the way to the toilets. 'Daniel? Hello, it's nice to meet you. Let me show you to your room.'

'Hello.' I recognised her voice from the phone.

I picked up my overnight bag and followed her to a small desk at the foot of the stairs. She offered me a payment terminal for my debit card and a registration form. While I filled that out, she got a key out of a locked cabinet tucked under the stairs. A proper key on a leather fob.

'I've put you in the end room at the back, so you'll be nice and quiet. Not that the bar gets too busy at this time of year.' She went up the stairs ahead of me.

The room was nice, with a king-sized bed flanked by side tables with lamps and facing a TV on a wall bracket. The en-suite had a bath with a shower over it.

'This is great, thanks.' I'd suggest coming here for a weekend break with Fin, once there was no danger of getting eaten.

'Tea and coffee.' Anne gestured at a kettle, two de-cent-sized mugs and everything else on an old chest of draw-ers. 'We'll be doing food from six in the bar. You can have a drink while you're waiting, if you like.'

'Thanks,' I said again.

'Right then, I'll leave you to it. And when you go out, you can always leave your key with me or Neil or whoever's in the bar. Better safe than sorry.' Anne smiled and closed the door behind her.

I would rather have a room at the front with a view of the river and the bridge, but I wasn't going to complain. I put the kettle on and admired the old chest of drawers. A crafts-man who knew his trade had made that from solid ash. The drawers slid in and out without a hitch. I ran a finger along one bottom edge and felt the smoothness of candle wax on the wood.

While I waited for the kettle to boil, I rang Eleanor and left her a voicemail to say I'd arrived. Then I spread her dad's map out on the bed. I had a mug of tea, and studied the map some more. Then I carefully folded it up and put on my coat.

When I got to the bottom of the stairs, I decided to hang on to my key. I wasn't going far, and there's a zip pocket in my combat trousers. I wondered again where the dead man's keys might have got to. How far from the water might Vatne be willing to look? She wouldn't want to handle the metal herself, but she could show me where to find them. If we couldn't find anything else, I could be a responsible citizen handing lost keys in to the police. That should get them searching for a vehicle.

I looked at the back door, but decided to leave through the bar. I grew up in a rural area and my dad taught me people will leave you alone if they think they know what you're doing. Then you can get on with what you really want to do. I waved the map in my hand when the men at the bar glanced my way.

'Getting my bearings before I head out tomorrow.' I didn't wait to see if that was worth a nod. The sun was sinking and I needed to talk to the naiads.

Outside, on the river side of the road, the tarmac gave way to a broad swathe of rough turf leading down to the water. The bridge itself was old but wide enough to have a decent footpath alongside the roadway. I stopped and carefully unfolded and refolded the map to show me the immediate area. I looked upstream, resting the map on the broad stone parapet. I kept a firm grip on it, and the piercing breeze made me wish I'd put my gloves on. I could feel the chill coming off the water, flowing fast and dark in the fading light. How long until sunset, and what did Vatne measure that by, anyway?

Mist surged up from the river and both naiads appeared. Blue figures with long blue hair slicked back from their faces, they reminded me of triathlon swimmers or divers in body-hugging suits. No one but me would see them. So I'd be talking to myself as far as any passer-by was concerned. To be fair, no one was out taking an evening stroll.

43

'Can you read this map?' I asked Vatne. 'Can you show me exactly where the man died?'

She studied the paper sheet for a moment, then looked at the hills rising steeply to meet the luminous westward sky. She tapped a spot on the map. 'There.'

Moisture from her fingertip spread across the paper. Bugger. I wasn't concerned about the map getting wet though, or the distance, even if getting there would be a hike and a half, and mostly uphill. The real problem was the solid red lines and triangles enclosing a chunk of land labelled 'DANGER AREA' in red capitals. 'That's MOD property.'

Both naiads looked at me blankly.

'Ministry of Defence?'

That got me another shrug from Vatne. Kalei didn't see a problem either.

'There's a fence, but it's only a few strands of wire.'

I suppose I shouldn't have been surprised. Water goes wherever it likes, and not a lot can stop it. Naiads are the same. Though this potentially explained a few things. If the fence was no real barrier, the cat could have easily got into the woods, and the dead man would have followed. The cat wouldn't have paid any attention to warning signs, and the dead man must have been desperate enough to go after it. Assuming he was chasing the cat. We still didn't know that for certain.

I turned to Vatne. 'How often do soldiers turn up? What do they use these woods for?'

She shrugged. 'I see men in green and brown chasing each other around a couple of times a year.'

I had to hope the dryad could tell me more. If I could get her to talk to me. 'What might a big cat find to eat in those woods?'

'Roe deer, and hares up on the fellside.'

JULIET E. MCKENNA

'A full-grown deer would fill the beast's belly, with meat left over,' Kalei commented. 'Let's hope it prefers to stay with a kill.'

'If it can hunt for itself – but if it was captured and sold as a cub? Maybe that's why it didn't eat the man after he died. It's used to getting its meat already cut up.'

I wondered where the nearest butcher was, and how much steak would keep a big cat occupied so I could take its photo. Getting close enough to toss it bloody lumps of beef would be a job for one of the naiads. If the cat tried to bite them, it would get a face full of water.

'Any chance the army will turn up any time soon?' I asked Vatne.

That could solve a lot of our problems, if the cat jumped a squaddie with a gun. If he had some bullets. I had no idea how often the army handed out live ammunition. Still, this theoretical unlucky squaddie should be wearing reasonably protective kit. There would be medics around. Assuming the cat didn't crush his throat with its first bite. I was starting to wish I watched fewer wildlife documentaries.

Vatne was shaking her head. 'I have no idea.'

Another question for the unknown dryad. Assuming I could give her whatever she might demand in return for answers. I folded up the map, relieved to see that the breeze had dried out that damp spot. 'I'll head for the woods after breakfast.'

'What's wrong with dawn?' Kalei objected. 'Your mother's blood gives you keener vision than most of your kind, even in the twilight.'

I shook my head. 'Setting out at daybreak will draw attention.' I wasn't going to walk through strange woods while the trees were still thick with shadows and a big black cat might be looking for its own breakfast. 'Where do you want to meet?'

45

'We'll find you.' Vatne vanished as abruptly as she had at Blithehurst. Kalei was barely a second behind her.

I went back to the pub. The bar was empty and the barman was restocking the bottled beers and ciders. He greeted me with a nod. 'Can I get you anything?'

I wouldn't be driving anywhere tonight. 'A pint of Black Sheep, thanks.'

While he filled the glass, I got out my phone and used the password on the notice behind the bar to log on to the pub's free Wi-Fi.

'Cash or card?'

'Card, thanks.'

'I'm Neil, by the way.' He put the pint glass and the payment terminal side by side on the bar.

'Dan. Nice to meet you. Okay if I sit at a table? Anne said there'll be food from six,' I added in case he thought I was expecting a menu. 'I'm happy to wait.'

He nodded. 'Enjoy your drink.'

I sat at a corner table, sipped my beer and read what the Internet could tell me about land owned by the MOD. The first thing I learned was it's called the Defence Training Estate. This adds up to more than 150,000 hectares from Scotland down to Cornwall. Major training areas, small ranges and camps are used for different things, from off-road driving training to practising urban warfare and a whole lot more besides.

Looking at the OS map earlier, I had been surprised to see a public footpath crossing the MOD land where the man had died. The official website said using that was fine, as long as people stuck to the right of way and didn't go wandering about. There were rules to follow. I would have thought these things were obvious, but common sense is often not very common. A pointed webpage listed the most ridiculous excuses the army had heard lately. 'I didn't see the signs' was familiar. Thinking red flags pointed in the direction of the danger was particularly special. I'd never met anyone who didn't understand how the wind works.

The website politely asked walkers to check posted training times for different sites before visiting, presumably to avoid civilians getting squashed by an unexpected tank or something like that. Military debris should be left where it was and reported. The military would come and dispose of it safely. So I didn't only have to worry about a big cat eating me. I might step on something that could blow my foot off.

Or maybe not. Over Cullen Wood wasn't on the list of big ranges where live firing exercises were scheduled. It must be one of those minor training areas mentioned in passing. Though I'd need to be careful in case the MOD was keeping an eye on the place. The official web pages were unsurprisingly vague about how they did that. Why tell people who are up to no good what they need to watch out for? Though the Ministry of Defence Police were happy to tell anyone planning some illegal off-roading or hare-coursing that they had used drones in successful prosecutions.

That wasn't good news for me, but if the army could search for an escaped big cat from the air, no squaddies would have to risk being eaten. Could I let the military know the animal was out there, ideally without telling them who I was? I looked across to the bar, where Neil was talking to a grey-haired couple. Regulars had started coming in for the evening.

The locals must have a pretty good idea of the times of year when the army turned up. I tried to think of ways to casually work questions about it into a conversation that wouldn't be massively suspicious. I've had people see my number-one haircut and my height and think 'right-wing skinhead, and big enough to be dangerous' before now.

I ditched that idea. Even if someone was willing to chat about whatever squaddies got up to around here, they'd ask why I was interested. I'd have to lie, and I'm crap at that. That's the price for knowing when someone's lying to me.

There was nothing more I could do tonight. When Anne put menus out on the dining tables, I ordered the trio of local sausages and colcannon mashed potatoes, with another pint of beer. After sticky toffee pudding and custard, I went up to my room. I rang Fin, and she agreed this sounded like a good place for a weekend away. I watched some telly and went to bed.

Chapter Four

Despite what I'd said to Kalei, I got up bright and early. I wanted to study the map before I set out. The good news was a right of way running through Over Cullen Woods and out the other side, cutting across the area labelled 'MANAGED ACCESS'. The path continued beyond the trees and passed a site labelled with olde-worlde printing as 'Over Cullen Priory (rems of)'.

The right of way continued beyond the priory, leaving the MOD jurisdiction behind. Following the path with my finger, I found it reached a narrow road. Was that where I'd find the dead man's parked car or a van that no one had noticed yet? An abandoned vehicle in Nether Cullen would have been reported, even if none of the locals here had mentioned that to a complete stranger for no reason.

The bad news was the stretch of riverbank where Vatne said the stranger had died. That was on the opposite side to the footpath. The water marked the edge of a stretch designated 'DANGER AREA'. There was no sign of anything like a bridge, though that wasn't necessarily a problem if I had two naiads to help me across. As long as no one with a gun turned up to arrest me, after spotting me on some patrolling drone's camera.

I measured the distances to the nearest houses and farms where a reclusive big cat owner might have lived. There was nothing anywhere close. So where had the dead man come from? Well, I wasn't going to find out by staying here. I folded the map to show me Over Cullen Woods and put it in the lightweight rucksack I'd brought with me. Then I went downstairs for breakfast.

Anne was wiping down the dining tables. 'Sit anywhere you like. There isn't a breakfast menu as such, not at this time of year. We can do you bacon and eggs, sausage, black pudding, beans, fried bread? If there's something else you fancy, I can see if we've got it in the kitchen. There's cereal if you'd rather,' she offered as an afterthought, 'or toast with butter and jam or marmalade.'

I took a seat at the closest table. 'Bacon and eggs and black pudding, please, and some toast. That'll be great, thanks.'

'Right you are. Tea or coffee?'

'Tea, please.'

She headed for the kitchen. Since I was the only guest, my breakfast soon arrived. Everything was as good as my dinner had been the night before. The bread for the toast was homemade and so was the raspberry jam. I was just about finished when Anne brought out a jug of hot water to top up my pot of tea.

'You're off out walking this morning? Have you some idea when you'll be back?'

'I think I'll make a day of it.' Then I realised what she was actually asking. 'I'll stop here again tonight, if that's okay?'

'Of course, that's fine. You'll want to be back before dark though. It gets right cold up on the tops once the sun's gone down.'

'I'll be back before then.' The last thing I wanted was the local Mountain Rescue sent to find me.

'You've got our number. You can always give us a ring if you're going to be a bit overdue.' She gathered up my plates and cutlery as I poured a last mug of tea. 'I could make you a packed lunch, if you like? Ham sandwiches, or cheese? It's no bother.'

'Ham, please, that'd be great.'

'Right you are.'

She went off to the kitchen, and I went back to my room. I'd brought some energy bars and I put those in the rucksack along with a water bottle which I filled from the en-suite tap. I was wearing my usual combat trousers, sweatshirt and boots. Clothes for a day's work in the Blithehurst woods would be fine for a bit of hill-walking. I went downstairs and into the bar.

Anne appeared with a brown paper bag. 'There you are.'

'Thanks very much. How much do I owe you?'

'You're all right. A bit of ham and bread's no bother.'

'Thanks.' I felt awkward about that, then I remembered why I had my room key in my hand instead of my pocket. 'I'll leave this with you. Do you want me to pay for tonight before I head out?'

'If it's no trouble.' She went to fetch the card payment machine.

I looked inside the paper bag. Salt and vinegar crisps and an apple, and two rounds of sandwiches wrapped in grease-proof paper. I'd have to remember to leave a tip in my room when I left. I paid for another night when Anne came back, and zipped my wallet into my waterproof coat's inside pock-et, together with my phone.

'Have a nice day. The weather looks pretty good.' Anne headed back to the kitchen.

I went out through the front door and put on my gloves and a woolly hat. The few clouds in the sky were high and light and hurrying on their way to somewhere else. The cold breeze was strong enough to blow a paper cup along the tar-mac as I walked up the road away from the river. Spring was noticeably further away here than it was back at Blithehurst.

Why hadn't the dead man been wearing a coat, if he had gone out in the middle of the night? In North Yorkshire at this time of year? The days might have been mild recently, but like Anne had said, it still got bitterly cold once the sun went down. A local would know the dangers of going out on the hills without proper gear. Was he so desperate to catch his escaped cat that he'd risk hypothermia?

These houses stood in their own neat gardens bounded by solid walls of grey stone. I reached the edge of the village, where the land started to rise more steeply. A sturdy wooden signpost directed anyone who wanted to get to Over Cullen Priory down a narrow lane alongside a dry-stone wall that bordered a field full of round-bellied ewes.

I followed the sign and left the village behind. A couple of fields later, the lane turned off towards a stone barn standing on its own halfway between me and the river. I carried on walking along a well-established path. No one else was around, which was probably why three curious ponies trotted over for a closer look at me. I fed them handfuls of the longer grass growing on my side of their wall until they lost interest and wandered off.

There must have been some rain overnight. The grass I pulled up for the ponies was damp, and so was the soil where hiking boots had worn away the turf on this path. No one had left footprints ahead of me this morning.

That made me wonder something else. How had this mysterious dead man been tracking an escaped cat? I couldn't believe the animal would leave much of a trail, prowling through leafless trees at this time of year. There was no undergrowth where it might break off usefully signalling twigs or crush greenery underfoot. The dead man wouldn't have had any moonlight to see by, even if the night skies had been clear.

Could the black cat have a radio collar? That would be incredibly helpful. The army should have no trouble finding that signal, for a start. It could explain a few other things too. Maybe the collar set off an alarm when the animal got out. If he knew he could find it, the dead man would have thought he would catch it quickly. So sure he went straight out in the clothes he was wearing.

Not even stopping to grab a coat? Maybe. Perhaps. What did I really know, for certain? Sod all. I hoped this unknown dryad had answers she was willing to share. I hoped I wouldn't have to pay too high a price. What sort of favour would a tree spirit in this neck of the woods want from someone like me anyway?

I left the neatly walled pastures behind and followed the path through rougher grazing as the land grew steeper. I kept an eye out for any livestock ripped to shreds. There was nothing amiss. The morning was calm and peaceful and filled with bird song.

When the valley sides drew closer together, I stopped and checked Eleanor's dad's map. The MOD's 'MANAGED ACCESS' land, and the trees that had taken advantage of this shelter centuries ago, would start just past that shoulder of land jutting out towards the river.

I walked on and found the fence. Like Kalei had said, it was a few strands of wire. Viciously barbed wire, to be accurate, chest high at the top and strung between ancient, crumbling concrete posts. I wouldn't fancy trying to get through that in daylight, never mind on a moonless night. Maybe the mystery man had scratched himself and died of tetanus, not thirst. I wondered how long dying of tetanus took. I unzipped my pocket and took out my phone. There wasn't a hint of a signal, so I wouldn't be looking that up online.

I didn't have to risk the wire. The footpath passed through a galvanised kissing gate that was a lot newer than the fence posts. Warning signs on solidly planted posts flanked it. They were clean and shiny yellow, with black triangles with symbols in them above stark black writing.

DANGER Military Training Area. That triangle had a big black exclamation mark.

WARNING Do not touch any military debris. It may explode and harm you. The black-and-yellow picture of an explosion should get that message across to the hard of understanding.

A smaller red-and-white sign warned people not to proceed beyond this point when the gate was locked and notice was posted that access was temporarily suspended. The gate wasn't locked and there were no extra notices today. I went through, walking more slowly and alert for any hint of movement in the trees, on this side of the river as well as on the opposite bank. Big cats can swim.

The scars on my arm weren't itching though, and the birds flitting from twig to twig weren't tweeting alarm calls because a predator was somewhere close. I carried on along the path until I found the stump of a tree brought down by a storm. I sat down and ate my apple.

I savoured the rich dark scent of the woodland deep in its winter sleep. These ancient oak trees were thickset and gnarled, with their grey branches twisting and reaching wherever they wished to go. No axe or browsing animal had touched them for centuries. I always enjoy seeing every tree's unique and fascinating shape before their leaves unfurl in the spring.

I finished my apple and chucked the core away. There was still no sign of the naiads. No sign of the dryad who tended these trees. There was nothing else for it. I'd have to see what Asca's dryad radar could show me. Getting up, I walked along the path until I found a sturdy oak, and I carefully laid my ungloved hand on its lowest branch.

It was like touching an electric fence, only ten times worse. The unexpected shock knocked me off my feet. I landed on my back, rolling sideways as my metal water bottle rammed itself hard into my left kidney. Fucking hell, that hurt!

My hand was absolute agony. Shit! Explaining a massive burn on my palm would be really difficult when I got back to the pub. Driving home with a barely usable hand would be impossible. If I needed a hospital, the nurses would know I was lying, whatever I said. There was every chance I'd get a visit from the authorities, because it wouldn't take them long to work out where I'd been. Some copper or an army official would ask me politely, 'What exactly did you pick up, sir?' They would call me 'sir' instead of 'you fucking idiot'. 'What part of "DO NOT TOUCH" was unclear?' would stay loudly unsaid.

Trying to catch my breath, I forced myself to look, to assess the damage. I stared at my familiar callouses with disbelief. There wasn't a mark. A voice cut through my confused thoughts with a challenge, harsh and hostile. I didn't understand a word of it, possibly because my head was still ringing. I got slowly to my feet.

A dryad appeared right in front of me, scowling and angry. As far as I could tell this time, she said something like, 'What dost tha want wi' me?'

I couldn't begin to guess how long she had been tending these trees. It had probably been decades, maybe even centuries, since she'd had any dealings with mortal people. I didn't imagine she'd risk being seen by soldiers, and those web pages had said the army had been buying up land for training before the First World War. Before that? I guessed the priory had been shut down by Henry VIII. Once the monks were gone, people would only come up this way for some occasional wood-cutting or snaring rabbits, maybe foraging for mushrooms in the autumn.

'I'm sorry,' I said cautiously. 'I didn't mean any offence.'

Like all dryads, she was beautiful, though in a 'look but don't even think about touching' way. She was taller than me, which was unexpected. Her eyes were dark green, not autumnal copper, but she was a lot older than Asca or my mum. Her face was deeply lined and she wore her long chestnut hair in a thick braid threaded through with strands of ivy as well as streaks of silver. The cloak she wrapped around herself looked like an artist's impression from one of those archaeology programmes, imagining how an Anglo-Saxon might have dressed, or maybe someone living in an Iron Age roundhouse.

She glared at me. 'What do you want in my wood?' She still had an accent three times as dense as Vatne's, but I could understand her now.

I chose my words very carefully. 'A daughter of the rivers told me a man had died here. She saw a wild cat as well, big enough to be a threat to the sheep and the people on these hills.'

The dryad's expression was impossible to read. 'What's that to you or your kin?'

Good question, and I wondered what she meant by my kin. On my mother's side or my dad's? 'We were concerned that other people might come looking for the dead man, and for the cat.'

'You fear their presence would disturb my peace? Unlike the other uses mortal kind makes of my woods these days?' Her sarcasm was withering.

Okay, I deserved that. I tried a different approach. 'If this man had been keeping other animals captive, they might be locked in cages with no one to tend them now he's dead.'

Her eyes narrowed, but I could see she was considering that. Dryads disapprove of cruelty to animals. Well, my mum and the Blithehurst dryads are against it.

'If we knew who he was, if we could find out where he lived, then we would know for sure.'

The dryad's opaque green gaze was seriously intimidating. 'How do you hope to learn such things?'

I made sure my voice was steady as I replied, 'May I ask you some questions? Naturally, I would expect to do something for you in return for any answers you might have.'

'Would you?' She was amused, which was even more unnerving. 'An interesting offer. I will consider it. What do you wish to know?'

'Do you know where the dead man came from? Did he follow the same path as me, or come that way?' I gestured in the direction of the priory.

'I have no idea.' And that was the simple, unhelpful truth.

'Did he drop anything in your woods, or maybe higher up on the fell? Something metal, like a bunch of keys?'

She looked at me, sardonic. 'No, he left nothing behind, and I know what keys are.'

I had wondered if I needed to explain. The dryad must have seen that in my face. Now I knew she might be isolated here, but she wasn't ignorant. Fine. If she was used to seeing the army around, I'd assume she knew what vehicles were too. 'Is there a car or a van parked somewhere, that might have been his?'

'There was a wagon without windows at the back.' Before I could get my hopes up, she went on. 'But that drove away not long after dawn, while I was ridding my home of the carrion.'

She scowled ferociously and I was very relieved I wasn't responsible for the dead man turning up in her woods.

'Can you tell me anything about him? Do you know how he died?'

It had occurred to me, walking up here, that Vatne could have conceivably misunderstood what she saw. If the man had fallen over in the dark, he could have injured himself. A sprained or broken ankle might explain why he was on his hands and knees. He could have died of internal bleeding. The cat might simply have been distressed, not realising what was going on, if it really was tame, or at least, as tame as a wild animal can ever be.

The dryad crushed that theory. 'The beast would not let him drink, just as it would not let him leave the trees. He died of thirst.'

But she had told me something new. 'How long did it keep him here in the woods?'

'Four nights had come and gone before he finally died.'

I remembered something my dad once told me. A person can survive for three minutes without air, three days without water, and three weeks without food without lasting damage. I'm sure Internet experts and real ones would argue about the fine details, but I reckoned that was good enough as a guide.

So the dead man had been trapped in these woods long enough to die of thirst, constantly stalked by the cat. He hadn't been able to slip past it and get back to wherever he had come from. If the cat had been stalking him, why didn't it attack? I'd hoped to find answers, but I was ending up with more questions.

'Have you any idea where the cat is now?'

'I haven't seen it since the man died.'

'Was it wearing a collar or anything else man-made?'

'No.'

'You dropped the dead man down a sink hole—'

'His bones can lie there with the rest.'

For a moment, I wondered what she meant. Then I re-membered reading about caves in Yorkshire with prehistoric animal remains at the bottom. Layers from mammoths to hippopotamuses. Any archaeologists who found that par-ticular sink hole were going to get a shock when they car-bon-dated what they thought was a cave man.

'Could the cat have fallen down there as well, or got trapped somewhere else underground?' Now I was clutching at straws.

The dryad shook her head. 'The animal is nowhere around here now.'

I couldn't think of anything else to ask. 'Thank you.'

She smiled that unnerving smile again. 'Then let us discuss how you will repay me for my answers.'

I tried to look relaxed. 'What do you propose?'

She gazed at her trees before looking straight at me. 'Ask your mother to give you a seedling oak from her wood to bring to me here. Ask her to accept one in return from me. Come back with her answer when winter's stillness turns on the longest night.' Her eyes were penetrating. 'Do I have your word?'

'Yes.' I was relieved she would know I was telling the truth. I didn't want to imagine what could happen to anybody stupid enough to lie. How else could I show her she could trust me? 'My name's Daniel, by the way. Dan.'

I waited to see if she'd tell me her name, but she only nodded and laid a hand on the oak branch I had touched earlier. 'You will be known here, next time.'

'Thank you.' I wondered if—

But she was gone before I could tell her about the dryads at Blithehurst.

Chapter Five

Perhaps that was for the best. I should probably talk to Asca and Frai before I came back here. They might not want me telling an unknown dryad about them, and getting on their wrong side wasn't a good idea. I wondered if the Blithehurst dryads had known I'd get knocked off my feet if I tried that dryad radar trick in an unfamiliar wood? Would they find that amusing?

I decided I'd talk to my mum first and see what she thought I should tell them. For the moment, I was glad this unknown dryad had answered my questions, even if I hadn't learned anything useful. Especially since I hadn't learned anything useful. I hoped my mum would be able to explain the deal I'd just made.

Slipping my rucksack off my shoulders, I found my water bottle and took a long drink. Then I looked to see what had happened to my lunch. The sandwiches were squashed flat and the packet of crisps had exploded. Salt and vinegar shards coated Eleanor's dad's map. Great. Still, at least I'd already eaten the apple.

I dropped my water bottle back into the rucksack. Slinging both straps over one shoulder, I carried on walking along the path. Since I'd come this far, I might as well go and look at Over Cullen Priory (rems of). Apart from anything else, if Anne or anyone else in the pub asked where I'd been today, an honest answer would be safest all round.

The sky opened up above me as I left the trees behind. Fluffy clouds were scudding across the blue. The path cut across the open fellside halfway between the crest of the hill and the river. I say river, but this high up, the water wasn't much more than a stream between scatters of rocks. The cold breeze was strong enough to qualify as a wind and I was glad I had my hat and gloves.

I nearly walked straight past the remains of the priory, hidden in last year's coarse, dry grass. No helpful weather-resistant board offered a potted history beside an artist's impression of what the place had looked like in its heyday, built on ground that had been levelled between the footpath and the river. Even looking down from above, I could barely trace the outlines of ancient masonry nearly hidden by encroaching turf. All I could say was the priory had never been a big place.

As I walked around the site, I guessed a fair amount of building stone for Nether Cullen had come from here. Carrying plundered blocks downhill until the river was deep enough for a flat-bottomed boat to take them downstream would be easy enough.

I found a dry place to sit on the turf and ate my squashed sandwiches. They still tasted fine. I took out Eleanor's dad's map and weighed it down with my water bottle and the energy bars while I ate what was left of the salt and vinegar crisps. I stuck the packet in a pocket and turned the rucksack inside out and shook it. I was going to have to buy Mr Beauchene a new map. This one had greasy marks and grains of salt all over it now.

A couple of magpies appeared. They decided that fragments of the crisps weren't worth having and flew off again. I put everything back in my rucksack and went to take a closer look at a little stream bubbling up out of the fell side. It flowed into a stone-lined gully and side channels disappeared under the turf. I took a few photos on my phone. Fin's interested in historical water management.

Vatne appeared beside me. 'The monks knew the value of cleanliness.'

I wasn't interested in the history of hygiene. 'I met the dryad.'

'We saw.' Kalei appeared. Neither naiad was bothering to masquerade as a human.

I wondered if the dryad had seen them. The spirits of wood and water who I've met can make themselves visible to ordinary people, or only visible to people like me and Eleanor who have inherited a bit more than ordinary blood. They can also keep themselves hidden from us, as Kalei and Vatne had clearly just done. I didn't imagine they'd say, so I didn't ask.

'She didn't have a lot to tell me.'

'We heard.'

'So what now?'

For the first time I could recall, I saw uncertainty ripple across Kalei's face.

'What more can we do?' she was asking me.

'There is no sign of the animal anywhere I can see.' Vatne glowered as if that personally offended her.

I knew how she felt. I wanted this sorted out. I racked my brains for something, anything else we could try. A buffet from the cold wind gave me an idea.

'Do you know any sylphs?' I asked her.

Sylphs are spirits of the air. They follow wind currents and eddies for hundreds of miles. They are also as fickle and unpredictable as the British weather. I couldn't see me per-suading one I didn't already know to do anything I asked, but maybe a naiad would have better luck.

'I do,' Vatne said, grudging.

'Would they be willing to search for the cat?'

She shook her head. 'I doubt it.'

But Kalei answered at the same time. 'We will find a way to convince them.'

'Okay. You do that, and tomorrow morning, after I leave the pub, I'll drive to every place I can find on the map where someone could possibly have parked a car before walking up here. We can meet back at the bridge around noon?'

But Vatne had gone. Kalei shimmered into a convincing appearance of a woman about my own age wearing the latest in hi-tech hiking gear. She spends most of her time in the Peak District, so that wasn't difficult.

'I'll walk back with you.' She started down the path to the woods. 'I should have thought of asking a sylph to help us myself.'

'We thought this dryad would know more.' I put my rucksack back on properly and caught up with her.

She didn't reply to that. We walked on in silence. When we reached the trees, I expected her to say something about me getting knocked on my arse. She probably thought that was hilarious. If she brought it up, I could ask what she knew about how the dryad radar worked. But she didn't say a word.

Would the dryad want to speak to Kalei? I tried not to make it too obvious that I was looking around at the trees. By the time we reached the kissing gate, I decided I need not have bothered. The dryad was nowhere to be seen.

We walked on. I was starting to wonder if Kalei was coming back to the pub with me. If she did, what was she planning to do? Then she stopped in the middle of the path.

'I will take another look at the body. If I find anything new, I will find you tomorrow.' She vanished.

Like me, she was clutching at straws. I walked on. My phone let me know I had reached civilisation, or at least somewhere with a mobile signal, by buzzing in my coat pocket. I leaned against the nearest dry-stone wall and regretted that as I felt the bruise my water bottle had left. I turned around and rested my elbows on the wall as I checked the screen.

A text from Hazel Spinner asked how I had got on and said to ring her back. I didn't have anything better to do. She answered the call at once.

'Hi, Dan. Just let me save what I'm working on...'

I heard a keyboard clicking.

'Right,' she said briskly. 'What can you tell me?'

'Nothing we didn't already know.' No, that wasn't precisely accurate. 'Well, the cat trapped the dead man in these woods until he died. The dryad is certain he died of thirst. That's it.'

'What's she like?' Hazel was intrigued.

'Not someone to get on the wrong side of. Have any of your contacts had anything useful to share?'

Hazel spends a lot of time replying to posts on her website about eerie and uncanny sightings with convincing reasons to explain them away. Even though she knows that naiads and dryads and so much more are absolutely real. She and her contacts don't want ordinary people to believe in the unseen and the supernatural. They're what used to be called wise women, and while they're wholly human, they have uncanny talents of their own. In the past, people who discovered that called them witches, and things went downhill from there.

'Nothing's got loose from a zoo, I can say that much for certain. Apart from that?' She sighed with exasperation. 'No one has heard a thing, but we'll keep our ears open.'

Their long ears? I was glad Hazel couldn't see me grinning. Wise women really can transform themselves into hares, like old fairy tales say.

'I'll check around for abandoned vehicles before I leave tomorrow,' I told her. 'The naiads will take another look at the body, and they're going to try to find a sylph who'll agree to look for the cat a bit further afield.'

'You've been busy.' Hazel approved. 'I know a couple of journalists up that way. I might make a few calls. See if any-one's heard rumours that haven't been worth pursuing for a story.'

As a cryptozoologist, she's often asked for a quote when a newspaper wants to run a story about the Loch Ness monster or sightings of escaped raccoons in the Quantocks. Calls like that can also give the wise women a heads-up about a prob-lem they'll want to deal with.

I tried to look on the bright side. 'At least we don't have to call out the army to track down a man-eating cat.'

'That's good news,' she agreed. 'But I'd still like to know more about this dead man. Maybe missing persons reports will give us a lead.'

Wise women make a point of getting unremarkable jobs in places where they'll see information that alerts them to strange goings-on. They work in hospitals, social services and, I'm willing to bet, the police. They're administrators, secretaries, things like that.

'Let me know if anything turns up.'

'I'll be in touch. Bye.' Hazel ended the call.

As I walked back to the pub, I texted Fin to let her know I'd had plenty of fresh air and exercise on my uneventful hike. I rang Blithehurst and got Eleanor's voicemail. I left a message saying I'd had a good day's hill-walking, that everything was peaceful up here and I'd be heading back tomorrow. They'd both understand what I wasn't saying. I didn't imagine anyone else would read my texts on Fin's phone, but there was no way to know who might be around when Eleanor played her messages.

A different handful of locals were propping up the bar in the Buck in the Dale when I had scraped the mud off my boots and walked in.

'Had a good day?' Neil asked cheerfully.

I thought back to the priory site and the water channels that had interested me. 'I have, thanks.'

'Can I get you anything?' He gestured at the gleaming coffee machine.

'Flat white?'

'Right you are.' He offered me the payment terminal to tap with my card while he got out a cup and saucer. 'I'll bring it over.'

'Thanks.' I sat at the closest table and got out my phone. While I drank my coffee and looked up the dissolution of the monasteries online, I listened to the regulars discussing bird flu. They were wondering how bad the outbreaks in wild birds were going to get. No one said anything about a missing man, a mysteriously abandoned car or a black panther roaming the dales.

After my coffee, I went up to my room. I had time for a shower before they'd start serving food. With a bit of twisting in front of the bathroom mirror, I saw the dark bruise where I'd fallen on my water bottle. It sodding well hurt, but thankfully my mother's blood means I heal fast.

I picked lingering bits of crisps off the map before I spread it out on the bed. I found every conceivable place where I could look for an abandoned car. Since I wasn't going to be giving the map back, I marked the most efficient route between them with a pencil. Remote lanes don't have postcodes to put into a satnav.

I had homemade steak and ale pie for dinner with local vegetables and chips, and a couple of pints of Black Sheep. Whether it was the meal, the beer or the fresh air and exercise, I slept for a solid eight hours.

I packed before I went down to breakfast. I'd told Anne the night before that I'd be on my way today. She'd said she hoped they'd see me again. I'd said I hoped so too. After another good breakfast I went upstairs to get my bag, trying to decide what to do about leaving some sort of tip.

Tipping is something I just don't get. If there's a price, surely that's the price? But Anne had made me those sandwiches and I should pay for those. Then I wondered how much cash I actually had on me. Everyone uses cards these days. I found I had a single twenty-quid note in my wallet. That would have to do. I put it on the tea tray, held down by a mug, and headed out before Anne could find it and we'd have to have an awkward conversation.

Checking out those places where I might find a car was a complete waste of a morning. I didn't see anything out of the ordinary, or either of the naiads, even though I pulled up and got out of the Landy every time I was near flowing water.

The last place I'd marked on the map was a sizeable thicket in a hollow halfway up a valley on the far side of the fell from the priory site. It would be a steep hike to the dryad's wood, but there was a footpath. When I got there, I found a dense cluster of holly trees which could have hidden a bus, certainly a single-decker.

I had better check. I made my way cautiously through the trees, in case the cat had come back here to wait for a lift home. I'd just decided nothing was in there when three roe deer sprang up from nests in the undergrowth. They bounded away and I waited for my heart to stop racing. I could have tried the dryad radar first to get some idea what I might disturb. Maybe next time. Maybe not.

I went back to the broad verge where I'd parked the Landy. I was about to get in when movement near the holly trees caught my eye. I looked over, expecting to see the

Green Man. It was about time he made himself known, if he wanted me to do something about this cat.

He wasn't there. This was someone else. He was massively muscled, bare-chested and barefoot, wearing ragged leggings, and could just about have been taken for human, if you didn't notice he must be over seven feet tall. If you didn't notice his antlers, as big and branching and dangerously eight-pointed as the oldest and wisest red deer stag's. His eyes were vivid gold, a bright contrast with his dark, bushy beard, his thick brows and curly, tangled hair.

I'd seen him before, a few years ago and a long way from here. The dryads called him the Hunter. I remembered that as I stood there like a rabbit caught in someone's headlights. I wondered what he wanted with me.

Then he was gone. I got into the Land Rover and closed the door. I waited for my hands to stop shaking before I tried putting the key in the ignition. Setting up the satnav, I told it to take me home.

I went over that encounter again and again while I was driving back to Blithehurst. Had the Hunter been there to give some clue or some message that I'd missed?

Chapter Six

February half term was busy at Blithehurst. As the days got longer and the weather began to warm up, the garden centre and the restaurant did good trade. March and the equinox came and went.

I didn't see either of the naiads again. That irritated me. I wanted to know if they had found a sylph willing to cooperate. Had they seen anything useful? At least the national news and the North Yorkshire local paper websites didn't report something was savaging sheep. That didn't stop me wondering what the hell had happened to the unknown man in Over Cullen Woods.

I visited my dad on my last Monday off in March. When I pulled up outside the cottage, he opened the front door. He was looking well, and I was glad to see it. I didn't have any reason to think he wasn't okay. We talk on the phone most weeks. All the same, he's over eighty. That's something else I prefer not to think about, to be honest.

He gave me a reassuringly firm hug. 'I put the kettle on when I heard your engine turn down the lane. I've baked a fruit cake. Do you want a slice with your tea?'

'Definitely.' I ate my cake and drank my tea while he brought me up to date with local news. I'd told him about my trip to Yorkshire on the phone. Now I told him about the deal I had made with the mysterious dryad.

'I haven't spoken to anyone else about this, apart from you just now. I thought I should tell Mum face to face.'

Dad was intrigued. 'I wonder what she'll say.'

'Same here.' I felt a lot better now I had told him. 'Do you know where she's likely to be?'

Now that my mum doesn't often have to pretend to be a mortal wife, she spends more and more time outside with her trees. My dad's happy with his radio and the telly and his library books. He's like me, or I'm like him. We don't have a problem spending time on our own.

Dad got up from his chair by the fireplace and collected our plates. 'Over on the far side, near the canal cutting most likely.'

I stood up. 'I'll be back in a bit.'

I crossed the quiet road outside the cottage and walked into the woods. A local birdwatching society had originally bought this overlooked patch of trees and scrub to save it as a nature reserve. Dad had been one of their first volunteers. That's how he met my mum. When he bought the semi-der-elict cottage on the other side of the lane, renovated it and moved in, the society decided to appoint him as their site warden. A nominal payment made that official and gave him a lot more authority if he had to ring the police to report something.

These days, the society has a visitor centre open at week-ends, and a roster of volunteers tackle whatever needs doing, from litter picking to recording when different species of birds nest and hatch their eggs. No one's suggested Dad should step down though, so someone else could take over as warden.

This Monday, the paths through the reserve were de-serted. Dog walkers would have been out earlier, and they'd reappear later on, but for now, I could enjoy the peace and quiet and the sweet spring air. Violets and primroses were dots of bright colour against the dark leaf litter. Other plants that gardeners call weeds were coming into leaf. Sorrel, ramsons and stinging nettles sent up clusters of shoots. The blackthorns were white with blossom and the faint pale green haze of new leaves softened the outlines of beeches and birches. A couple of grey, fluffy squirrel tails went bouncing along high branches. A pair of goldcrests were single-mindedly hunting for nesting material, and any number of other birds flitted around. Insects gleamed when they passed through patches of sunlight, vanishing as they moved on into shadow.

Most of the oak trees are on the far side of the wood. There never was a canal here, but back when barges were the latest innovation in industrial transport, whoever had owned this land was suckered into a get-rich-quick scheme. Unfortunately, it didn't occur to him to ask anyone who knew about geology and geography if this was a workable idea. The digging was abandoned and the only trace left is the long, shallow trench that marks the edge of the nature reserve.

My mother was talking to her favourite trees, gently rousing them from their deep winter sleep. No one but me would be able to see her, so I checked there was no one else around.

'Daniel!' She was right in front of me, wrapping me in a hug. Dryads can move quick as thought through woodland. 'How lovely.'

She smiled, delighted, as she took on the human appearance she has carefully maintained and updated ever since I was born. As far as Dad's friends are concerned, she's a lot younger than him, so these days she pretends to be somewhere in her fifties. Today she wore a pair of old jeans, a faded jumper and a well-worn fleece.

'It's good to see you.' I held her tight for a long moment.

'Daniel?' She pushed me gently away to look up and study my face. She could tell this wasn't some casual visit. 'What have you come to tell me?'

She often joins in with our conversations when I'm on the phone to Dad. Don't ask me how, but dryads can tune in to things like radio waves and mobile signals. That cuts both ways, of course. I'm absolutely certain that Asca and Frai are responsible for the lousy phone reception at Blithehurst. Or maybe it's just Frai. Anyway, Mum already knew as much as Dad did about my trip to Yorkshire. Now she saw something else was up. So I explained the deal I had agreed with the dryad.

'Are you okay with this? Giving this stranger a seedling oak from your own wood?' If not, I would need her to tell me what to say to that other dryad. I'd promised to take Mum's answer to her, whatever it might be.

Mum thought for a few more minutes, then she nodded. 'I am willing, and I will care for her seedling in return. You can give her my word on that.' Her eyes momentarily gleamed as bright green as the sun shining through spring leaves. 'How fascinating.'

'Fascinating how?' I asked immediately.

'We can talk about that later, when you come to collect my seedling. Tell me, how is Fin? How are the trees and the gardens at Blithehurst? Is Eleanor Beauchene well?'

I knew she was asking all these questions to stop me asking her anything else. I would have to wait and hope she would share whatever lay behind this tree swap later. Since she wasn't going to tell me anything about that today, there was something else I wanted to talk about. Something I hadn't mentioned to anyone, not even Dad.

'Asca, the dryad at Blithehurst, showed me how to do something...' I flexed my fingers and reached out to the nearest oak, holding my open hand a few centimetres away from the tree. 'May I?'

I wasn't sure if I was asking Mum or the oak, but she nodded anyway. 'Go on.'

These trees knew me, so I wasn't expecting the same brutal shock I'd had in Yorkshire. Even so, I braced myself as my palm brushed against the rough bark. I could tell at once I was welcome, so I tightened my grip.

Now I sensed the deep, deep drowsiness of the slumbering oak. Slowly, steadily, my awareness spread through the wood. I could feel the blackthorns' sharp alertness. A surge of sap was stirring the silver birches with an urgency that wouldn't be denied. Violets and primroses were eager to swap their pollen and offered up their nectar to those who could help. I sensed moths and butterflies looking for such life-giving sweetness. They had overwintered in the shelter of long trails of ivy or in the nooks and crannies of fallen trees. Those trees were left where they lay, to return everything they had taken in life to the woodland as they decayed. I could feel the pale creamy-brown frills of a bracket fungus feasting on a dead birch.

I looked at Mum. 'How—?'

She laid her hand over mine. Now I could feel right down to the oak's roots as they reached out in all directions. Some were as thick as my forearm while the smallest tendrils were as fine as hairs. I sensed the intricate network of different unseen fungi woven throughout the woodland under the ground. Some trees sustained each other, connected by these thin, pale threads. Others were alert for the chance to seize resources from the soil ahead of their rivals.

Mum smiled sunnily as she lifted her hand. 'So now you know.'

'You didn't show me.' My voice shook as I took my hand off the oak tree. I wasn't complaining, exactly.

'I knew you would come to it in time. Let's go and tell your father.' She threaded her arm though mine and held me close as we started walking towards the cottage.

Realising she wasn't going to explain why she hadn't told me about dryad radar, I asked something else. 'Do you think I should tell the Blithehurst dryads about the seedlings?'

She considered that for longer than I expected. 'Wait for them to ask what this unknown dryad wanted in payment from you,' she said eventually.

'Okay.' I hadn't realised, but she was right. Neither Asca nor Frai had asked me what deal I had made in return for the dryad's answers.

I wondered why not, until we arrived at the cottage and my dad got the dominoes out.

When I got back to Blithehurst, the dryads didn't ask me about anything at all. March slid into April and the Easter school holidays came and went. I saw Asca and Frai every so often while I was busy around the estate. They were only ever interested in discussing the coppices or the fir plantation. They were happy to lend a hand making sure the trees thrived.

May arrived, and by then, the visitor season was well under way. Everyone was busy. The house and the gardens were open six days a week, as well as the restaurant and the garden centre. I was checking the Wilderness Garden for litter late one Friday afternoon when Sarah, who's in charge of the cafe in the castle gatehouse, came to find me.

'Dan!' she called out from halfway across the lawn. 'Eleanor rang down from the house. She says can you pop up to see her? She needs a quick word before the next tour.'

I raised a hand to show I'd heard her. 'No problem.'

The Spring Bank Holidays had Eleanor constantly adjusting the staff rota. I checked the time on my phone and saw the last guided tour of the house today would start in fifteen minutes. I walked up to the manor and went in through the side door. Eleanor was in the entrance hall, waiting for everyone in the final tour party to remember they had timed tickets and to realise where they were supposed to be. She checked her wristwatch as soon as she saw me.

'I'll keep this quick. It's about Sophie's wedding. Well, about weddings in general. I've been thinking. We can't close the house, but maybe there's some way we could use the ruins as a venue. The cafe's already there for catering facilities and we could keep the whole event private by closing the bridge over the moat. We would need some sort of canopy though, or maybe a marquee. Otherwise, Sod's Law guarantees a day pouring with rain. Or a heatwave and everyone getting sunstroke if there's no shade. What do you reckon?'

'It's worth thinking about,' I said cautiously.

'Just as a concept initially. I'm not getting Soph's hopes up until we have a workable solution and know roughly what that would cost—' She broke off and fished her phone out of her jeans pocket. She checked the screen and immediately answered the call.

'Hazel?' She glanced at me to be sure I'd heard.

I waited while Eleanor listened. She looked increasingly concerned.

'Let me call you back. Give me a couple of minutes.' She beckoned to Denise, the member of staff on duty in the dining room. 'Can you take the next tour around the house, please? Something has come up.'

'Of course, my pleasure, you know that.' Denise smiled brightly.

She was a new hire, recently retired from some civil service job. She already knew more about the manor's history than people who'd worked here for years. She kept trying to persuade me to join her Friends of Blithehurst group on the Internet. I told her I don't do social media. She said I was being silly. She knew I'd enjoy it. She'd help me set up some profiles. I said no thanks. She tried to insist. I said no, and this time, she got the message. Now I avoided her as much as I could. I could see she wanted to know what that phone call was about.

'I'm happy to help. You know, if—'

'Thank you.' Eleanor was already heading for the back stairs, and I followed.

The upper door opens right by the gallery. Eleanor only had to cross the corridor to unlock her sitting room door. We had it locked behind us before any visitors gazing at the family portraits had time to wonder what we were doing. Eleanor's phone buzzed again. She answered the call.

'Let me put you on speaker. I've got Dan with me.' She walked over to the bay window and put the phone on the table. As she sat down by her laptop, I pulled up a chair.

'Go ahead,' Eleanor prompted.

'I've had a call from a journalist.' Hazel spoke fast. 'In Devon, not in Yorkshire. He's looking for a quote because the Beast of Bodmin has gone to the seaside. To Darley Combe on the North Devon coast, to be precise.'

I didn't know what to say and Eleanor was lost for words. Hazel's laugh floated up from the phone.

'Cat got your tongue?' She got straight back to business. 'Someone sent my mate a photo they say they took on their phone this morning. It shows a big black cat up on some cliffs. He says it's crystal clear it's not some wandering pet. Obviously he's got someone checking every possible way the pic could have been faked, and he's waiting to hear back from the Defence Infrastructure people, because, guess what? Those particular cliffs are where some MOD land reaches the sea. There's public access along the shoreline though.'

I was pretty sure no one passing the door would overhear us, but I kept my voice down. 'Have any dead bodies turned up?'

'Not yet.' Hazel sounded grim regardless. 'As soon as my mate can stand the story up, he'll publish. He can't risk anyone else getting in first. His editor would kill him. Once this hits the Internet, the place will go nuts. If we're going to have a look, we need to get down there right away.'

'Daniel?' I saw Eleanor looking past me at the fireplace.

Five or so years ago, I had carved some images of the Green Man. They look like masks because I had left holes for his eyes framed by the overlapping oak leaves that make up his face and beard. I'd given one to Eleanor and she keeps it on her mantelpiece. I turned and saw the vivid emerald gleam in his eyes. There was no point in any more discussion. The Green Man would turn up in my dreams to make it clear I had to do this if I didn't agree. I wondered what we were going to find out.

'Are you still there?' Hazel thought she'd been cut off.

'How do you spell the name of that place?' Eleanor opened up her laptop and started typing as Hazel told us.

I shifted my chair so we could both see the screen. Darley Combe turned out to be a miniscule dot of a place west of Ilfracombe, on the coast where Exmoor comes down to the sea. Bodmin is miles away in Cornwall, but that wouldn't get in the way of a good headline.

I did a quick calculation. 'It's at least a four-hour drive. It could be twice that with bad Friday traffic on the M5. I'll be lucky to be there before midnight. With no moon to speak of, we won't be able to see a thing.'

'Fin's working from home this week.' Eleanor looked at me. 'You could stay overnight with her and set off bright and early tomorrow morning.'

'The earlier the better,' Hazel agreed. 'We want to get out to the foreshore before anyone else is around.'

'You're driving up from Exeter?'

'I'm already here.'

I looked at my phone screen. If I rang Fin, of course she'd say I could stay with her tonight. Then she'd come with me to Devon in the morning. There was no question about that. What if I didn't ring her? Was I going to keep this trip a secret? Hardly. She already knew what had happened in Yorkshire. Was I going to tell her she shouldn't be involved in solving this mystery? That this big cat might be too dangerous? I'd tried to keep her safe like that once before. It had almost ended our relationship. She'd told me in no uncertain terms that she made her own decisions.

'Let me check with Fin.'

Her phone rang a few times, then she answered. 'Hello there.'

'I'm with Eleanor, and she's got Hazel on speaker,' I said quickly, before Fin could say anything that should be private. 'Are you at home? In the flat, I mean.'

'What's going on?' She didn't need telling something strange had come up.

I explained. I didn't even need to ask if I could stay with her.

'Stop here tonight, and we'll get on the road first thing. What sort of time do you think you'll arrive? What do you want to do about food?'

'I'll eat here and drive down later, when the Friday traffic has cleared.'

'Makes sense,' she agreed. 'Text me when you set off?'

'Will do.'

'Love you.' Fin ended the call.

'Right then,' Hazel said briskly. 'I'll see you both tomorrow, as early as you can.'

Eleanor's phone screen went dark. She stuck it in her back pocket. 'I'll need to think up a good excuse for giving you the weekend off and buggering up the staff rota.'

'Sorry.' I genuinely was.

Still, Fin and I hadn't thought we would get together before the end of the month. Though we would have to get some sleep before we drove to Devon. We couldn't spend the whole night making love.

Chapter Seven

Fin shares the flat near Bristol with her sister Blanche. They run their water consultancy business out of the spare room. Blanche was away for the weekend, and she had left by the time I arrived. That suited me. We can find it hard to relax around each other.

Fin opened the door wearing a silky dressing gown. I left my clothes where I dropped them on our way to her bedroom. We took our time enjoying ourselves, and finally set our phone alarms for 4.30 a.m. In the morning, a quickie before we showered meant cereal for breakfast. Totally worth it.

As we walked down the stairs, Fin jingled her keys. 'I went out and filled the tank yesterday evening.'

'Good thinking.' I'd left my keys on the dining table and my Land Rover was parked in a visitor's space. Fin prefers her own car. She prefers just about anything to the Landy for a long drive. I'm not bothered.

The sky grew lighter as we reached the motorway. Fin put her foot down and the little Toyota clocked up the miles. The sun rose and strengthened, though I could see plenty of clouds. Fin switched on the radio to get the forecast and the news headlines on the hour. Apparently the weather was going to be changeable.

Motorway traffic wasn't too bad for a Saturday. It wasn't peak tourist season yet. When we left the A361, I called Hazel to let her know we weren't too far off.

'Though this isn't the fastest road.' I looked at the twists and curves ahead on the navigation app Fin used, clipping her phone on the dash. The road was lined with hedges on top of earth banks reinforced with stone.

'Watch out for tractors,' Hazel advised.

We reached Darley Combe just before seven. The village was strung out along the last mile or so of the narrow road heading to the coast. Narrow terraced cottages that had to be centuries old gave way to bigger, double-fronted houses closer to the sea. This must have once been a place where Victorians had come for their holidays. These days most of the houses would be self-catering rentals. The place would be a ghost town in winter.

The road sloped steeply down to the sea. Side streets claimed whatever flat land they could. We passed several pubs and a village hall. The High Street was barely wide enough for two vans to pass each other. Here and there, I caught sight of a little river racing the road.

The only bridge was just before the beach, where the road ended in a T-junction. Go left, and an even narrower road headed west, winding up the headland in tight bends. From what Hazel had told us, that must be the way to find the MOD land where the cat had been prowling.

Go right, and we'd drive over the little bridge. Then we could go straight ahead into a car park overlooking the beach or follow the road as it doubled back to head inland. The land didn't rise so steeply on this side of the river. Clusters of modern houses had been built to enjoy unobstructed views down the steep-sided cove. Somewhere behind those little developments, the road must turn east. I could see the coast route climbing the other headland to carry on over the hill.

Fin pulled into the nearly empty car park. On the left, as we looked out at the beach, a broad concrete ramp led down to the shore. Beyond that, the stony bed of the little river spread out to merge with the beach and the fresh water disappeared into the sea. On the right-hand side of the car park, a white-painted block of public toilets stood next to a flight of steps down to the sand. A tarmac path carried on past the toilets to follow the coastline all the way up to the edge of the cliffs.

Fin switched off the engine. 'I'm going for a pee.'

I got out of the Toyota and did a few stretches before I did the same. There's barely enough leg room in that car, even when I slide the seat all the way back. A strong breeze gusted around me, but I didn't think it was going to rain.

'I've got a ticket. The tide's on its way in, but that shouldn't be a problem for several hours.' Fin walked over from the pay and display machine as I got back from the Gents.

'Right.' She would know. Fin grew up not far from the sea in the Fens. I was born about as far inland as it's possible to get in Britain.

The car park was significantly higher than the beach. A white-painted three-barred iron railing stopped people walking off the edge and finding that out the hard way. I looked down to see three metres of smooth concrete wall disappearing into dull grit banded with ridges of shingle. Victorians expecting expanses of golden sand must have been disappointed. Maybe it would look better in the sunshine, but I wasn't convinced.

A couple of gulls were pecking at stranded clumps of seaweed. I looked out to sea. Dark cliffs rose steeply from the water on either side of the narrow cove. Stones that had fallen or been dug out of those headlands were piled up to make a breakwater about halfway to the open sea. Any boatman looking for safe harbour there would have to get through a whole lot of other rocks first.

Four other cars were parked here. I recognised the muddy white Ford Fiesta. Hazel wasn't anywhere to be seen, so I guessed she was in the coffee shop or the small supermarket. The chip shop on the right of the modern building on the far side of the tarmac was clearly closed. The supermarket in the middle was twice as wide as the other two units. I watched a teenager prop the door open. He brought out two big mesh bins full of vividly coloured footballs and frisbees, followed by a rack of plastic buckets and spades which I couldn't see making a dent in that beach.

Hazel came out of the coffee shop with a takeaway cup in her hand. 'Morning,' she called out cheerfully.

Fin put the parking ticket inside the Toyota. 'What do you want?' she asked me. 'Tea or coffee?'

'Coffee, thanks. Ordinary coffee. Milk and two sugars, please.'

'Right you are.' She headed for the cafe.

'Reasonable journey?' the wise woman asked when she reached me.

'Not bad.' I didn't ask what she'd found out so far. She could tell us both when Fin got back.

Hazel walked over to look out at the sea. I didn't know how old she was, and I wasn't about to ask, but I saw more grey than I remembered in her dark, collar-length hair. The lines around her chestnut-brown eyes were deeper too. I guessed she was somewhere between ten and fifteen years older than me.

The gulls who had been down on the beach flew up to perch on the railing not far away. Close to, they were bigger than I expected, with snowy-white heads and breasts and black-tipped wings with the same pale grey feathers as their backs. I didn't want to get any nearer to their hooked yellow beaks, as their beady eyes assessed whether or not we had anything to offer them.

'Herring gulls.' Hazel sipped her coffee. 'Noisy bastards and a right menace. They rip open bin bags looking for food. Rubbish goes everywhere and attracts rats.'

'Do any of your contacts know of a naiad with any interest in this river?' I watched the fresh water carving grooves in the gritty sand. 'Or maybe a nereid?' I'd met one of those in East Anglia. They live in estuaries, riding the ebb and flow of the tides.

Hazel shook her head. 'Sorry.'

I knew that was as much as she would tell me. The wise women keep each other's names and personal information secret. I leaned back on the rail to watch Fin walk across the car park with a cup in each hand. The clouds overhead were breaking up. Her pale blonde ponytail gleamed in a moment of sunshine. I could watch her all day.

'Americano with cold milk and sugar.' Fin handed me a cup. She took the lid off her latte and sipped cautiously. 'So what do we do now?'

'We find the place where that photo was taken and see what we can see from the foreshore.' Hazel finished her drink and threw the cup in the nearest bin. The gulls watched her intently.

My coffee was stronger and more bitter than I like, but it would keep me awake. That was what counted today.

Hazel clapped her hands to scare the herring gulls away. She glanced at Fin. 'Are you seeing much bird flu when you're doing fieldwork?'

Fin grimaced. 'More than we'd like. We report the dead birds, but we don't go near them.'

I didn't like the sound of that, but that was a conversation for another time. Fin and I drank our coffee as quickly as we could.

Hazel watched us. She was worse than those herring gulls. 'I did a quick recce yesterday, before I gave you a call.'

I'd drunk as much of the coffee as I wanted. 'Let's go. If you've finished that?'

I held out a hand. Fin gave me her empty cup. I shoved them in the bin as we followed Hazel. She was already half-way down the ramp, which I realised was a slipway for boats. Fin followed her across the grey sand and I followed Fin. The river fanned out into shallow channels across the beach, easy enough to step over. On the other side, ribbed slabs and ridges of grey rock jutted up from the water.

'I thought you said there was a path along the foreshore,' Fin called out to Hazel.

'I said there was public access.'

We picked our way carefully over the rocks, avoiding pools of seawater that would soon be reclaimed by the tide. The water on our right-hand side looked dark and deep. Every so often, we had to step over gashes cut through the grey stone where runnels of rainwater came off the cliffs. I looked up and saw dark earth and lighter turf marking the edge of the solid ground up there. Clumps of gorse bushes and stunted pine trees stirred in the breeze.

Say 'cliffs' and people think of Dover. This ragged coast-line was nothing like those white chalk heights. Short stretch-es of fractured rock headed inland until another headland stuck out into the sea. Down by the water, waves broke against low ridges of stone. Rounded lumps further out showed how they would look worn down by time and tide.

'How far are we going?' Fin wanted to know as we reached the mouth of the cove. 'We need to keep an eye on the time.'

'We're nearly there.' Hazel crossed a flat expanse of rock and began picking her way around a tall wedge of stone that was stubbornly resisting the sea.

I glanced back to calculate how far we had come. I was surprised to realise the car park was already hidden by the ir-regular line of these cliffs. I told myself that was a good thing. No one would see us out here. No one would see us if we got into trouble either. I felt unpleasantly exposed as we left the debatable shelter of the cove and the open sea stretched out to the horizon.

'Watch your step here.' Fin was being very careful where she put her feet as she edged around the big stone wedge.

When I got there, I found the exposed rock was uncomfortably narrow for size-fourteen boots. If I slipped, I'd go right in. The water was clouded with seaweed, so I couldn't see how deep it was, but that wouldn't be good. My wallet and phone were in a zip pocket, but that wouldn't keep seawater out. I tried to find handholds as I inched along, but the grey stone offered sod all help. I finally got safely to the far side of the rock and found a small cove with a crescent beach of steeply shelving grey sand. I tried not to think about having to go back.

Fin gazed up at the cliffs, shading her eyes with one hand. 'This is where that photo was taken?'

'That's right.' Hazel was looking at her phone. 'The metadata checks out, and my journalist friend has looked into the bloke who sent it in. Checked his social media for red flags. He's convinced the picture's genuine. His editor's waiting to see if they can get an official quote before they run the story.'

'What do the army use this place for?' I had found the relevant OS map in Blithehurst's library. This bit of land was marked as MOD property with no public footpaths we could use to get a closer look. The only information online were some ancient by-laws from the 1920s which didn't say anything useful.

'It's more likely to be the Royal Marines.' Hazel offered me her phone. 'My mate says they practise climbing these cliffs in all weathers, at all times of year, and at night as well as in daylight. The lad who took the photo is thinking of joining up, so he came to take a look. His grandad was a Marine.'

'Fair enough.' I studied the picture.

I couldn't say if this big cat was a leopard or a jaguar, but I knew black panther was the name used for variants of both species. I'd looked it up. Right now, what a zoologist might call it wasn't relevant. A sizeable wild animal was perched on the edge of the cliff, snarling to show vicious white fangs. Its vivid yellow eyes were looking straight into the camera. From the way its front feet were placed on the rock face, with its backside and long tail still higher up on the turf, it looked as though the big cat was trying to find a way down to the sand.

'What did this lad do, when he saw it up there?' Apart from wondering where he could find a change of underwear.

'As soon as it saw him, he said it backed off. They do prefer to avoid people, as a rule.'

Hazel's certainty reminded me her cryptozoology expeditions had taken her to places where big cats still survive.

I had a lot more questions. 'How the hell did it get here from North Yorkshire? Do we seriously think it walked all the way without being seen? Someone must have brought it here, surely?'

'Assuming it's the same animal.' Hazel held out her hand for her phone.

I handed it back. 'You think some network of illegal jaguar breeders is letting them loose around the country?' Even if there was, why would that concern the Green Man? Though I could see that might well piss off the Hunter.

'I don't know what to think,' Hazel admitted, frustrated.

'Do we think it's still somewhere up there? How about I go and take a look?'

Fin handed me her shoulder bag. I closed my eyes against a flash of blinding light, for people like me at least. Ordinary people wouldn't notice a thing.

I opened my eyes and watched a snowy-white swan paddling out to sea. Fin sees uncanny things because she's a swan maiden. A shapeshifter, like her sisters and her mum. As far as I know, pretty much all her relatives on that side of her family can do it, including the men.

Living in the Fens in days gone by, they could keep their secret with some careful subterfuge. These days, the challenges are different. Some things are easier, and some are more difficult. That's modern life for all of us who have one foot in the ordinary world and the other in the unseen.

Hazel and I watched Fin take off. She wheeled around in a wide arc, gliding on long, strong wings. As she swept over our heads, heading inland with her neck outstretched, I reminded myself she wasn't stupid. She would fly so high even the most ambitious big cat couldn't jump up and grab her.

There was no reason for me to stand there, staring up at the cliff. I didn't move all the same. Hazel didn't speak and neither did I. There was nothing to be said until Fin came back. Thankfully, we didn't have to wait long. She soared back out to sea, landed on the rippling surface and paddled back to shore. As she waddled up the gritty sand, I couldn't help grinning. Swans are graceful in flight or on the water, but they really aren't built to be pedestrians. I closed my eyes as she transformed back.

'You do remember that a swan can break a man's arm?' She took her shoulder bag off me.

'Sorry?' Hazel was confused.

'Family joke.' Fin grinned.

'I see. Well?' Hazel was far more interested in what Fin might have seen.

'No sign of the cat anywhere.' She shook her head, apologetic.

'Damn. Though if it's found a sheltered spot for a lair, somewhere quiet, it'll be well hidden. I need to get in there myself and look for traces on the ground. There'll be a scent trail for a start. I can't get up this cliff though. We need to find a quiet spot where I can slip through the MOD perimeter. I had a quick recce when I got here yesterday, before it got dark. It's a serious fence, with razor wire and an overhang at the top, but there has to be a weakness somewhere.'

Hazel was talking about looking for the cat while she was transformed into a hare. As far as I was concerned, that was quite literally a hare-brained idea. 'It'll pick up your scent as soon as the wind blows its way. Hello, lunch.'

'How long should we give you?' Fin asked. 'You had better leave us with a number to ring, to let someone know you've probably been injured or eaten.'

Hazel looked as if she wanted to argue. I was relieved to see her shake her head, silently admitting that this predator was too great a threat. 'So what are we going to do?'

She was still frustrated, and I couldn't blame her. So was I. I looked up the cliff with a hand shading my eyes. I didn't want to meet Fin's gaze or Hazel's. Fin would see I was hiding something, and Hazel would have her suspicions. I had a way to find out where the big cat was lurking. If we went inland and if there were trees on both sides of the MOD wire, I could try the dryad radar.

Would I get the same shock I'd had in Yorkshire though? And how was I going to explain what I was doing? I wasn't sure I wanted Hazel to know about the dryad radar before I'd talked to Fin. I was pretty sure whenever one wise woman learned something new, the rest of them found out as soon as they checked their email or their crystal ball.

Would knowing where the cat was hiding tell us anything useful? We would still have to get through the fence or an MOD gate to get to it. I didn't fancy our chances of doing either. What could we do if we did corner the cat in its lair? I wasn't going to try wrestling a black panther into submission and carrying it off to cram it into Hazel's Fiesta.

Seawater surged up the beach. I looked down to see a ruffle of foam sweep past my boots and soak away into the sand.

Fin looked over her shoulder. 'The tide can't already be...'

I turned to see why she had stopped talking. Wide-eyed, Hazel pressed a hand to her mouth.

A mermaid floated lazily on the surface of the sea, as relaxed as someone sprawled on a sofa. 'You're not the usual sort of tourists we get around here.'

Chapter Eight

The mermaid was gorgeous. Golden-haired with wide blue eyes. Her cheeks dimpled as she smiled, and her mouth was full, soft and kissable. Forget any clam-shell bra. I could see her rosy nipples through the long, smooth curls that brushed her fabulous, lightly tanned tits. If she had been standing up – assuming she was ever able to stand up – she'd have a narrow waist and rounded hips that promised a temptingly curved backside. Her long tail was covered with pale scales tinged with gold, and tipped with a delicate, translucent fin.

She gave Fin a swift glance, and assessed Hazel just as fast. As she turned her attention to me, her gaze didn't waver. We could have been the only two people for miles around.

'You're a long way from home. Can you swim? It will be my pleasure to teach you. I can show you so many wonders of the seas.' She was breathlessly intense, as if I was the most fascinating man she'd ever seen. She stretched a hand towards me, incidentally giving me a better view of her tits.

'I'm fine, thanks.' I hoped my lack of interest in whatever she might be offering was clear. I didn't want to piss her off, but I wasn't even going paddling with her around.

I'd never met a mermaid, but I had encountered fearsome mermen, or tritons, or whatever they call themselves. I don't know because we didn't stop to chat when they were rescuing me from something even scarier. Recalling what I'd seen of them, I reckoned this tempting fantasy was nothing like the mermaid's real appearance. As I knew from dealing with the naiads, water takes on whatever shape it likes. I wondered how many porno mags had been lost over the sides of fishing boats before adult entertainment had gone online.

The mermaid laughed, and that wasn't a sweet, seductive sound. If I hadn't known better, I'd have thought I was hearing seabirds calling on the wind. She raised her arms like a diver and jack-knifed to disappear beneath the water.

'Damn it,' Hazel said, exasperated.

The mermaid reappeared, much closer to us now. Lean, lithe and muscular, she hoisted herself up to sit on a convenient rock. Think marathon runner, not Marilyn Monroe. Her hair was short, sleek and silver. Translucent fins stretched from her elbows to her armpits. Her pale skin was faintly tinged with blue, and while she was clearly female, she barely had any breasts to speak of. Silver scales started high on her torso and darkened to blue-grey as they ran down the length of her powerful tail to reach a broad dark fin. Her face was sharper, with thin pale lips, and her lidless blue eyes were penetrating.

She gave me a very different smile. 'I see you have both feet firmly on the ground, as befits a son of the greenwood. What brings you here?'

I couldn't think of any reason not to tell her. 'A big cat was seen on the top of this cliff yesterday. We want to know more about it.'

'Do you?' She smiled again, showing unnervingly sharp teeth.

Given sex with a mermaid could surely only be oral... I quickly ditched that thought.

'How did you know we were here?' Hazel asked.

The mermaid stared at Fin with unnerving curiosity. 'It's rare enough to see a swan in my waters. I have never met such a swan as you.'

Dryads, naiads and the like can see at once when some-one like me or Fin is a bit more than ordinarily human. I wished we'd thought there might be mermaids around here before Fin had gone into the water. I thought about her in swan form, paddling on the sea's surface as the mermaid came up from the depths below. I pictured those sharp-nailed hands reaching up to grab her. I tensed every muscle to stop an instinctive shiver. You don't show fear to a preda-tor.

The mermaid's glance flickered to me all the same. 'What do you want to know?'

'What might you ask from us in return?' I countered.

The mermaid folded her arms. 'If you can rid my coast of this beast, that will be service enough to settle any debt between us.'

Once I'd unravelled her reply, that sounded promising. 'Did you see the cat yesterday?'

She nodded. 'And the day before.'

'What was it doing?' Hazel asked before I could.

'He pursued a man to the edge of the cliff several times. When the man finally fell, he left him to die broken on the rocks.' The mermaid didn't share our shock. 'What of it?'

'Never mind. Please, go on,' Hazel said quickly.

The mermaid studied each one of us before she contin-ued. 'He chased the man off the cliff in the dead of night. At first light, he returned, to climb down without risk of break-ing his own neck. Once he was satisfied the man was dead, he filled his pockets with stones and hauled him out onto those rocks.' She gestured, but wherever she meant must already be covered by the returning tide. 'He dropped the body into a narrow cleft. He dropped rocks after, to hold him there until the scavengers have stripped the flesh from the bones.'

Like the skeleton that would be left when the dead man in the Yorkshire sink hole had rotted away. Then something she had just said struck me like a slap to the back of the head.

'How does a cat do any of that?' I could just about imagine a big cat dragging a body if it could get a good mouthful of clothing, but filling its victim's pockets with stones?

'He does that as man, not cat.' As far as the mermaid was concerned, that was nothing remarkable.

'Fuck.' I stared at her.

'He could shift from one shape to the other?' Hazel had to be absolutely certain. 'From man to cat and from cat to man?'

'Yes.' The mermaid looked surprised that we were surprised.

I realised she'd said 'he does that', not 'he did that'. This was getting worse and worse. 'You've seen him before? Has he killed other people and hidden their bodies in these rocks?'

'For a few years now, though there is no pattern of the moon or the tide in his visits.' The mermaid scowled. 'If I had known he was coming again, I would have been ready to deal with him. Warn me beforehand next time, and I will be in your debt.'

I was pretty sure that encounter would put an end to these killings. These murders. I saw Hazel and Fin wanted to get off these rocks and back to the car park as urgently as me. We needed to talk this through without anyone listening in, human or otherwise.

'How can we let you know when we wish to speak to you again?' Hazel asked politely.

The mermaid stared at Fin for a long moment. 'Ride these waves, swan maid, and I will know you are here.'

94

'Of course.' Fin sounded a lot calmer about doing that than I felt. 'We had better get back to the beach now, before the rising tides cuts us off.'

'Please excuse us,' Hazel agreed quickly.

Fin was already heading for the wedge-shaped pillar of rock. I waited for Hazel to follow her. I wondered if the mermaid was going to watch us leave. I wondered what she might do if one of us slipped and fell into the sea. A moment later, she slid back into the water and disappeared with a twist of her powerful tail.

I made my way safely around the big rock and followed the others along the foreshore. We got back to the beach without anyone getting soaked or breaking an ankle.

'Coffee,' Hazel said emphatically. She climbed the slipway with long strides.

I wasn't going to argue, though I was thinking about something else. 'I've got an OS map in the car. Let's take a look at this MOD site's boundaries before we do anything else.'

'You two do that and I'll get more coffee.' Fin tossed me her keys.

'Good idea.' Hazel headed for the Toyota. 'Latte, no sugar, thanks.'

I got into the front passenger seat while Hazel sat behind the steering wheel. I reached around to get the map off the back seat and unfolded the uncooperative paper. I'd already gone online and ordered a new copy of this particular OS sheet for Eleanor's dad's collection.

'And we are... there.' I found Darley Combe and folded the map into something more manageable.

'Here be mermaids,' Hazel remarked. 'It's a shame they don't put that on maps these days.'

'Have you ever met one before?'

'Have you ever heard of anyone who could shift into a big cat?' The wise woman spoke just quickly enough to avoid answering my question.

'No.' And since she was asking me, I guessed Hazel hadn't either.

'Fin's never mentioned anything?'

'No, but we don't exactly sit around swapping monster stories. That said, we've gone through enough books and websites about weird things. If I'd read about something like that, I'd have told her, just out of interest. I think she would have told me.'

'May I?' Hazel reached for the folded map. She looked at the coloured sheet as if she was studying the coastline. I wasn't convinced. I reckoned she was deciding what she was going to tell the other wise women. That was fine with me. The sooner we found someone who could shed some light on this puzzle, the better.

Fin wasn't long getting the coffees. I saw her coming with a cardboard tray holding three cups that had a brown paper bag balanced on top. I got out, and so did Hazel. I took the tray so Fin could get into the car. I handed everything back to her and went around to the passenger door again.

'Blueberry muffins.' Fin was passing the paper bag back to Hazel. As I sat down, she handed one of the coffees to me. 'NATO standard.'

'What?' I looked at her blankly.

'White with two sugars. That's NATO standard coffee, according to the soldier who tried to chat me up while I was waiting to be served.' Fin wasn't particularly amused.

Those legends about men so infatuated with swan maidens that they stole the feathers the women must possess if they're to transform themselves into birds? Unpleasantly true, according to Fin. Meeting her had made me see that having more than ordinarily human allure was very different from her point of view. When I was younger, once I'd left home, it didn't bother me that a girl who invited me into her bed didn't realise she was drawn to my greenwood blood. Now I knew better.

'That answers one question.' Hazel handed me the brown paper bag.

'The Royal Marines have arrived,' Fin confirmed. 'What do you suppose they'll do?'

'Does it matter?' I put my coffee in a cup holder so I could take out a blueberry muffin and a couple of paper napkins. 'They can beat the bushes on top of those cliffs for as long as they like. That cat is long gone, and he won't even be a cat any more. He has to have had a vehicle somewhere close, so he could be anywhere in the country by now.'

'The dryad said a car had been parked not far from her woods for a day or so,' Fin recalled.

I swallowed a mouthful of muffin. 'She said it drove off once the man was dead. This bastard must have been driving. Job done. Home for tea and biscuits.'

I guessed this explained why the cat hadn't eaten its – his victims. I really hoped so. Things were bad enough without adding what must surely count as cannibalism.

'So we're dealing with a cold-blooded killer.' In the back seat, Hazel sounded uneasy.

'A serial killer,' Fin pointed out. 'There have been at least three murders. There's the dead man in Yorkshire, and the mermaid said he'd done this here before.'

'Shit. When the dryad told me about dropping the dead man down the sink hole, she said, "His bones can lie there with the rest." I thought she was talking about animals that had fallen down there and died. She could have meant more murder victims.'

'Quite possibly,' Hazel agreed, 'but it's hardly worth the mileage to go and ask her.'

'Not really, no.' I was irritated with myself all the same.

'He's not only a killer.' Fin was still thinking about the murderer. 'He torments his victims. He wants them to die in pain.'

'And he's put some thought into that.' Hazel sounded grim. 'How precise do you think the mermaid could be about the dates when she's seen him before?'

I shook my head. 'Not very, if dryads and naiads are anything to go by. You could probably get the time of year, but that'll be about it.'

Fin was trying to make sense of this. 'I can see how a big cat would find it easier to get over the fencing, but how did he force his victims to climb over?'

'I imagine being chased by an enormous cat with razor-sharp claws would be an incentive. Does it matter?' I asked.

Hazel wasn't going to be distracted. 'He knows where to find these bits of MOD land. They're nothing special and tucked well out of the way, hundreds of miles apart. Could he be an ex-soldier? That could explain why he's not bothered by dead bodies.'

'Or he could have worked as a paramedic, or as a hospital porter, or for an undertaker, or in a slaughterhouse.' I'd read a book by a pathologist who'd got over any squeamishness about blood and dead meat when she'd had a teenage Saturday job in a butcher's shop.

'What good would that be, knowing what he used to do?' Fin demanded. 'It's not as if ex-soldiers have to register their addresses for someone to look up.'

'I'm just trying to think how we might find some leads.' Hazel heaved an exasperated sigh.

I stared out through the windscreen and wondered if some wise woman worked in whatever government department dealt with ex-soldiers' pensions and things like that. But official records wouldn't carry useful notes like 'transforms into a black panther at will'.

The only sound in the Toyota was the three of us drinking coffee. Fin offered me the paper bag for my empty cup and other rubbish. She scrunched the top closed. I had been thinking about the whodunnits I get from the library.

'If we can't find out anything about the killer, how about his latest victim? Would it be a big story for your mate the journalist if a dead body washed up on this beach? Would he want to find out who it was and what had happened?'

'He would,' Hazel agreed, 'though I expect this corpse's pockets will be empty, like the one in Yorkshire's.'

'He'll still have fingerprints, won't he, if he only died the night before last?' I hoped I was right about that. 'There's DNA. If his isn't on file with the cops, there'll be dental records. Maybe they'll issue an artist's impression for the papers and the telly.'

'Someone must be missing him.' Hazel was starting to like this idea.

'Once we know who he is, maybe we can get some idea of who wanted him dead.' That might not be much of a starting point, but it had to be better than nothing.

'Assuming the mermaid is willing to fetch him up from the depths. Fin?' Hazel leaned forward between the front seats.

Fin folded her arms and stared out through the windscreen. 'What then? Suppose we find out who's killing these men – and that's a long shot if you ask me. We can't go to the police and expect them to believe us. I don't imagine they'll find any useful forensic evidence after this man's been soaked in the sea. We have no proof or witnesses who could stand up in court. What are we going to do then? This isn't a shadow giant trying to get a foothold in reality, or a lake monster drowning teenagers. We're talking about...' She struggled to find the right word. 'A person. A person like us.'

'Nothing like us,' Hazel said instantly.

Fin looked at me. 'If he's got a car, he's got a driving licence and insurance – most likely,' she added before I could point out how many fuckwits don't bother with those things. 'He must do something to earn money for fuel. We have no idea who might miss him, if we... if we...' She couldn't go on.

She'd made her point. The menaces the Green Man had sent me up against before now had been creatures of wood or water or of shadow. When I'd managed to defeat them, the greenwood, the waters or the darkness had reclaimed them. However hard I'd had to fight to win, I hadn't had to dispose of a body afterwards.

That wasn't even the biggest challenge I could see. There was a world of difference between the idea of fighting some creature from a folk tale and killing a man I might pass on the street. Someone as human as me, Fin or Hazel, even if he was a murdering bastard. He might beg for mercy, or yell with pain. Thinking about any of that made me feel sick.

How was I supposed to kill another human being? Shotgun? I'd have to get hold of one just for a start, and I didn't have a licence. Use a knife? I honestly didn't think I could. My fighting experience is limited to dickheads in pubs out to make a point by taking on the biggest man in the bar. This bastard was a murderer. I'm really not.

'The mermaid said she would deal with him,' I said slowly. 'If we can tell her to expect his next visit.'

'Get her to do the dirty work, you mean?' Fin wasn't happy with that idea.

'That's a big "if".' Hazel wasn't convinced. 'And someone else will have to die first.'

That was undeniable. I thought about the two dead men. One had died of thirst within sight of a flowing river. How sadistic was that? How long had it taken the poor sod here to die in agony from broken bones and internal injuries after he'd been forced off that cliff? This killer was a vicious fucker. And those were only the victims we knew about, even if we still didn't know who they were.

I decided I had no problem with turning this killer over to the mermaid. More wet work than dirty work if the thrillers I read were accurate. That was appropriate. I didn't say that out loud.

'Someone must be missing this dead man. Even if we can't find any clues to tell us who could have killed him, once his body turns up, at least whoever cares about him will know what's happened.'

Fin stared at me for a long moment. Then she heaved an irritated sigh and opened the driver's door. She didn't exactly slam it, but she used more force than was strictly necessary to shut it. I watched her walk down the slope of the slipway.

Hazel was already thinking ahead. 'Let's hope we get an ID quickly. Then we can find out a lot more about this victim.'

I didn't say anything. I was still watching Fin walk away.

Chapter Nine

We waited. When I glanced over my shoulder, Hazel was doing something on her phone. From the speed her thumbs were working, I guessed she was emailing some other wise women. Probably the two she worked with most closely and most often. They seem to work in threes. I didn't bother asking.

To my relief, Fin didn't take long. She got back into the Toyota and pulled the black stretchy loop off her ponytail. 'Soldiers are searching along the top of the cliff. There are more of them down on the rocks. It doesn't look as if they've found anything.'

'Were you able to talk to the mermaid?' That was Hazel's main concern.

'I flew a bit further along the coast and she came to find me.' Fin smoothed her blonde hair back and twisted the elastic around her ponytail. 'She'll make sure the body washes up here on the beach at the next high tide.'

'When's that?' I asked.

Hazel was already checking on her phone. 'Half past ten, as good as.'

I checked the clock on the dashboard. More than an hour to wait. It was hard to believe it was still so early, but we had been up since sparrow fart.

'That's going to spoil their day.' Fin watched a mum walking across the car park with two boys somewhere around ten years old. The kids carried buckets and spades. Their mum had a big holdall slung over one shoulder.

'There are other beaches.' Hazel was busy on her phone again.

Expecting that little family to drive somewhere else assumed they had a car. They had walked down here. I was going to say that to Fin when she leaned back in her seat and closed her eyes. I wasn't sure if she was taking a nap or if she just didn't want to talk about what we were going to do next. Either way, she'd made her choice, so I left her alone.

We sat and waited. We each made a trip to the toilets. The car got stuffy, so I lowered my window a few inches. Hazel didn't comment and nor did Fin. More vehicles arrived. A family of five had crammed themselves and what looked like enough gear to camp for a week into a Renault hatchback. Three solidly built white-haired men unloaded rods, folding stools and tackle boxes from a plain white van. They clearly knew where they were going as they walked over the rocks and out along the breakwater to set up for a day's fishing.

Six determined swimmers got out of a people carrier. They were already wearing dark wetsuits, slick rubber hats and goggles. They chucked plastic slip-on shoes through the open door and ran down to the water. As they raced each other towards the open sea, the grey-haired man who'd driven them headed for the shops. He came back with a newspaper and a coffee.

More vehicles came and went. A Land Rover in army green turned up to collect the squaddies from the coffee shop. Some people weren't even interested in going down to the beach. They had come for a coffee and a bit of fresh air, happy to sit at the tables and chairs on the paving beside the cafe. Others went into the supermarket without even glancing at the sea. I watched a thin-faced woman heave two heavy bags into the back of her Kia and drive away. As she passed the pay and display machine, a council notice caught my eye.

'Shit.'

Startled awake, Fin's hands hit the steering wheel, though thankfully not the horn. I heard a thud from the back as Hazel dropped her phone.

Fin recovered first. 'What is it?'

'CCTV.' I read the warning sign out loud. 'Cameras in operation. Images are recorded and monitored for the purposes of crime prevention and public safety.'

Hazel found her phone on the floor and straightened up. 'So what?'

'So we should leave. Shit. The cops will still have this number plate, and yours. They're going to want to know what we're doing here, once a body turns up.'

'What's the problem?' Hazel was unconcerned. 'I drove up from Exeter to meet Fin. You came along for the ride, since you were visiting her this weekend.'

'Why are we meeting?' Fin asked, curious.

'To discuss local concerns about the quality of the water. There isn't an outfall here any more, but these sewers are well over a century old and they might be leaking.'

I should have remembered Hazel and the other wise women have no problem bending the truth, or even lying through their teeth when they need to. 'Those concerns are on record somewhere, are they?'

'They will be by the time the police go and check,' Hazel assured me.

I guessed arranging that was at least some of what she'd been doing on her phone.

'If they check,' Fin commented. 'It should be obvious that body's been dead for more than twenty-four hours. They won't find us on the CCTV before this morning. Your number plate will be on motorway cameras to prove where you were last night, and we've all got alibis for the past couple of days.'

'If we need to provide alibis,' Hazel agreed. 'The police won't find any link between us and the dead man.'

I wasn't convinced. If they couldn't find any better leads, the cops would dot every 'i' and cross every 't'. Then it couldn't be their fault they were making no progress. 'I still think we should leave before—'

'I don't,' Hazel said firmly. 'If we're part of the crowd when the body turns up, yes, we may be asked for our details, maybe even to give a statement. If we say our piece now, we'll be on the first list of people who are ruled out of any involvement. While everyone else is milling about, we might overhear something useful.'

'What's that?' Fin leaned forward. 'In the cove.'

I saw commotion out on the water. I reached for my door handle.

'Sit tight,' Hazel advised.

'What's going on?' Fin asked, frustrated.

'It's those swimmers.' At least I had a decent view of the sea from my seat. Then I realised Fin didn't know what I was talking about. 'Half a dozen swimmers headed out a while ago. I guess they're coming back.'

'Has one of them found the body?' Fin wrinkled her nose as if she could smell the corpse from here.

'Could be.' As long as none of them bumped into the mermaid. 'They're swimming in a circle around something. Now one of them's heading for the shore.'

That swimmer was a real athlete, cutting through the water in a rapid crawl. They soon reached the shallows and staggered to their feet. The driver got out of the people carrier and met the swimmer halfway down the slipway. After a quick conversation, the driver ran back to the vehicle. The swimmer followed more slowly as his surge of adrenaline faded.

'Those fishermen are packing up.' Fin pointed at the breakwater.

Two fishermen were gathering up their gear. The third was already making his way along the rocks as fast as he could. Back at the people carrier, the driver was making a call on his mobile. He gestured urgently at the sea with his free hand. The swimmer sat on the sill of the open side door, his head hanging. He was exhausted.

The families who'd been enjoying the beach came hurrying up the steps by the loos. The kids looked confused. The two boys with their mum kept half turning back to ask her what was going on. She shook her head and chivvied them along. The other parents ushered their two girls and a boy to their car with outstretched arms, determined to protect them.

'I don't envy them the questions they'll get at bedtime,' Hazel remarked.

I realised I didn't know if she had any kids. Maybe she had nephews and nieces. I didn't ask.

The Renault hatchback left with a screech of tyres as the upset dad over-revved the engine. Even without that noise, people using the cafe and the supermarket had started to notice something was going on. A middle-aged couple with a dog on a lead walked past my window. They leaned over the white-painted railing to see what was happening down on the beach. More people followed them. The people carrier's driver went to speak to a man and a woman in supermarket uniforms. They soon looked appalled.

'Let's see what we can find out.' Hazel was already opening her door.

I was glad to stand up straight, and to feel the sun and the breeze on my face as I stood beside the Toyota and counted the people gathering at the railing. Seventeen in all, from teenagers to retirees. They stood elbow to elbow, asking each other the same questions.

'Do you know what's happened?'

'Has there been an accident?'

'Has someone drowned?'

Hazel went to join them, but as far as I could tell, no one had any answers for her. Fin snapped her fingers to get my attention. I followed her gaze. The fisherman who'd left his mates to pack up was getting an old green tarpaulin out of their white van. He didn't stop to talk to anyone as he went down the slipway with the tarp tucked under one arm. He passed two of the swimmers coming the other way, but they didn't say anything. They headed for the people carrier, where the first one had recovered enough to hand them both a towel.

Fin slid in close to the rail beside Hazel. I walked forward to see if I could see what was happening down on the beach. Being tall enough to look over most people's heads has its uses. The three remaining swimmers were spreading the tarp over something where dry sand showed the high-water mark. The fisherman fetched sizeable stones to weigh down the corners. The murmurs from the watching crowd ranged from vague distress to disappointment. Hazel and Fin left them to it, and I backed off as well.

'How soon will the cops get here?' I asked Hazel when we reached the Toyota.

'Coming from Barnstaple?' She pursed her lips. 'Twenty to twenty-five minutes with blue lights and sirens, depending on the traffic. That's where the hospital is, if they think it's worth sending an ambulance.'

Then we wouldn't have much longer to wait. Given the choice, I would still much rather leave. Hazel could ring her journalist mate later to find out what he discovered about the victim. I saw other people didn't want to be involved. They got into their cars and drove inland. The crowd in the car park was still getting bigger though. More people who lived locally walked down to see what was going on.

We stayed beside the Toyota. I watched idiots holding their phones up, trying to video the beach. I'd be amazed if anyone got anything more than blurred shots of the sky or the water. If they did, I couldn't imagine a green tarpaulin held down with stones would go viral online.

One of the fishermen from the white van took a Thermos flask and a lunch box down to his mate standing watch by the tarp. Wearing their towels like cloaks, the swimmers were guarding the slipway. Several teenagers kept trying to edge past them where the river ran across the sand. The closest swimmer barred their way, shouting angrily. One of the teenagers yelled back, just as aggressive. It was a shame those squaddies had left. Someone in uniform, any uniform, needed to take charge.

'Here they are,' Hazel said with relief.

She was looking inland. I turned my head to see a police car and then an ambulance cross the bridge and drive into the car park. Both vehicles had their blue lights flashing. As the cop car pulled up, its siren yelped to get everyone's attention. Two officers got out, a man and a woman. The man went to talk to the swimmers and their driver. The woman headed down the slipway to the sand. The teenagers abandoned the beach, racing past her. They ran across the car park. I watched them follow the coast path past the coffee shop and disappear.

'Do you suppose they know anything?'

'I expect the police will know where to find them and ask. This is a small enough place.' Fin was watching the paramedics in their bright green overalls take a couple of heavy bags out of the ambulance.

They hurried down the slipway. I moved until I could see the fisherman and one of the swimmers hold up the tarpaulin to make a screen. Both turned their faces away from whatever was lying on the beach. One of the paramedics spoke to the woman copper. She nodded and reached for the radio clipped to her stab vest. While she was talking to HQ or whoever, the swimmer and the fisherman laid the tarp back down and the other paramedic stood up. The first one, a woman, patted the younger man's shoulder, reassuring. They gathered up their bags and walked back to the slipway. Their faces were resigned.

'Whoever that is, they're dead then,' someone in the crowd remarked.

'Talk about stating the bleeding obvious,' someone else murmured.

I heard the crackle of an official radio. The copper who'd been talking to the swimmers was heading this way.

'Good morning.' He smiled, brief and business-like. 'As you can see, there's been an incident. Please clear this area.' This wasn't a request. 'We are expecting more vehicles. Thank you.'

'Officer!' Whoever spoke first was drowned out by other voices asking what the policeman knew. He didn't say anything as people crowded around him.

I looked at Fin. She pressed the remote to unlock the Toyota. I expected Hazel to head back to her Fiesta, but she got into the back seat instead.

'What now?' Fin turned the key one click in the ignition.

'Pull up by the chip shop.' Hazel was still watching the crowd intently.

Fin shrugged and drove over to the closest empty space to Hazel's Fiesta. She kept her speed to a crawl. The car park was crowded with people on foot. 'How much longer do you want to stay here?'

'Let me make a quick phone call.' Hazel got out of the car.

Fin heaved another sigh. 'I really don't see the point of this.'

I watched the woman copper halt vehicles trying to leave with an upraised hand. At her nod, the ambulance went back across the bridge. Then the copper stood at the car park exit with a notebook in her hand. The swimmers' people carrier was first in the queue. The driver pulled up and lowered his window. They had a brief conversation. The copper wrote something down and waved them on their way.

Her partner took a thick roll of blue-and-white tape out of the boot of their car. He tied one end to the railing and walked over to a lamp post on the other side of the slipway, just before the bridge. 'POLICE LINE DO NOT CROSS'. That was clear enough.

'How much longer is she going to be?' Fin twisted to try and see where Hazel had gone.

I looked the other way. People who'd retreated from the car park were shifting and shuffling in front of the supermarket as customers wanted to get in and out. I also noticed the chippy's lights were on. I checked the time. Nearly midday.

'How about fish and chips while we're waiting? Haddock?'

Fin smiled for the first time since we'd met the mermaid. 'If they've got it. Cod'll be fine if not. And a can of Sprite or 7UP or whatever. Thanks.'

'Right you are.' I got out of the Toyota and joined the queue by the chip shop door. I still couldn't see Hazel.

The chip shop had opened at half eleven and was already busy. A man in white overalls and a paper hat was working the fryer while a lad in the same workwear prepared the next batch of things to cook. At the front counter, a woman in a white polo shirt and a black apron with the same logo was wrapping orders in layers of white paper, fast and efficient.

JULIET E. MCKENNA

A teenage girl who was surely her daughter was busy with a tablet screen and a payment terminal.

When I got to the front of the queue, the girl entered our order into their system and passed me the ticket it printed out. To get out of everyone else's way, I went to read the flyers and notices cluttering a pinboard on the opposite wall. There was plenty going on for a small place. The Anchor had regular music nights with visiting bands. The village hall offered karate and yoga classes, a mums and tots group, a photography club, 'knit and natter' and a weekly food bank where people could also make appointments for debt advice and other counselling needs. Notices for one-off events were layered over each other by people who had apparently forgotten to bring their own drawing pins.

'Excuse me,' someone said, loudly annoyed.

Two teenage girls had come in and gone straight to the counter. They ignored the man they had irritated by jumping the queue. No, I realised, they weren't ignoring him. They were so intent on talking to their friend taking orders that they hadn't even heard him. The three girls hurried to the far end of the counter, raising hands to hide their mouths as they whispered to each other.

I stared at the noticeboard and concentrated on listening hard. I couldn't tell who was saying what, but that didn't matter.

'What if it's Taser?'

'Is it?'

'I dunno, but what if it is?'

'That's quite enough, thank you!' The woman wrapping orders paused long enough to clap her hands. 'Emma!'

The visitors scurried away and the chip shop girl got back to work, red-faced. Her mum called out my order number and I collected our fish and chips. As I walked back to the Toyota, I saw the two girls go into the supermarket. I

111

followed and pretended to be choosing a drink while they talked to the lad I'd seen putting out those beach toys first thing. He was restocking the chiller cabinet with sandwiches. An unexpected death was good for business all round.

The supermarket was bigger, full of people and noisier than the chip shop. I caught the same name though. Taser. The lad didn't have an answer, shaking his head. As I paid for a Coke and a Sprite at the self-service check-out, the girls hurried off.

While I was cancelling my transaction and starting again, because I'd put the fish and chips down on the wrong bit of the automated check-out, the lad went behind the row of tills to talk to the woman who was serving the customers who would rather deal with a human being.

'Can I take my break now?' he asked.

'Just fifteen minutes.' Her gesture at the packed shop explained why.

The lad went through the staff door at the back. I hurried out to the car, knocked on Fin's window and handed her the food and bottles of drink as soon as she slid it down. 'Back in a minute.'

I skirted the chippy and followed the path to the back of the supermarket. A sizeable yard there had a high fence, so I went around that as well. I reached the far side just in time to see the lad in the supermarket uniform walk up the path that followed the coastline away from the car park. I followed, trying not to look too conspicuous.

The lad didn't bother looking behind him. He headed straight for a weather-beaten man with a fringe of white hair around a bald patch, who was sitting on a bench overlooking the cove and having a cigarette. He was one of the three fishermen who'd been out on the breakwater.

The lad sat down and started talking, waving agitated hands. The older man listened for a moment, then stopped smoking to interrupt. The gusting wind meant I heard barely half of what he said, and they didn't talk for long. The lad got up, fished his phone out of a pocket and started texting as he walked back. I stopped pretending to admire the view and hurried back to the car park. Fin was eating her fish and chips. Hazel was in the back seat with a packet of sandwiches and another coffee.

'What have you been doing?' she asked when I opened the passenger door.

I got into the seat and took my lunch off the dashboard where Fin had wedged it. 'The local teenagers are desperate to know if the dead man is someone called Taser. The lad who works in the supermarket has been to ask his grandad, who was one of the fishermen out on the breakwater. Grandad thinks it might be, from the lad's description, though he can't be certain.'

Hazel didn't waste time asking how I'd learned this. 'Taser? I don't suppose that's on his birth certificate.'

'No, but your mate the journalist might have heard of him.' I unwrapped my fish and chips. 'Those kids are scared. I think they're hoping it is this Taser, but if it isn't, they really don't want him knowing they would like to find out he's dead.'

'Interesting.' Hazel might have said something else, but a plain black van drove into the car park and stopped at the top of the slipway.

The driver and another man got out. They both wore dark grey suits. The copper standing guard untied his blue-and-white tape from the railing. The two men were getting a wheeled gurney out of the back of their van. The flat black thing strapped to that could only be a body bag.

'No prizes for guessing who they are,' Hazel remarked. 'I don't think we're going to learn much more here today.'

'So we can go home?' Fin folded the paper around what was left of her fish and chips and put the bundle in a rubbish bag she'd ripped off a roll in the glove box.

'Might as well.' Hazel opened the back door to get out. 'I'll ring you later.'

As the wise woman headed for her grimy Fiesta, Fin glanced at me. 'Are you okay to eat on the move?'

'Fine.' I stuck my bottle of Coke in the cup holder.

Fin started the engine and drove slowly across the car park. The policewoman was still expecting every driver to stop and roll down their window, but she only asked for Fin's name, address and phone number.

'In case we need to follow up. I don't expect we will.' She waved us on our way with a smile.

Hazel's car followed us out once she'd answered the policewoman's questions. Fin indicated and turned left. When I checked the wing mirror, I saw Hazel wasn't following. I twisted around to see the Fiesta take the narrow road that led up to the headland. Towards the land the MOD had fenced off.

Fin had seen what the wise woman was doing in her rear-view mirror. 'Do you suppose she's going to try to get through the fence anyway?'

'It wouldn't surprise me.' I really hoped the killer black cat was long gone.

We left Darley Combe behind. I ate my fish and chips and cleaned my greasy fingers with the wet wipes Fin keeps in the glove box. I put my rubbish in the bin bag. The narrow road twisted through a series of bends that kept the traffic cautious. I looked for a place where Fin could pull over. A blue sign promised parking not far ahead. When we reached the next straight stretch, I saw a lay-by halfway before the next bend.

'Can we stop, please?'

Fin glanced at me. 'We can put the rubbish in the bin at home.'

I shook my head. 'That's not it.'

Chapter Ten

Fin pulled into the empty lay-by and switched off the engine. 'What's the problem?'

'We need to talk to those kids.' I undid my seatbelt and twisted around to get the map off the back seat. Long arms are useful in a small car. 'Today, while they're still off balance. Tomorrow, they'll have got their story straight and they won't say a word. We need to know more about this Taser.'

Fin drummed her fingers on the steering wheel. 'You don't think we should leave that to Hazel's journalist?'

Something in her voice made me look up from the map. 'Do you?'

She ran a hand over her hair. 'Those girls you overheard in the chip shop? I watched them leave the supermarket. One of them wasn't just scared. She was terrified. Seriously, I thought she was going to pass out. If her friend hadn't been there to hold her up...' She shook her head. 'Give me that rubbish.'

I handed her the bag. Fin got out and dumped it in the closest lay-by bin. I sat and waited.

'If the dead man was – what could he be, how bad could he be, to scare those kids like that?' she asked as she got back into the car.

'I don't know, but it might explain why I saw the Hunter up in Yorkshire.' The last time I had seen him, he had intervened in a problem the Green Man had sent me to sort out. He dealt mercilessly with a man who'd been menacing kids. Maybe I wouldn't have to confront the cat man myself, if he was already on the Hunter's shit list.

Fin came to a different conclusion. 'Maybe this cat man is working for him. If this Taser person was such a threat.'

That was a startling idea. I took a moment to consider the possibility. It didn't feel right to me. 'I still want to see what we can get out of those kids.'

'Why don't we wait to hear what Hazel's journalist can find out about the dead man?' Fin countered. 'If he is this Taser person. We still don't know that for sure.'

I shook my head. 'It could be weeks before this reporter can find out who wanted this arsehole dead. He might not be willing to tell us what he knows. He could say it's a job for the police. Those kids though, they know something. Things that could help us right now.'

Fin had thought of something else. 'Who wanted this Taser dead and who actually killed him might not be the same person. That could explain a dead body up in Yorkshire and another one down here months later.'

'You think this shapeshifter is some sort of hitman?'

'Who knows?' Fin was as frustrated as me.

I wondered how many other possibilities we could come up with. One thing would stay the same though. 'Whatever he is, he's not only a danger to the people he's killing. If he gets caught by the cops, or the army, if they find out what he can do, everything changes for us.'

'A black swan moment.' The slipstream from a passing car buffeted the Toyota as Fin smiled without humour. 'You think he'd be that stupid?'

'He got himself photographed,' I pointed out. 'I bet he didn't plan on being in the papers.'

'At the risk of sounding like a bad movie, he must know he'll never see daylight again if someone official sees what he can do.'

'Unless he does some sort of deal. Unless he tells them he can help them find other people who can do the same sort of thing.'

Fin looked at me, incredulous. 'You think he would do that?'

'I have no idea.' But even the possibility was enough to convince me we had to find this bastard before anyone else. 'We can't guess what he'll do, or what he knows, until we know who he is. Finding out why he killed Taser is the first step to working that out.'

'If Taser is the dead man.' Fin looked thoughtful for a moment. 'Okay. How do you propose to get these kids talking to two complete strangers about someone who scares them witless?'

I handed her the map. 'We look for places where they'll go to hang out in the evenings. We see what we can overhear without them knowing that we're listening. Then we decide the best way to approach them.'

'You do realise they could be staying in their bedrooms, talking to each other online?' But Fin studied the map all the same.

'Maybe, maybe not. If they're outside, they can be sure no one's listening on the other side of a closed door or getting into their phones to read their messages.' I shrugged. 'If we can't track them down, we head back to yours. We'll wait and see what Hazel's journalist comes up with.'

'Fair enough.' Fin tapped the map. 'If these kids are going to get together, somewhere their parents will be okay with, I reckon they'll be here.'

She'd found the same place as me. As the coast road climbed up the eastern headland and left the newer houses behind, it passed a short spur to a dead end. The Ordnance Survey had labelled the cliff top with 'Viewpoint' and 'Picnic Site'. The coastal path from the beach car park went straight there. Another blue symbol promised parking, and beyond that, a patch of woodland reached the cliff edge. That was ideal. The time had come for me to find out if the Green Man really could help me hide myself when I didn't want to be seen.

'Looks the most likely spot,' I agreed. 'What time do you suppose they'll meet up?'

'After the ones with jobs finish work,' Fin guessed. 'After they've had something to eat.'

'Around half eight, maybe nine o'clock?' I hoped the girl from the chippy and the lad from the supermarket weren't doing the late shifts. 'What shall we do until then?'

Fin started the engine. 'Let's see what Ilfracombe's got to offer.'

As it turned out, the little seaside town had enough to keep us interested. The local museum was set up in what had once been a grand hotel's laundry. The exhibits had started out as an eccentric Edwardian's personal collection. He travelled around South America collecting natural history specimens. All sorts of things had been added since then. Household artefacts and farm tools were displayed alongside pictures detailing local life in days gone by. Photos and military artefacts told the local history of both World Wars. After we'd seen everything there, we went for a walk along the sea front. When we decided it was time for dinner, it was easy enough to find a decent restaurant.

As we walked back to the car, I took Fin's hand. 'We should have more days out like this.'

'Without the dead body and the crack-of-dawn start, don't you think?'

'Agreed.' As we reached the Toyota and Fin found her keys, I checked my phone again. 'Still nothing from Hazel.' I was starting to get uneasy.

'She'll be in touch when she's got something to tell us, won't she?' Fin sounded as if she was trying to convince us both.

'Hopefully.' Unless the wise woman had been eaten or arrested. I didn't say that out loud. Once we were in the car, I changed the subject. 'So how are we going to do this? Are you going to do a flyover first?'

I hoped the drive back to Darley Combe would give me enough time to work out how to explain to Fin how I was going to test some previously unsuspected how-to-not-be-seen talent.

'Let's keep things simple until we know the kids are actually there.' Fin concentrated on making the turn we needed. 'It's a viewpoint. We'll be a couple out for a walk to admire the sunset. Then we'll stroll back to the car and work out how to get close enough to listen to whatever they're talking about.'

'Sounds like a plan.' I settled myself for the drive back. It didn't take long. As we crossed the little bridge, the setting sun was framed by the dark mouth of the cove and gilding the sea. The supermarket and chippy were doing a decent trade, though the coffee shop was shut. There was nothing else to see. Not even a scrap of blue-and-white tape tied to the railing.

'You'd never know that anything had happened.' Fin turned the steering wheel to follow the road winding through the houses on this side of the river.

'I don't suppose they want to encourage that sort of tourism.' I concentrated on the road ahead.

A few minutes later, Fin indicated and turned the Toyota into the dead end. The tarmac gave way to a car park surfaced with coarse gravel. There were no other vehicles, which was a relief. Fin pulled up and we got out of the car. A gravelled path headed towards the sea, showing us the way to go.

I got my coat out of the back of the car and so did Fin. The evening was getting chilly. It was still only the first week in May. Fin reached for my hand. I laced my fingers through hers as we walked down the path. It ran straight to a half-circle of stone paving where a waist-high wall stopped people with binoculars wandering off the edge of the cliff by mistake. The wooden fence on either side was lower and mostly hidden by dense gorse bushes.

The picnic area was over by the trees. Without looking too obviously in that direction, I counted four of those tables with fixed bench seats which are such a pain to get in and out of. A gang of teenagers, eleven of them in total, were sitting on the table tops as well as the benches. Bottles passing from hand to hand gleamed bright green in the last of the sunlight.

Fin walked on my right, on the side of the path closest to the teenagers. We strolled towards the sea. A handful of lads and two girls left the picnic tables and walked towards us. That was unexpected. I recognised the boy from the supermarket and the girl from the chip shop. Nobody was smiling.

Fin let go of my hand. The lads stepped onto the path, blocking our way. The girls were hanging back, but I didn't like the way they looked at Fin. The supermarket lad squared his shoulders as he challenged me.

'We know who you are, and you can fuck right off.'

That might have sounded menacing in a different part of the country. The north-east, say. It was hard to take a threat in a broad Devon accent seriously. He was also barely five foot ten. I could flatten the skinny little sod with one punch. But I was careful not to grin. If he was prepared to face up to someone my size, that earned him a bit of respect.

'I'm sorry.' Fin smiled. 'I have no idea what you mean.'

He glared at her, hostile. 'We seen you. Coming here first thing, hanging around all day. Couldn't get hold of Taser?

Not since last weekend? Well, he's gone. Gone for good. Dead and gone. If you know what's good for you, you'll – you'll sling your hook an' all.'

His voice rose as his throat tightened with tension. That undermined the hard-man effect he was hoping for. That and his obvious reluctance to swear at Fin.

I tried to look friendly. 'Listen, we really don't—'

'You think you can step in and take over where Taser left off? You think we're stupid?' One of the girls stepped forward. Not the one from the chip shop. She glared at Fin, venomous. 'We ent going to fall for your bullshit a second time.'

Fin shook her head. 'I don't know—'

The supermarket lad took a step forward and scowled at me. 'I told you to fuck off. I'm telling you again.'

'Or what?' Playing Mr Nice Guy was getting us nowhere. Let's see what Mr Nasty could provoke.

The little fucker punched me. A quick snap with his fist went straight into my gut, and he stepped back just as fast. I saw the blow coming in time to tense my stomach muscles, but it hurt a lot more than I expected. Close to, he wasn't such a skinny little sod. Wiry would be more accurate, and I guessed he went to those karate classes at the village hall. He was waiting for me to make a move, light on his feet and balanced. He had both fists clenched and kept his elbows tight to his sides.

I waited. He waited. I sneered at him. He still didn't move. I faked a step forward. I know nothing about guns and I'll never be dumb enough to carry a knife, but I know what I'm doing in a fist fight.

The lad reacted the way I hoped he would, throwing another hard punch. I moved faster, though only barely. I side-stepped and blocked his fist with my open palm. The impact stung but I gritted my teeth as I clamped my hand around his fist. Fingers the size of mine may struggle to hit tiny icons on a phone screen, but they have their uses.

He stared at me, confused. This hadn't come up in karate class. He hesitated just long enough for one of his mates to decide to help. This lad didn't do any martial art. He tried a straightforward punch to my face. If he had managed to hit me, he might have pissed me off, maybe even given me a nosebleed if he got really lucky.

He didn't get the chance. He was no taller than his mate, which meant my reach was a lot longer than his. I grabbed him by the throat. Panicked, he tried to rip my hands away. Not a chance. Trying to twist out of my grip, he clawed at my coat sleeve. His hands didn't even reach my shoulder, so that wasn't going to be a problem.

I looked at the third lad. 'Don't even think about it.'

His hasty step backwards didn't deter the two girls. They went for Fin. One darted around behind her and grabbed her ponytail. The chip shop girl went for her face with long nails crooked like claws. The two lads I was holding thought this was their chance. They started to struggle to free themselves. The third boy grew some balls and charged at me. I threw the lad I was holding by the throat straight at him. They fell over like skittles in a bowling alley.

I tightened my grip on the karate kid's fist. I have very strong hands. He yelped. One of the girls squealed a whole lot louder. We both looked over to see what had happened. The lass from the chippy stumbled backwards, rubbing the inside of her upper arm.

'You pinched me!' She stared at Fin with disbelief. 'You bitch!'

'I'll do it again if you don't stop playing silly buggers,' Fin said forcefully. 'We didn't come here to fight you.'

'That's right. Pack it in.' I looked the karate kid straight in the eye. Then I glanced at the chip shop girl. 'Emma.'

That scared her. She had no idea how I knew her name. The other girl pressed close to her side. She was cradling one wrist in her other hand and looked ready to cry. What had Fin done to her? What were we going to do now?

Fin snapped her fingers at the kids still sitting on the picnic benches. 'BFW Environmental. One of you must have a signal. Look it up. Quickly!'

Two of them did as they were told. I looked at the karate kid. He still wasn't going to back down, even though he was gritting his teeth against the pain in his hand.

The kids looked up from their phones. The lad looked confused. The girl looked worried.

'Find the "About" page on the website,' Fin ordered. 'Look at the photos. See anyone you recognise?'

The teenagers who had challenged us retreated to see what their mates were finding out. Apart from the karate kid, because I wasn't letting him go just yet. A moment later, I saw dread on several faces, even in this fading light.

'Look up Blithehurst House,' I snapped. 'Find the page about woodland walks.'

In general, I hate being photographed, whether I'm expecting it or not. I either look like a complete idiot or someone the police advise members of the public not to approach. Right now though, I wasn't going to complain about the picture of me making hazel hurdles on the Blithehurst website. Thankfully the caption didn't give my name. If these kids googled that, they'd find news stories which would complicate this conversation horribly.

'That's who we are. Now, what are you lot talking about?' Fin demanded. 'Who the hell is Taser?'

'Someone you're glad to see the back of, by the sounds of it.' I relaxed my grip on the karate kid's hand, though I still didn't let him go. 'How about we talk about this? Like sensible people?'

JULIET E. MCKENNA

'I guess we can give you five minutes.' He made that sound as if we were making a deal, though I could see in his eyes that he realised he had no choice. He could see that I knew it too.

I grinned as I released his hand. His lips thinned as he stretched his fingers out wide a couple of times, but he resisted the urge to rub away the pain. Never show weakness to your enemy.

'How about we all sit down and calm down?' Fin sounded like a schoolteacher. Maybe that was why the kids mumbled agreement.

I followed Fin to the empty picnic table furthest away and closest to the sea. It wasn't real wood, but a convincing fake made out of recycled plastic. Fin sat on one end of the bench that faced the teenagers. I sat at the other end. We had the tabletop at our backs, and if we had to, we could move fast. I didn't think these kids would try anything else, but we would be stupid to take any chances.

'So what the fuck are you doing here?' One of the girls spoke up, belligerent. 'If you ent nothing to do with Taser.'

'Take a look at my company website,' Fin shot back. 'Ever heard of agricultural run-off causing algal blooms? There's a possibility that might be an issue in your river.'

That confused half the teenagers. The rest looked even more apprehensive.

'How do we know you ent really the Feds?' A boy at the back of the group still wasn't convinced.

'The police, you mean?' That stupid slang from TV really irritates me. 'Do I look like a fucking copper to you?'

'You think we've got fake identities set up on the Internet and going back years, just so we can nick a bunch of teenagers for underage drinking?' Fin spoke up before any of them could answer me. 'Don't be stupid.'

THE GREEN MAN'S QUARRY

I looked at the karate kid and shrugged. 'It's none of our business what you're doing up here, as long as no one gets hurt.'

'We're not police,' Fin said firmly. 'I promise you that.'

A few of the kids looked at each other. Hopefully that meant our words were ringing true. But the boy who wasn't convinced stood up. 'Fuck it. I'm out of here.'

He might not know what was going on, but he knew he didn't want any more trouble. We had to get them talking and fast, otherwise we'd lose this chance to learn whatever they knew.

'This Taser was someone you're glad to see the back of, wasn't he? How much trouble has he been making for you?'

Fin followed my lead. 'What you're doing is none of our business, as long as no one gets hurt. But if someone has been hurt, maybe we can help with that.'

'How?' I heard desperation in the not chip shop girl's demand.

'It's over,' the karate kid said curtly. 'Taser's dead. Drowned.'

'He was who they fished out of the sea this morning?' Fin prompted.

Emma from the chip shop nodded. 'Fell off the cliff path. That's what they're saying.'

I heard a couple of murmurs from the kids behind her.

'Or got pushed.'

'Good riddance.'

'But you thought we had come to take over his operation.' I spoke slowly, as if I was thinking this through. 'We're not, but maybe someone will. We could probably help stop that happening. If we knew what Taser was doing, we could make sure the cops knew what to look out for. Get whoever might try to take over here arrested?' But I saw unease and mistrust on the faces looking my way.

'We can tell a journalist we know,' Fin said quickly. 'Journalists protect their sources. No one will ever trace anything back to you.'

I don't know how many of the kids believed that. All I could see on their faces was stubborn refusal to talk.

'Fair enough,' I said briskly. 'We'll go to the cops with what we've got. They can take it from there.'

'No, wait,' the karate kid protested.

'But you promised,' one of the girls wailed.

'Talk to us or talk to the cops,' I said, uncompromising. 'Your choice.'

None of them spoke, but at least the boy who'd stood up to leave sat down again.

'You live Bristol way?' Chip shop Emma had been looking Fin up on her phone.

Fin nodded. 'Well away from here.'

The karate kid looked at me. 'Your mate works for the Bristol papers?'

Since I had no idea where Hazel's journalist pal was based, I just shrugged. To my relief, the lad took that as a yes.

The teenagers looked at each other. Don't ask me how, but they silently elected the karate kid as their spokesman.

Chapter Eleven

The supermarket lad's voice was thick with hatred. 'Taser come up here last summer from Exeter, or maybe Plymouth. South coast, anyway. Said he'd been moved here by the social because of the housing shortage. Him and his girlfriend. He told different people different stories. Nice and friendly to start with, both of them were. That was a whole lot of lies an' all.'

Another voice spoke up. I recognised the third girl, the one who had been so upset. Perhaps she found it easier to talk now the dusk was deepening.

'She's called Willow. Taser's girlfriend. That's what she says, anyway. Fuck knows if that's her real name. Whatever. Made friends with my sister. Told her about her hard life. Said she was a looked-after kid ever since she was born. Foster home after foster home till she turned sixteen and social services dumped her. That's why she did the drugs, she said. Just a bit of weed at first. I mean, that's nothing, right?'

From the shuffling around the tables, I guessed that was the general opinion. I didn't care.

'Smack though, that's what Willow got my sister on. Heroin,' the girl added in case Fin and I were so old we needed that explaining.

She couldn't go on. Tears running down her face shone silver in the fading light from the west. The karate kid took up the tale.

'Taser said we had to work for him. Different one of us holding the phone each week, someone else holding the stash. Once everyone had done it, we had to take another

128

turn. He said we could sort that out between us. If we didn't, bad things would happen. Especially to Chelsea. She might overdose. That could happen any time he wanted. He was the only one who'd know what was in the smack he gave her. She needed to pay him for her gear an' all. As long as we were earning, and keeping his stash safe, doing his deliveries when he called us on the burner, then she'd be fine. He'd take what she owed him out of our cut. If not? He'd stick Chelse in his car and drive her to Devonport. He'd put her to work in a place he knows with her knickers off. Quickest way to pay back what she cost him. She'd collect a few bruises, but that's the price of that sort of business.'

The girl who wasn't Emma chipped in. 'If we didn't make enough deliveries, if we got ripped off, if we tried to rip him off, he said we'd better know we'd get shoved in his car an' all. We'd be taken to fuck knows where, to be – to be—' Terror choked her.

'Any of us.' A boy spoke up at the back. 'Not just the girls. Maybe our little brothers and sisters. Taser said he knows paedos who pay good money for fresh meat.'

The karate kid looked at me. 'If we even thought about fighting back, we'd find out why they called him Taser. He's got one, a really boss one from America. Not like those shit police things the coppers here shoot you with, with wires and that. He's got one that'll drop a full-grown man. He said he'd kill my nan's old dog to prove it if we didn't believe him. He'd make us watch.'

'Said we better know there was a chance it could stop our hearts too if he ever had to use it on us,' someone added.

'Has anyone gone missing?' I had to ask.

'Do you think we're fucking stupid?' a sarcastic voice spoke up from the back of the group. 'We did what he wanted.'

The murmur from the rest agreed.

'Holiday lets and second homes. Weekenders.' The kara-te kid shrugged. 'Plenty of that lot down from London like their coke and shit. Stag and hen parties at the caravan parks come looking for pills round the pubs here. Taser made sure they got told he could get whatever anyone wanted.'

'But now he's dead and we ent doing that shit no more.' Chip shop Emma was defiant. The murmurs from the others weren't quite so confident, but these kids definitely wanted out.

'Where's this Willow now?' I was more than willing to scare her shitless to get her talking after what I'd just heard.

'She fucked off the same day Taser disappeared. A week ago. Do you reckon she's drowned too?' If not, the karate kid was afraid she'd reappear.

'What about Chelsea?' Fin asked. 'Where is she?'

The crying girl's answer surprised me.

'She's good. Well, she's okay. My aunt's yoga teacher got her into counselling and detox and that. Private, off the books. My mum don't know nothing about it,' she added hastily. 'She doesn't know about Willow or Taser or anything.'

'We won't be talking to anyone's parents,' Fin assured her.

I didn't think private rehab was cheap. 'Who paid for that?'

'We dint have to. Some sort of charity took care of it all.'

'Taser didn't care about Chelse getting clean,' Emma said bitterly. 'Said he could get her back on the smack any time he wanted. If we wanted him to leave her alone, we better do what he said.'

'Can you really send the Feds after Willow? Get whoever Taser was dealing for arrested? Get them to leave us the fuck alone?' The crying girl stood up. She was ready to leave now. So were the others.

'Taser said—' The karate kid's voice shook. 'If we thought he was bad news, he said we ent seen nothing like the people he works for.'

'We'll do everything we can.' That was a promise I was happy to make. I had no clue how I was going to keep it, mind you, but that was a problem for another day.

'No one will ever know you talked to us,' Fin assured them.

'Yeah, right.' The girls walked off together with their arms wrapped around each other's shoulders and waists. The boys followed, kicking up gravel. The further they got from us, the faster the kids walked. They had unloaded their troubles, and they wanted to leave the whole mess behind.

The karate kid was the last to leave. 'You better do what you said.' He was still trying to sound like a hard man. To me, he sounded desperate.

'Leave it with us.' I hoped I sounded more confident than I felt. The last thing I wanted to do was take on some gang of drug dealers. 'These burner phones, where are they? We could hand them over to the police without saying where we got them. That sort of evidence could get these dealers locked up.'

But he was shaking his head. 'We chucked them in the sea this afternoon. As soon as we knew Taser was dead. The drugs an' all. No one can tie any of that shit to us now.'

'Fair enough.' I could understand that.

Fin and I watched the boy follow the other teenagers towards the path back to the beach-front car park. She shook her head, incredulous.

'Do you really think their parents have no idea what's been going on?'

'I'm the wrong person to ask.' I got up from the bench. 'Did you keep secrets from your parents?'

A second later, I realised that was a stupid thing to say. Fin and her sisters had the secret they shared with their mother and their aunts. They had to keep that from their entirely ordinary dad. Unsurprisingly, her parents' marriage had ended in divorce, even if they were still on good terms. 'Sorry.'

'It's okay.' She got out her phone. 'Well, we've got plenty to tell Hazel now.'

I waited while Fin tried to call the wise woman.

'Voicemail.' She didn't leave a message. She stood up and we started walking back to the car park. 'Let's hope her journalist pal is willing to pass on this Willow's name to the police. Or maybe the wise women can help. If they can trace her, maybe that will help them find this Taser's suppliers. Then the cops can take over.'

'Right.' I wouldn't argue with that. Coppers are good for some things. 'This Taser sounds like a right—'

Movement caught my eye. The scars on my forearm burned. A black shadow broke away from the dense darkness under the trees. It raced across the grass straight towards us. I realised it was an enormous black cat.

I pushed Fin behind me. The creature slowed to a lope and then to a walk. It stopped on the path a few metres ahead of us. We'd have to go around it to get back to the car. I moved as if I was about to step right. It moved just as fast to stop me. No, the cat moved even faster. It read my intention as soon as I tensed a muscle. I wondered if it could smell my fear.

This cat was easily as big as a full-grown man. Every scary thing I had ever seen in a wildlife programme was standing right in front of me. The beast drew back dark lips in a silent snarl. Its fangs were the colour of ivory in a jaw powerful enough to split bone. It swiped a warning with a forepaw, showing me its massive claws. I took a step backwards. I couldn't help it. That paw was as big as my head and those talons could rip my face off.

Most terrifying of all, this creature wasn't an "it". This wasn't some animal doing what came naturally, hunting its prey without any malice. The shapeshifter's yellow eyes gleamed with human intelligence in the sun's afterglow.

'If you go—' Fin broke off as the cat's gaze flickered to her.

We had no chance of making any sort of plan. This cat would understand whatever we said to each other. Fuck.

It – he – sank lower. His belly pressed to the ground. I sensed rather than saw the flicker of his black tail against the dark gravel path. I did see his shoulder blades tighten and a faint wriggle of his haunches. I reached back blindly, shoving Fin away towards the viewpoint.

The cat didn't spring. As I saw him relax, his jaw hung loose. His scarlet tongue lolled as he lifted his nose and sniffed the air. The bastard was laughing. Ha sodding ha. Before I could feel relieved, he stalked forward. Now he'd had his fun, he growled a warning. I felt the low noise as vibration in my breastbone rather than hearing it.

The cat came closer. His steps were measured and menacing. We retreated as slowly as we dared. The cat came forward again. We backed off some more. I desperately tried to calculate how far we were from the cliff edge. Was this how Taser had died, driven backwards step by step until he fell to his death? Payback for the way he'd terrorised those kids.

'Dan,' Fin said behind me, warning.

I felt stone paving under my feet instead of the gravel path. We had reached the viewpoint. There was nowhere left for us to go.

'Give me the car keys.' I held out my open hand, reaching back towards her. 'Give me your bag.'

I didn't think I had any chance of getting past the cat, but if Fin wasn't holding anything metal, she could shift into her swan form and fly away. If she headed straight out to sea, the cat wouldn't risk trying to jump up and catch her. Or if he was stupid enough to try, maybe I could get underneath him as he sprang. Maybe I could throw him over the cliff edge. Then we could see if cats can swim.

But the cat was in no hurry. He had us penned. He paced to and fro with his eyes fixed on me, unblinking. Was he considering what to do next? How long before he made some decision. Was there any point in waiting? We knew he was a killer. If I slammed Fin's bag into his face, would that distract him long enough for me to get past? Maybe, but I was kidding myself if I thought I could outrun him. He'd be on my back with one spring and his weight would knock me to the ground. His claws would tear me to pieces.

Where would that leave Fin? Flying away, I sincerely hoped. I would have to trust her to use her own abilities to get out of this mess. Then she could take what we'd learned to Hazel. I had to hope that seeing Fin leave would convince the shapeshifter he'd better run before she came back with reinforcements. I'd have to hope my greenwood blood could cope with healing whatever damage he did to me first.

I only had myself to blame. I'd been a fool. Instead of pissing about back at Blithehurst, wondering if I really wanted to discover what Annis Wynne had meant, I should have tried to summon a fucking shuck. Right now, I could really do with one of those on my side.

Something growled behind me. That wasn't a big cat. I smelled something like hot iron on the breeze. The hairs on the back of my neck stood up like a dog's hackles. Fin stifled a squeak and burrowed under my left arm. She held me tight around the waist. I wrapped my arms around her shoulders. Now I knew what frozen with fear really meant.

A four-legged shadow far blacker than the cat stalked slowly past us. Its ruffed shoulders were on a level with mine. The ridge of its spine barely sloped down towards its powerful hindquarters. I felt the shuck's warm breath on my cheek. I saw its sunken eyes glowing bright, as red as embers in a forge woken by a blast from the bellows. Its long, feathered tail swept slowly to and fro, scattering rags of shadow.

The shuck stood on the path between us and the cat. Red light slipped like liquid from its jowls, though the ruby drops disappeared before they hit the ground. The creature's ominous growl shook me from my skull to my toenails. Fin's hold on my waist tightened, leaving me breathless.

The cat was retreating. Belly to the ground, he backed away, step by reluctant step. His tail thrashed furiously as he growled a higher-pitched threat. He'd rip the shuck to bloody, quivering shreds. At least, he'd try to. I wouldn't fancy his chances, but the shapeshifter would still have no trouble killing me and Fin.

The cat sprang. I stumbled backwards, dragging Fin with me. We slammed into the stone wall at the edge of the viewpoint. But the cat wasn't coming for us. He twisted in the air so fast he jumped over his own tail. He raced away into the darkness, faster than I could imagine. I couldn't even see where he had gone.

The shuck didn't chase him. The shadow creature turned its fearsome head and looked at me instead. Its eyes were glowing more dimly, so it was easier for me to see it prick its ragged ears.

What was I supposed to say? Good boy? That'll do? I settled for 'Thanks', although my mouth was so dry I could barely whisper.

The shuck made a sound that could have meant anything. It was fading, disappearing into the night. The glow of its eyes lingered last of all, diminishing to a bright scarlet pinprick. Fin and I didn't move until the last hint of red blinked out. Then we waited a few minutes more.

Fin drew a deep, shaking breath as she released me from her crushing hold. 'Let's get out of here.'

'Fuck yes,' I agreed as soon as I could speak again.

We hurried back to the car. Fin was pretty much running, trying to pull me after her. I forced myself to walk, taking the longest strides I could. I knew if I ran, I wouldn't stop until I got home to my mum's wood.

We reached the car park. Fin fumbled her keys out of her coat pocket. She tried to press the button on the electronic fob but dropped the whole bunch instead. 'Fuck!'

'I'll get them.' I knelt on the ground, not caring about sharp-edged gravel digging into my shins. To my relief, I found the keys with the first sweep of my hand. 'Here you are.'

Fin unlocked the Toyota and we got in. Fell in, to be more accurate. For a second, I welcomed the courtesy light pushing back the darkness. Then I realised the glare meant I couldn't see through the windows. Anything could be sneaking up.

Fin got the key into the ignition on her second attempt. 'I don't think I can drive home,' she said abruptly. 'Not safely.'

I wasn't at all sure I could. 'Let's find a room somewhere close for the night.'

She nodded and started the engine. She didn't slow down as we drove through Darley Combe and I didn't suggest it. We wanted to get well away from this place. I was already using my phone to look online for the closest modern, anonymous chain hotel.

'Head for Barnstaple.'

Fin tossed her phone into my lap. 'Directions?'

I found her satnav app and put the phone in the holder clipped to the dashboard. Then I used my own phone to call Hazel.

'Voicemail, still.' I didn't leave a message. I couldn't think what to say.

Neither of us spoke on the half-hour drive. Just before we reached the hotel, Fin saw an open supermarket and pulled into the car park. She didn't ask me and she didn't need to. We bought toothbrushes and other essentials. Walking through the brightly lit aisles, we both breathed a little easier. This was closer to normal life. Safer.

At the hotel, an incurious receptionist welcomed us with a well-trained routine. 'Just the one night? Do you want to book breakfast? Full or continental?'

I glanced at Fin. She shrugged.

I went with the simplest option. 'Full breakfast for us both.'

'Right you are.' The receptionist explained how that would be served in the steak house across the car park.

We nodded to confirm we understood. I paid with my bank card while Fin put her car's number plate into the parking system. We headed up the single flight of stairs to our designated room.

I opened the door. Fin stuck her card key in the slot on the wall that made the lights work. She dropped the shopping bag on the desk under the wall-mounted TV. I checked the door was properly closed and fastened the security lock just to be sure. Hanging my coat on a convenient hook, I turned around to see Fin was lying on the bed. She was still wearing her coat and had a forearm over her eyes.

'Tea?' I went to fill the kettle from the bathroom tap.

'Camomile, please.' Fin had dropped some herbal teabags into the basket on our quick tour of the supermarket. She sat up, took her coat off and hung it up. 'Have you got any idea why that shuck turned up so handily?'

I switched on the kettle. I turned the two mugs on the tray the right way up and dropped a hotel tea bag in one. Reaching for the shopping bag, I found the camomile infusions and opened the box. I put one in the other mug. Then I turned to Fin.

'I think so,' I admitted.

I sat on the chair by the desk and we waited for the kettle to boil. I explained what Annis Wynne had said to me in North Wales. Fin sat on the bed sipping from her mug while I told her about the hints that Frai had dropped. I told her about the dryad radar and what my mum had said about that. It was time she knew.

'I haven't said anything before now because I've been trying to get my own head around it.' My mouth was dry again. I drank the last of my tea and wished hotel mugs were bigger. I was more relieved than I can say to see Fin nodding.

'Yes, I get that. Are you planning on telling Hazel?'

'Only if I have to.'

Fin nodded. She understood that as well. She put down her mug and stretched her arms over her head with a yawn.

'Let's be thankful you were able to whistle up a shuck when we really needed one. I'll be a lot happier when we hear from Hazel. I want to know what she's been doing today.'

'Right.' I wished I could be as sure as Fin that was a question of when. I'd been thinking *if* we heard from the wise woman. Jokes about getting eaten weren't funny any more.

Fin yawned again. 'Bed?'

'There's nothing we can do before morning.' I reached for my phone to set an alarm. 'Breakfast at eight?'

'Fine with me,' she agreed.

We stripped off and got under the covers. Fin curled up with my arm around her, resting her head on my shoulder. She was soon fast asleep and snoring softly. Even though I was absolutely knackered, I lay awake for a while longer, trying to make sense of what we'd seen and heard.

Chapter Twelve

My phone woke me up. That wasn't the alarm I'd set last night. I grabbed and stabbed the screen with my finger to answer the call. Fin opened her eyes.

'Good morning,' Hazel said cheerfully. 'Sorry I didn't get back to you last night. Where are you at the moment? Did you go back to Fin's?'

'Hi.' For a moment, that was all I could say. I put the call on speaker so Fin could hear. 'Sorry, I just woke up. We're in Barnstaple.'

'Great.' Hazel was pleased. 'I'm in Exeter right now, and I have a couple of calls to make, then I'll be heading your way. I know you both have to get home, but can we meet for coffee first? Say, eleven o'clock?'

Fin propped herself on one elbow. 'Yes, that's fine. Where?'

'There's a good place in Butchers Row.' Hazel gave us directions.

'See you there.' I ended the call and looked at Fin. 'Do you want to shower first?'

'Okay.' She threw back the duvet. 'That sounds as if Hazel's got something to tell us.'

'Hopefully.' I got up and switched on the kettle. 'Tea or coffee?'

'Coffee.' Fin headed for the bathroom.

Whatever Hazel had found out, we would know soon enough. What we'd learned from those kids should be news to her. Would putting everything together tell us more about the shapeshifter? Hopefully. If it didn't, I couldn't see what else we could do.

I left Fin drinking coffee after her shower and took my turn in the bathroom. By the time we were both dressed, I had more questions.

'What did you do to those girls last night? Did one of them say you had pinched her?'

Fin was putting last night's supermarket supplies into the calico shopping bag from her car. 'Do you think I do field-work in the middle of nowhere without knowing how to defend myself? Blanche and I took a course.'

'Good to know.' I hadn't actually thought about that.

Fin put the bag down on the desk and turned her back to me. 'Grab my hair.'

'Sorry?'

'Grab my hair. Like that girl last night.'

'Okay.' I reached for her ponytail, not liking this very much.

My fingers barely touched her hair before Fin clamped her hand on top of mine. She pressed down hard. I couldn't have let go if I'd wanted to. A minute later, I wanted to, as Fin bent her knees and spun under my arm. Now she was facing me, and that quick move had put a twist in my wrist. I could feel enough pressure to know it would be agonising if she hadn't relaxed her hold.

She grinned as she let me go. 'First lesson. If you're grabbed, get free. Go for their eyes or their nose, if you can, or surprise them with something like this.'

Before she finished speaking, she pinched my bicep, on the inside of my upper arm. She twisted a fold of skin between her finger and thumb hard enough to convince me she could really make that hurt if she wanted to.

I held up my other hand, surrendering. 'You're free. What now?'

'Get away.' Fin mimed stamping hard and downwards on the side of my knee. 'How fast can you hop?'

'Ouch.' I decided I was glad she could defend herself. 'Breakfast?'

'Let's.' She picked up the calico bag and we went downstairs.

After we put the bag in the Toyota, we crossed the car park to the steak house. I had the full English and followed that with some mini pastries. Fin had a bowl of fruit and a plateful of vegetarian options from the cooked breakfast menu.

'We'll make better time on the motorway if we don't have to stop for lunch,' she pointed out.

'Fair enough.' I got some more toast.

Checking out was dropping our card keys in a Perspex box beside the reception desk. Fin found a town centre car park on her satnav app, and we had enough time to walk around for a bit before we were due to meet Hazel. Barnstaple's an interesting place, with medieval buildings down narrow alleys and unexpected side streets. Memorial plaques commemorated men and women who had endowed alms houses and schools. Mrs Alice Horwood had been a wealthy merchant's widow who didn't only see her husband's projects completed after he had died. She set up a school for twenty poor girls in her own right.

Opposite the Pannier Market, Butchers Row had been built in the mid-1800s. Now the shops offered beer, cheese, artisan bread and lots of other things. We found the cafe Hazel recommended. When the alarm on my phone said it was eleven, we went inside. Sunday morning meant it was pretty busy, but we were able to grab a table. We sat and stirred our coffee, and I hoped Hazel wouldn't be long. She arrived five minutes later, got herself a drink and joined us. She leaned forward and got straight to the point, speaking quietly to avoid being overheard.

'Terence Atwill, known to his friends as Taser, is well known to the Devon police. So are his father and grandfather before him, also both called Terence.'

That can't have done him any favours in the school playground. The only Terence I knew was a farm worker in his sixties who lived not far from my dad. Everyone called him Terry or Tez. Tez to Taser wasn't much of a step. Perhaps that had given this bastard the idea to get hold of the weapon he had used to threaten those kids. If everything he had said wasn't bullshit and bluff.

Hazel listed a string of magistrates' court convictions. 'None of this comes as any real surprise to his teachers or to the authorities, so my journalist friend says. The whole family's been neck deep in local crime for generations: smuggling, car theft, whatever's most profitable at the time. Taser dropped off the radar last summer. My pal reckons the police will be very interested to hear he's turned up dead in Darley Combe. He's pretty curious himself.'

'We can save him some investigating,' Fin told her. 'We found out Taser was dealing drugs.'

'We promised we'd keep the kids who told us well out of it,' I added quickly. 'They've had a hell of a time. They don't need coppers knocking on their doors. They didn't have a choice.'

'How so?' Hazel took a notebook and pencil out of her jacket pocket.

I explained, keeping my voice low. Fin added a few details. Hazel made unintelligible notes in what I guessed was shorthand. When we finished, she tapped her notebook thoughtfully with her pencil.

'So Taser was running a county line. His suppliers will realise there's a vacancy as soon as his body's formally identified. They won't be the only ones. Someone will want to step into those dead man's shoes. The kids were right about that.'

'Will the police be able to stop them?' Fin was concerned. So was I.

'Finding this woman Willow should be a good start. With luck, she'll have a record, or be a known associate of the Atwill family.' Hazel sounded optimistic, which was encouraging. 'I'll ask my own contacts to trace her too.'

'Can you keep these kids out of it?' That was my priority. 'When you tell your mate about the drugs. Are you certain he'll agree not to drop them in the shit with the cops?'

Hazel drank the last of her cold coffee. 'With luck, only Taser knew exactly who was working for him. He'd want to keep his operation secure from anyone who might try to cause trouble by sending the cops after his crew. If those kids have chucked their phones into the sea, his suppliers won't be able to reach them, even if they've got hold of Taser's phones or have a list of those numbers.'

'Which means what, as far as your journalist mate is concerned?' I had to be sure about this.

'I have no reason to give him their names,' Hazel assured me. 'Come to that, we don't even know their names. All we can tell him is where a couple of them are working. Anyway, without those burner phones, there's not much they could offer the police. If they've ditched the drugs, there's no evidence to link them with anything illegal. If I told my pal and he went to the cops, it would be his word against theirs. Besides, what would be the point? Taser can hardly be prosecuted now. As long as his death looks like an accident, the police will be a lot more focused on catching whoever tries to take over his operation. That's where the story will be for my mate.'

She tapped her page with her pencil again. 'Our friend did those kids quite a favour. How do you suppose he knew they needed help?'

I'd been thinking about that, though I hadn't come up with any answers. 'It makes me wonder about his trip to Yorkshire and the man he – met there.' It was probably best if no one heard me say 'murder' in this nice cafe.

'You think the man in the sink hole was a similar prize specimen?' Hazel sighed. 'I wish we could find out who he was, but I can't see that happening now, not after three months.'

'He knows we're on his trail,' Fin said abruptly. 'This – the man doing this.'

Hazel stared at her, shocked. 'What?'

'Let's go for a walk.' This definitely wasn't a conversation to have in the nice cafe.

We left, and I led the way. I'd noticed a small park by the river when Fin and I had looked at a tourist map on a notice-board. It wasn't far and it was a sunny morning. The three of us sat down on a bench with a good view of the medieval stone bridge that crossed the estuary. Fin was in the middle and Hazel and I sat sideways, looking at each other. We could stop talking before anyone got close enough to hear us.

'So?' Hazel demanded.

We told her about the black cat turning up to scare us shitless after the kids left. Fin explained how a shuck had scared the shapeshifter away. That was all she said. Sharing anything else was up to me. I kept my mouth shut. Hazel could assume the Green Man had sent the shuck. For now, anyway.

'He had to realise we could see the shuck,' Fin concluded. 'Even if he can't know anything else about us.'

I hoped she was right about that. Dryads and naiads and the like can recognise a shapeshifter or someone like me with more than human blood in their veins. I can't and neither can Fin. As far as we knew, the wise women couldn't pick us out of a crowd either. Hopefully this shapeshifter had the same limitations. He still had one advantage over us, even so. He knew what we looked like. We could pass him on the street without knowing who he was when he wasn't being a cat.

Uneasy, I looked around the little park. A fancy eighteenth-century building with a colonnade had been turned into a posh cafe at the far end. It didn't seem to be open, but plenty of tourists were admiring it. In the other direction, more people were going in and out of an impressive Victorian building between us and the bridge. Any one of them could be the shapeshifter. Though I couldn't see how he could know to come here looking for us. That wasn't much of a relief.

Hazel was thinking about something else. 'Why on earth did he come back to Darley Combe?'

'How do you mean?' Fin queried.

'Yesterday, before I went back to Exeter, I took another look at that MOD land. It took a bit of doing, but I found a place where I could get through the fence. That cat's scent was days old. He hadn't been there since he chased Taser over the cliff. Trust me, I wouldn't have set foot inside that fence, in any shape, if I wasn't a hundred per cent certain he was long gone.'

'He came back when he heard Taser's body had been fished out of the cove.' Fin didn't see a mystery. 'He must have expected the corpse would stay where he had put it.'

'Why?' Hazel persisted. 'What was he going to do about it?'

I was more concerned with what might lie ahead. 'What's he going to do now he knows we've seen him?'

'He doesn't necessarily know that we know he's a shapeshifter,' Fin pointed out. 'And I don't suppose the mermaid will tell him about us if he asks her what happened to Taser's body?'

'Not if she's still pissed off with him for dumping bodies in her bit of the sea.' I wondered if the shapeshifter would be the next body found floating in the cove. Maybe we should go to see the mermaid ourselves.

'Do you suppose those other bodies she was complaining about were drug dealers as well?' Fin wondered.

Hazel waved exasperated hands. 'You're missing the point. Who told him about Taser's body washing up yesterday? How did he know what had happened so fast? The police haven't released any details about the body. There was no briefing for journalists yesterday or this morning. Whoever told him, how did they contact him?'

Fin frowned. 'Could it have been one of those kids?'

'Maybe,' I said reluctantly. 'But they really seemed to think Taser's death was an accident. Until yesterday, they thought he had just gone missing.'

'Whoever told our killer that the body had turned up had his phone number,' Hazel persisted. 'They know who he is when he's not being a cat.'

'Shit.' I realised she was right.

Fin looked across the river. 'If it was one of those kids, I can't believe they know he can turn into a cat.'

'If they did, it would be all over the Internet,' I agreed. 'Even if people thought it was a hoax.' That made me think of the photo that had brought us here. I looked at Hazel. 'What's happening with that picture of the cat on the cliff?'

'I expect it'll end up on an inside page. A dead body makes for much more interesting headlines. Never mind that. We have to know which one of these kids told the shapeshifter about Taser if we're going to have any hope of finding him.' She looked at us, expectant. 'You need to go and ask the lad who works in that supermarket. If he can't help you, try the girl in the chip shop. I'd go myself, but they don't know me. They already trust you two.'

'They might not be working today.' I knew she was right, but I didn't have to like it.

'There's only one way to find out.' Hazel got to her feet.

Fin took the hint and stood up. 'We can make a quick stop before we head for the motorway. We can tell them nothing ties them to Taser now they've got rid of the evidence. As long as they don't say anything, everything should be fine.'

'Let's hope so.' I reckoned the fear of getting dragged back into that nightmare should keep their mouths shut.

'Ring me this evening.' Hazel patted her pockets to find her car keys. 'I'll go home and make a few calls. Let's see if anyone can trace this Willow woman.'

The way she said that made me wonder something. 'Is she a woman called Willow or could she be a willow spirit?' That would be an unexpected and unwelcome complication.

Hazel considered that for a moment. 'Who knows? I'll see what I can find out.'

It turned out we had left our cars in the same town centre car park. We walked back together, and Hazel headed off in her grubby Fiesta. Fin drove slowly through the Barnstaple traffic and we headed for Darley Combe.

The seafront car park was crowded. Fin circled slowly, looking for a space. 'Do you think these people are here because they heard about the body being found?'

'Why? There's nothing to see.' Though people do very strange things. I unclipped my seatbelt as Fin crawled past the disabled parking bays across the front of the shops. 'Let me get out. I'll be as quick as I can.'

The chip shop was rammed. As Fin continued her circuit of the car park, I didn't even bother going in to see if Emma was taking orders. If she was, she'd have no time to talk. I went into the supermarket. The karate kid was on the till beside the automated check-outs. He recognised me and looked sick with apprehension.

I took some chocolate from the nearest display and joined the queue of people who wanted a human being to scan their shopping. The lad beckoned to someone behind me. I turned to see an older woman parking a trolley stacked with cartons of milk beside a glass-fronted fridge. She came to take over from the lad at the till. He headed for the milk and began refilling the shelves. I went to join him. I kept my voice low.

'People we trust are looking for Willow. When they find her, they'll tell the police. No one official knows anything about you or your friends.'

He was more scared than reassured. 'What do we do if Willow comes here? What if she tells Taser's bosses how to find us?'

Shit. He had a point. 'Then you go straight to the cops. Tell them you're being threatened. She's trying to force you into dealing for her. Tell them this is the first time you've ever met. Tell them where to find her, if you possibly can. You got rid of the evidence and you haven't told anyone else what Taser had you doing, have you? Anyone at all?'

'Fuck no,' he said with absolute sincerity. 'You and her last night, you're the only ones. I swear.'

'So if anyone asks you about Taser, say you have no idea who that is. You never had anything to do with him. Tell your mates to say the same. If Willow says different, it's her word against yours.'

I really hoped so. The bitch might have something to give her a hold over these kids. Photos on a phone? There was nothing I could do about that. I was here to ask him what we needed to know.

'Did you tell anyone else it was Taser who got pulled out of the sea? What about your mates? Is there anyone they might have told?'

I was asking too many questions. The lad looked confused. 'No.'

That was the truth as far as he knew it, for whatever that might be worth.

'Okay. Keep your heads down and don't say a word about any of this to anyone.'

I left him filling the fridge with milk and paid for my chocolate at an automated check-out. Leaving the supermarket, I saw Fin's Toyota on the far side of the car park. I walked towards the exit, so she could pick me up there.

A sudden shiver ran down my spine. My dad calls that a goose walking over his grave. If this was some new dryad sense, I had no idea what it was telling me. I rubbed the scars on my arm, but they weren't itching. Fin pulled up and I got into the Toyota.

'Anything?' she asked as we left the car park.

I told her what the lad had said. I rang Hazel's number and left a message telling her the same. I mentioned the possibility that Willow might be able to tie the kids to Taser with photos or some other evidence. 'If your wise women find her before the cops, deleting any blackmail material on her phone would be a good idea. Right, talk to you later.'

150

'The kids said Willow disappeared at the same time as Taser.' Fin changed gear. 'If the shapeshifter got her too, he could have dumped her body somewhere else.'

'That would make life simpler.' I wasn't going to waste any sympathy there.

As we headed for the motorway, I wondered if Fin had the same questions as me chasing each other round and around in her head. Were we ever going to find this killer? What were we going to do if we did?

Chapter Thirteen

While we were on the motorway, I asked Fin if I could stay over on Sunday night. She said yes, so I rang Eleanor to tell her I'd head back to Blithehurst first thing in the morning while the roads were still quiet. Then I told her what we'd discovered about the mysterious, murderous cat.

'A shapeshifter?' She was as baffled as us. 'I'll ask Asca and Frai if they know anything useful, if I get a chance. I'll take a look through the library this evening.'

'Thanks.' If we were going to find some clue, it would most likely come from some old, overlooked book. A lot of old myths never get onto the Internet. That's a good thing for us, until we need to do some specific research.

As soon as I ended that call, Hazel rang me. She had nothing new to tell us. The wise women had barely got to work.

The roads were busy but the traffic was moving. We skirted the south of Bristol to avoid the city centre. Cainescombe, where Fin and Blanche live, is far enough from the city to avoid being sucked into a suburb, but just about everyone who lives there these days works somewhere else. Fin's flat is the upstairs left in a block of four, tucked behind some barn conversions with three other identical new builds. Each flat has two designated parking spaces. When we pulled up, I saw Blanche's Honda in her spot.

Up in the flat, she was sitting on one of the sofas, watching what looked like a crime drama in France. She hit the pause button when we came into the lounge-diner. 'Hi. What have you two been up to?' She must have enjoyed her weekend, if she was in such a good mood.

'I'll put the kettle on.' As I went through to the kitchen at the other end of the room, Fin told her about our eventful few days in Devon.

'Wow.' Blanche was astonished and then concerned. 'He has to be stopped. If he gets caught by someone official who sees what he can do, that's a threat to us all.'

'We have to find him before we can stop him,' Fin pointed out.

I put tea and coffee on the low table between the sofas and the TV. 'You don't recall seeing anything that might help us in your grandad's old books and magazines?'

Eleanor saying she'd look through the Blithehurst library had reminded me about the substantial stash of folklore-related stuff at their mum Helen's house.

Blanche shook her head. 'Nothing comes to mind.'

'I'll ask Mum to have a look.' Fin reached for her phone.

While she brought Helen up to date, I took my mug of tea out onto the flat's small balcony, overlooking the farmland at the edge of the village. I checked there was no one in the ground-floor flats' small gardens and that their patio doors were shut. Then I rang my dad. Mum must have been close by, because she joined in the call. She was astonished when she heard what had happened to me.

'A man who can become a cat. A hunter who protects the weak from predators. I've never heard of such a thing.' She corrected herself. 'I've never heard of a mortal capable of such a transformation. Woses would defend the helpless who sought sanctuary in the greenwoods in days gone by.'

I wasn't so sure about that. The way I read those stories was woses didn't hesitate to go after any potential threat they found in their remote woods. A wose had done its best to kill me once, and that bastard thing had been a lethal threat to mortal girls as well as to dryads.

I didn't remind Mum about that. 'Let me know if you remember anything else.'

Then I did my best to reassure my dad, stressing how fast the shuck had appeared and scared the killer away. We chatted for a bit longer, then I went back inside.

'If you have the vegetable pakora and I have the onion bhaji, we can share.' Blanche was making notes on a Post-It stuck to a takeaway menu.

'And I'll have king prawn masala with pilau rice.' Fin looked at me. 'What do you want, Dan?'

'Sheik kebab and chicken dansak, please, with pilau rice and a naan. Oh, and a vegetable curry. If you ring the order in when they open, I'll go and pick it up.' They must have both done enough driving this weekend.

Fin put her coffee mug on the table. 'Mum says hello. She says she'll tell Will and everyone else about the cat man. Hopefully someone will know something that'll help.'

'Let's hope so.' Between Hazel's network of wise women and our own contacts, questions about this shapeshifter would be spreading outwards like ripples from a stone thrown into a pond.

Later on, as I drove back from the Indian restaurant with our takeaway, I wondered if Fin's cousin Will's nereid girlfriend could find out if more bodies had been dumped in the sea somewhere. I wondered how long it might take her to get a message to the mermaid in Darley Combe. What more could she tell us about the corpses still hidden there? This wasn't a conversation to have over dinner. I pulled up outside the flat, picked up the takeaway bag in the passenger footwell and went inside.

Fin and I had an early night. We more than made up for going straight to sleep in Barnstaple. I got up bright and early and ate half a naan and leftover vegetable curry for breakfast. I had an easy run back to Blithehurst.

I drove straight to the Dairy Yard and parked there. I hadn't forgotten what Eleanor had asked me before I went to Devon. I needed to measure the ruins before I could work out how to keep a wedding dry. Doing that would be easiest without visitors around.

Besides, I needed to think about something else. I'd been racking my brains all the way back, trying to think of some way to trace the sodding shapeshifter. I hadn't come up with a thing. I made a quick pot of tea and ate some biscuits out of the tin while I found a pad of paper, a short metal ruler and a sharp pencil. I got my laser distance meter out of its case and locked the workshop door behind me.

The gates were open as I walked through the grounds and past the manor. Down by the river, Sarah and her team were cleaning the loos and restocking the castle gatehouse cafe. I used the laser to measure the open space that had once been the central courtyard. That's where a marquee would have to go. I measured the rest of the space around it as well, where low walls marked out what had once been servants' quarters and storerooms beneath the family's luxurious apartments. There had been a lot more of the building left until some dim-witted eighteenth-century Beauchene decided a bit of demolition would make the ruin more romantic. There was no such thing as the Health and Safety Executive in the good old days. Seven estate workers had nearly been crushed by falling masonry.

I sat on the remnant of one of those walls and drew a plan on my pad. I added dimensions and thought about possibilities. If there was a way to use the space around the courtyard, that would give Eleanor a lot more options. The old stone walls would also be much more interesting to look at than a white canvas marquee's interior.

I looked up at the great hall's arched windows and wondered if the old lime mortar was solid enough to take a few anchor points. How would we go about rigging a canopy? I'd never done anything like that. On most building sites where I'd worked before I got this job, if it rained, we just got wet. I decided to ring Chris. His mum runs the marquee firm which Blithehurst uses for special events like craft days or metal detectorist weekends. He might have some useful ideas.

'Penny for your thoughts?'

'What?' I looked up to see Denise walking towards me, carrying a couple of mugs.

She offered me one. I didn't want a drink, but I took it to be polite. It was coffee. I put it down on the wall beside me.

'I heard what Miss Eleanor was asking you last week.' Denise gazed around the ruins. 'About having Miss Sophie's wedding here. Won't that be lovely? It's so wonderful when families carry on their historic traditions.'

She was talking bollocks. There hadn't been a wedding here for centuries, and a fugitive Catholic priest had married that particular rebellious Beauchene. It probably hadn't even been legal. And why was she talking about 'Miss Eleanor' and 'Miss Sophie', like some servant in a Sunday-night drama? Nobody called them that.

I looked at my plan and calculated floor areas. Denise didn't take the hint. She sipped her own coffee, gazing up at the great hall.

'Miss Sophie will be the first of her generation to be married. Perhaps Miss Eleanor will be next. You two are very close. She lets you set your own hours and you take days off whenever you like.'

'I've got a girlfriend who lives in Bristol.' I still didn't look up, and I wasn't going to say anything else about Fin.

156

'Oh, well. Has Miss Eleanor got someone special, do you know? Up in Durham, perhaps? A boyfriend or a girlfriend? We're all open-minded these days.' She forced a fake laugh.

I looked up from my pad and scowled. Most of the time, I try not to be intimidating. Sometimes, though, I do. 'Why the hell do you think I know Eleanor's private business? And why the hell should I tell you?'

Denise took a hasty step backwards. Since I had said that fairly loudly, she didn't realise Eleanor had walked up quietly behind her.

'As it happens, no, I don't have a boyfriend in Durham, or a girlfriend.'

Denise spun around, spilling coffee down her sweatshirt.

Eleanor carried on. 'Since you're so curious, I can tell you I've been to bed with women as well as with men from time to time. Honestly, I'd rather go to bed with a good book. Any other questions? No?' She didn't give the embarrassed woman any chance to reply. 'Then I suggest you go and see where Sarah needs your help.'

Denise hurried away. The back of her neck was bright red with humiliation. That served her right.

Eleanor watched her go into the gatehouse. 'I wish we could put a tick box on our application forms. Are you a nosy old gossip who assumes she has a right to know everyone else's business? Tick the box for yes or no. She's been asking what happened to Robbie. Apparently she's sure there must be juicy details which didn't make the local press.'

Now I understood why Eleanor had been so brutal. As far as the rest of the world knew, Robert Beauchene, the oldest of the four of them, had died in a tragic accident no one could have foreseen. Only Eleanor and I and the dryads knew what had really happened.

I held up the pad of paper to show her the plan I had drawn, to change the subject before she got too upset. 'We

157

could set up a marquee, but some sort of canopy would be better. Tables and chairs could be more spread out. If there was going to be dancing, that could be set up in the great hall.'

To be honest, I was pretty hazy on what happens at weddings. I vaguely remembered a service in the local church when I was a little kid. There'd been sandwiches and cake in the function room at the back of The Two Magpies. That had been the first time I'd eaten marzipan. I have no idea who got married or why my parents were invited.

Eleanor managed a smile. 'Let's talk about that later. I actually came to give you this.'

She pulled a sheet of paper off her clipboard. She'd printed out an email. Fin had forwarded a message she'd got this morning through the BFW Environmental website's contact form. The four words would be meaningless to anyone else.

'Chelsea told her therapist.' I didn't have to explain to Eleanor. 'How do we find out who that is?'

'And what links the therapist and the shapeshifter?' Eleanor added.

'One of the girls said a local yoga teacher helped Chelsea get clean, on the quiet so her parents didn't have to know. I can't remember if we told Hazel about that.'

'Come up to the house and email her,' Eleanor suggested. 'Better safe than sorry.'

'Right.' I picked up the coffee I hadn't asked for and followed Eleanor towards the gatehouse. As she went over the footbridge, I stepped into the cafe kitchen to pour the coffee down the sink.

Sarah appeared in the doorway and held out her hand for the mug. 'I'll deal with that.'

A glint in her eye made me wonder if she'd sent Denise in my direction earlier. I didn't ask.

'Thanks.' I gave her the mug and went after Eleanor. By the time I'd closed the sitting room door behind me, I'd remembered something else.

'There was a noticeboard in the Darley Combe chip shop. Someone teaches yoga classes in the village hall. You'd join the closest class, wouldn't you, if you were interested?'

Eleanor was already busy with her laptop. 'I'd give a class within walking distance at least a try. Let's see if the village hall has a website.'

I didn't sit down. I wanted to go and look at the screen over Eleanor's shoulder, but there wasn't room.

'The yoga teacher is called Jenny Damerell and she has her own web page. Let's see what that says.' Eleanor moved her mouse and clicked. 'She teaches classes at several different places. Oh, this is interesting. She spends Wednesday mornings at the Pedrick Wellness Centre. That has to be worth a look, if we're trying to find a therapist.'

'Got to be,' I agreed.

'It's not too far away from Darley Combe, up on Exmoor, and based in what looks like an old farmhouse.' Eleanor started reading aloud. 'We offer a range of therapies with an emphasis on holistic and integrative care to offer relief from acute and chronic pain, chronic fatigue, headaches and migraines, digestive disorders, sleep disorders, and mental and emotional health issues. Please get in touch to arrange an initial in-depth consultation. Individual treatment plans are created to address each patient's specific needs.'

She clicked through a few more pages. 'It looks completely legit, established in 1976. As well as yoga and tai chi, they offer acupuncture and shiatsu, chiropractic therapy, hypnotherapy, reiki, herbal medicine and counselling.'

I saw her raise her eyebrows before she went on. 'It's not cheap, but plenty of satisfied clients are offering glowing testimonials.'

'What does it say about getting teenagers off drugs?'

'Nothing, but that's probably not something they'd adver-
tise. Maybe one of these practitioners does that as a sideline,
in their own time. Apart from the couple who founded the
place, they seem to be self-employed, working in different
places as well as at the centre.'

'How do we find out if they treated Chelsea – whatever
her surname is? There's no point in me going down there.
No one will believe I'm a junkie, or Fin.'

'No.' Eleanor grinned. 'Let's see what Hazel and her network can find out. Everyone who works there has a page with
a photo listing their professional qualifications.'

Eleanor turned the laptop around so I could see the
screen. I ignored the women on the list and checked out the
four men. Two were chiropractors. One was a medical herbalist, and one was a hypnotherapist. Two had beards, one was
bald. They were all middle-aged and white. None of them
looked like a ruthless murderer.

I was annoyed with myself. 'We should have got a better
description of the bastard from the mermaid.'

Eleanor reached for the laptop. 'Maybe Hazel can find out
if any of these guys cancelled appointments or were away
from home when we know the shapeshifter was in Yorkshire.'

She finished typing. 'There. Sent. Now we just have to
wait.'

Hazel emailed back at once, saying we could leave that
with her. She didn't contact us again that week. When
I texted to ask how she was getting on, she messaged back
saying these things took time.

When she did get in touch in early June, she said she had
talked to the mermaid at Darley Combe. She didn't recognise any of the four men from the wellness centre website.

I got the Blithehurst dryads to look at them on my phone anyway. Neither of them saw anything out of the ordinary. When I told Fin, she said I should show Asca and Frai a photo of her. It turned out that neither dryad could tell she was a swan maiden from a picture on a screen or when it was printed out. I suppose that was useful to know. It was sodding frustrating all the same.

I wanted to go to Yorkshire, to ask the dryad why she hadn't told us the black cat was a shapeshifter. Kalei turned up before I could arrange the time off, so I asked her. The naiad said she could recognise a shapeshifter in a crowd of people, but she couldn't pick Fin out of a flock of swans. My mum said the same. So that was something else that was interesting which didn't get us anywhere.

Hazel gave me a quick call at the start of July. Taser's girlfriend had been arrested in Plymouth for drug-related offences. A week or so later she told us the wise women were confident that Willow was just ordinarily human. She also seemed to have done some sort of deal, presumably to reduce her own sentence or because she didn't believe Taser's death was an accident and she wanted revenge. Either way, the cops were making lots of arrests. Hazel's journalist friend saw no sign of anyone trying to set up a new county line to Darley Combe. That was good news as well, but we were still nowhere near finding the killer.

Chris came up with a solid plan to use scaffolding and canvas to set up a massive gazebo inside the castle ruins. The scaffolding poles could be hidden with garlands of artificial flowers, and long canvas curtains on each side could be lowered if a cold wind got up or the sun was scorching.

Eleanor set up a spreadsheet and worked out the costs. She discussed the plan with her mum and dad, and then gave

Sophie a call. Sophie was delighted. Her wedding was going ahead at Blithehurst.

Fin and I spent a few days away in the Fens. Her mum's a freelance graphic designer, and she was working a big project so she hadn't had much time to spare for searching Grandad's books for clues. Fin and I took a look for ourselves. I had just opened the window overlooking the back garden when Fin sat up straight on the ancient, sagging settee.

'This is—' She sneezed. Old books and papers shed a lot of dust. That's why I'd opened the window.

Fin found a tissue and blew her nose. 'This might be worth following up.' She held up a small, thin book with a faded red cover. The title in black was clear enough. *Cat Myths and Legends.*

'There's a chapter about Scottish witch trials.' She wrinkled her nose. 'They did horrible things to cats, or at least, doing that was supposedly part of their spells. But listen to this. One coven was accused of riding on gigantic black cats. Grandad or someone else has underlined those last three words. Whoever did it, they've written "the cunning men" in the margin.'

She looked at me. 'What do you think? Could this mean these cunning men were shapeshifters?'

'That's quite a leap, but it's the only thing we've found that might be even vaguely relevant. We have to ask Hazel.' I knew a cunning man had been the equivalent of a wise woman in days gone by, but as far as I knew, none of them were still around.

I got my phone out, expecting to leave a message, but Hazel answered my call. I sat next to Fin on the settee and put my phone on speaker. Fin explained what she had found in the tattered old book. Hazel didn't say a thing.

'Are you still there?' I checked in case the phone signal had dropped out.

'That's very interesting,' Hazel said slowly. 'We've finally made some progress working out who could have heard first when Taser was found dead. One of the counsellors at Pedrick Wellness treats substance abuse very discreetly and not through the centre itself. She charges rich addicts an arm and a leg so she can take on poor patients pro bono. She's the Darley Combe yoga teacher's girlfriend. She has to be Chelsea's therapist.'

'She?' We weren't looking for a female shapeshifting murderer.

'She's a fully qualified medical herbalist who gets her tinctures and such from a Scottish supplier. He travels the country, selling to the alternative medicine trade. The thing is, he seems to have disappeared. No one's seen him since the start of May. I was wondering if he could have fallen foul of the cat somehow.'

'But he might be who we're looking for instead. Does he have a name?' Fin got up to fetch her laptop from the table.

'William Halsbury.' Hazel spelled out his surname.

Fin typed quickly. 'He has a website.'

I stared at her. Finding the bastard couldn't be this easy.

Chapter Fourteen

It wasn't. It was August before we made any progress. That website was no damn use. The only photos were plants and herbs. We still had no idea what the man we were hunting for looked like. There was no address given for his business, and the only way to contact him was through an online form.

We found people to do that, asking for details of William Halsbury's herbal products. People the shapeshifter shouldn't be able to link to me, Fin or Hazel. We didn't know if the bastard had seen the three of us together at Darley Combe, but we weren't taking any chances. We asked them to just make one enquiry, to avoid making him suspicious. I don't know why we bothered. No one got a reply. I reckoned that had to mean something. If he disappeared so suddenly and without any warning, he had something to hide.

On Sophie Beauchene's wedding day, we finally got a lead. That was great, but I could hardly tell Eleanor I was setting off to hunt the bastard down. I had to be on hand in case Chris needed help. He and his team had rigged the canopy over the castle ruins the day before. The scaffolding was solid and the canvas wasn't going anywhere unless an unexpected tornado arrived, but lowering the curtain panels on the sides would be a two-man job. Those two men were Chris and me.

Hopefully the side curtains wouldn't be needed. The sun was shining but the day wasn't too hot, thanks to fluffy white clouds drifting overhead. It was a bit humid down in the valley beside the river, but the breeze kept the air moving.

The wedding ceremony would start at midday. Then the guests would be ushered out of the castle for the wedding photos and champagne would be served in the Wilderness

Garden. Inside the ruins, Sarah and her team would be rushing around to set up tables and rearrange the flowers and the chairs so lunch could be served at one-thirty. After the speeches and the bride and groom cutting the cake, the guests could go home or to their hotels, unless they were staying on for the evening party. That was the plan anyway.

I was on duty from ten in the morning. A lot of guests were only coming for the day. Eleanor was right about the lack of places to stay overnight locally, especially in the middle of the school summer holidays. Besides, Blithehurst is under two hours' drive from Manchester. The best man had been busy arranging lifts in spare seats for anyone who needed one.

Sophie and the bridesmaids were staying with Mr and Mrs Beauchene at the Dower House. David and his best man were staying with one of the local Beauchene cousins. Everyone would arrive by limo just before the ceremony.

The manor house itself was still open to the public, along with the restaurant and the garden centre. Like Eleanor said, the business couldn't afford to close down completely. At the staff meeting to discuss arrangements, everyone had agreed the wedding guests' cars would be better parked somewhere out of the way. The best place was the Dairy Yard. We also agreed some would turn up early. Anyone with half a brain would allow extra time in case they got caught by bad traffic in peak holiday season. With luck, the roads would stay clear, but those early arrivals would need somewhere to go.

Lynne, who works with Sarah in the castle cafe, suggested setting up the cafe's tables, chairs and umbrellas in the Wilderness Garden. Guests could be offered tea, coffee or a cold drink there, and the use of the castle cafe loos. They could sit and chat, or go for a walk around the manor grounds. Everyone agreed that was a brilliant plan.

So my job was walking thirty-something couples up to the manor house and showing them the path to follow. As I got back to the Dairy Yard, I tried to ease my new shirt's stiff collar. Finding formal clothes in my size isn't easy and I don't like wearing shirts with collars anyway. I really don't like wearing ties. Putting a noose around your own neck isn't smart, it's stupid.

But Eleanor said members of the public and the guests would need to know who was Blithehurst staff and who was involved with the wedding. So I was wearing my only pair of formal trousers and a new short-sleeved grey shirt, and Eleanor had given me a dark red tie. Thankfully she'd found one long enough to reach my belt. At least she hadn't asked me to wear a suit, so I didn't feel like I was going to court.

My phone pinged. I'd politely asked Asca and Frai to make sure everyone had decent phone reception today, as a wedding favour from them to the bride. Mark had texted me two more car registrations. He'd usually be supervising the main car park, but today he was on duty on the estate's back gate, checking arrivals against the list of drivers which David's best man had emailed to Eleanor.

As I waited for the two cars to turn up, I remembered something Fin had said about the shapeshifter.

"If he's got a car, he's got a driving licence and insurance – most likely. He must do something to earn money for fuel."

That wouldn't have changed. The man we wanted to find still needed to eat and to pay his rent or his mortgage as well as his other bills. Unless he was spending all his time as a cat, and catching rabbits for his dinner. I doubted that. Fin and Hazel both said they could only stay transformed for twenty-four hours at most before the urge to change back overwhelmed them. So what was William Halsbury – if that was even his real name – doing for money? He wasn't doing any business through his website. Unless he was living off his savings, of course.

Then I remembered something Chris had said. All their marquees were booked for events over the August Bank Holiday weekend. One was a craft fair not far away. I had been a regular at craft fairs and living history days before I started working at Blithehurst. I sold the wood carvings I did in my spare time, usually for beer money and sometimes for rent and food. I thought about the other traders I used to see when I was sitting at a table I'd paid for, hoping to make more than the trip cost me.

It's a fair drive from the estate's back gate. I had a few minutes before those cars would appear. I didn't want to let go of this idea. I scrolled through my phone contacts and called Aled James. He's a silversmith who rents a workshop in a crafts and cultural centre in the North Wales mountains, in the village where I'd met Annis Wynne. I knew he sold his jewellery at craft fairs from time to time.

'Hiya, Dan.' He answered the phone as cheerfully as he always does. A moment later, he was suddenly concerned. 'Everything's okay, isn't it? With the candlesticks?'

It took me a moment to work out what he meant. 'They're fine. They're in Eleanor's safe.'

A set of Tudor altar silver had turned up at Blithehurst: a cross, two candlesticks, a chalice, a plate and a round silver box with a lid. Back in Elizabeth I's day, the ancestral Beauchenes had worshipped in a tiny secret chapel. A carpenter who travelled between quietly rebellious wealthy households had built that inside the manor for the family to use, as well as constructing a priest hole for Jesuits to hide in. His ghost had shown Eleanor enough clues to convince her the altar silver had been hidden and forgotten.

The modern-day Beauchenes hadn't hesitated to auction the treasure off. The complete set was so valuable, it would have cost a fortune to insure. The major injection of cash would secure the manor house's future. The altar pieces wouldn't be forgotten again though. Eleanor's dad had commissioned Aled to make a replica set to go on display with the story of the silver's rediscovery. He'd also commissioned another pair of candlesticks as a surprise wedding present for Sophie. Aled had delivered them personally the week before last.

'This is about something else,' I quickly explained. 'You know this shapeshifter we're trying to find? What if he's working the summer fair circuit, selling herbal remedies to earn cash in hand. What contacts have you got with traders and organisers?'

'That's an interesting idea,' he said thoughtfully.

I didn't need to say anything else. Aled had been the first person I called when I'd realised we might be looking for a cunning man. Generations back, there had been one in Aled's family. A Welsh cave spirit, a coblyn, had fathered Elias Pritchard. That's why Aled can see the same things as Fin and me, and he's more comfortable in pitch-dark tiny spaces underground than anyone I've ever met.

I remembered him telling me how cunning men travelled around Wales in days gone by. They sold cures for various ailments, as well as setting bones and pulling teeth, working charms and lifting curses. I hadn't seen those services on offer at any craft fairs, but I'd seen herbal teas that promised to ease all sorts of problems. Nothing guaranteed, of course. Notices made it very clear these stall-holders weren't selling unregulated medicines.

'Right you are. I'll ask around,' Aled said. 'Still no luck with that website?' He had filled in William Halsbury's contact form for us.

JULIET E. MCKENNA

'No, and I don't think anyone will ever get a reply.' I heard a car engine. Two car engines. 'Sorry, I've got to go. Can you ask around about craft fairs?'

'Leave it with me.' Aled ended the call.

I put my phone in my shirt pocket and went to direct the new arrivals into their designated parking spaces. Four couples got out of the two cars. The women wore bright summer dresses. Two carried fancy hats and the others had twists of ribbon and feathers fixed to their heads somehow. The blokes were in suits, or jackets and chinos. I noticed two of them wore open-necked shirts.

'Good morning. Welcome to Blithehurst.' I waited for the woman who'd been driving to change her trainers for strappy high-heeled shoes. 'This way, please.'

I gestured towards the path that led to the front of the manor house. It cut through a gap in the tall yew hedge that had been planted to hide the outbuildings from the house's windows. They followed me through the ornamental shrubs and dwarf fruit trees that Eleanor's great-grandmother had planted on the east side of the house. I heard the drivers compare the traffic they'd encountered while the others swapped news of people the four of them all knew.

When we reached the front of the manor house, Eleanor stood by the porch. I recognised the photographer with her. He'd taken that photo of me making hazel hurdles. Eleanor had been talking about getting some publicity photos to use if today was a success and the family decided to try offering the castle as a wedding venue.

I let the guests catch up with me and pointed to the sign directing them to the wedding. 'If you go down to the castle, Lynne will show you where to get a drink.'

She would be standing on the footbridge over the moat, explaining the ruins were closed for a private function. Some of the other visitors would manage to miss hearing that when

169

they bought their tickets, and wouldn't see the polite notices saying the same thing.

Eleanor acknowledged the guests with a wave as she carried on giving the photographer his instructions. 'Try to get the lunch set-up fully covered before everyone comes in to sit down. The bride and groom are fine with you taking pictures of the ceremony as long as you take those from a distance. Do your best to avoid getting anyone else in shot. I don't want to have to ask for releases from the guests.'

The photographer nodded. 'Anything else, or shall I make a start?'

Eleanor managed a smile. 'I think that's it. Thanks.' She turned to me as he walked away. She looked tense again. 'What do you need?'

'Nothing. You look nice.' She was wearing make-up that made her look like a model or a film star, and a silky plum-coloured dress that really suited her.

'Thanks.' She raised a hand but remembered just in time that her long dark hair was plaited and pinned up. She had a spray of red and white silk flowers fixed to the back on a silver comb. She checked her wristwatch instead. 'I should go and see if Sarah needs anything.'

This wasn't a good time to talk to her about craft fairs. 'I'll get back to the Dairy Yard.'

Eleanor headed for the castle and I turned around to go the other way. I got out my phone and rang Hazel. I told her why I had rung Aled, and what I thought the shapeshifter might be doing to earn some cash.

'That's probably worth following up.' Hazel sounded as if she was willing to try anything by now. 'Isn't the wedding today? How's it going?'

'Fine. Do you know anyone you can ask about craft fairs? Maybe up in Scotland, in case he's gone back there? If he wanted to get as far away from Devon as possible?'

'Yes, that was my first thought,' Hazel said crisply. 'The problem is, we don't have much of a network north of the border. With everything that happened back in the day, most of our people left. No one's had much reason to go back.'

'Right.' After Fin had found that old book, we'd looked up the history of witch trials in Scotland. What we found had been gruesome. It was hardly surprising that any wise women who stayed out of trouble had decided to get out while the going was good.

We found enough stories of men being accused of working magic to convince me we were on the right track. This shapeshifter was a modern cunning man. We needed to find him before any more murders risked him being caught, putting the rest of us in danger. Then we had to convince him to stop. These were murders, even if he was killing scum like Taser Atwill. Like my dad says, two wrongs don't make a right. Even if three lefts do, he usually adds.

'We don't have much to do with craft fairs, but I'll see what I can find out.' Hazel ended the call.

By the time I got back to the Dairy Yard, I'd had another text from Mark. More guests had arrived. I was soon too busy to think about anything else. When everyone we had been told to expect was finally parked, I muted my phone, stuck it in my shirt pocket and followed the last four guests up to the manor.

They had cut this very fine. The first of the wedding cars had just driven carefully along the wide gravel path that runs through the centre of the knot garden. I'd never seen vehicles use that before. As the limo drew up in front of the porch, a handful of people who'd only come to see the Tudor house gave David and his best man a round of applause. The two men managed a tight smile with a brief wave of thanks. Then they headed for the ruins.

Sophie and the bridesmaids were in another limo a few minutes behind them. Everyone's parents arrived right after that. Now a sizeable crowd of visitors had gathered to cheer and clap everyone getting out of a car. I went over to the signpost pointing to different places in the grounds to clear people off the path.

Sophie took her father's arm. She was wearing a stylish long white dress with a lace-edged veil that brushed her shoulders. Eleanor had said her sister always swore she wasn't getting married looking like a meringue. The head bridesmaid was about the same age as Sophie, in a dress the same colour as Eleanor's. She looked like a woman not to be messed with today. She ushered three little girls in matching pale pink dresses down the path ahead of her. Mrs Beauchene followed with a couple who had to be the groom's mum and dad. More visitors called out congratulations, hoping everyone had a lovely day.

I followed ten paces behind. Looking over everyone's heads, I saw the guests who'd been waiting in the Wilderness Garden were crossing the footbridge over the moat. As Sophie and her dad went through the gatehouse arch, I heard the string quartet set up in the great hall start playing.

I went over to the Wilderness Garden and helped myself to a long, cold drink. The leaves on the trees were limp and dull at the end of the summer, but their shade and the river close by meant the grass here was green and lush while the lawns were parched and faded. I sat on the bench I had made and wondered if maybe I should ask Fin if she wanted to talk about where we might be headed as a couple.

The ceremony went smoothly, as far as I could tell. When everyone came out for the wedding photographs, the bride and groom, the head bridesmaid and Eleanor looked a whole lot more relaxed, even before they'd had some champagne. The best man was still pretty tense, but he had to give a speech.

Sarah came over the footbridge to tell Eleanor they were ready to serve lunch. Everyone headed back inside the castle. It was still a nice sunny day, and I could feel a gentle breeze by the river. I didn't think the canvas curtains would be needed. In any case, Chris could always text me. I was thinking about heading up to the restaurant to get some food when Frai and Asca appeared. They looked like Greek goddesses crowned with garlands of flowers. That was something I hadn't seen before.

'It looks like it's going well.' There was no one close enough to hear me talking to them.

'You had better come with us if you want to be sure of that,' Frai snapped with a glint in her eye.

'Quickly,' Asca urged. 'We don't want anything to ruin this day.'

I got to my feet. 'What's the problem?'

'This way.' She was already beyond the trees that mark the boundary of the formal gardens, taking the path that leads to the meadow.

I followed her into the meadow. On the other side, the path follows the river through a stretch of rough pasture. Beyond that, the water has cut its course through a shallow ridge of higher ground. On the far side of that, sluices draw off water to fill the old millpond. That's a little way upstream of the derelict watermill. There's no way to reach that building now. The path is fenced off with so many 'Danger – No Entry' notices the MOD would be impressed.

Asca was getting too far ahead. I started running. According to the official record, Robert Beauchene had died when the mill collapsed. Eleanor and I knew he had been killed by a shapeshifting menace who wished their family no good at all. Was it possible she had somehow come back?

Chapter Fifteen

When we reached the rough pasture, I saw a woman stumbling around in circles. I breathed a whole lot easier when I realised who she was. 'Denise?'

After she'd embarrassed herself so thoroughly back in May, she'd handed in her notice that same day. No one seemed particularly sorry to see her go, though no one would say why. I wondered what I'd missed. Janice who runs the restaurant said something a few weeks later about a surge of bad reviews online. She suspected Denise was posting those, although she couldn't prove it.

'What's she doing here?' I asked Frai.

The old dryad's smile promised nothing good for the nosy woman. 'We saw her trying to slip through the gate-house early this morning, when Sarah needed Lynne's help with something.'

'She was here before the gates were open to visitors,' Asca said severely. 'We cornered her and asked what she was doing. She said she had been asked to help out for the day. That was a lie.'

Denise wouldn't have realised who she was dealing with, or known that she had no chance of deceiving them.

Frai nodded. 'She reeks of malice and she has no invitation to this wedding. So we led her away.'

They had done a lot more than that. 'What's she doing?'

'We have mazed her.' Asca shrugged.

I didn't know that's what it was called, but I'd seen my mum send a hiker walking in circles, unable to find his way out of her woods. She said he'd been offensively rude to a birdwatcher. If the Blithehurst dryads had done that to Denise, she wouldn't have any idea where she was, or how long she'd been stuck there.

'You need not look so concerned,' Frai said, exasperated. 'No one who comes this way will see her. We have seen to that.'

Denise was wearing jeans and a Blithehurst sweatshirt even though I knew staff who left were asked to return those. I had no idea why she had come here. I knew she wasn't welcome, not today, not any time.

'Do you know where she left her car?' If the dryads had seen her skulking around the castle before the main gates were open, she couldn't have parked by the garden centre.

Frai nodded. 'That is on the grass where the path along the valley side reaches the road.'

Oh, great. The public footpath was on the other side of the river. The footbridge that linked that with the mill had been destroyed when Rob Beauchene died. It hadn't been rebuilt, to limit access to the derelict building.

I looked at Asca. 'Can you get us both across the water? And keep her—' I waved a hand at Denise, trying to find the right word. 'Oblivious but cooperative? Until I can get her back to her car?'

'She will stay suggestible until you leave her.' The younger dryad was watching Denise as intently as a hawk watching a mouse.

'Come on then.' I hurried across the rough grass, hoping as hard as I could that the dryads' powers would mean no one could see me either.

When I reached Denise, I realised she wasn't just stumbling on uneven ground. She was close to collapse. She'd been out here for hours without anything to drink, walking in circles the whole time. Shit. Was she going to pass out with heatstroke before I could get her back to her car?

I saw she was gripping her phone tight in her sweaty hand. That struck me as odd. I took it off her and looked through her recent photos. I swore under my breath. She didn't only have pictures of the set-up inside the ruins for the wedding. She'd photographed Mr and Mrs Beauchene outside the Dower House at what looked like different times of day, going back months. She had lots of pictures of Sophie and Eleanor, together and on their own, going in and out of shops. She'd been stalking them all.

I deleted every photo and stuck the phone in my shirt pocket with my own. I snapped my fingers in front of Denise's face. She stopped walking so abruptly that she nearly fell over. As she blinked and grabbed my arm, she peered at me like somebody drunk.

She sounded absolutely plastered as well. 'Dan? Dan'l? S'that you?'

'Come on.' I took her elbow and forced her towards the path that ran alongside the river. She couldn't have resisted me if she'd been able to try.

Asca and Frai walked on either side of us. When we reached the splintered footings where the footbridge had once been, Asca took my free hand. Her grip was cool and gentle, but when Frai seized Denise's wrist, I felt the woman flinch.

I didn't have time to spare her any sympathy. The dryads continued walking at the same even pace. A moment later and we were crossing the fast-moving water together. I focused on the far bank and hoped that neither dryad would let go. If they did, I – or more likely Denise – would sink like a stone. Dunking the intruder might amuse them, but that wouldn't help me if I had to fish her out of the river.

We made it safely across. Now I forced Denise through the hazel coppices that I was steadily bringing back into productive use. She staggered along. Her breathing was harsh and her face was sweaty and pale. I kept her moving as fast as I could up the sloping side of the valley. I hoped she had some water in her car. For her, not me, even though my shirt was damp with sweat. The dryads strolled beside us, serenely unconcerned.

Denise was still just about able to walk when we reached the public footpath. Then a basset hound waddled into view around a bend not far away. The middle-aged woman with its leash in her hand was chatting to the grey-bearded man walking with them.

I froze as the dog looked at me and barked, loudly baffled. Denise's knees buckled. I wrapped my arm around her waist, struggling to keep her on her feet. How the hell was I going to explain what I was doing out here with a semi-conscious woman? The dog stopped and looked over its shoulder as if it expected its owners to clarify this situation.

'Get a move on, you daft old girl,' the woman said fondly.

She didn't glance in my direction. Nor did the man. Since they weren't concerned, the dog decided I wasn't a problem. They went on their way.

I waited until they were a good long way further down the path before I glanced at Asca and Frai. 'Thank you for that.'

'For what?' Frai said tartly. 'It's long past time you drew on your greenwood blood when you wish to go unseen.'

I looked at her for a long moment. I decided I'd come back to that later. For now, I had to get rid of Denise. Thank fuck we weren't too far from the stile where the footpath met the road. As we got closer, I saw a black Volkswagen estate parked on the wide grassy verge. It was the only vehicle there, which was another stroke of luck.

I draped Denise face down over the stile. As I patted her pockets, looking for her keys, I really, fervently hoped that whatever greenwood power I might have was keeping us hidden from anyone who might drive by. A lump in her back pocket clinked, metallic. Keys. I took them out and pressed the black plastic fob to unlock the car.

I climbed over the stile and dragged Denise across it. She was pretty much senseless by now. I laid her down in the scrap of shade cast by the Volkswagen. Opening the driver's door was like opening an oven after the car had been sitting for so long in the sun.

I saw a bottle of water in the cupholder in the central console. It was unpleasantly warm, but I poured about half over Denise's face. To my relief, she blinked at me, though her unfocused eyes were still confused.

I forced her into a sitting position, determined to strip off that Blithehurst sweatshirt. Nothing was going to link Denise to the manor on Sophie Beauchene's wedding day. As I pulled up the hem, I saw bare skin and the edge of her bra. For one awful second, I thought the sweatshirt was all she wearing. Then I saw the edge of her grey T-shirt had got caught up inside. I dragged the thin material down to her waist. After a lot of effort I got the sweatshirt over her head and off her limp, unresisting arms. The dryads watched my struggles, demurely amused. Ha fucking ha. I didn't find any of this remotely funny.

'Will she remember what's happened? Is she going to remember me doing this?'

'Oh no,' Frai assured me.

'She will recall nothing from the moment we mazed her,' Asca agreed.

That was good to know, but before I could ask the dryads anything else, they vanished. I bit back an urge to shout after them, telling them to come the fuck back here. I didn't have time to waste on losing my temper. I had to get away from here before anyone turned up.

I put the cap on the bottle of water and left it beside Denise. Taking her phone out of my shirt pocket, I dialled 999.

I didn't say anything when the call was answered, dropping the phone on the grass. I used the Blithehurst sweatshirt to rub any possibility of my fingerprints off everything I had touched. That meant I accidentally cancelled the 999 call, but they should still be able to locate the phone, if TV cop shows are to be believed. I hurried back to the stile, taking the sweatshirt with me. Coming up with some explanation for the cops or the ambulance that found her out here with sunstroke was Denise's problem, not mine.

I walked fast along the crest of the valley towards the ornamental temple. Once I was out of sight of the road, I slowed down a bit. The breeze cooled me down too. By the time I had walked down the path through the wooded pasture, the sweaty patches on my shirt had dried. Even so, I'd better not stand too close to anyone until I'd had a shower, and I really needed a cold drink.

I was so focused on that, I almost didn't register my muted phone was buzzing in my shirt pocket. Fuck. The last thing I wanted to do now was sort out those canvas curtains with Chris. I stopped just short of the footbridge to take the call. It wasn't Chris on the phone.

Aled got straight to the point. 'A man calling himself Will Hall is selling herbal teas at craft fairs. A Scotsman by all accounts.'

Will Hall? William Halsbury? That couldn't be a coincidence. 'Up in Scotland?'

'Dorset. Last weekend anyway, at a place called Bindon House. That's on what they call the Jurassic Coast.'

'Can you find out where he might be going next?'

'I'm on it,' Aled assured me.

I still couldn't just tell the satnav to take me to Dorset. The castle and the gatehouse cafe had to be open to the public again as soon as possible. The day after the wedding I was up bright and early to help Chris and his team take down the canopy and dismantle the scaffolding. Then everything had to be carried back to the Dairy Yard and loaded onto their flatbed lorry.

While we were working, I kept my ears open for any mention of Denise. To my relief, nobody said anything, not even Lynne when she brought us tea and biscuits. She's usually the first to hear local news. I put Denise out of my mind. I wouldn't worry about her until somebody gave me a reason.

I followed Chris and his lorry to the estate's back gate in my Land Rover to let them out and relock the gate. When I got back to the Dairy Yard, I collected my laptop from my workshop along with some sandwiches I'd made first thing. Going over to the manor, I went into the staff room to log on to the Wi-Fi. Typing with one hand, I ate my lunch as I looked up the place Aled had mentioned. I found Bindon House a mile or so inland, about halfway along the Dorset coast between Purbeck and the Isle of Portland.

Once upon a time, the family had owned a lot of land, in Dorset and elsewhere. They had been rich enough to build themselves a Georgian stately home on the south coast. The good times didn't last. By the start of the twentieth century, they had fallen on very hard times. Several heirs died unexpectedly, which meant paying brutal death duties. The ones who didn't die tried to restore the family fortunes but made catastrophically bad investments. The family started selling land, slowly to begin with, then more and more often. They were probably relieved when the War Office requisitioned their Dorset house during the Second World War and handed it over to the US army.

The Americans left but the family never came back. After the war, the house became a naval signals training base, and then a police training college. When the coppers moved somewhere more convenient, the house was leased to researchers working for an international consortium searching for oil along the Dorset coast. These days, the place was an outdoor education centre offering residential accommodation for school and university groups as well as bed and breakfast for anyone keen to go digging for dinosaurs.

A few things that had nothing to do with fossil hunting struck me as I studied various online maps. Firstly, this coast was dramatically different to the convoluted, rocky shoreline of North Devon. The broad sweep of these cliffs plunged straight down into deep water, and sandy beaches for tourists were scarcer and more spread out than I expected.

The second thing I noticed was Lulworth army camp. This massive area of MOD land had a sizeable chunk completely off limits. Exactly the sort of place where the shape-shifting murderer liked to dispose of his victims. Was he stalking someone new or had he already killed again and moved on? I hoped Aled would have an update for me soon. My phone had stayed stubbornly silent all morning.

I was so focused on thinking about what we might do next that I didn't even notice Eleanor had come into the staffroom.

'What are you looking at?' She broke off and yawned.

'What?' I looked up, and then I looked at her more closely. 'Late night?'

'Very,' she said wryly.

'Worth it?'

'Definitely.' She grinned as she brushed her hair back over her shoulder.

She looked less stressed than I'd seen her for weeks, and much more comfortable in jeans and a staff sweatshirt. I turned the laptop screen towards her.

'Aled might have a lead for us.' I quickly explained.

'At very least, we need to find out who this Will Hall is, if only to rule him out.' Eleanor pulled up a chair to look through the browser tabs I had open. 'If he is our man, he didn't go as far as we thought he might do. I wonder why. Do we know where he is right now?'

'Not yet.'

'There's no website for this Will Hall and his teas, I take it?' Eleanor clicked and scrolled. 'Okay, let's say Aled finds out where he is now and you can get a look at him. How will you know for certain that he's this shapeshifter you're after? Who will be able to tell you that?'

'I've been wondering,' I admitted. 'There's not a lot of woodland around there, and nothing much by way of streams.'

Eleanor nodded. She'd seen the same thing on those maps. 'How do you go about calling up a dryad or a naiad anyway?'

For a moment, I thought she was actually asking me. Then I realised she was just thinking aloud. That was a relief. I should probably tell her what I was learning about my greenwood blood sometime, but I wasn't ready for that conversation today. I definitely wasn't going to tell anyone what had happened with the Blithehurst dryads and Denise until I had told Fin and I knew what she thought about it.

Eleanor sighed. 'We know the obvious people to ask.'

I nodded. 'For a price.'

The staff room door opened and Lynne's teenage daughter Briony came in with a can of Coke. 'Oh.' She stopped in the doorway, not sure if she'd interrupted something.

I closed my laptop and put the lid back on my plastic sandwich box. 'I'll get up to the temple so Mark can have a break.'

I took my laptop back to my workshop first. When I reached the temple, Mark was happy to see me, and even happier to head back to the garden centre. Blithehurst had loads of visitors today. I must have told the story of Edmund Beauchene's grand tour of European capitals, when he collected paintings and Greek and Roman statues, twenty times before I could start reminding people that the house and gardens would be closing soon, and they probably wanted to get back to the car park with enough time to visit the garden centre and the restaurant before they left.

When the last of the tourists had gone, I waited for Asca or Frai to appear. They didn't. I waited a bit longer. Still nothing. I checked my phone and saw I should be clocking off by now. I looked at the closest oak tree and walked across the grass. Taking a deep breath, I laid my hand on the lowest branch. I didn't get the shock I'd had in Yorkshire, but I was startled to realise Asca was a long way outside the Blithehurst estate boundary. It took me a moment to work out she was over at the Dower House. I wondered what she was doing there.

Frai chuckled. 'You're a slow learner, but at least you learn.'

I decided to ignore that. 'If I wanted to find a dryad or a naiad in a place I didn't know, somewhere without many trees or streams, how would I go about doing that?'

She blinked her copper-coloured eyes, surprised. Whatever the old dryad had expected me to ask, that wasn't it.

'You owe me after yesterday,' I reminded her.

Frai narrowed her eyes. 'You think so? I would say we helped you to help Eleanor by ridding the wedding of that woman.' But now she was curious. 'Why do you ask this of me?'

'You know we're hunting a killer.' I explained what we needed to do, as soon as we found Will Hall.

Frai shrugged. Unless the big black cat turned up at Blithehurst, she and Asca wouldn't consider he was their problem. Part of me almost wished he would find us here, so I could see how the dryads dealt with the bastard. If past experience was anything to go by, he wouldn't know what hit him. I was wondering how to ask Hazel if the wise women had any way to verify who was or was not a shapeshifter when the old dryad surprised me with an answer.

'You would do better to summon a sylph.'

'How do I do that?' I didn't think she'd tell me for free, but I had to ask.

'You don't.' But Frai was smiling. 'Your swan maiden could try.'

I waited for her to tell me her price for whatever instructions Fin would need. At that exact moment, my phone rang. I checked the screen, ready to dismiss the call. It was Aled, so I answered him instead.

'What can you tell me?'

'This craft fair I was telling you about, turns out it's a twice-weekly event through July and August. Wednesdays and Saturdays, alongside a farmers' market kind of thing. My friend's checked, and this Will Hall has booked a stall to sell his herbal teas until the end of the month.'

'Thanks. That's great.' Unless this was just some random Scotsman and not the bastard we were looking for. If he was the bastard we wanted, I hoped Aled's contact hadn't asked any questions that made him suspicious.

'Sorry, mate, I've got to go. I'll talk to you soon, yeah?'

I heard voices at Aled's end of the call and the distant jingle of a little bell. He would be in his workshop today and the cultural centre would be full of tourists, the same as here.

'I'll let you know as soon as I have news,' I assured him.

As I ended the call, I realised that Frai had vanished. That was sodding typical. I didn't reach for the oak tree's branch to find her though. I started walking back towards the manor house and called Fin on the way.

She answered at once. 'I've been wondering when I'd hear from you. How did the wedding go?'

'What? Sorry, yes, it went fine. Everything was fine.'

'Did you take any photos?'

'No.' I hadn't realised she might expect that. 'Sorry.'

'It's not a problem. I'm sure Eleanor will have plenty to show me.'

Fin sounded amused. I also heard Blanche saying something about Fin owing her a tenner. They must be in the office they shared, in the middle bedroom of their flat.

Fin spoke over her sister. 'If you're not ringing to tell me about the wedding, what's up?'

'We may have a lead on the cunning man. He might still be in Dorset.'

'Let me put you on speaker.'

I told Fin and Blanche everything that Aled had told me. Then I told them what Frai had said. 'Do you have any idea how to summon a sylph? Might your mum or one of your aunts know?'

I knew Fin's relatives knew a whole lot more about sylphs than I did. The air spirits like to ride the winds that sweep across the flat Fens. A few visited Helen's house and garden fairly regularly, or at least they had done in the past. That's where I'd first met one, though they hadn't been particularly friendly or helpful, not until there was something in it for them.

'No, I mean, I don't know how,' Fin clarified. 'But I can ask Mum.'

'I'll give Iris a call,' Blanche added. 'If she doesn't know, maybe Conn can help.'

'That's an idea.' It hadn't occurred to me to ask their older sister's Irish boyfriend. Why not? He was a swan-shifter as well.

'This place, Bindon House, is pretty much exactly two hours' drive due south from here.' Blanche was clearly looking at maps online.

'How soon can you get a day off to check it out?' Fin asked me.

'I'll have to see what Eleanor says.' I should be owed some time in lieu after the work I'd done for Sophie Beauchene's wedding.

Chapter Sixteen

Perhaps my mother's blood means I'm happier in woodland, or maybe it was because I'm six foot four. Either way, I felt unpleasantly conspicuous on the edge of a Dorset clifftop overlooking the dark blue sea. If a thunderstorm arrived, I'd be the tallest target for a lightning strike for miles around.

I looked down and that was a mistake. That was deep water way down there. I'm not a fan of enclosed spaces, and on the narrow path cutting along the contour of this steep slope, I decided I wasn't a fan of heights above sheer drops either. Fin wasn't bothered. She'd be fine if she fell off. She can fly.

She shaded her eyes with her hand as she looked in both directions, even though she was wearing sunglasses. It was noon and the day was hot and cloudless, with barely a breeze to cool us. 'This really isn't a place for naiads or dryads.'

She was right. The straggling gorse bushes dotted across the rough turf a little way inland were barely knee high. I couldn't even see a tree. As for streams, Fin had explained to me on the drive here how no flowing water reached the sea for five miles in either direction, thanks to the local geology.

'What about sylphs?' If I focused on why we were here, I didn't have to think about that drop.

'They should love it.' Fin smiled as she turned her face into the breeze.

Looking out towards the horizon, I could see ruffles and ripples on the water's surface that hinted at shifts in the wind. Fin was instinctively aware of currents and eddies in the air that were invisible to anyone else. I wondered if she felt something like the connection with a woodland that I made using the dryad radar. I might ask her sometime. Not now.

'So?' I prompted. 'Shall we see if there's one around?'

'Let's give it a try.' Fin slipped her backpack off her shoulders and handed it to me.

She took a skein of thread out of the side pocket. It was loosely wrapped around three white feathers. Fin's feathers. Not the downy ones that cling to her human skin, which she keeps safely hidden beneath her clothes, or locked away at home if something like a doctor's appointment means someone will see her undressed. Someone apart from me.

She'd plucked these feathers from underneath her own wings in her swan form last night in the flat's living room. You don't realise how big an adult swan is until you're indoors with one. Their hiss is a lot louder as well. Fin hadn't said plucking those feathers hurt, but I'd noticed her rubbing her forearm a couple of times. But there was no chance this would work with ordinary feathers, even if you could get them off a live swan without ending up in hospital.

Fin carefully unwound the thread. Hazel had provided that. I still wanted to know how. This wasn't thread anyone could pick up from some sewing shop. Sheep's wool gathered from tufts caught on hedgerows had been combed and carded with teasles. The thread was spun using a drop spindle weighted with a whorl made from fallow deer antler. That had been carved with a bronze knife. Nothing iron had touched the thread at any stage.

Fin's aunt Stella insisted this was essential, if there was any chance this would work. I wanted to know how Stella had learned the secret to intriguing a sylph, and why, and if she'd ever got hold of the thread to give it a try herself. But she hadn't said, and I could hardly blame her for keeping family secrets. I keep plenty of my own.

Fin wound the end of the thread securely around her right hand. The three feathers were already tightly knotted to the other end. She tossed the feathers into the air. The breeze caught them and swept them higher.

'So far, so good.' Fin was relieved.

So was I. The three of us had been dubious about this last night. I slung Fin's backpack straps over one shoulder and checked the coastal path again. Hopefully fewer walkers would come along here in midweek, even in peak tourist season. From a distance, with luck, they would think Fin was flying some sort of kite. She was ready to reel the feathers back in before anyone got close enough to ask.

We had debated whether to come here on Wednesday or Saturday. I still felt it was a toss-up. More people around at the weekend would give us more cover. Fin pointed out our quarry would also find it easier to hide in a crowd. He'd have more chance of losing us if he spotted us on his trail. It would be a lot harder to park and the roads would be busier on a holiday change-over day. She had a point. Several good points. Also, me asking for a Wednesday off would cause less disruption to the Blithehurst staff rota. I hadn't forgotten what Denise had said.

'Dan...' Fin was looking upwards.

I squinted and shaded my own eyes as I watched the feathers zipping to and fro. This slight breeze couldn't be doing that.

'What brings you here, swan maid?' A shimmering figure appeared beside Fin, slender and as pale as a summer cloud. The feathers on the thread fell out of the sky and landed on the path.

Anything the sylph was wearing that counted as clothes was skin-tight. If they weren't wearing anything, that wouldn't matter. I'd learned in the Fenland that concepts like male or female aren't relevant when you're dealing with sylphs. They take on whatever form they feel like.

This sylph turned piercing blue eyes on me. 'You're a long way from home, son of the greenwood.'

That was just a passing comment. The sylph wasn't interested in me. They looked at Fin and smiled, charming and growing more solidly distinct every moment. 'Who taught you how to pique my curiosity, gracious bird?'

'My aunt.' Fin knew she must tell the truth. She also knew not to say any more than she absolutely had to.

'I do not believe I have met her.' The sylph gazed at Fin, fascinated.

'I don't think so,' Fin agreed. She picked up the feathers and began carefully winding the thread around them.

A glint came and went in the sylph's vivid eyes. 'Then what business do you have with me?'

I tried not to react to the sharp edge in those words. I knew a sylph's mood can be as fickle as the weather.

'We would like your help.' Fin turned to me to put the skein of thread and feathers in her backpack's pocket.

'You are so bold with such a request?' The sylph was genuinely surprised.

'We need to know if a man who threatens us can change his shape. We think he can become a great cat. You could see him for what he truly is. You could tell us that.'

The sylph blinked. 'You are very free with your wants. In days gone by, your kind would woo us with honeyed words when you sought our aid.' Their disappointed glance included me.

We knew we were taking a risk with this straight-talking. Every story we knew of said that sylphs like to tease mortals with promises of favours when they bargain and barter. More often than not, the human making the deal ends up disappointed. When it was time to deliver, the sylph would vanish like morning mist, citing some carefully phrased loophole in their assurances. Even when they stuck to an agreement, I'd learned how deftly they would wring every possible advantage out of it.

'These are very different days,' Fin said steadily.

'That is very true.' The sylph sounded more curious than offended.

'When did you last see one of my kind?' Fin asked. 'Or one of his?'

The sylph's gaze flickered to me before they answered. 'I have not seen a swan maid in many long years.'

Fin nodded. 'This man is killing people. Ordinary people, who have no idea what he is. If he's caught, if his true nature is discovered, that will endanger all of us who have to live in the mortal world as well as in yours.'

The sylph shrugged. 'What is that to me?'

Fin didn't blink. 'You say it's been years since you last saw a swan maid. If we have to hide our nature from mortals who don't understand us, because they will fear what they don't understand, it will be even longer before you see another.'

This was the best we had been able to come up with, to persuade the sylph to help us. Yesterday evening, Fin and Blanche and I had sat at their dining table, with Stella and Helen and other aunts and cousins on a Zoom call. We'd gone round in circles. No one could imagine what a sylph might want that we could possibly offer. Then Stella and Helen's sister Sylvia remembered something that had happened when her children were small.

A sylph appeared in her garden and stopped to watch the kids play. The sylph didn't ask Sylvia for anything, but they kept turning up and hanging around. They'd told her tales of days gone by, getting more and more wistful with each recollection. Sylvia was convinced they were lonely.

My mum had told me sylphs found humans entertaining. I told everyone what she had said. As people made more use of metal and pottery, sylphs were fascinated by the thermals that rose from hearths and kilns and forges. They would often lend a hand, in the days when people accepted sylphs and similar folk existed.

By the seventeenth century, wealthy and powerful men learned about sylphs when they got interested in alchemy and astronomy and ceremonial magic. They weren't interested in negotiating. They wanted ways to compel sylphs and hobs and the like to do as they were ordered, and ways to inflict punishments if they didn't. That turned out as badly as you might expect. Hobs and sylphs started keeping their distance from mortals.

That sylph visiting Sylvia's garden had vanished as unexpectedly as they had appeared. Sylvia thought they had got bored and gone looking for amusement elsewhere. Sylphs like to be entertained. Which was good, because the prospect of a new and unexpected shapeshifter was all we had to offer.

'Have you ever met a man who can become a cat?' Fin asked.

'No.' The sylph angled their head. 'Where might I find such a thing?'

I tried not to look too relieved. Thankfully, the sylph was focused on Fin.

She smiled. 'Do you know a place called Bindon House?'

'I do.'

'Can you meet us there? Where the people are gathered today?'

The sylph grinned. 'At the craft fair? Do you want to meet me inside the gate or out in the car park?'

Fin blushed. 'Inside will be fine.'

So this sylph wasn't nearly so isolated and out of touch as they had let us assume. Our mistake. Still, they had told the truth about not seeing a swan maid for years. Hopefully that mattered. Hopefully they'd enjoyed taking the piss with this little game, talking like someone who'd strolled off stage at the Royal Shakespeare Company. There had to be more chance that an amused sylph would be a helpful sylph.

'I'll meet you by the hog roast.' Our new friend vanished.

I looked at Fin. 'We'd better get a move on.'

We hurried back to the car park where we'd left the Land Rover. We didn't know if the cat man would recognise Fin's Toyota from Darley Combe, but we had decided not to risk it. As we got in and I started the engine, Fin got out her phone.

'The sylph said yes. They're going to meet us by the hog roast. Is he still there?' She pressed the screen to put the call on speaker.

'Yes,' Blanche assured us. 'He's doing good business and he seems to have plenty of regular customers coming back. I'm starting to wonder what he puts in those teas. Maybe I should buy a packet.'

I wanted to tell her not to go near him. We couldn't take the chance, in case he had some way to sense she was more than ordinarily human. I reminded myself that Blanche knew that. She was probably winding me up.

'Is the hog roast anywhere near his stall?' I asked instead. 'We have to stay out of his eyeline.'

That's why Blanche had come with us, following the Landy in her Honda. She had pointed out someone needed to keep an eye on Will Hall or whatever his name might be, in case he left his stall, even just to go for a pee. We couldn't risk turning up with the sylph and have nothing to show them. If we couldn't find a sylph, it was even more important that someone kept watch, alert for any clues that might possibly help us.

She was right, but I wasn't keen and I said so. Even though Blanche has short, spiky hair and Fin keeps hers long, they're clearly sisters. One strikingly pale blonde was unusual enough to be noticeable. Two would draw twice as many eyes. I didn't want to risk the cat man going after Blanche while she was on her own.

She hadn't argued with me. When we'd finished talking to Helen and Stella and everyone, she disappeared into her en-suite bathroom. I assumed she wanted a shower after the hot day. When Fin and I were thinking about going to bed, she reappeared with damp turquoise hair. She'd found a box of temporary dye which she'd bought for a party that never happened. She asked what time we were leaving in the morning. I said I'd like to be on the road by nine-thirty, and we'd gone to bed.

Right now, Blanche was telling Fin where to find Will Hall. 'He's on the outer edge of the farmers' market stalls over by the hedge. The food tents and trucks have their own patch by the house. He shouldn't be able to see you.'

'Where are you?' I hoped the shapeshifter hadn't noticed her loitering.

'Round and about,' Blanche said airily. 'Let me know when you arrive. I'll come and find you.'

It didn't take us long to reach Bindon House. When we arrived, a chalk board by the gate said the car park was full. Police cones along the grass verges meant no one could stop on either side of the road.

'Sod it.' I wondered where the hell we were going to park.

'Wait a minute.' Fin pointed at a BMW convertible cautiously coming out through the gate. 'People who came first thing this morning are starting to leave.'

While the BMW driver decided which way he wanted to go, I edged the Landy forward, getting closer to a middle-aged bloke with a hi-vis waistcoat standing by the chalk board. 'Wind down your window, could you?'

Fin smiling at him got his attention. I ducked my head and leaned over so he could see me. 'Any chance of a space opening up in there?'

He shrugged, amiable. 'You can take a look. No promises.'

That was good enough for me. 'Cheers.'

I put my foot down to get into the car park ahead of a Vauxhall. The first space we saw was big enough for the Land Rover. I parked and turned off the engine. 'Got the tickets?'

Fin was already finding the email on her phone. 'Right here.'

At the car park's inner gate, she showed the screen to the lady asking people if they had booked online. Two solidly built men in hi-vis were directing people who hadn't to the ticket tent.

'Thank you. That's fine.' She gave us each a red paper wristband.

We moved out of everyone's way so I could put Fin's on her and she could do mine. The men in hi-vis waved us into Bindon House's extensive grounds.

Between the car park and the cluster of Georgian buildings hemmed in by newer, uglier extensions, the craft fair and the farmers' market spread out across what must have been an impressive lawn. The craft stalls were on our left. The closest open-fronted tents sold candles, jewellery and glass ornaments. Off to the right, I saw an artisan baker, a cheese maker and someone offering unusual jams. People selling food to eat right now were straight ahead of us in front of the house. So where was the hog roast?

'There's a map.' Fin walked over to a helpful noticeboard and scanned a QR code to download a site guide to her phone. 'This way.'

I followed her through the crowd. It was unpleasantly hot. Any hint of a breeze from the coast wasn't making it past so many tents and people. We hadn't got anywhere near the hog roast when we saw Blanche approaching.

No one would think she and Fin were sisters today. Fin wore lightweight brown trousers with a flowery green-and-yellow tunic. Blanche was wearing about twice as much make-up as any of the women at the wedding. Her long, floaty skirt matched her turquoise hair, and she wore a long-sleeved white blouse with white embroidery and dangling tassels as well as umpteen beaded necklaces and bracelets.

Blanche stopped beside us, but didn't say hello. She looked at her phone screen as if she was checking something.

'So where is he?' Fin asked quietly as she looked at her own phone's black screen.

Before Blanche could answer, the sylph arrived. For an instant, they were the pale figure we'd met on the clifftop, invisible to anyone except the three of us. A moment later, they looked as human as anyone else, wearing baggy trousers the same colour as Blanche's skirt and a loose cotton vest top that could have come from the same shop as her blouse. He – at least that's what anyone else would see – had wiry, muscular arms, lightly tanned skin and a shaven head. Those bright blue eyes were the same, and they were gazing at Blanche with unnerving intensity.

'A second swan maid in one day. This meeting would have been sufficient payment for many more favours, my new greenwood friend.'

I couldn't tell if the sylph was mocking me or challenging me. I didn't care. We had more important things to do. 'Can you take our friend to look at the tea seller?' I asked Blanche.

196

'Follow me,' she invited the sylph.

'To the ends of the earth, should you wish it, graceful lady.'

Fin watched them walk away towards the farmers' market. 'Get your coat, girl, you've pulled.'

I didn't want to have that conversation. 'How about we find some lunch?'

I might not be able to see the hog roast, but I could smell something a lot more appetising than crushed grass, sweaty people and umpteen different brands of sunscreen.

Fin nodded. 'We might as well.'

I found the hog roast and got a big floury bun loaded with succulent pork, crisp crackling and apple sauce. Fin bought a paper plate of falafel from a vegan food truck proudly proclaiming it ran on biodiesel. We headed for the beer tent, where local craft brewers were quenching thirsts. It was stuffy and noisy in there, but it was good to get out of the sun. Fin managed to sit down at a little table with two folding chairs.

I put down my roll. 'I'll see what's non-alcoholic. Do you want a half or a pint?'

'A pint, thanks.'

When I got back with two plastic glasses of what claimed to be an alcohol-free IPA, Blanche and the sylph were carrying a couple of spare chairs over to join us. I noticed the sylph was wearing beaded necklaces and bangles now. I wondered if they were real or spun out of thin air.

'Well?' Fin pushed her paper plate towards her sister.

Blanche accepted the invitation and took a falafel. 'It's him.'

The sylph leaned their elbows on the table and cupped their face with their hands. 'Who has the beast been killing, and why?'

Our new friend was intrigued.

Chapter Seventeen

We told the sylph what we knew. There wasn't much risk of being overheard in the noisy beer tent. The sylph asked the crucial question.

'Why is the beast here now?'

'He has to earn money.' But I was starting to think there was more to this.

'He's not only taking cash,' Blanche said thoughtfully. 'He has no problem accepting card payments.'

'So "Will Hall" must have a bank account.' Fin's expression put quotes around his name. 'He had this identity ready to pick up as soon as he left "William Halsbury" behind.'

I wondered how the bastard managed that. The days are long gone when someone could travel a hundred miles from home and reinvent themselves. Computerised records and checks on everything from renting a flat to starting a new job have put an end to that. The only people who can still steal a dead child's identity from a gravestone to get a birth certificate are undercover cops.

'Why is he here today, in this place?' the sylph persisted. 'Is he hunting some new prey?'

That's what I wanted to know. I looked at Fin and Blanche. 'Do you think we can follow him when he leaves? If we can find out where he's living, that would be a start.'

Fin nodded. 'Hopefully he's based somewhere close if he's paid for a stall until the end of the month.'

'We have got two cars between us.' But Blanche didn't sound convinced, and Fin looked dubious.

I didn't blame them. Tailing a vehicle might look easy on the telly or in a film, especially for private eyes in some American city where parallel streets conveniently cross each other. I didn't reckon much for our chances in Dorset's narrow, winding lanes choked with summer holiday traffic.

The sylph laughed at me. 'I expect your kind to be earthbound in his thinking, but not swan maidens.'

'I suppose we could try—' Blanche began, but the sylph laid a hand on hers.

'I can follow him to his lair and he will never know it.'

'That would be very helpful.' I waited to find out what this assistance would cost us.

Sly, the sylph smiled at Fin. 'Give me those feathers and I will be able to find you, to tell you what I learn.'

She didn't reach under the table for her backpack, looking at me instead. 'How late can we stay here today? We really should get as much info as we can.'

I couldn't argue with that. 'If it gets really late, I can head back to Blithehurst from here and you can go home with Blanche. The gates close at five, so he should be packed up by six. If we find a pub with a decent beer garden while you follow him wherever he's going—' I nodded at the sylph '— we can decide what to do next once we know where that is.'

'Sounds good.' Fin picked up her backpack, unzipped the pocket and carefully unknotted the thread to release a single feather. She held it up, out of the sylph's reach. 'I want your word that you'll give this back to me when I ask you for it.'

The sylph pouted dramatically, but nodded. 'I promise.'

As Fin handed over the feather, Blanche stood up. 'We ought to keep an eye on him. We'll look like right idiots if he's already packed up and gone.'

That was a nasty thought. 'Text us if he shows any sign of leaving.'

'Will do.' She grinned at the sylph, who grinned back and followed her out of the tent.

I looked at Fin. 'Shall we get out of here?'

'Let's take a look around,' she agreed.

We found the right recycling bins for our rubbish and left the stuffy tent. The sun was still blazing outside but the fresher air was welcome. We wandered around the farmers' market and through the craft stalls. Now we knew where the cat man was sitting, we could avoid going anywhere close.

Some of the tat for sale looked mass-produced to me. I wondered how closely the organisers vetted their stall-holders. Other stuff was handmade by enthusiastic amateurs who'd be lucky to cover their costs. Here and there, we saw unique and distinctive items in pottery, glass, silver, copper, enamel. Skilled artists were using every sort of paint and materials. I didn't find any of the woodwork for sale overly impressive though.

Fin stopped to buy a dozen greetings cards from a woman selling striking linocut prints. I was tempted by the next stall along, where photographs of ancient oak trees were mounted and ready for framing.

The sylph appeared beside us. Fin looked around. 'Where's Blanche?'

'Watching the beast. Come quickly. There's something you should see.' The sylph was already walking away.

We followed. As we got close to the grassy aisle where the cat man was selling his teas, I thought very hard about just how much I didn't want the bastard to see us.

The sylph glanced back, suddenly curious, before laughing softly. 'So you are your mother's son.'

Before Fin could ask what was so funny, Blanche saw us and beckoned. She had found a good spot. We could look across a corner stall and see the herbal tea seller otherwise known as the murderous bastard at the other end of a long row that marked the edge of the craft fair. He had a hot-water urn set up with a sign inviting customers to taste any of his blends. His brown paper packets had neatly printed labels. This wasn't a business he'd thrown together in a hurry because we'd scared him away from Devon.

The woman running this corner stall seemed happy enough to let us browse. She was selling anything you could imagine could be made from multi-coloured wool knitted into tubes of different sizes. She was making them on a Victorian circular knitting machine.

I knew that's what she used because she had the intricate device set up behind the table. Whenever she wasn't taking payments from customers, she was making more stock. A display board at the end of her table explained how she had restored the machine. That looked like interesting reading, as well as stopping passers-by from knocking fingerless mittens off the table onto the trampled grass.

It also helpfully obscured the cat man's view of us. Not that he was looking in our direction. His attention was focused on a young woman trying to buy a packet of tea.

'She's come down this way three times,' Blanche said quietly. 'This is the first time she's stopped at his stall.'

'What's he doing?' Fin asked no one in particular.

The woman was trying to take the brown paper packet he offered her, but he was holding on to the other end. He leaned forward, talking to her, intent. I took a moment to make certain that I'd know him again, when I saw him on two feet instead of four.

He was average height, maybe five foot ten, and average build, though he was wearing a dark T-shirt and his arms looked muscular enough to be a threat. He had sallow skin and dark eyes, and his ragged black hair looked as if he cut it himself in the dark. Even if I hadn't known what he was,

I'd have called his face cat-like, with sharp cheekbones and a narrow chin.

I'd have steered clear of him in a pub. He was shifting from foot to foot, tense with pent-up energy, as he talked to the woman. Unpredictable. A toss-up whether he'd start a singalong or a fight.

The cat man let go of the packet of tea. He sat down on his chair as he watched the woman walk away. She was coming towards us. Fin and I took a step backwards to stay out of the cat man's line of sight. Blanche and the sylph moved smoothly forward to fill the space where we had been.

The woman stuffed the brown paper packet into the tote bag she had slung over one shoulder. She hurried past, glancing behind her, but not at the tea seller. She looked as if she didn't want to be noticed, wearing faded old jeans and a loose, long-sleeved check shirt. Her mid-length, mid-brown hair half covered her face. She was skinny, but not in the way that comes naturally. She didn't eat enough.

'She didn't pay for that.' Blanche quickly corrected herself as the knitting woman looked up with sharp concern. 'I mean, that man let her have that packet of tea for free.'

'It looks like they know each other.' I wondered what that meant.

'I think I know her from school.' Fin's surprise probably sounded convincing to anyone else. 'I'll go and say hello. Buy me a draught-excluder, darling. Whichever one you like best.'

'Of course.' Once I'd got over being called 'darling', I took out my wallet and pretended to compare a knitted snake with a tree branch with knitted green leaves and some crochet snails. I had seen what Fin had seen. We'd both noticed the man who had been watching the woman while she talked to the man selling the tea. Now he followed her past the knitting stall.

Apart from a chunky gold watch on one wrist, he was unremarkable in chinos and a navy polo shirt. I wondered if he was responsible for the fading bruise the nervous woman was trying to hide as she pulled her hair forward to cover her cheek. When the loose cuff of her shirt sleeve slid back, I saw newer bruises ringed her wrist.

'I'll take this one, thanks.' I waved the knitted branch at the stall-holder. She offered her payment machine and I hit it with my bank card. 'I don't need a receipt, thanks.'

I glanced at Blanche and the sylph. Her nod told me she'd seen those bruises too. The sylph's nod confirmed they would stay to keep watch on the cat man. I risked a quick look in his direction. He was staring after the prick I was about to follow. Talk about a murderous expression.

I walked after the prick, trying not to hurry. Fast movement alerts a predator. Knowing there was a killer behind me made my skin crawl all the same. But the scars on my arm weren't itching. That had to mean he wasn't a threat to us. For the moment.

I wanted to find Fin. We needed to find out what we could about the woman with those bruises. I wasn't sure how we'd do that, so I hoped she had some ideas. I scanned the crowd ahead and saw the bruised woman first.

She had reached the open space between the craft fair and the farmers' market. There were noticeably fewer people around. Tourists must be heading to their hotels or camp sites or holiday lets. The woman stopped to search for something in her tote bag. She didn't notice the man who was stalking her. He was walking more slowly as he got closer.

I moved around the edge of the grassy space to get to a place where I could see them both. The prick's expression was repellently smug. I looked around for Fin, but she was still nowhere to be seen.

The woman took a packet of tissues out of her bag. As she looked up and realised he was only a few metres away, she gasped, horrified and terrified. He strolled forward with his hands in his pockets, grinning like some clown in a horror movie.

Fin hurried up to the woman and took both her hands in her own. She turned the woman around so she couldn't see the grinning prick. Ignoring him completely, Fin talked to the bruised woman, still holding her hands. The woman nodded a few times, though I couldn't tell if she was saying anything.

Fin's arrival had wiped that smile off the smug arsehole's face. He stopped, red-faced and furious. He clenched his fists. I didn't like that at all. Fin had proved she could defend herself, but could she protect the other woman as well?

I started walking towards them. The prick could reach them before I did and a knitted draught-excluder wouldn't make much of a weapon. I'd still smack him around the head with it as soon as he laid a finger on either woman. As soon as he raised a hand. Before he laid a finger on anyone. That would surprise him, if nothing else. On the bright side, I couldn't get done for ABH. Not this time.

The prick stopped dead. Now his face was wary. I tried to see what he had noticed. A moment later, that was obvious. Two community coppers were coming through the crowd, bulky in black uniforms, hi-vis vests and utility belts. People quickly got out of their way.

The shorter one pointed and I realised they were looking for Fin. When they saw her, they strode over. Fin had an arm around the other woman's shoulder. The stranger was fumbling with her packet of tissues, trying to wipe away her tears.

The bruised woman started talking to the community coppers. The prick with the gold watch wasn't grinning now. His glower said this wasn't over as he backed off. When he

204

reached the edge of the farmers' market, he turned and hurried away. I took a deep breath and walked over to Fin. I stopped with a lot more than an arm's length between us and did my best to look unthreatening. Just a tourist with a woolly draught-excluder, officer. 'Is everything okay?'

'We've got this, thank you, sir,' the woman copper said firmly. She didn't care I was ten inches taller than her.

'This is my boyfriend,' Fin said quickly. 'I sent someone to find the security people, like you suggested, darling.'

'We'll take this from here, sir.' The other copper was a younger bloke, maybe my age, but his expression said he'd been around the block a few times. That was reassuring. The police do have their uses. 'Thank you for your concern.'

'You take care of yourself.' Fin gave the crying woman a quick hug. She was overwhelmed by her distress as the coppers led her away.

Fin came over and tucked her head under my chin. I held her tight. 'What did you find out? Darling.'

I felt her tension ease as she laughed. 'Sorry about that. I didn't want to use your name anywhere near the sylph or the cat man.'

'Just don't call me that when anyone else is around.' I took a step back to look down at her. 'Did you get any idea about what's going on?'

Fin nodded. 'Her name's Ashley and he's Ryan, her soon-to-be-ex-husband. Ex as soon as possible. He was sweetness and light when they first met. It was a whirlwind romance, and they got married inside six months just over a year ago. As soon as she had his ring on her finger, everything changed. She couldn't see her friends, couldn't go out on her own. The usual crap you read about.'

The crap that's in the news after a woman's been murdered, along with shit like 'the neighbours said he was always so helpful'.

'Any idea what he was doing here today?' I asked.

Fin nodded again. 'She got up the nerve to ring a helpline a month ago. It's her house, and they have no kids, so he was told to get out and stay away. She's got a restraining order or whatever it's called, so he hasn't been back. But he keeps turning up when she's out and about. He says it's a coincidence. How's he supposed to know where she's going?'

I didn't bother wondering. 'He's doing more than just turning up. Those bruises on her wrists are recent.'

'He grabbed her in a supermarket car park last week.' Fin shivered. 'Tried to force her into his car. A white van man stopped him, thank goodness.'

'Didn't anyone call the cops? Wasn't there any CCTV?'

'No idea.' Fin was as frustrated as me. 'That's all she said before those officers turned up and took over.'

'Getting them involved was a good idea.'

'It was the only way I could think of to stop another woman getting to Ashley first,' she admitted. 'I asked her to go and find them.'

'Quick thinking.' I hugged her and wondered what the hell we were going to do now.

Before I came up with any answers, the sylph appeared. 'The beast is leaving.'

'What?'

Which was a stupid thing to say, and the sylph gave me the look it deserved.

'He has put his goods and gear on a handcart and left his table. Blanche is following him.'

'Following him on her own?' Fin didn't like that idea.

'She won't be alone when I rejoin her.' The sylph disappeared.

'Come on.' Fin started walking, fast.

'Can I have a quick look at your phone?' I gave her the draught-excluder and found the plan of the site she'd downloaded earlier. The stall-holders had a separate car park with a separate entrance and exit. Sod it. Even if we got back to the Landy in time, I couldn't see anywhere to pull up on the narrow lane where we could wait and watch for the murderous bastard to leave. Apart from anything else, blocking traffic would make us far too noticeable. He'd recognise us as soon as he saw us.

Back in the car park, Blanche was waiting behind the Landy. The sylph was nowhere to be seen.

'What's going on?' Fin was puzzled as well as relieved to see her sister was safe.

'See that red Mazda?' Blanche nodded to show us where to look. Doing that was less obvious than pointing.

'Yes.' It was much easier to pick out individual cars now that people were leaving gaps in the rows the hi-vis blokes had organised this morning.

'That's the stalker's car. See that grey van three rows behind, off to the left? That's the herbal tea guy. I thought I'd lost him when he loaded up his stuff and drove off. I couldn't even ask Zan to follow him. But when I came back here, I saw he'd only driven around the corner. What's going on?'

Fin quickly told her what we'd learned from the bruised woman, Ashley. Blanche found the story as disturbing as we did. She scowled at the red Mazda.

'What's he going to do now?'

The prick Ryan was sitting in the Mazda's driver's seat, staring straight ahead. Every couple of minutes, he slammed his hand against the steering wheel. I reckoned that frustration made him even more dangerous.

'I don't think he knows what to do. He must realise Ashley will be telling the cops everything. He must already be on very thin ice with the law. The cops will find out where he lives easily enough, if they don't already know. He'll find them waiting on his doorstep with questions he won't want to answer. I think he's trying to work out where he can go to avoid them.'

'Wherever Ryan goes, I'm guessing he plans on following.' Fin looked around the side of the Landy to check the grey van hadn't moved.

'I think we've found his next victim.' I wondered how the cat man planned to torment Ryan, to pay him back for Ashley's bruises. Terror for terror, like Taser before he died, after his threats had made those kids' lives a living hell.

'No great loss.' Blanche raised a hand as Fin shot her a sharp look. 'I know, I know. Even complete bastards have the right to a fair trial. But what can we do about it?'

'I could happily walk away and leave the prick to take his chances,' I admitted, 'but it isn't that simple. The police will be looking for him, at very least to give him a caution and to warn him to stop harassing Ashley. If he's crossed far enough over the line, if her lawyer's any good, they might be ready to arrest him. Either way, he's on their radar in a way that Taser wasn't. If Ryan turns up dead or goes missing, the cops are going to want answers.'

Fin was watching the grey van. 'He'll want to get hold of him before the police do.'

'Why don't we give them both what they want?' The sylph appeared beside us. 'Or the promise of that, at least.'

'Hang on, let's talk—' I don't know why I bothered. The sylph had already gone.

'There. Over there.' Fin took a step forward, then quickly retreated, remembering we couldn't risk being seen.

'Shit.' I saw the sylph was hurrying through the car park, cutting between lines of cars. What everyone else would see, especially that prick Ryan, was Ashley. The sylph mimicked the bruised woman to perfection, and not only with every detail of her appearance. The way she kept looking back over her shoulder was utterly convincing. So was the way she swept her hair forward to hide her face. Her awkward, uneven steps made it seem she was trying not to break into a run. To run for her life.

Chapter Eighteen

I heard the Mazda's engine. The grey van started up. Both vehicles manoeuvred out of their spaces.

'What now?' Blanche demanded.

'We follow them.' I unlocked the Land Rover.

Blanche reached into her skirt's deep pocket for her keys. 'I'd better take my own car. I can't risk getting it locked in here overnight.'

She ran off to wherever she'd parked the Honda. I got into the Landy and started the engine. Fin was already in her seat, leaning forward and searching for the other vehicles.

'There's nothing else we can do.' Clearly, she reckoned our chances of catching up with the two men were slim. I couldn't argue with that.

'What can you see?' I made sure I wasn't about to hit anything and pulled out.

'The red car's reached the gate. The van's two cars behind him. The red car's turning right.'

If I'd been on my own I'd have had no chance. I had to concentrate on getting safely through the car park. When we reached the gate, we had to wait. A lot more traffic than I expected was crawling along the narrow lane. Every car that passed in front of us meant the Mazda and the Nissan were getting further away. I gripped the steering wheel. Getting pissed off wouldn't help. Seeing the hint of a gap, I inched the Land Rover forward. That forced cars coming in both directions to pull up and let me out. I ignored a driver flicking me two furious fingers as I turned right. 'Can you still see them?'

Fin was sitting up as tall as she could, trying to get a better view. 'I can see the van.'

The line of cars edged along for the next half mile. At least we were still moving. Of course, as soon as I thought that, a rush of red brake lights coming towards us warned me everyone was stopping.

'What's happening?'

'I can't see.' Fin shifted in her seat, frustrated.

I could make out an indicator flashing up ahead. 'Someone's trying to turn right.'

They'd have to cut across the continuous stream of cars coming the other way. Those drivers were more interested in going home or wherever they were headed. Finally someone took pity on the indicating vehicle and let them cross. I caught sight of the car's tail end. 'That's the Mazda. Where the hell is he going?'

The traffic started moving again, then everything stopped just as abruptly. The grey Nissan van risked losing a headlight, indicating and sitting right on the line in the middle of the road. 'Our man's making the same turn.'

I had to follow them. We had no options. Hopefully the cat man was too focused on Ryan to check his rear-view mirror. With any luck, he'd assume the Landy belonged to some local farmer.

Fin was checking behind us in the wing mirror on her side. 'I can't see Blanche.'

Blanche could look after herself. I was concentrating on the grey van. A handful of cars were coming out of that side road, filtering into the traffic going in both directions. The van driver saw a chance and went for it, provoking an angry blast from somebody's horn.

The cars ahead of me pulled away now that the road was clear. I moved more slowly to let a gap open up between the

Landy and the next set of tail lights. A Ford coming out of that side road was trying to turn right. Even if I couldn't see their indicator, they had ignored two decent chances to go left. I pulled up a few metres short to let them out and saw this wasn't a side road at all. It was another car park, though it didn't have a gate or any sort of barrier. A long line of cars was trying to leave.

A people carrier coming in the other direction took pity on the Ford as well. As the grateful driver pulled out, I cut across behind him to go into the car park. It was nearly empty, which wasn't good for us.

Fin pointed. 'Over there.'

The Nissan was parked next to the Mazda. I couldn't see either driver. Had the cat man already grabbed Ryan and shoved the prick into his van? I pulled up some distance away. 'If the van heads for the exit, do I try to block it?'

I was thinking aloud as much as asking Fin. She twisted in her seat to assess that situation.

'He won't get far. There's still a queue of cars trying to leave. Oh, there's Blanche.'

She was relieved and so was I. The fewer people I had to keep track of, the better. The Honda pulled up on my side of the Landy. I looked down to see Blanche looking up at me, wanting to know what to do now.

I looked at the Nissan and the Mazda. There was still no hint of movement inside either vehicle. Could the cat man have forced Ryan into his van without any sort of struggle? I didn't think so. I undid my seatbelt. 'I'm going to take a look.'

I didn't waste time telling Fin to stay put. She got out too, and so did Blanche. At least they waited by the Honda, letting me go on ahead.

A quick look inside the Mazda confirmed it was empty. I gave the Nissan a hard shove to rock it on its suspension. That got no reaction from inside. No warning blast from an alarm deafened me either. I realised a moment too late I'd risked setting one off. I thought about that for a moment. Disabling the alarm made sense if the cat man often kept prisoners in his van.

'Well?' Fin called out.

'They're not here.' I moved to see the far side of the car park more clearly.

A dozen or so men, women and children were coming down a path flanked by thorn hedges. The three dogs they had between them were so eager to leave they were straining against their collars and harnesses. Soon the last few cars joined the queue to get away.

I pictured the maps of this area online. As Fin and Blanche reached me, I realised where we were. 'The hillfort's over that way.'

Fin nodded. 'There's nowhere else they could have gone.'

Blanche had no idea what I was talking about.

I waved towards the fingerpost pointing the way to an ancient monument. I'd noticed hillforts were scattered right across Dorset. This one had been marked as 'not surveyed'. 'It still belongs to the house. I guess no one had any use for a load of earthworks when the farmland was being sold off.'

Blanche started walking towards the path. 'What is Zan doing?'

Zan. So that was the name the sylph was going by. Useful to know, but I was more concerned that Blanche had told Zan her name too. What else had she said? What had she said about me and Fin?

That would have to wait. At the far side of the car park, we could see down the chalky path that led to the earthworks. The Hunter barred the way with his bare feet planted wide and his muscular arms folded across his massive chest. When he saw me, he smiled with grim satisfaction.

213

'Who is...' Blanche's voice faded away.

'What do you think he wants?' Fin and I had talked about the Hunter, but she'd never seen him for herself before.

I thought back to our last encounter, when he'd involved himself in the Green Man's business. 'I don't think he likes to see people who can't defend themselves abused.'

'He's here to save that bastard Ryan?' Fin was appalled.

I shook my head as the Hunter's impenetrable golden gaze met mine. 'I think he's the reason those people who came out here for a nice walk changed their minds so suddenly. That way, they can't get caught up in whatever's going to happen. I think Ryan's on his own.'

'So the cat's going to kill him and there's nothing we can do.' Fin didn't like that idea any more than me.

I don't know if the Hunter heard her, but he angled his head as if he was considering something. A moment later, he stepped aside with a sweep of his hand to indicate we could go on. A second after that, he vanished.

'Let's see what we can see.' Fin had her backpack straps in one hand. She unzipped the top and held it out to her sister. 'Keys? Purse? Phone? Anything else?'

Blanche emptied her pockets. Fin handed the backpack to me. 'With any luck, the sylph will come to see what we're doing. We can ask what the hell they're playing at.'

'Zan—'

Fin spoke over her sister, talking to me. 'Are you going to wait here?'

'I'll try to get a closer look.' I could see she wasn't keen on that idea. 'Remember how the shuck scared him off the last time.'

She bit her lip. 'Be careful.'

'You too. Both of you.'

I couldn't tell if they heard me. I'd barely raised my hand to shield my eyes from the flash when they shifted into their swan forms. They launched themselves into the air, flying towards the hillfort.

As I walked down the path, I adjusted the straps and settled Fin's backpack on my shoulders. I wanted both hands free. Watching and listening for any hint of movement ahead, I tried to take every step as quietly as possible.

All I could see at the far end of the path was an indistinct mass of green, even with plenty of daylight left. It would be hours before the long summer evening deepened into dusk. The cat shouldn't be able to creep up on me this time. I would see the bastard in time to summon the shuck.

Nothing happened. The summery perfume of the thorn thickets was reassuring. No squawk of feathered alarm interrupted the cheerful birdsong. When I reached the end of the path, a wide space opened up. To my left and to my right, pale lines on the turf showed where walkers circled these earthworks. The hillfort rose up straight ahead.

An archaeologist turning up here with a trowel would have to go home and get a chainsaw. 'Not surveyed' was an understatement. The substantial hillock was covered in thorn scrub, brambles and countless other plants taking advantage of the shelter offered by whatever earthworks they now hid. I couldn't guess how many ditches and banks ringed the raised expanse in the centre. Mature trees had claimed that open space decades ago.

I saw no sign that anything had disturbed the impenetrable thickets in front of me. Where had that prick Ryan gone? Where was the cat man pursuing him? Had we got this completely wrong? Had they gone in some other direction? Was Ryan already dead?

I looked up, but I couldn't see Fin or Blanche in the cloudless late-afternoon sky. I flexed my hands, stretching my fingers wide, as I looked for a decent-sized tree. I chose a flourishing dogwood, growing on the lip of a steep-sided ditch. That must be the first of the hillfort's defences, though I couldn't see how deep it went beneath the tangled undergrowth. Good luck to anyone whose dog decided to go exploring down there.

'Excuse me,' I said to the dogwood tree. 'Please, may I...?'

Taking firm hold of one of its branches, I braced myself for the shock of rejection. Instead I saw the whole hillfort's layout. Three roughly oval rings of steeply banked earth overlooked three deep ditches. Away to my right, at about three o'clock, three slightly offset gaps offered access through all three ramparts to the innermost enclosure. On the other side, between ten and eleven o'clock, the outer two rings weren't nearly so close together. Several gaps in those outer earthworks overlooked the more open areas between them.

In the same instant I knew where Ryan the prick and the cat man were. Ryan was caught between the second and third rings. The cat man prowled through the trees at the heart of the site. So Zan had lured Ryan into the car park and along this path, pretending to be Ashley. Given how slowly the traffic had been moving, I guessed it was just about plausible that she could have got here on foot while Ryan followed in his Mazda. I don't suppose he'd wondered about that. He just wanted to get his hands on her with no one around to stop him.

The cat man had followed Ryan, planning to do the same. Now they were both going in circles and I knew why. They weren't alone. Hamadryads had claimed this place. No wonder the hillfort stayed unsurveyed.

I let go of the dogwood's branch. 'Thank you.'

'I'm sure that you're most welcome to whatever aid these trees can offer.' Zan the sylph was beside me. 'You wanted these fools taught a lesson. My friends are happy to help.

216

Don't worry. The cat and the brute will exhaust themselves. Their paths will not cross.'

Bloody sylphs. What about asking us if we agreed with your not-so-brilliant plan? I didn't say that out loud.

Zan smiled cheerily. 'By the time dawn follows his night of terror, the brute will no longer see women as playthings. He will know he had better hunt elsewhere.'

'How can you be so sure?'

'Go and see for yourself.'

The sylph wasn't smiling now that I hadn't been suitably impressed or grateful. An instant later, Zan vanished. Great.

The brambles choking the deep outer ditch unravelled themselves. I looked warily at the gap that opened up. Thorny tendrils were still moving though there wasn't a hint of breeze. Sprays of pale flowers waved alongside clusters of small green berries as well as larger red ones. There'd be plenty of blackberries in the next couple of months for the local birds and animals, but if those brambles closed up behind me, I would get scratched to bits as I fought my way out. Assuming I could even get up the steep bank.

'You will pass safely, stranger.' A hamadryad looked up from the bottom of the ditch between the writhing brambles. She seemed friendly enough.

Fuck it. I had to know what was going on. I made my way cautiously down the slope, holding on to the dogwood trees to avoid sliding the rest of the way on my arse.

'Follow me.' The hamadryad turned clockwise and the brambles opened up ahead.

She walked quickly and I stayed close. It was distinctly unnerving to hear the trees and undergrowth rustling as they settled themselves behind me. I decided there was no point in worrying how I'd get back right now. What lay ahead was more important, as well as a lot more dangerous.

I'd met hamadryads before, in a beech wood. They're different to dryads, irrevocably bound to one tree. When that tree dies, or if it's cut down, the hamadryad dies too. Unsurprisingly, the ones in that beech wood had been hostile towards humans who had so many uses for timber. I wouldn't recommend any archaeologist turn up here with a chainsaw.

This hamadryad had the same opaque steely-grey eyes, but she was a lot shorter, with a reddish tinge in her dark skin and long hair. Not a redhead but actual scarlet. The sleeveless dress that reached her knees seemed to be sewn from bright green leaves.

The space between the steep earth banks widened and the hamadryad glanced back at me. As she waved a hand, the undergrowth obligingly offered us a way up onto a shallower section of earthwork. I realised we'd reached the gaps I'd seen at the ten o'clock mark. The hamadryad sat down and gestured for me to join her. So I did.

Below us, someone was whimpering and thrashing as they tried to fight through the undergrowth. The dogwood trees drew their branches back. I saw Zan the sylph pretending to be Ashley again. Ryan appeared. His clothes were torn and filthy with grass stains, green smudges from tree branches and a fair amount of blood. He was covered in cuts and scratches. The deeper gashes would probably need stitches.

He fought his way towards what he thought was Ashley, yelling abuse. Zan shimmered and transformed. Now the sylph looked like the hamadryad beside me. Ten or more other hamadryads appeared. I realised Ryan hadn't got those cuts trying to force his way along the ditch. The hamadryads were hitting him, shouting. I knew from experience how hard their slaps and punches would be.

Ryan fell to his knees. The hamadryads stepped closer, hiding him from view. A moment later, they vanished.

Ryan struggled to his feet. I could see his chest heaving as he gasped for breath.

'Now the brute knows what it feels like.' Zan was smug with satisfaction, sitting on the bank beside me. 'To be helpless against a greater strength's cruelty.'

'To fear for your life.' The hamadryad spoke up unexpectedly. 'The terror of not knowing where or when the next threat will appear.'

Ryan backed away as fast as he could, which wasn't very fast at all. The trees and shrubs were in no mood to let him pass. He tried to rip fronds and branches apart with his bare hands. I sensed rather than saw something lurking some distance away, in the shadows where the tall earth banks drew closer together again. This wasn't a hamadryad. It was something ominous and ancient. Something that had lived here since long before the hillfort had been raised.

My pulse raced and my gut felt hollow. I had encountered something like this before. Not the same, but similar. This was one of the stronger and stranger powers that linger deep below ground. Perhaps that's why the hillfort had been raised here. There's no way to know. So many things have fallen out of folklore. No one knows why giant figures of men and horses were once carved into hillsides. I only knew that's where I'd last felt something like this.

Ryan had disappeared. Shivering treetops showed me where he was fighting to get away. The dark shadow swept along the ditch to pursue him. That would be another reason why this place had stayed unsurveyed.

I heard rustling and turned to see another hamadryad leading Fin and Blanche to join me. That was a definite tick in the plus column. Not just because now I knew they were safe. I hoped they'd have some ideas about what we should do next.

'What did you see?' Swans aren't exactly suited for aerial surveillance. They can't hover and they can't perch on a branch to keep watch.

'We made several passes, north–south and east to west.' Fin sat down beside me. 'The cat's in those trees in the middle and he can't find a way out. And I do mean he's a cat now. I'm surprised we can't hear him snarling.'

'I guess we have our friends to thank for that.' The hamadryads must have mazed him.

'Shall I show you how we are repaying the brute for his cruelty towards his wife?' The sylph was clearly expecting Blanche and Fin to offer the gratitude I'd failed to show.

'We saw.' At least Blanche smiled, appreciative.

'Is he going to die here?' Fin asked bluntly.

'Perhaps, if his heart fails him. Though he is young and strong.' Zan wasn't concerned.

There was an awkward silence. I tried to work out how much that possibility bothered me. Not much, I decided. Not at all.

Blanche spoke first. 'If that happens, Ashley will be rid of him.'

'How will she ever know?' Fin gestured at the dense vegetation. 'It could be months before anyone finds him in here. There won't be anything to see from outside the fort, and if anyone smells him rotting, they'll think it's a dead fox or deer. Ashley will still be looking over her shoulder every day, terrified he's about to appear.'

Zan scowled. I talked fast before the sylph vanished again.

'If he dies, he's no great loss. He deserves everything he's going through. Thank you for that. If he dies here though, that will make trouble for our friends.' I gestured at the two hamadryads. 'The police will be looking for him after what happened this afternoon, and his car is back there.'

I kept talking. I didn't want Zan or one of the hamadryads to realise any one of us could move the Mazda. There was no way Fin or Blanche or I was getting in that car and leaving some trace for a keen CSI.

'Once they start searching this place, as soon as they find him, even if they think he died by accident, they'll cut down trees and clear away the undergrowth to get his body out.' I didn't look at the hamadryads, but I could see their concern in the corner of my eye.

'They might suspect Ashley had a hand in his death,' Fin added. 'If anyone saw you, Zan, when you were leading him here, they will most likely come forward when the police appeal for witnesses. If they think he was murdered, they'll strip the ground where they find his body down to bare earth looking for clues.'

Zan's expression was thunderous. The hamadryads were scowling at the sylph.

'That's only a problem if he dies,' Blanche said quickly. 'If he leaves alive, no one will ever know he was here. What were you planning to do with him next?'

'That can be your task, son of the greenwood. I have done enough, and for little thanks.'

But I had seen the uncertainty flicker across Zan's face before they vanished. The sylph hadn't thought that far ahead. They didn't know as much about mortals and the world we live in as they liked to think.

Chapter Nineteen

The hamadryads sitting together on the earthwork looked worried.

'Give us a moment to think. I'm sure we'll find an answer.' They would know I meant that, even if they also knew I couldn't guarantee a thing.

Fin reached for her backpack. I handed it over and she got her water bottle out. She took a drink. 'What now?'

I wondered where the cat was. Never mind. Ryan was our immediate problem. 'We need the police to arrest him, so Ashley knows he's locked up. How do we make that happen?'

'If the police get hold of him while he's raving about trees turning into women and women turning into trees, they'll section him, won't they?' Blanche took the water bottle when Fin offered it. 'Locked up on a psych ward is still locked up.'

'Please, could one of you get his wallet and bring it to us?' I asked the hamadryads. I got my own wallet out to show them what I meant. 'He should be carrying something like this.'

The hamadryads exchanged a glance and one disappeared. The other one stayed where she was, watching us intently with steely-grey eyes.

'What are you thinking?' Fin screwed the top back on her water bottle as Blanche handed it over.

'He's not supposed to go to her house,' I reminded her. 'If the police catch him there, he'll be arrested.'

'As long as they arrive before he can break in and attack her.' Fin was dubious.

'Then someone needs to be there, ready to call 999 as soon as he arrives. Ready to get in his way until the cops turn up and able to disappear as soon as they do.'

Blanche saw what I meant. 'No one will believe him if he says two women stopped him, then turned into swans and flew away.'

The hamadryad reappeared and offered me a mono-grammed maroon leather wallet. Ryan really was a wanker. I found his driving licence and checked when it had been issued.

'This hasn't been updated, so this must be the address where they lived. You said it was her place originally.' I'd need the satnav to be certain, but I didn't think that was too far away.

Fin took the licence from me and read the address. 'She might not be there. Especially after this afternoon.'

'Does that matter?' Blanche was getting impatient. 'If he starts a row with the neighbours, that'll get him arrested, won't it?'

'Hopefully.' I saw Fin was trying to think of every pos-sibility. 'I should wait here and follow him, in case he goes somewhere else. If not, if you two are waiting by Ashley's house, I can ring you when he's getting close. If he doesn't go after her, we'll think again.'

Though I was already thinking how I could improve those odds. I looked at the hamadryad. 'Can you keep the cat mazed here for the rest of the night? Until one of us comes back to say you can let him go?'

She nodded, confident. I looked at Fin and Blanche. 'Once we've seen Ryan thrown into a police van in handcuffs, we can come back here. We can be waiting when Will whatever-his-name-is gets back to the car park.'

'We're going to confront him?' Blanche looked apprehen-sive. 'What are we going to say?'

223

I hesitated. 'Let's work that out once we've dealt with Ryan.'

Fin stood up. 'Let's get on with it then.'

'Ring me when you get to Ashley's house. Then our friends can let him go.' I looked at the hamadryad and she nodded. 'Give me that licence back. I'll leave his wallet on the ground by his car so it looks like he dropped it.'

'What's the phone signal like here?' Blanche asked.

I was about to suggest she look for herself, then I realised her phone was still in Fin's backpack. I checked my screen. 'Not great,' I had to admit, 'but it should be enough.'

'Look again,' the hamadryad who was sitting listening to us said quietly.

I saw I had maximum reception. 'Thank you.'

Fin looked at the brambles. 'How do we get out of here?'

The hamadryad rose gracefully, smiled and led them away.

Sitting alone on the top of the earthwork, I tried to work out what we could have forgotten. Was it something that could come back to bite us in the arse? The only thing that occurred to me was the police might trace Fin's phone when she made that call.

Could she say Ashley had said where she lived when they were talking earlier in the afternoon? Fin and Blanche could say they had popped by to check on her after what had happened. That was sort of true. Was it true enough to convince the cops? If they checked with Ashley, was there any chance she was so focused on Ryan that she wouldn't remember what she had said?

We'd have to talk about that later. Hopefully Fin or Blanche would come up with something better. Meantime, the sun was sinking and the shadows were lengthening around the hillfort. Birds settled into their roosts, chattering amiably. The rustles in the undergrowth told me the animals who lived here were going about their business. I felt welcome, if not at home precisely. I didn't press my luck by trying the dryad radar again. Wherever Ryan was, he was far enough away for me not to hear him. I was enjoying the peace and quiet.

When my phone rang, I was so startled I nearly dropped it into the ditch.

'We're here and the lights are on, so it looks as if she's home. There are two cars parked outside, so hopefully someone's with her.' Fin sounded relieved.

'Great. I'll let you know when he's getting close. Bye.'

I looked around for a hamadryad. One appeared. She had boosted the phone signal for us. I was starting to be able to tell them apart. She gestured, and the brambles opened up to show me the way out through the earthworks.

'Please, can you keep the brute suggestible for as long as you can?' That was the word the Blithehurst dryads had used. 'And have him forget he ever met me here.'

As the hamadryad cocked her head, I saw a faint crease between her eyebrows.

'Please. I will owe you a favour in return.' Once this was over, the Landy would be racking up the miles settling my debts in Dorset and North Yorkshire.

The hamadryad gave that some thought and nodded. 'I can ensure the effects of the mazing will linger. We will decide how you can repay us in due course.'

'Thank you. For all your help.' I hoped Zan owed the hamadryads so many favours by now that they'd keep the sylph busy until midwinter.

I made my way out of the hillfort and hurried back along the path. Dusk was thickening in the shadows of the thorn hedges. The Mazda, the Nissan and my Land Rover were the only vehicles in the car park. I didn't know if we had the Hunter or the hamadryads to thank for that. I unlocked the Landy and put Ashley's address into the satnav. Then I found the notepad and pen I keep in the driver's door pocket and wrote down both the other number plates.

If Ryan didn't go after Ashley, I'd ring the cops myself and report him as a dangerous, possibly drunk driver. As for the cat man, I went to check the tops of the Nissan's tyres in case he'd left his keys hidden in one of the wheel arches. No such luck. Well, that had been a longish shot. Never mind. As long as I was back here before the hamadryads let him go, I could stop him leaving until we had talked. We knew he was going after utter scum now, but there had to be some way to convince him to stop.

I waited by the Landy and listened. Stumbling footsteps were coming along the uneven path. Harsh breathing echoed back from the unsympathetic trees. Ryan staggered into the car park and stared at me, confused.

He was swaying and covered with muck and blood. Any copper would be convinced he was drunk. Even when he passed a breath test, they wouldn't let him go. Someone would insist he needed first aid. Once they'd got him to a hospital, surely they'd do a blood test? If he wasn't drunk, they'd think he had to be on drugs. After that, I didn't care if the prick spent the night in a cell or a hospital bed with a copper standing guard.

'Who – you—' He blinked.

'It's all her fault, isn't it?' I moved closer. 'Ashley. The bitch. She did this to you, didn't she?'

I'd decided not to tell Fin when I'd had this idea. I probably wasn't ever going to tell her. But I could see my vile plan was working.

'Ash?' Hatred burned through the haze in his eyes. 'Bitch.'

'You should go and tell her what you think of her. Make her listen.'

'Make her listen,' Ryan repeated venomously.

'Go over there now. Right away.'

'Right away.' He fumbled in his pocket.

For one heart-stopping moment, I thought he'd lost his sodding keys. If he had, we were royally fucked. The hamadryads wouldn't be able to fetch them. How long would it take for them to find them and lead me through the brambles to pick them up?

'Go there now.' Ryan jangled his keys with a vicious smile.

I wanted to punch his filthy face and keep hitting him after he was down. But me doing that wouldn't help Ashley.

Ryan unlocked the Mazda. While he was fighting with his seatbelt, I lobbed his wallet in through the open door. He needed two tries to get the door closed before he drove off. I was starting to worry that the prick would drive into a lamp post. If he did, I'd better be on the scene to play the good Samaritan.

I took out my phone as I hurried back to the Landy and called Fin. 'He's just left.'

'Right.' She ended the call.

I got into my seat, shoving the key into the ignition as soon as I slammed the door. The other door opened as I reached for my seatbelt. Will whatever-his-name-was slid into the passenger seat.

'Right, ya cunt, it's time we had a wee chat.' He showed me the knife in his hand. The double-edged steel was an inch wide and six inches long. Twice as long as anything legal. Long enough to go deep enough to be lethal. I didn't need the scars on my forearm to start burning to know this threat was real.

227

The cat man was Scottish. We were right about that. More to the point, his low, rasping voice was Glaswegian. A few years ago, I'd worked on a reforesting project in Lanarkshire. A couple of that team had been from Glasgow. Nice guys who you really didn't want to annoy.

'Hands on the steering wheel, pal, if ye dinna want me tae cut ye. Eyes front an' all.'

I did as I was told.

'Ah kennt they birds wi' ye, but whit the fuck are you?'

He sniffed, and not because his nose was running. As he drew in a long, deep breath, I realised he was trying to get a better sense of my scent.

There'd been no hope of a TV signal at that Lanarkshire hunting lodge, and the only box set for the DVD player had been a season of Taggart. The ancient cop show had been set in Maryhill, where a detective solved murrrderrrs. One of the lads from Surrey asked if there were subtitles. He could barely follow the stories. The blokes from Glasgow had laughed themselves silly. As far as they were concerned, those gangsters and lowlifes were ridiculously well spoken. When they gave us a taste of what they'd grown up with, no one else had understood a word.

'I asked you a question, pal.' Menacing, he tapped my forearm with his knife. 'Ye know I'll ken if you're lying.'

To my relief, I was hearing him a bit more clearly. I told him the truth. There was no point in doing anything else. 'My mother is a dryad.'

'Is she now?' That genuinely surprised him. 'That explains a few things. Called in some family favours, did ye?'

I shrugged. The less I told him the better. He didn't like that.

'Who told you tae get into my business? That cunt Ryan was mine,' he growled. 'That puir wee lass—'

'We know what he did to her. She needs him locked up, not dead where no one will ever find the body.'

If keeping my mouth shut wasn't an option, maybe I could get him talking. Not only to see what I could learn. So he'd ask fewer questions. Assuming he could hear me lying, I'd have to answer him as close to truthfully as I could. That risked me giving too much away.

I went on the offensive, verbally at least. 'Those kids in Devon were scared sick that arsehole Taser would be coming back. Him disappearing did them no favours. What about that bloke you killed in Yorkshire? Who's spent the last few months worried shitless, waiting for his knock on their door?'

'You know—?' He recovered quickly. 'That cunt? Loan shark. Bleeding folk dry. Taking their gear when they could-nae pay. Breaking their fingers when they had nae more stuff he could sell. If they didnae want a broken arm, he tellt them to borrow from family or steal from any job they could get.'

The fury in his words was as clear as a bell. I wasn't going to argue. The dead man sounded like scum.

'If some daft bastard tells the polis? They useless jobbies wouldnae do fuck all. On the take mebbe, or covering for some grass. Or too fuckin' idle. Same as all the rest.'

He was even less of a fan of the cops than I was. But we had to convince him to stop taking the law into his own hands.

'If no one knows where that loan shark has gone, what are those poor sods going to do if someone turns up on their doorstep saying they're holding their debt now? Who's going to say different, when nobody knows you killed—'

'I didnae kill the fucker,' he snarled. 'I dinna lay a hand on any o' them. And if yer ma was so put out, why did she get rid o' the body? Aye, an' the others an' all? She's no said a word before.'

He thought I was the dryad in the Over Cullen Woods's son? I decided not to correct his mistake. 'You haven't only pissed her off. I know a couple of naiads who don't like what you're doing. A mermaid in Devon will give you real trouble if she sees you again.'

'They've sent you to tell me?' he said, scornful.

'Yes, and they know where I am. If I disappear, they'll come looking. All of them.'

'Then they can get tae fuck.'

But I saw uncertainty in his eyes. Just a hint, but I followed that up all the same.

'You're not only fucking with folk like my mother. Those swans you saw? What happens to them and their families if you get caught? If someone sees what you can really do?'

His laugh was harsh and loud inside the Landy. 'If the polis pull me over and find some cunt they cannae be bothered with tied up inside my van? They can try putting the cuffs on a panther, if they've got the baws, but I dinna see that happening. They'll pish their breeks and bolt, pal. And tell naebody wha' happened. Who'd believe them if they did?'

'You can't be sure of that.' But his words had the ring of truth.

'I know it, pal,' he assured me. 'There's naebody better than the polis when it comes to hiding shite they dinna want folk to know. Apart from the British army mebbe.'

I had a nasty feeling he could be right. He'd been getting away with these deaths for years. He might think twice about killing me, now he knew that I'd be missed by folk he didn't want for enemies. He wouldn't hesitate to cut me though, to make a point. I could hear that for a stone-cold certainty.

What was I going to do? Close to, he was quite a bit older than I'd thought when I'd seen him this afternoon. In his fifties maybe, with acne-scarred skin and crooked, stained teeth. He looked as hard as nails, with muscles like steel ropes in his tanned forearms. I didn't think he'd risk shifting into his cat form in this confined space, but that wasn't much comfort. I might be able to get out of the Land Rover while he was doing that, but I'd have a big cat hunting me through the evening shadows. He had my scent, and I had no idea if dryad hiding powers would cover that as well.

I didn't reckon I had any realistic chance of getting that knife off him. What would I do with it if I did? Cut his throat? Gut him? Stab his thigh and hope I hit the femoral artery? Then I'd have a dead man in my Land Rover and everything would be covered in blood. What was I going to do then? Set the Landy on fire in the car park? Find some way to send it off the nearest cliff with the body inside? It would be found, traced back to me, and the police would want answers.

All I could think of was keeping him talking. Buy enough time and maybe I'd think of some way out of this mess that wouldn't end up with one of us dead. Most likely me. I gripped the steering wheel tight and stared out through the windscreen.

'What is your real name anyway? Will Hall? William Halsbury?'

'Done your homework, have ye?' He looked momentarily uncertain, then he grinned with some secret satisfaction. 'You can call me Billy. Billy the Cat. What does yer mammy call you?'

'Dan. Daniel.' I was trying to make sense of what he had just said. Somehow, in some sense at least, Billy the Cat truly was his real name. But that couldn't possibly be on his birth certificate.

'Nice to meet you, Dan Daniel,' he said, mocking. 'Right, here's what's gonnae happen the morra' and every day after that. I'll stay out of your way, and you can tell your people I'll be more careful where I throw out my trash. You stay out of my way, or I'll catch ye and send ye back to yer ma wi' a smile. Do we have a deal?'

I didn't answer right away. I was still trying to work out what that name he had given me could mean.

'I asked you a question, cunt.' He slid the point of his knife between my lips. As he pressed the razor-sharp steel into the corner of my mouth, I felt the delicate skin parting. I had to fake a sickly grin to stop the blade doing any more damage.

'Good lad,' he said, approving, as he withdrew the knife. 'And in case you were thinking of following me—'

If he said anything else, I didn't hear it. Imagine the worst cramp you've ever had, buckling your foot or knotting a calf muscle into a solid lump. Imagine that in every single muscle from head to toe. My whole body was wracked with agony. I couldn't get away from it. I couldn't move. I could barely breathe. The pain kept coming, relentless. I was getting dizzy and feeling sick.

I vaguely registered the passenger door opening. Billy the Cat was getting away. I managed to jerk my hand towards my own door handle. That proved there was fuck all I could do to stop him. My balance and coordination were shot. If I opened my door and managed to get out of the Landy, I'd fall flat on my face. I could only sit there and listen to the Nissan's engine as Billy the Cat drove away.

Fuck.

Chapter Twenty

I have no idea how long I sat in the Land Rover. I kept my eyes closed, trying not to throw up. Trying to work out if I could get the door open before I did. Then someone opened the door. I opened my eyes. The courtesy light shone brightly enough to make me squint.

'Dan?' Fin reached for my hand.

I was surprised to realise I was still gripping the steering wheel. I tried to speak. Sharp pain in the corner of my mouth reminded me of Billy the Cat's promise. I touched the cut gingerly with my tongue.

'Is that blood?' Alarmed, Fin leaned closer to look at my face. Blanche was standing behind her.

'It's okay.' No, it wasn't, but it was the least of my worries. I carefully straightened my hands. To my relief, that didn't trigger any fresh muscle spasms. I found the trickle of dried blood by my mouth with a fingertip. I did my best to lick the smear and wipe it away. That made the cut a lot more painful.

I pulled up my T-shirt and cautiously felt my side. Slowly taking a deep breath didn't hurt, so I didn't think any ribs were broken. I did find two sore points close together, as if some insect had stung me. I realised Terence Atwill hadn't ever had a taser, never mind what he'd told those kids. He'd had a stun gun and Billy the Cat had it now. Spoils of war.

'What happened with Ashley?' I spoke over whatever Blanche had started to say. 'Did Ryan—?'

Fin nodded. 'He turned up and left his car blocking half the road. He started hammering on her front door, yelling and swearing, threatening her.'

'A neighbour was out walking her dog,' Blanche added. 'We saw her get out her phone and the cops were there inside five minutes. No lights or sirens, so they didn't scare him off.'

I was relieved to know the cops wouldn't have Fin's or Blanche's mobile number. 'Did they take him away?'

'In cuffs,' Fin confirmed with satisfaction. 'Ashley has a couple of people with her tonight. We saw them when they opened the door to the cops.'

'Then we went back to my car and came here.' Blanche wasn't interested in Ashley any more. 'What the hell happened to you?'

A voice from the twilight answered her. 'The cat escaped when we unwound the maze to release the brute. We had no idea he would be able to break free.'

I reached up to switch off the light above the windscreen. As my eyes adjusted to the pale summer night, I saw the hamadryads standing in a wide circle around us.

'We are deeply sorry.' Whichever hamadryad was speaking sounded distraught. 'We will repay you—'

'Forget it.' I had far more important things to worry about. 'We're quits. Seriously.'

The hamadryads must have believed me. At any rate, they disappeared before I could change my mind.

'Have you any idea where he's gone?' Blanche looked around the car park.

I don't know how she thought doing that would help. Her Honda was the only other vehicle there. 'No.'

'We need to get you home.' Fin was still concerned. 'I'll drive.'

I shook my head. 'I have to get back for work tomorrow.'

'Sod that.' Fin pulled my keys out of the Landy's ignition before I realised what she was doing.

I swallowed hard. 'Listen, Eleanor said—'

But Blanche was talking over me, speaking to Fin. 'Dan's got to get back to Blithehurst somehow. If you drive him there now, I can follow in my car. It'll be stupid o'clock by the time we arrive, but we can stay overnight. There's nothing urgent in the work diary for tomorrow. We can tell Hazel everything that's happened, as well as Eleanor, and it'll be better if we do that together. Then I can drive us home.'

'That sounds like a plan,' I agreed.

Fin narrowed her eyes at me, but I could see she knew this made sense. 'I suppose so. Move over.'

'I'll go around.' I was about to swing my feet out over the door sill when I realised I still had my seatbelt on. At least undoing that proved my hands were working properly. 'Ring Eleanor. Tell her to expect us.'

Fin's lips thinned in the way that tells me she's annoyed, but she found her phone. I managed to get out of my seat at the second attempt. I was steadier on my feet than I expect-ed, but it was obvious Fin would have to drive. I wasn't going to trust my reactions to some sudden emergency on the motorway.

By the time I walked around to the passenger seat and set-tled myself, Fin was finishing her call to Eleanor. 'He hasn't said what happened, but we can go through that tomorrow.'

So that's what we did. Fin didn't ask any questions as we drove though unlit country lanes. When we reached the motorway, she hit the CD player button and turned up the volume. I didn't say anything, finding a new CD each time whatever was playing ended. That didn't stop me thinking about Billy the Cat and his knife. I wondered where he was. Tucked up in bed? I was sure the bastard wouldn't lose a minute's sleep over what he had done to me.

We got back to Blithehurst in the small hours of the next day. When I got out of the Landy to open the back gate, I found a note in a plastic wallet drawing-pinned to the wood.

Text me when you arrive. I'll meet you at the cottage. E

So I texted her, once I'd closed the gate behind Blanche's car. Eleanor was waiting by my front door when we arrived. I couldn't tell what she was thinking. Mostly, I was just glad that the dryads weren't around. I couldn't see Frai waiting until the morning to interrogate me.

Blanche had driven cautiously along the dark estate road. The Honda pulled up as I got out of the Landy. I was horribly stiff, from the long journey and from being hit with that sodding stun gun. I arched my back and stretched my arms out wide.

Eleanor nodded now she could see I was basically okay. 'Give me a ring when you're ready to come up to the house tomorrow. You're off the staff roster, so you can sleep in.'

She walked over to Blanche as she lowered her car window. 'You're welcome to one of the guest rooms up at the house. I'll show you where to park.'

By the time Eleanor was in the Honda's passenger seat, Fin was unlocking the cottage's front door. I followed her in and we went to bed.

I woke up hearing Fin in the shower. Stretching under the duvet, I found I was pretty much back to normal, which was a relief. I checked the time and saw it had gone ten. That was less good.

'Bathroom's free.' Fin passed the bedroom doorway. 'I'll put the kettle on.'

I showered and dressed and checked that cut at the corner of my mouth in the mirror over the sink. It was already healing, thanks to my greenwood blood. I cleaned my teeth very carefully. Then I followed the smell of frying bacon to the kitchen. Two rounds of sandwiches were ready on the table.

Fin was making herself cheese on toast. 'Tea's in the pot.'

'Great, thanks.' I poured myself a big mugful and ate my breakfast, careful not to reopen that sodding cut.

Fin sat down and reached for the Worcester sauce. She keeps some spare clothes at the cottage, so she was wearing clean summer trousers and a pink T-shirt. 'There's no point going over everything twice. Just tell me you're okay.'

'I am now.' It was a relief to know that she would know I was telling her the truth.

'Blanche is up and about.' She nodded at her phone lying on the table. 'I told her we won't be long.'

My phone buzzed while we were putting our mugs and plates in the dishwasher. I wiped my hands and checked the message. 'Eleanor says to meet in her sitting room.'

We walked up to the house, went in through the side door and straight up the back stairs. Blanche was sipping a mug of coffee and reading the manor house guidebook. Eleanor must have lent her the jeans she was wearing and a Blithehurst staff polo shirt. The light blue went well with her turquoise hair.

She waved the guidebook. 'In case anyone asks me where's the closest loo. Eleanor's in the gallery.'

But the door opened as she said that, and Eleanor came in.

'Give me a moment to set up the laptop. Then I'll let Hazel know we're ready.'

She locked the door behind her. The plaque on the outside says 'PRIVATE', but I've lost count of the times I've been in there when some visitor has tried the handle.

We arranged three upright chairs and Eleanor's office chair in a half-circle on one side of the table. That way we could all see the computer screen. When Hazel logged on, we saw two faces we didn't know and one we recognised. Gillian Adams lived and worked in Cheshire. She'd alerted us to the problem in North Wales that led to me meeting Aled and Annis Wynne.

Hazel didn't introduce the two other women and their webcams didn't show us any clue about them. One was probably in her fifties, and the other one was maybe ten years older. The younger one had short, greying hair and wore a plain beige jumper. The other one had white hair and her dark green cardigan was buttoned to the neck. Like nearly every wise woman I'd met, there was nothing memorable about them.

'Right,' Hazel said briskly. 'Let's hear how you got on.'

I looked at Fin and Blanche, to see who wanted to go first.

'We were right about how to lure a sylph.' Fin ran through everything that had happened calmly and clearly. Blanche chipped in here and there, explaining what she had seen and done while Fin and I had been doing something else. They each described their own flights over the hillfort, and told the wise women how Ryan had been arrested.

Since I didn't have anything to add, I watched the wise women. They kept glancing down. I was sure they were taking notes. Hazel did that all the time and I hadn't much liked it at first. Then I'd seen her handwriting and the weird abbreviations she used. I'd be amazed if another wise woman could make sense of her notebooks, never mind anyone else.

'We flew back to my sister's car and drove back to the car park by the hillfort,' Fin concluded.

I wondered if the dog walker had wondered what two swans were doing in the housing estate at night.

Gillian Adams raised a hand. 'I wonder... It does seem likely he heard about the drug trouble in Darley Combe from the counsellor who was treating the girl Chelsea for her addiction. If this woman Ashley rang a domestic violence helpline, perhaps he has a contact there.'

'Someone recommended his teas to her,' Hazel agreed. 'Though that may well be all they did.'

Neither of the other wise women spoke, studying their notes. Hazel looked through the screen at me. 'Daniel?'

'I waited in the hillfort until I got the call from Fin.' I told them the rest, up to and including Billy the Cat's threat to scar me for life. 'You've heard of a Glasgow smile?'

'I have.' Hazel looked worried. None of the other women commented.

'Then he hit me with the stun gun he must have taken off Taser in Devon. Game over.' I didn't go into any more detail about that.

'We found Dan when we got back.' Fin covered the rest of the night's events in a couple of sentences.

'Thanks.' Hazel's gaze was going to the different corners of her screen. 'We'll need to discuss this. We'll be in touch, hopefully soon.'

'What do we do in the meantime?' Blanche asked her, but the other women had already logged out of the meeting.

'I do wish they wouldn't do that.' Eleanor shut down the software. 'I'm not sure we can do anything to track down this Billy the Cat.'

That was good news as far as I was concerned. I'd be happy to never see the Glaswegian bastard again. He was a killer, even if he claimed what he was doing wasn't murder. He also had that fucking knife and he wouldn't hesitate to use it.

Would I hesitate, if it came down to him or me? I honestly wasn't sure. I do know I'm not a killer. That could be a problem if that ended up being the only way to stop him killing. He had to be stopped. That hadn't changed. What he was doing was a threat to so many of us, even if the world without his victims would be a better place for a whole lot of people.

If I couldn't kill him, could I find someone – or something – to do it for me? The shuck? I had no idea how I'd even propose making a deal like that. If I did find a way, what sort of price would I have to pay for ending Billy the Cat's life? I wasn't at all sure I wanted to find out.

Fin looked at Blanche. 'Do you think Conn might know anything useful?'

She shrugged. 'We can ask. Do you want to call Iris or shall I?'

A week or so later, Fin got in touch. 'Iris said that Conn told her he wasn't going to get involved.'

'That sounds as if he knows something,' I said cautiously.

Fin nodded. 'Iris thought the same. She asked Conn to explain what he meant. He wouldn't, and they ended up having a hideous row. Iris seems to think that's my fault, and Blanche's. We've had a bit of an argument.'

She was unhappy about that, but I didn't have any advice. I have no idea what it's like to have brothers or sisters. All I could offer was my own lack of progress. 'I've asked Aled, but that's a dead end as well.'

I still couldn't decide if I was disappointed or relieved. Until we had some idea how we were going to tackle the bastard, we had agreed we were going nowhere near Billy the Cat. I only hoped we wouldn't find him turning up on one of our doorsteps.

Fin was making the video call on her laptop sitting in her living room. I caught sight of someone I didn't recognise passing behind the sofa and heading for the kitchen. A moment later, I realised that was Zan, with waist-length blonde hair and wearing what looked like Blanche's dressing gown.

The shape the sylph was wearing underneath the thick tow-elling looked more female than male. That was none of my business. I was more concerned that the sylph knew where Fin and Blanche lived.

As soon as Zan left the living room, Fin got up and closed the door. That seemed pointless to me. I was pretty sure the sylph would be able to hear everything we said regardless. I didn't say anything, though, as Fin came back to the sofa. 'I forgot to ask for that damn feather back before we came home.'

'You didn't get a chance,' I pointed out.

'At least I've got it now, and without any fuss, as soon as I asked.' But Fin didn't sound as happy about that as I expect-ed.

I wondered if Zan had intended to keep hold of that feather all along. The sylph was clearly fascinated by Blanche. I wondered how long that was going to last.

I worked every day for the rest of August. No one at Blithe-hurst was going to be able to bitch about me getting special favours or taking too much time off. I did go home for an overnight stay at the equinox in September. Mum was mildly interested to hear about the hamadryads I had met in the hillfort. Mostly, she wanted to show me the oak sapling she had chosen for me to take as her winter solstice gift to the dryad in the Over Cullen Woods.

After I had admired the tiny tree, I went back to the cot-tage and brought Dad up to date with our lack of progress over a pot of tea and some biscuits.

'No news is good news as far as I am concerned,' Dad said. He went on before I could admit I felt the same. 'Billy the Cat? That reminds me of something, but I'm blowed if I can place it.' He shook his head, dismissing it. 'Just promise me you won't go up against the bastard on your own.'

'I won't,' I assured him. I didn't want to go up against him at all. My cut mouth had healed without leaving a mark, but I wasn't going to forget the feel of that razor-sharp blade any time soon.

September turned into October. Life at the manor got less hectic. I overheard Lynne telling Sarah that Denise's Blithehurst fan site hadn't been updated for a couple of months. They wondered why she'd lost interest. I didn't care why, as long as she had. Asca and Frai agreed with me. They were a lot more concerned with that than they were about me meeting some hamadryads or solving the mystery of the murderous black cat.

Eleanor checked her spreadsheets and decided the house should go back to closing on Mondays and Tuesdays. Apart from half term week, ticket sales wouldn't justify the costs of keeping the lights and heating on. From the start of November, the manor would only open for the Christmas fairs at weekends. She did tell me she'd done some research in her spare time, since she was curious about the ominous presence at the hillfort. She hadn't found any hints about what that might be though.

Kalei didn't introduce me to more naiads outraged by dead bodies being dumped in their rivers or lakes. None of the newspapers ran stories about big black cats roaming the countryside. News bulletins didn't mention the police discovering evidence of some previously unknown serial killer. The Green Man didn't appear in my dreams or while I was working in the estate woods. There was no sign of the Hunter.

We started making plans for the Christmas craft fairs. I rang Aled to pass on Eleanor's offer of a free table, to see how his jewellery might sell.

'That's good of her. Tell her I'll accept, with thanks. I've asked Annis Wynne if she knows anything about this Billy the Cat,' he went on, before I asked. 'She says she won't betray any confidences, but to be honest with you, I don't think she knew what I was talking about. She's getting very frail. Mostly she talks about her sister and their life before she was mortal. Don't worry about that though. Anyone who hears her just thinks she's away with the fairies.'

'Right. Well, thanks for asking anyway.'

If we couldn't find the bastard, wasn't this over and done with? If no one was finding any more dead bodies, maybe I had managed to convince him to back off, at least for a while. Once he'd had time to think about what I'd said, maybe he realised he was putting other people like himself in danger. Maybe I'd seen the last of him for good.

I hoped so. Then Eleanor texted me first thing one Monday morning. It was the week before half term and a fortnight before Halloween. It was seven o'clock in the morning.

Come up to the house asap. Email from a colleague of Hazel's. Needs to speak to us both before work.

Chapter Twenty-One

When I went in through the side door of the empty house, Eleanor heard my boots on the flagstone floor. She called out from the kitchen, 'I'm making some coffee. Do you want a cup?'

I went through the old kitchen with its massive black-leaded range and rows of copper saucepans for visitors to admire. Modern units and appliances had been fitted into what had once been a scullery.

'I'm fine, thanks.' I'd had a quick mug of tea and some toast before I walked up from the cottage. 'Where are we doing this? In the library?'

Eleanor poured hot water from the kettle and carefully put the plunger in her cafetière. 'Let's go upstairs.'

I followed her up to her sitting room and opened the door so she could go through with her tray. Her laptop sat between piles of paperwork.

'Move that lot so I can put this down.' Eleanor nodded at a stack with a brochure for Halloween tat on top. 'Anywhere will do. It's for recycling.'

I dumped the pile on the floor. Every year or so someone in the Beauchene family has the bright idea that Blithehurst should do something special for Halloween. Bring in more kids and their parents to spend money, they say. Eleanor has to convince them it's not a worthwhile investment of staff time. She can hardly say the dryads forbid it, threatening dire consequences which they refuse to explain.

Eleanor added milk to her mug and checked the time. She settled in her office chair and reached for the mouse. As she clicked on the meeting link, I sat on the upright chair beside her. I tried not to look too surprised when we saw who had emailed. This wise woman was a goth, with long black hair, dark eyeshadow, pale make-up and lipstick the colour of clotted blood. She also looked to be somewhere in her twenties, though it was hard to be sure with that make-up. I wondered what sort of day job she had to get to. She wore a black leather collar with a single row of spikes around her neck, and some sort of black lacy top over a sleeveless black T-shirt.

'Hi there, I'm Carmen. Right, let's get to it. For a cunning man, our man's no been too clever.' She was another Glaswegian, but her accent was light and lilting. 'From what you said about the way he talks, and what he thinks of the polis, we thought he could well be a schemie. That was as good a place as any to start looking.' She grinned and explained before we had to ask.

'After the Second World War, the authorities in Glasgow were desperate to clear the city's slums. Bombs meant for the shipyards had left a lot of folk homeless as well. Housing developments were built around the outskirts of the city, with tower block flats offering indoor plumbing and all mod cons. Who knows, the schemes might even have worked, if the geniuses in charge had remembered that folk would need jobs they could get to on the bus, as well as shops where they lived and a couple of pubs, mebbe a cinema, things like that.'

She raised an apologetic hand with black-varnished fingernails. 'Sorry, I work in planning. We're still trying to sort out the mess. Anyway, we reckoned if our man had been a schemie kid, he'd likely be in his teens in the eighties, right in the middle of the ice cream wars.'

Now Eleanor raised a hand. 'I think I've heard of that. Something to do with drug dealing from ice cream vans?'

Carmen nodded. 'Some folk swear they saw dealing going on, as well as stolen property sold out the vans. The authorities will tell you that's an urban myth. Whatever the truth of it, there was more than enough violence and intimidation going around.'

I must have been looking completely blank. Carmen backtracked.

'With no shops in the schemes, a couple of firms set up business sending vans out there. They sold ice cream, as well as cigarettes and sweeties. It wasn't long before they were selling a whole lot of other things. Since they made a decent profit, the local gangs moved in to take over. Rival gangs wanted to control the most lucrative routes and that meant scaring off the opposition. Windscreens were put in with shotguns. Drivers who didn't back down took a beating. To be fair, the cops stood no chance when they tried to investigate. Witnesses kept their mouths shut. They were too afraid of the gangs. Eventually there were some horrible deaths when a flat went on fire.'

Carmen grimaced. 'The police locked up a couple of men for those murders, but there were doubts about the case from the start. The men who were convicted were eventually freed on appeal, but no one else was ever charged. Some reckoned the cops were protecting an informant, even though he was responsible. Other folk are convinced some detectives were paid to look the other way. There's no way to know what really happened.' She shook her head.

'That would explain why the man we're looking for despises the police,' Eleanor said cautiously, 'but do you have anything more than this theory?'

Carmen didn't take offence. 'We took a closer look at schemies who ended up in court. Ones who'd be about the right age to be the man you're wanting. William Smith. By the time he was twelve or thirteen, he was palling around with neds who'd left school with no qualifications and no prospects. They turned to petty crime, paying tax to the gangs to keep them sweet. Young William was a lookout to begin with, before he graduated to breaking and entering. He had quite a talent for climbing, apparently, getting in through windows no one thought a burglar could reach. He got pulled in for questioning a couple of times, and several interview records note his nickname as Billy the Cat.'

Not for the first time, I wondered how the wise women got hold of records like this. I wondered how many records they had gone through before they found a lead worth following up. No wonder it had taken them months. I didn't ask for details though. What I didn't know couldn't get anyone in trouble.

'Here's a picture of him.' Carmen looked down at her keyboard.

The laptop screen showed me and Eleanor a mugshot. The photo was a few decades old, but I recognised the bastard who had threatened to slash my face open. 'That's him. No doubt about it.'

Eleanor was concerned about something else. 'Are you saying these other crooks knew he could change into—?'

'No.' Carmen shook her head. 'There's nothing to suggest he could do anything like that, not back then. We've looked hard to be sure, believe me. That has to be something he learned later—'

She broke off and cleared her throat. 'Billy the Cat was a kid superhero in *The Beano*, back in the late sixties and early seventies. We're guessing his pals who were a few years older started calling him that when he showed a talent for climbing up balconies.'

I didn't care how he'd got his nickname. What interested me was the wise women's certainty that Billy Smith could have learned shapeshifting, as opposed to being born able to do it. That was as close as I was going to get to confirmation that the wise women themselves learned to transform into hares.

Eleanor tried to hide her impatience. 'How do we get from William Smith to Will Hall aka William Halsbury dishing out his own brand of justice as a big black cat?'

'How exactly is still a mystery. Mebbe we can join a few more of the dots now we know for sure he's our shapeshifter. Any road, Billy Smith's luck ran out just after he turned twenty. He got caught with a couple of others burgling a house in Bearsden. That was him locked up in Barlinnie for the next three years. When he came out of prison, he dropped off the grid. Completely. We couldnae find a trace. Seriously. People thought he was dead, but there was no certificate registered. We checked.'

Carmen grinned. 'A month or so ago, we heard something new. Apparently, fifteen years ago near enough, Billy Smith started visiting his old mum. We checked this out and it's true. He doesn't come by too often, but he's given her enough cash to do up her flat and buy some smart new furniture and a big fancy fridge. The neighbours are convinced he works on the rigs, and not only in the North Sea. They say he must be travelling to the Gulf, or West Africa, or wherever companies drilling for oil pay over the odds. We've checked that out and we can't find any evidence of him working offshore. He's getting money from somewhere though. The neighbours say he drives a Nissan van, and one of them had a picture showing that number plate you gave us.'

'Has anyone—?' I began.

"That registration gives William Halsbury as the van's owner, at an address that turns out to be a farmhouse in upper Argyll.' Carmen shook her head, apologetic. 'It's a holiday let, rented out through an agency. On paper, William Halsbury owns the place, but there's no sign that he ever goes there. Billy Smith visited his mum six weeks ago, and we'll hear if he's seen there any time soon, but to be honest, I'm not holding my breath.'

I tried not to look too pleased to hear that. I still had no idea how to convince the bastard to stop killing, short of killing him myself. Hand on heart, I knew I couldn't do that, even if by some miracle I got him at my mercy and I had a knife in my hand. Even if we knew his next target was even worse scum than the loan shark in Yorkshire, or Taser the blackmailing drug dealer.

'You've done a fantastic job piecing this together,' Eleanor congratulated Carmen. 'We'll just have to wait till he shows up somewhere.' She tried to sound optimistic.

'I think we can do better than that,' Carmen said cheerfully. 'Like you said, Dan, he needs to earn money and he knows we're on to two of his aliases, so I don't suppose he'll be using those, though we're keeping an eye out all the same. We've also been looking for anything out of the ordinary that might lead back to him. A friend of a friend heard there's some trouble in a wee castle over on the west coast. People are talking about a poltergeist. Doors slamming, pots smashing, the water going on and off, and screams in the night scaring the shite out of the owners' paying guests. It's one of these places that runs arts courses and yoga retreats and the like.'

She raised a black-taloned finger. 'There's two things not right about this. Firstly, there's never been a hint of a ghost about the place. Westerknowe Castle was only built in the 1780s and nothing much has ever happened there. Secondly, we've heard that a letter arrived at the castle last week from someone claiming to be a cunning man. Says he can feel a disturbance in the force or whatever. Says he can lay unquiet spirits to rest – for a hefty price which he wants paid in cash. Payment on completion, mind you. Full refund if not completely satisfied. Ring this mobile number for immediate service. How convenient is that?' Carmen asked with wide-eyed sarcasm.

'He?' Eleanor queried.

'Liam McGowan, according to the letter. That surname means "blacksmith" in English,' Carmen added.

'How soon can you check him out?' I wondered who had told the wise women about the letter. 'Has anyone looked into that mobile number?'

'That's way above my pay grade.' Carmen shook her head cheerfully. 'I've a note here says you need to talk to – Hazel, is it? Sorry, I've got to go for my bus now. Email me if there's anything I can help with, mind. Cheerio.'

She gave us a quick wave as she closed her window. Eleanor's screen automatically asked for feedback on our meeting. I don't think what I wanted to say was what the software developers had in mind.

Eleanor closed the laptop. 'That surname can't be a coincidence.'

'No,' I agreed reluctantly.

'When do you want to talk to Hazel?'

I wanted to say, 'How about never? Does never work for you?' Because it was obvious who was going to be sent up to bloody Scotland to see if Billy the Cat was behind this.

'Can you email her to ask when she'll be free? I'm going for a walk.' I needed to think about this. I kept recalling the cold, sharp edge of that knife pressed against the corner of my mouth.

'You've got your phone with you?'

My hand went instinctively to my trouser pocket. 'Yes.'

'Okay then.' Eleanor swivelled her chair back to the table and opened up the laptop.

I left the sitting room and went downstairs. When I walked out of the side door, I couldn't decide which way to go. I didn't want to talk to Frai or Asca, so I wasn't going to walk up to the temple. The dryads would say that some ghost in a Scottish castle or a shapeshifter killing lowlifes wasn't their problem, and I'd be very tempted to agree. Why couldn't the wise women deal with this themselves?

The path to the temple crossed the river. On the remote chance that Kalei was around, I didn't want to talk to her either. She would insist I had to deal with Billy the Cat to make sure no more dead bodies were dumped in rivers. That was easy enough for her to say. I couldn't see how she could help me. Could she even find a way to get up to Scotland? That wouldn't stop her making my life uncomfortable though, until I agreed to go and sort him out. There were a whole lot of ways a naiad could screw with me if I pissed her off.

I thought about calling Fin, but I kept hearing Billy Smith's rasping voice. He'd known that Fin and Blanche were swan maids as soon as he'd seen them. I had no idea how he'd sensed that, but being stuck in the Landy with him and his knife and his stun gun was enough to convince me I wanted Fin and her whole family to stay as far away from him as possible. Blanche was also still seeing Zan on and off. The sylph was the last person I wanted to know about any of this. Their bright ideas had already caused more than enough trouble.

I headed for my workshop. Working with my hands and focusing on a practical task is always a good way to distract myself from a problem I can't see how to solve. Quite often, I'll come up with an answer later, when I'm not even thinking about it.

I reached the gravel sweep in front of the porch. Over to my left, the knot garden's herbs and flowers had lost their fragrance, sinking into winter dullness. Ahead, between the yew hedge and the side of the manor, the ornamental shrubs

and dwarf trees that Eleanor's great-grandmother had select-
ed were bright with autumn leaves.

The Hunter barred the way to my workshop. He stood
on the path winding through the little trees with his hands
clasped on the top of a yew staff that was planted solidly
between his feet. The fallen bough had been stripped of its
bark and polished, but the shape of the wood was untouched.
I could see expectation in his face.

Heavy footsteps crunched on the gravel beside me. I
turned my head and saw the Green Man, wrapped in a cloak
of autumn browns. The mask of oak leaves that makes up his
face means his expression rarely changes, but the piercing
emerald light in his eyes gets his meaning across. Today that
message was clear. I wasn't finished with Billy the Cat.

My phone buzzed in my pocket. I checked the message
from Eleanor. Was I free to talk to Hazel right now? I looked
at the Green Man. He nodded his approval and his eyes
shone brighter.

I sent Eleanor *OK* in reply and turned to retrace my steps.
I did look back just once, when I reached the corner of the
house. The Green Man and the Hunter were standing side by
side in the knot garden. The Hunter raised his staff and they
disappeared. So that was a fat lot of help. Frustrated, I went
back inside the manor.

Upstairs, Eleanor had her laptop ready when I came
through her sitting room door, but she didn't reach for the
mouse. 'Is there anything you want to discuss before we do
this?'

'How badly will it screw up the staff roster when she tells
us I've got to drop everything and go to Scotland?' I tried not
to sound too grumpy.

'I'll sort that out.' Eleanor knew as well as I did that's what
Hazel was going to say. She was also bothered about more
than sorting out lunch breaks. 'I'm not at all sure this is a

good idea, Dan. He pulled a knife on you. He's been in prison and he's been mixing with gangsters ever since he was a kid. What are you going to do if he really is whoever's causing this trouble at this castle?'

'I'll stay out of his reach. Come on, let's get this over with.' I sat on the chair beside her.

Eleanor didn't look happy as she opened the meeting and Hazel logged on. I spoke before the wise woman could open her mouth. I was going to have my say first this time.

'Why me? Why have I got to go and sort out whatever shit Billy Smith's stirring up now?' I took a breath and that was a mistake.

'He already knows you,' Hazel shot straight back. 'That won't risk Carmen or anyone else—'

'So you do have wise women in Scotland. You said—'

'I said we didn't have *many* people there. Many isn't none. But that's all the more reason not to put a single one of them in danger.'

'But you've got no problem sending me to find a violent criminal who's already threatened me with a knife?'

'When you can whistle up a shuck to chase him off? When Billy Smith clearly thought twice about making an enemy of the dryads, the naiads and whoever else he thinks you've got on your side? Yes, I'm fine with that.'

This conversation wasn't going the way I had planned it as I was coming up the stairs. 'Can't you let the police know he's trying to extort a payday from whoever owns this castle? The cops don't have to believe in ghosts to warn him off.'

'What will he do then? Something desperate that puts us all at risk? He has to be stopped. Besides, someone needs to sort this nonsense at the castle, even if our man isn't behind it. You can see ghosts,' Hazel went on, 'and so can I, so—'

'You're coming too?' That knocked me off my stride.

'Of course.' She was surprised that I had to ask.

'Why?' Since I'm not a sodding psychic, she had better explain.

Hazel took a moment before she answered, making an effort to speak more slowly and reasonably. 'Whoever he is, whatever else he might be, Billy Smith's a cunning man. We need to talk to him. We have to find out what he knows.'

'You just want to speak to him?'

'If possible.' Hazel stared at me as if that should be obvious. 'What did you think we were going to do?'

'Nothing.' I could hear for myself that wasn't exactly true, so I picked up something Eleanor had said earlier. 'He's a violent criminal who's been mixing with gangsters since he was a kid. How the hell do you think you'll get him to sit down for a chat? Are you going to invite him for afternoon tea?'

'I'm hoping you will be able to persuade him to at least hear me out. I'm hoping he'll want to know why you've turned up. If he knows we've been able find him again, maybe he'll think twice about running this time. At least until we've talked.'

I could hear that's what Hazel hoped for, but I could tell she was far from certain.

'He said he'd cut me if he saw me again,' I reminded her.

'I know.' She sighed. 'I'll do everything I can to keep you safe, I promise, but we have to try. We can't leave him doing whatever he wants until he causes some trouble that threatens us all. I've got to try and make him see sense.'

'You think you can convince him to stop what he's doing because you say so? He goes after these arseholes because he's convinced the cops won't touch them.'

Hazel hesitated before she answered. 'If necessary, we're prepared to discuss how we might work together to address such problems. We're hardly fans of loan sharks, drug dealers and wife-beaters. If we can do that, we'll know where he is and what he's up to. We can take steps to deal with any disturbances.'

'You'd rather have him inside the tent pissing out, instead of outside the tent pissing in?'

Hazel grimaced at that mental image. 'Yes, I suppose so. It's in everyone's best interests. Even Billy the Cat's.'

'What about Fin and Blanche?'

'It's as much in their interests as anyone else's.' Hazel was confused.

I realised she was only asking me to go with her to Scotland. Since I didn't want her rethinking that, I moved on quickly. I had to admit this did change things. Especially now the Green Man and the Hunter had both turned up to give this plan their backing. Why else would they have been here?

I took a deep breath and turned to Eleanor. 'How soon can I have some more time off, boss?'

We really were going to have to talk about what the rest of the staff thought of that. But not today.

Chapter Twenty-Two

Scotland is a lot further away than you might expect if you've only ever lived in the southern half of England. If you're driving up the west coast, you'll pass Carlisle and see the signposts for Gretna Green. Everyone's heard of Gretna, haven't they? First town across the border where runaway brides in the olden days could get married without their parents' permission. See that and you think you're nearly there. Not so much.

Once you've crossed the Scottish border, you've got an hour or so of driving through farmland and trees and another hour or more after that of hills and moors dotted with sheep, forestry plantations and wind turbines before you get to Glasgow. The motorway takes you through the city easily enough, and all you'll see of the place is tree-lined cuttings alternating with views of industrial estates and retail parks from the elevated sections. You might catch a glimpse of a few Victorian redbrick remnants among the featureless modern buildings.

If you're heading for Argyll, there's another short stretch of farmland before you cross the Clyde on an angular steel bridge, followed by some stop-and-go driving through the towns along the river. After that, the road heads up the western side of Loch Lomond. Hazel kept pointing out interesting things to me, but I barely glanced at the bonnie banks or anything else. Cars heading south on this single-carriageway road had a tendency to drift away from the rail of rusted Armco. That was the only thing between them and a plunge into dangerously deep water. That was understandable, but there was no room to spare on my side of the road and I had nowhere else to go if an oncoming vehicle strayed too far. The steep hillside on the passenger side came right down to the tarmac, with rock faces alternating with stretches of dense woodland still bright with autumn reds and golds. I noticed those trees were choked with enough invasive rhododendron to convince me there were no dryads around.

Those twenty-five miles or so set the pattern for the rest of our journey. The main routes skirted the edges of seemingly endless lochs with dour mountainsides looming overhead. Side turnings were few and far between. Traffic lights controlled access to narrow bridges built back in the days when lorries and cars had been a lot smaller and nowhere near so much traffic came this way. I hated to think how much disruption trying to upgrade those routes would cause nowadays.

Every so often red-painted poles bracketed the road, to show drivers which way to go in deep snow. I really hoped the weather forecast was right and the worst we could expect was rain. I drove carefully and steadily, letting locals prepared to take more risks overtake whenever they wanted. As long as they didn't crash and block my way, that was up to them.

By the time we arrived at the holiday let we had booked in North Argyll, Hazel and I had been on the road for just over eight hours with a couple of breaks and a stop at what looked like the last petrol station we'd see for a while, to top off the fuel tank. I didn't want to risk getting stranded out here.

I was ready to admit the Land Rover wasn't the most comfortable vehicle for doing that sort of distance. Even so, I hadn't changed my mind about refusing to come in Hazel's Fiesta. On the cusp of autumn and winter, and when we were going somewhere this remote, I wanted the Landy's four-wheel drive and solid weight on my side. Hazel's car could stay parked back at Blithehurst.

She got stiffly out of the passenger seat and went to the door halfway along the side of the low, white-painted cottage. I heard her muttering, exasperated, as she pressed black buttons on the grey metal lockbox that should hold the key.

I got our bags out of the back of the Landy. 'Do you want a torch?' In theory, the sun hadn't set, but the clouds meant the light was fading fast. At least it wasn't raining. Yet.

She struggled with the lock for a moment before she opened the door. 'I've got it.'

I followed Hazel inside, stooping through the low doorway and wary until I could be sure I wasn't going to hit my head on an equally low ceiling. I put down our bags and looked for a light switch. Hazel found it first. Recessed lights overhead showed us the place had been recently renovated. An L-shape of kitchen units on the right-hand side included a dishwasher, a washing machine and an oven. The counter-top had a microwave, a toaster and a kettle to the left of the hob. Wall cupboards presumably held crockery and glassware.

A dining table with four chairs was just to the left of the door we'd come through. On the other side of the room, two sofas at right angles made a square with the television on the interior wall and a wood burner on the back wall. Paintings of a shaggy Highland cow and of a couple in evening dress dancing on a beach brightened up the white walls.

Hazel had hung her coat on a hook and opened the door on the other side of the table. 'The bedroom's through here. You'd better take it. I'll be fine on the sofa bed.'

'Thanks.' I wasn't going to argue. I opened the other door at this end of the kitchen counter and found a fancy wet room with a tiled floor. I closed the door behind me and had a pee. That felt a lot better. When I went back into the living room, Hazel had put the kettle on.

'Tea or coffee?' I asked as she headed for the bathroom.

'Coffee.'

I fetched the crate of supplies we'd brought with us from the back of the Landy, along with the cold box. We were miles from any shops, but that wasn't the only consideration. Hazel and I needed to keep a low profile for as long as we could. Billy Smith couldn't be too far away if he was making trouble for the Pennants, the owners of Westerknowe Castle, where these ghosts were supposedly wreaking havoc. When they got desperate enough to call him, the sooner he did his job, the sooner he'd get his payday. We couldn't risk me and Hazel bumping into him in some bar when we were out looking for a steak and chips. Not until we knew exactly what he was doing to screw with the Pennants. That's what we had to find out first.

The cold box held supermarket milk and eggs and a few nukeable meals, along with cheese, bacon and sausages we'd bought at the Tebay Services farm shop. Since we were coming up the M6, I wasn't missing the chance to stop there. We'd also had a substantial lunch in the restaurant. I put everything in the fridge and opened cupboards until I found some supermarket crockery. I made two mugs of instant coffee. It had been a long day and a very long drive.

Hazel came out of the bathroom and rubbed her hands together. 'It's none too warm.'

'I'll light a fire.' I put down my coffee and went to open up the wood burner.

I didn't think it was particularly cold for the last weekend of October, though I was still wearing my fleece. A last trace of lingering heat in the soft, fluffy ashes said the guests who'd checked out this morning had disagreed. The chimney must draw okay since the place didn't smell of smoke.

'Firelighters and matches are in the wooden box behind the full log basket.' Hazel was sitting on a sofa and turning the pages in a ring binder I'd seen on the dining table.

'Got them.' I used my penknife to feather the bark on a couple of smaller pieces of birch tree. 'What are we going to do now?'

'Let me check my email.' Hazel looked from the information folder to her phone and back again as she entered the code to log on to the Wi-Fi.

I put a match to the firelighter and the birch wood caught nicely. I closed the wood burner and went to fetch my coffee. I noticed that the plugs for the kettle, the toaster and the microwave had current electrician's inspection stickers.

'Right,' Hazel said a few moments later. 'As of today, Mr and Mrs Pennant over at the castle are just about ready to try anything. Even calling helpful Liam McGowan, self-proclaimed ghostbuster, especially if he doesn't want money up front. If he can end the upheavals wrecking their business, they'll pay up.'

'Who's telling you this?' I sat down on the other sofa.

'Carmen's friend knows one of their cleaners.' Hazel summarised the email she was reading. 'Even if their guests believe the hideous noises in the night are really just owls or foxes, they're still getting next to no sleep. Most mornings, there's no hot water and some of the toilets have been backing up. Half term week was a disaster, and the latest online reviews are brutal. Carmen says the Pennants are getting cancellations every day, including for bookings over Christmas and New Year.'

'They can't afford that.' I didn't need a spreadsheet to tell me the Pennants could be facing disaster.

'Whatever's going on, sorting it out can't wait,' Hazel agreed. 'Well, Katie Pennant says she'll meet us any time we like.' She raised her eyebrows at me. 'Shall we go over there now?'

'Might as well.' More driving didn't appeal, but the alternative was a microwave lasagne.

Hazel got up from the sofa and fetched her coat from its hook. 'Let me do the talking.'

What she meant was let her tell the lies we'd concocted to get ourselves inside the castle.

'Fine with me.'

As we went back outside and Hazel locked the door, a skein of geese passed high overhead, heading west and barely visible in the last of the light. I wondered what Fin was doing this evening. Telling her I was coming here with Hazel had gone okay, much to my relief. I'd told her more than once that I'd only agreed to this plan because Hazel promised we were only going to talk to Billy Smith.

I'd made my conditions clear and told the wise women they were non-negotiable. We'd meet Billy the Cat out in the open. I'd make sure to keep my distance. I wouldn't threaten him in any way, so he'd have no excuse to retaliate. I'd be ready to summon the shuck the instant he threatened Hazel or me.

Fin had offered to come to Scotland with us all the same, but she had also agreed pretty quickly that just the two of us might be better. If Billy Smith felt outnumbered, that might be enough to provoke him. She also told me she and Blanche had just signed a big new contract. They'd be working flat out gathering water-contamination data for what could end up in a very high-profile court case.

We got into the Land Rover and Hazel put our destination into my satnav. It felt odd having her in the passenger seat instead of Fin. I started the engine and followed the route the satnav highlighted. The narrow, uneven road was barely wide enough for one vehicle and didn't have many passing places. I really hoped we didn't meet something coming the other way as we crossed a steeply hump-backed bridge over a stream I could barely see in the dusk.

I was about to put my foot down, seeing a straighter stretch of road ahead on the satnav map. A dark, four-legged shadow sprang out of the roadside bracken. I slammed on the brakes and stretched out my arm to stop Hazel hitting the dashboard even though she was wearing her seatbelt.

'Bloody hell,' she said, shaken. 'I thought the ponies on Dartmoor were a menace.'

We watched a roe deer's white arse bound off into the twilight. That was another reason I'd wanted to come in the Landy. I'd seen the mess that a deer strike could make of a bigger car than Hazel's Fiesta. Ben Beauchene's expensive Audi had been a write-off the year before last.

I changed down a few gears and accelerated slowly. We both watched the roadsides for any more deer. I noticed that silver birches dominated the woodland around here, though taller sycamores and beeches were doing pretty well. We arrived at Westerknowe Castle's East Lodge without any more excitement. Hazel got out and used the combination Katie Pennant had sent her to unlock the chain that secured the gates. The weathered wood swung open. Hazel pushed the gate wider and I drove the Landy through to park behind the lodge, out of sight of the road.

The building looked deserted, but I was still going to check. Like I said, if Billy the Cat was Liam McGowan, he'd be somewhere close and this was a prime location. I pulled on the thickest and most waterproof coat I'd been able to order in my size for next-day delivery. Even though it wasn't raining. This coat was the best protection I could come up with against unexpected claws in the night. If luck was on my side, even a knife blade might skid off it.

The back door of the lodge looked secure, but I could see the windows were warped and loose in their flaking frames. Anyone willing to spend a bit of time and care could get inside without leaving much of a trace. Especially someone who'd learned how to break into houses when he was a teenager. For the moment though, I didn't think he was in there.

I walked around to the front. Hidden from the road by a tall stone pillar, Hazel waited by the relocked gates. She didn't move as I approached the door, set back under a porch between two bay windows. All very picturesque, but the place would need a new roof before the Pennants could start renting it out to tourists.

I pulled on a pair of work gloves. My hands weren't cold, but I wanted a decent thickness of coarse leather between me and any chance of a blade. I gripped the door-knob and tested it. The varnished wood rotated. I eased the door open a crack, ready to back off fast if Billy Smith was in there, whether he was on two legs or four.

'Who you gonna call?' an American voice said with a shaky laugh. 'Hi, I'm Katie Pennant.'

I opened the door wider and saw a figure outlined against the grey window. 'Hello.'

As I stepped back out onto the porch, Hazel hurried over from the gate. She reached me at the same time as Katie Pennant came out of the empty lodge.

'Hello, it's so nice to meet you. I'm Hazel Spinner and this is Dan, my research assistant and driver.' She offered her hand and the American woman shook it. 'Thank you for meeting us here. I know you said you check the lodge every few days, but it never hurts to be sure.'

'You seriously think this could be someone shaking us down with some sort of trickery?'

I heard the strain in Katie's voice as she locked the lodge's front door and shoved the keys into a pocket of her battered waxed thornproof coat.

'It's one possible explanation. Nearly every case we've investigated has come down to deceit or an overactive imagination. I'm keeping an open mind all the same. Do you believe in ghosts?' Hazel asked.

'Well, there are some pretty convincing stories...' Katie was torn.

Now I understood. She liked the idea of ghosts in a theoretical sort of way. If she caught a glimpse of something uncanny, that would be fine, as long as she could still tell herself it was probably just her imagination. Whatever was going on now though? This wasn't anything she wanted to be real.

'Let's see what we can find out. We go this way?' Hazel started walking along the track that led away from the gate. 'What a lovely place. I can't wait to see it properly in the daylight. Was this the deer park originally?'

Katie walked beside her. 'We are so grateful you've come such a long way. I mean, when we found your website, I didn't think this was your sort of thing...'

'Oh, Dan's intrigued by ghosts. Now, tell me, when did all this start?'

I got a holdall out of the back of the Land Rover and followed them, trying not to grin. Seeing Hazel being so chatty and reassuring was bizarre. Still, that was what she was here to do. The wise women must have worked non-stop for several days and nights putting up convincing posts and comment threads about ghost-hunting on Hazel's website. I have no idea what the Bigfoot fans had made of these conversations suddenly appearing. Presumably, their comments asking WTF was going on were being mercilessly deleted.

Meantime, Carmen and her friends had been busy on local social media. They'd posted stories of ghosts, real and invented. They'd linked to ghost-hunting websites and blogs, only to immediately share their doubts under different usernames. Apart from whenever they mentioned Hazel's website. They'd agreed she was the real thing. Hazel Spinner would get to the truth, whether some supposed apparition was a spiteful hoax or a genuine haunting. I assumed the wise women had also been deleting indignant protests from outraged ghost-hunters pointing out they had years more experience with this sort of mystery.

Most importantly, a thread had been discussing the uncanny goings-on at Westerknowe Castle. Thanks to some search engine optimisation trickery, that was soon one of the first results a search for the place would show. The sort of search a desperate owner would do, looking for the latest updates on their struggling business. Katie Pennant got in touch within the week. Hazel agreed to come up to take a look. Once we knew what was going on, and hopefully put a stop to it, she'd persuade Katie to ring that mobile phone number. We would see what Liam McGowan had to say for himself when he turned up expecting to get paid. Assuming he was Billy Smith, he'd recognise me. He was bound to want to know how I had found him. Once I explained that, Hazel was convinced he'd want to hear what she had to say. That was the plan. I tried not to remember how often things don't go to plan.

Chapter Twenty-Three

As we walked along the track, I tuned out what Katie was saying to Hazel. The wise women had created their own virtual reality online, but the danger we could be walking into was very real indeed. I searched the shadows under the ornamental pine trees planted on either side of the track, looking for any hint of movement. If Billy Smith wasn't lurking in the lodge, Billy the Cat could well be prowling this parkland. He'd be the ideal shape and colour to keep watch on the castle from the darkness.

Hazel and I had discussed this possibility. She argued if he saw us with Katie Pennant, he had no reason to attack her, so he should leave the three of us alone. Even if he suspected we were here to put an end to his scam, he would want to talk to us, to find out what we knew. I reminded her he liked asking questions while he was holding someone at knife-point. Hazel assured me that wouldn't be a problem.

The track led us towards one last stand of Douglas firs. I looked at the nearest tree. Hazel and I had also discussed the pros and cons of me using dryad radar. That could tell us if Billy was lurking somewhere close. Then I remembered the Over Cullen dryad had known I was in her wood as soon as I'd tried to find her in Yorkshire. A quick phone call to my dad got my mum to confirm that dryad radar worked both ways. Hazel and I agreed I should hold off, at least until we knew what was causing trouble here. We didn't want to alert any creature that might be working with Billy Smith.

We rounded the clustered fir trees and saw the castle ahead of us. To be honest, I hadn't been impressed when I'd looked at the photos on their website. My idea of a castle was somewhere more like Kenilworth and Warwick, where I'd gone on school trips.

Westerknowe Castle had four towers, each one set deep into the corners of the solid square building. I guessed it was built from local stone, but the masonry was hidden by a whitewashed coat of render. The four towers had pointed caps like a fairy tale illustration and little windows ran around their outer curved sides in diagonal lines. Bigger windows opened onto the larger rooms between the towers. I counted four storeys in all.

The trees and the coarse grass on either side of the track gave way to an immaculately mown lawn that almost ringed the building. A broad strip of raked gravel circling the base of the castle wall cut through the lawn to head down what must be the driveway to the main entrance. Stone steps led up to a suitably impressive dark wooden door reinforced with metal bars and studs. As we got closer, half-windows at ground level showed there was a basement floor as well. Electric lights down there were lit on the right, though the left-hand side was dark.

'We do B&B in high season, and we host weekend and full-week residential courses year round,' Katie was saying to Hazel. 'Creative writing, poetry, painting, music sometimes. Basically hobbies and activities where people can bring their own equipment. Some groups organise themselves. Sometimes we'll hire a tutor, and obviously that'll be someone who comes well recommended. We provide the workspace as well as accommodation and meals.'

'And you've been open for seven years now?' Hazel knew that already, of course.

'We've had our ups and downs, like everyone else. Renovating the lodges had to be put on hold. But we keep our overheads as low as we can and we haven't had to borrow from the bank. Generally, things were going well.'

Until this bizarre nightmare hit them out of the blue. No wonder Katie sounded so unhappy.

A tall thin man with short steel-grey hair must have been watching from a front window. He opened the front door and came down the steps to meet us. 'Hi. I'm Henry Pennant.'

We did handshakes all round and went up into a sizeable hall that ran the full width of the building and went back about a third of the depth. For a Scottish castle, there was a noticeable lack of deer skulls with antlers on the walls, or artistic arrays of daggers and swords.

'Please,' Henry offered, 'let me take your coats.'

'Thanks.' I was glad to put down the heavy holdall and strip off my bulky waterproof.

Katie hung up her own jacket. Seeing her in the light, I guessed she was about my age. She was blonde and pretty in a way that made me think she should be wearing a cheer-leader's uniform instead of dark corduroys and a creamy Aran sweater.

'You've no guests here at the moment?' Hazel handed her coat to Henry.

'Correct,' he confirmed.

Eleanor had looked into both of the Pennants as well as into their business. She told me they'd made a decent-sized fortune in California, selling some sort of electronic pay-ment protection software they had invented between them. Nothing to do with cryptocurrency, but something genuinely useful. For whatever reason, they'd decided to move to Scot-land. Henry's grandparents on his mother's side had come from Argyll. Wiry in loose jeans and a dark blue cable-knit sweater, he looked quite a bit older than Katie.

'We live in the gatehouse, so you'll have the run of the place to set up your equipment. We're saying we've had to close temporarily on account of a plumbing issue.' The frown line between his eyebrows got deeper and his voice was tight with frustration.

'Do you want to get started, Dan?' Hazel turned to Katie. 'While you show me around?'

Henry looked at me as if he'd only just realised I was there. 'Where do you want to start?'

'In the basement?' I picked up the holdall.

'This way.' Henry crossed the room to open a door to the turret in the corner.

I followed him down a wide stone spiral stair and into a brightly lit kitchen that took up a full quarter of the building's footprint. It was fully equipped with a commercial-sized range cooker, spotless steel work surfaces and what looked like every appliance a caterer could possibly need. Only the stone vaulted ceiling overhead would remind you this was a castle.

Henry looked around. 'There's been no trouble in here, but do you want to set up – whatever it is you're here to set up?'

'Not where there hasn't been any trouble.' That didn't surprise me, standing there surrounded by all this metal.

Henry shook his head and sighed. 'Please don't take this the wrong way, but do you seriously believe in this supernatural BS?'

He clearly didn't, but equally, he hadn't been able to come up with any other answers. I was willing to bet he had tried. He looked utterly exhausted in the harsh fluorescent light.

'A lot of people do believe it, and frauds take advantage of that if they see a chance.' Like Billy Smith, if he was behind this. I remembered what Hazel had said earlier too. 'Most reports of ghosts turn out to be fakes, or a figment of someone's imagination, but we keep an open mind.'

Henry tossed his keys from hand to hand. 'Have you ever heard of this McGowan guy?'

'Not until a couple of weeks ago.' That was the honest truth.

'Yeah. Well, whatever he's selling, I don't buy it.' Henry turned to push open the door to the next room and switched on another light. 'But I can't explain this. Every morning, we come down here first thing and something else has been smashed or ripped open. Pickles, jams, pasta, flour, tea bags, you goddamn name it.'

I followed him into a storeroom that took up another quarter of the basement. Now I could see how these thick stone walls were taking the load of the floors and the rooms up above. Wooden shelves on all sides were stacked high with catering-sized packets, jars and tins as well as enough standard groceries to stock a corner shop. Cupboard units made an island in the centre topped with a composite work surface. I put the holdall down on that.

Henry looked at the bag, still sceptical. 'Do you need power for your equipment? Shall I clear some shelf space?'

'The units are self-contained, thanks. Let me see all the rooms down here first. Then I can decide what goes where.'

Making his fortune in software wouldn't necessarily mean Henry Pennant was good with technology, but now that I'd met him, I didn't think he'd be too impressed by what I had in the bag. Fin's cousin Will, the photographer, had found us some cheap battery-powered, Wi-Fi-enabled surveillance cameras online. When they had arrived, I'd stayed up late fitting them into black-painted wooden boxes along with sound-activated recorders. Everything worked, obviously, in case the Pennants insisted on taking a closer look, but anyone with a credit card, an address for deliveries and a few basic tools could have put them together.

I looked at the door in the far corner. 'Is that another staircase?'

'There's one in each turret, leading all the way to the roof. Watch your step here,' Henry warned as he headed for the door leading to the rear basement. 'This morning's surprise? Cooking oil all over the floor. We've cleaned up, but...'

I'd bet that had been sunflower oil in a plastic bottle. I'd bet those big tins of olive oil were never touched. I wondered about the coffee beans I could see stacked in foil packets, but I didn't ask as I followed him into the next cellar. Three big upright steel freezers stood against the wall to our right and the wooden shelves in here had wicker baskets for storing fruit and vegetables.

'Fresh produce is the only thing that goes missing. Who breaks in to steal five goddamn zucchini? Why not the venison out of the freezer? And we've got a goddamn state-of-the-art security system. How come that never goes off?'

Henry stared at me as if he expected me to have some answers. A moment later, he shook his head. 'I'm sorry. It's just... it gets to me. You know?'

'I can imagine.' I could have given him some answers now, if there was any way he would believe me.

A boggart eating a carrot squatted under the lowest shelf over in the corner by the turret door. It was smaller than the ones I was used to seeing, with a thicker pelt of darker hair. If it came out and stood up to challenge me, it would be barely more than knee high. Those clawed hands and feet were the same though, along with its stubby, twisted limbs and barrel-shaped body.

No medieval stone mason had ever carved a gargoyle this grotesque, with its squashed muzzle and randomly sticking-out teeth. Imagine a cartoon bulldog that's been smacked in the face with a frying pan. Its pointed ears were scarred and torn. Every boggart gets bitten and clawed from its earliest days by the rest of its gang as they squabble over food or fight over some small creature one of them has caught to torment and eat.

Seeing me, it shuffled backwards to hide in deeper shadow. All I could see was the malevolent gleam of its piggy little eyes as it watched my every move. For the moment I gave no sign that I knew it was there.

The door to the rear turret was half open, and a faint sheen of light fell on the stone stairs. More light than I would expect from the small windows I'd seen from outside. 'Does that go up to a back entrance?' I asked.

Henry nodded. 'With motion sensors, pressure pads on the glass, the works.'

Which meant someone had let these boggarts in here. Billy the Cat might be selling herbs and teas these days, but I guessed he'd kept his house-breaking skills up to date. However good the Pennants' alarm system might be, it looked as if the cunning man was better.

'This used to be the scullery. Now it's where we've put the dishwashers and the laundry.' Henry opened the final door and took a hasty step back from the foul smell. 'I swear, we've had every plumber within fifty miles in to check these goddamn drains. We've had the septic tank pumped as well.'

That wouldn't help. Boggarts reek. I heard hasty claws scrabble on the stone floor in the darkness, though Henry clearly didn't. I'd been wondering where the rest of them were. See one boggart and there'll be more nearby. Like sewer rats, only not as appealing, and not just because they stink. Their spite and malice seeps into everything around them once they make a lair.

'Do you want to see in there?' Henry closed the door while he waited for my answer.

'Let's go back upstairs. I want to talk to Hazel about where to site the monitors.'

'Fine with me.' Relieved, Henry headed for the turret.

I quickly retrieved the holdall before I went after him. Boggarts will smash things just because they can. I still didn't look directly at the little bastard lurking under the shelves in the corner. As long as it wasn't sure I had spotted it, there was a chance it would stay put.

I followed Henry up to the ground floor. We found Hazel and Katie in the big wood-panelled room that took up the rear two-thirds of the ground floor. Dining tables for two or four had been pushed to one side with chairs stacked beside them. There were some very nice paintings of what I guessed were local scenic views. The countryside around here must be impressive in the daylight.

'I swear, one bride-to-be had three different swatches in her purse,' Katie was saying. 'The family tartan which her father and brothers would be wearing, then the groom's, and the best man's. So I decided on plain dark grey carpets. At least the floor wouldn't clash.'

She was clearly used to telling that story, to put guests at their ease with a laugh. Right now, she could barely force a smile. She looked at Henry, anxious.

'One of us should get back. We've left the kids with a sitter,' she explained to us, apologetic.

'You could both go,' Hazel suggested. 'We can call you when we're ready to leave. One of you can come over and lock up, and walk us back to our car.'

Then you can be sure we haven't stolen anything, she didn't say. I could see that Henry appreciated what she meant. I could also see that Hazel wanted time alone in the castle with me. I backed her up.

'It will be easier to set up our monitors if I don't have to worry about someone tripping them accidentally.'

Henry stood motionless, then nodded abruptly. 'Okay. Fine.'

He held out a hand to Katie. She took it and they went through to the entrance hall without a word. We heard the main door slam a moment later.

'I'm not surprised they can't wait to get out of here,' I commented. 'The basement's full of boggarts.'

'They really must love each other. A lot of couples would be at each other's throats by now. Let's be thankful their children aren't sleeping here.' Hazel walked towards the rear turret door. 'Unfortunately, that's not their only problem.'

'What else have you found?' I'd guessed there had to be more to this. Boggarts are vile, but they're stupid. Their limit would be breaking things, eating things, making a mess of the stores and shitting down plugholes. Interfering with hot-water systems would be way beyond them.

'Up here.' Hazel went up the spiral stair. She waved at the first door we reached, but she didn't stop to open it. 'This floor is just one big hall with a partition to divide it into two, front to back. There's nothing to see.'

I followed her to the next floor, and we walked out into a half-panelled passage. I saw this corridor linked the four turrets in a broad H-shape, lit by windows beside each stair door.

'Bedrooms with en-suites.' Hazel gestured as we passed them. 'Two at the front, two at the back, one on each side, all spacious and luxurious with mountain views. The layout's the same on the top floor. And then there's this.'

A hob sat cross-legged on the pale grey carpet. It – he – wore a long tunic of some coarse, ruddy material with another length of the same stuff draped over one shoulder. His wiry brown hair had hints of green and purple that reminded me of heather while his skin was as dark as the granite rock faces we'd driven past on our way here. His golden eyes shone as he looked me up and down, getting my measure and looking very unimpressed.

I'd met hobs before. I knew they could be appallingly inventive and persistent if they decided to make some unsuspecting mortal's life a misery. I had no reason to think this one would be any less capable.

On the plus side, hobs love to make a deal. Once we knew what Billy Smith had promised, as long as we could come up with a better offer, we had to be in with a decent chance of getting them to leave the Pennants alone. Then we could deal with the boggarts, which should be easy enough.

The hob stood up and took his time settling the drape of his wrap. He was about half my height, but his shoulders were easily the width of my hips. Hobs are strong. I decided not to get too close. If he attacked, his first blow would be a straight punch to my balls.

Satisfied with his wrap, he looked at Hazel. 'Dè tha sibh ag iarraidh sassenachs.'

I hadn't got a hope of understanding that.

Hazel looked at me, equally at a loss. 'I saw another one upstairs. I'm guessing she's his wife or his mate or whatever. But how do we negotiate if we can't even talk to them?'

'Is he speaking Gaelic?' I'd guessed that was the second language I'd seen on local road signs.

'I wouldn't know it if I heard it,' Hazel admitted.

I stared at the hob. He stared back at me. His lip curled with contempt, and he walked away, straight into the nearest wood-panelled wall.

We went back down to the rear hall on the ground floor. Hazel stared out of the windows, not focusing on anything in particular. 'What do we do now?'

The black nylon holdall was where I'd left it on one of the dining tables. I unzipped it. 'Let's get these set up.'

Hazel looked at me. I answered her unspoken question. 'That's what the Pennants are expecting us to do. And if we can't talk to those hobs, at least we can deal with those boggarts. They won't know what these are, but they'll know we brought them into the castle. You know they're wary of anything unfamiliar. With any luck, they'll stick to the back basement tonight, just to be on the safe side.'

If they didn't, they wouldn't get picked up on audio or video, so the end result would be the same if Henry Pennant asked to see what our supposed monitors had recorded.

Hazel came over and took four of the wooden boxes out of the holdall. 'Anywhere in particular?'

'Tuck them in corners. Point them at the doors.' I went down to the storeroom with the holdall and put one on the shelf by the door from the kitchen. I flicked the switch and a pinprick of red light glowed on the side of the box. Any boggart sneaking in here couldn't fail to see it. Red for danger, like a shuck's gaze.

I put another fake monitor in the back basement where the freezers were and stuck the rest around the rooms on the ground floor. Then I went up the spiral stair, looking for Hazel. I met her coming down from the floor where we'd met the hob we couldn't talk to.

'Right, that's done,' she said briskly. 'So how do you suggest we get rid of those boggarts?'

I'd been thinking about that. 'I generally throw six-inch nails at them until they bugger off. They're cowards when they're faced with someone bigger than they are. But chasing them off might not be so easy here. They know these cellars are an all-they-can-eat buffet, and someone must have opened that back door to let them in. I reckon it was that bastard Billy Smith, and there's no guarantee he won't just do that again as soon as we leave. They obviously like it here. I mean, they don't normally lair in places where people are coming and going all day.'

'Let's go back to the cottage and make some calls. Some-one might have some bright ideas to get rid of them for good.' Hazel held her phone to her ear as we walked back to the entrance hall. 'Hello, Mr Pennant? Of course, excuse me. Henry. We've got everything here set up now, so if you want to come and lock up, we can be on our way. We'll come back first thing tomorrow to see what the monitors might have recorded.'

I wondered how much sleep she planned on getting. I wondered how much sleep she was going to allow me. I might have to remind her how many hours I'd spent driving today. Thinking about going to bed was a mistake. I felt an overwhelming urge to yawn, even though it wasn't actually that late. The darkness outside was deceptive this far north at this time of year.

Hazel listened to Henry. 'Of course. That's very kind of you. He's going to give us a lift back to the East Lodge,' she explained as she ended the call.

That was the best news I'd heard since we got here. 'How about we suggest Henry locks those connecting doors in the basement? If the boggarts can't get from one cellar to the next, that should limit the damage tonight.' I was still trying to think of ways to help the Pennants, even just a little.

'Can you explain how a locked door is supposed to stop a ghost?' Hazel wasn't being critical. If I could come up with an answer, she'd back it. Unfortunately, I couldn't think of one.

She took her coat off its hook. 'Besides, if those vermin realise they can't get out, they could trash the room they're in completely. What do we say when Henry or Katie asks if our supposed monitors recorded what did the damage? If they ask to take a look?'

'I'm starting to think this ghostbusters bollocks is going to be more trouble than it's worth.' I found my heavy waterproof but didn't put it on. I'd be warm enough in my sweat-shirt.

'Feel free to suggest something else.' Hazel shrugged herself into her coat.

A few minutes later, we heard a powerful engine outside. At least a V6. When Henry Pennant opened the door, I saw he was driving a black pick-up truck with a crew cab.

He stood outside on the steps. 'Ready to go?'

'All done, for now.' I was folding the black canvas holdall flat so Henry could see that was empty. I draped it over my arm with the waterproof on top of it.

'Let me set the alarm.' We waited while he activated the security system using an app on his phone. He drove us back to the East Lodge without saying another word until we arrived. 'I'll get the gate.'

'We'll see you first thing tomorrow,' Hazel said cheerfully as we got out of the pick-up.

Henry didn't answer. He was already walking over to undo the combination lock on the chain.

Chapter Twenty-Four

I looked at the lodge, alert for any sign that anyone had been here since we had arrived. I couldn't see any cause for concern. We got into the Landy, and I drove out through the gate. It really was pitch dark out here, even with my green-wood night sight. Going carefully along the narrow, uneven road, I was glad the satnav map was showing me the shape of the route ahead.

Hazel started listing things to do. 'I'll call Carmen first. We need to get in touch with someone, ideally someone not too far away, who'll be able to see those hobs, and who can tell us what language they're speaking. Once we can talk to them, we can find out what they want. We'll have to find some excuse for calling someone else in. And we'll have to come up with a reason to keep the Pennants out of the castle while we're trying to make a deal with them. It would be good if we could show some rapid progress. Like getting rid of those filthy boggarts. Dan?'

'What?' I'd been thinking about some supper. One of those microwave lasagnes would be quickest, but a sausage sandwich wouldn't take too long. Thick, buttered bread, a smear of mustard on one slice, not too much tomato ketch-up on the other.

'Sorry. I reckon I should try the dryad radar tomorrow. To see who else might be around. Maybe a local dryad or a naiad who could help us talk to the hobs.'

I hadn't seen any rhododendrons around here, though that might not mean anything. I knew the National Trust and other organisations were busy eradicating the damn things. The satnav display showed me the corner coming up as we approached the little bridge. I adjusted the steering wheel, ready to make the turn.

'Perhaps,' Hazel said, thoughtful, 'if—'

'Quiet.' The steering felt wrong. The sound of the tyres on the tarmac was wrong. Fuck. If we didn't make the turn to the bridge, I had no idea what the drop to the stream might be like. I changed down the gears and braked as fast as I dared. I pulled up as far to the side of the narrow road as I could get without risking leaving the tarmac. There was no verge, and I had no way to know how soft the ground under the heather might be.

'What's wrong?' Hazel demanded.

'I'm not sure.' I got out before she could say anything else. I put the sole of my boot on top of the closest tyre and leaned my weight on it. That one was fine. It should be. I'd checked the pressures on all four wheels at the garage when I'd fuelled up for this trip. The tyre at the back on my side was okay as well. The rear tyre on the passenger side wasn't. I felt it give under my weight. I got my phone out to use as a torch as I squatted down and checked the tyre valve. That wasn't damaged.

'Dan?' Hazel lowered her window, concerned.

'Wait a minute.' I checked for traffic before I walked back around the Land Rover to the front passenger tyre. This was a bloody awful place to have to stop. Anyone approaching in the dark would see the Landy's headlights, but keeping those on would run the battery down. If we were still here when it got light tomorrow, a local belting along familiar roads would be on us before they realised they didn't have room to get past.

I tested the other front tyre with my boot. This one was even softer. The valve was also intact. Fuck.

Hazel opened her door and got out. 'What's going on?'

I was kneeling down, holding my phone torch in one hand as I ran my fingertips carefully over the thick tread. I'd replaced all four tyres just over a month ago. I could probably have got another couple of hundred miles out of the best two old ones, but I had at least one long winter journey ahead of me, going from Blithehurst to Warwickshire to Yorkshire and back again.

'Daniel?' Hazel was getting impatient.

'Hang on.' I had to lie down on the road to get a good look at what I could feel on the underside of the tyre. It was a shiny new nail. Bastard. Fucking bastard. He must have been lurking in the castle grounds after all. I was too used to dealing with creatures who'd steer clear of vehicles. I should have thought he might go after the Landy.

'You've got a puncture?' Hazel had seen the flattened base of the tyre. 'Where's the jack? You get the spare.'

'Wait.' I got to my feet and checked for approaching headlights again. No help was coming. 'We've got two punctures. Both tyres. I've just found a nail and I'll bet anything you like there's another one at the back.'

'Billy Smith?' Hazel turned in a slow circle, staring out into the darkness.

'Who else?' I looked and I listened hard. All I heard was the untroubled rustle of vegetation and the soft patter of the stream trundling along its rocky bed.

'I haven't got a signal.' Hazel was looking at her phone. 'Have you?'

I switched off the torch function and checked my screen. 'No.'

Did Billy Smith know there was no reception along here? Had he stuck enough nails in tyres to know precisely where we'd be likely to stop? Was he just hoping we'd crash and end up injured or dead? Either way, had he been following us since we left the castle? I hadn't been driving fast and a big

281

cat could make decent speed over this terrain. The darkness wouldn't bother him.

I wondered about driving on with those two slow punctures regardless. That would most likely ruin the expensive new tyres, and that pissed me off. When we caught up with Billy Smith, I'd sodding well bill him. But if we got back to the cottage, we'd have broadband and a whole lot more options.

Something growled in the darkness.

'Get in the—'

Hazel was already moving. She hit the lock on her side as I slid into my seat and slammed my own door.

'What—?'

The cat landed on the bonnet. The whole front end of the Land Rover sank down on its suspension. Thank fuck we weren't in a Fiesta. The cat crouched low and snarled, looking from me to Hazel through the windscreen and back again. Those teeth were sodding enormous. Saliva sprayed across the glass as it roared. I hit the wipers and pressed the button for screen wash. The cat recoiled, falling backwards off the dented bonnet.

'Dan!' Hazel protested. 'Don't provoke him!'

I wasn't listening. I'd turn the fucker into a rug if I could. I turned the key and put my foot down hard. The Land Rover lurched forward. I didn't feel the bumper hit anything and there was no sign of the cat in the headlights.

Hazel screamed as the passenger-door window smashed. Billy Smith stood there, grinning with a lump of granite in one hand and his gleaming knife in the other. I threw open my door and grabbed Hazel's arm. She yelped as I dragged her across both seats, out of his reach. A shower of broken safety glass hit the tarmac around my feet.

Billy hadn't tried to stab Hazel. The bastard had disappeared. I pressed my back to the side of the Landy, ready to use the open door as a shield, as best I could. 'Where did he go?'

'I don't know.' Hazel twisted around so she could sit in the driving seat instead of lying across it.

I didn't feel sleepy now. The darkness pressed close all around us, but nothing disturbed the peaceful night-time sounds. It took me a moment to realise the Landy's engine had stalled.

'Move over. I'll drive.' I'd take it as slow as I could, but we had to get out of here.

Hazel slid over to the passenger seat, keeping as far from the broken window as possible.

I turned the key and the bridge collapsed. Tarmac sagged and tore as the steep span crumbled from the centre. The arched walls on either side fell outwards with their stones still mortared solidly together, landing in the water with loud splashes.

'What did that?' Hazel demanded. 'What's out there? What can you see?'

'Nothing.' I was straining my eyes, searching the edge of the darkness beyond the headlights.

I thought about getting out and going around to the back of the Landy. A tyre iron would be a useful weapon against any supernatural creature. It would do Billy Smith no good either, whatever shape he was in. Of course, hitting a badger baiter with a spade and breaking his arm was how I'd ended up with a criminal record. Could I claim self-defence if I showed the cops his knife? Hazel would be a witness that he'd threatened her.

What if I killed him though, if I hit his head by mistake? I'd be in a shitload of trouble. Unless we dropped his body down some rocky crevasse or in a bog. I remembered stories of lost hikers whose bodies weren't found for decades, and no one would even be looking for Billy Smith. He'd been successfully dumping corpses for years. Maybe I was going to find out if I could kill a man after all. If it really was him or me or Hazel.

Fuck that. Trying to get a tyre iron was a stupid idea. As soon as I stepped out of the Landy, Billy would see his chance to attack. If he took me down, Hazel was completely screwed.

'What now?' Her voice was taut, but she wasn't panicking. Not yet.

'Time to run away and live to fight another day. We can't drive on with no bridge, so we'll have to go on foot. If you do that as a hare, I can use my greenwood blood to not be noticed.' I reached for the satnav and zoomed out on the map, to show me the whole shape of the route back to our rental cottage. I concentrated on fixing the way we had to go in my mind's eye.

'Can you indeed?' Hazel's surprise told me she'd be asking for details later. 'Where are we going?'

'Not back to the castle. The Pennants have kids. It's a fair way to the cottage, but we can follow the road once we get over the stream. Well?' I looked at her, reaching for my door handle.

'Let's go for it.' She handed me the rental cottage keys.

I thought for a moment about grabbing my big waterproof. No, I'd get too hot, and I'd move more easily without its restricting bulk. Buying that had been another half-assed idea. This whole trip had been nothing but rushed decisions we were going to regret.

I left the Landy's lights on and locked it, for whatever that might be worth. I zipped my keys and the cottage keys in the secure pocket of my combats, along with my wallet and phone. I only hoped I would get back to find the Land Rover hadn't been stolen or totalled by some wanker crashing into it. But that was a problem for later.

We walked forward to the broken edge of the bridge. Trying to clamber down that rubble was asking for trouble. I looked upstream and down. Nowhere looked promising, but going upstream would mean we were heading in the right direction.

'Where are we going to cross?' Hazel hadn't changed into a hare yet, still looking around for any sign of the enemy.

'Let's try this way.' I stepped off the road, testing every step before I trusted my weight to the uneven ground. Now I was more concerned about stepping into a bog than a rabbit hole. I'd seen how these little streams – burns – cut through marshy meadows along the valley bottoms. The steep span of the bridge showed me how much higher the water could get when snowfall that made those red-painted poles necessary was melting.

Plants I couldn't identify in the darkness clawed at my bootlaces and trouser legs. I thought very hard about not being seen. Since the footing seemed pretty good, I walked faster, heading for a spindly birch sapling.

'Please.' I grasped the little tree firmly by the trunk. I sensed nothing, apart from Hazel. At least, no hint of any presence that might be Billy the Cat. There were sleepy animal presences, clusters of roosting birds and a flurry of indignant fish. All of those were pretty close. Was that because this tree was so small, or because it wasn't an oak? I wished dryad radar came with a bloody handbook. My satnav did, even if I hadn't read it.

Still, something was better than nothing. I started walking again. We reached the stream and I searched the water for white ruffles that might show us a shallower stretch where we could cross. We'd end up with wet feet, but that was the least of my worries.

Hazel was still walking beside me. 'Don't worry,' she said quietly. 'He can't see me, and I can't see you at all, unless I focus my third eye.'

Her what? I'd ask her later. We walked along the winding stream. I tried to concentrate on finding a place to cross, but I couldn't help looking over to the road or back towards the castle. Where was the bastard? Every time I looked behind me, I half expected to see that big black cat. This was like some sodding horror movie. Ten times scarier when you can't see the monster. I rubbed the scars on my forearm through my sweatshirt sleeve. Not so much as an itch. But how much warning would I get if the cat was moving really fast?

Then I realised the stream sounded louder. I saw a scatter of flat stones and gravel breaking through the water. This had to be the best place to cross that we were going to find. I stepped down, testing my footing yet again. This wasn't the time to get careless. Cold water seeped through my lace holes to soak my socks. Never mind that. I took another step and another one. Something shifted underfoot when I was halfway across, and I flung out my arms to keep my balance. I managed not to fall over.

When my heart rate had slowed to something approaching normal, I went on. By the time I reached the far bank, my feet were freezing. When I tried to step out of the water, the ground crumbled under my boot, throwing me forward. I twisted to fall onto my side, shielding my face with my arm. Hiking at night is all fun and games until someone loses an eye or breaks their bloody wrist.

A hare bounded up the disintegrating bank beside me. I sat up and found I had a few nasty scratches, but my sweatshirt had been thick enough to stop anything worse. I scrambled out of the stream and saw Hazel was human-shaped again, motionless and tense as she looked towards the road we were trying to reach.

JULIET E. MCKENNA

The rumble and crash of falling rocks ahead told me we had something new to worry about. One of the tall dark outcrops we'd passed earlier had collapsed. The boulders rolling furthest tumbled across the tarmac and into the meadow. The road was completely blocked. If this was some random rockslide, I had the wreckage of a little stone bridge for sale.

Something moved in the darkness. A massive figure was squatting by the freshly scarred rock face. It was roughly human-shaped, and if it stood up, it would be as tall as one of the castle's turrets. The night air was filled with the smell of newly turned earth, and of water bubbling up from deep underground.

A noise so low it was on the edge of hearing sounded like mocking laughter as the thing turned its head our way. I saw two pale glints that must be its eyes. The thing's gaze was as cold as winter snow.

'If we were on Dartmoor, I'd say that was Old Crockern.' Hazel was intrigued.

Seriously? I wanted to know how we were going to get past the sodding thing without it stamping on our heads. I guessed it couldn't move very fast, but something that size wouldn't have to. A couple of strides and it could squash us flat.

I swallowed hard. 'What's that, exactly?'

'Old Crockern?' Hazel whispered like a birdwatcher who's spotted something really rare. 'Legends say he's the spirit of the moor. I've been doing a bit of exploring up around the tors. I'm trying to work out where giants could have come from.'

If she said anything else, I didn't hear it. I was face down in a clump of dead bracken with a cat as big as I was crouching on my back. I could barely breathe with his weight pressing down on me. Just when I thought I was going to pass out, his back feet shifted to straddle my legs. That relieved some of the crushing pressure, but other than that, I wasn't any better off. I felt the pinprick of lethal talons through my sweatshirt and my T-shirt as the shapeshifter pawed at my shoulder. He wanted me to roll over. I really didn't want to.

We didn't have pets when I was a kid. Mum dislikes the idea of captive animals, though she agrees most pet dogs couldn't fend for themselves and they would be miserable on their own. Dad wasn't bothered either way. But Nick, my mate from primary school, his family had three cats. I sometimes went to his house to play, until his mum got a new job and they moved to Oxford. Their white cat with patches of every other colour was the oldest and the cleverest. She would jump onto the sofa beside you and tug at your hand with her paw when she wanted to be stroked. If you were a bit slow, she'd tug harder, with her razor-sharp claws pricking your skin to make sure you got the hint.

The shapeshifter's claws dug in deeper. He growled, low and insistent. I got the message. If he had to roll me over, I'd lose a sizeable amount of skin. I got my hands underneath my chest and pushed myself up a few inches, to show I was cooperating.

The cat planted his front feet on the ground either side of my shoulders. Struggling over onto my back wasn't easy with the bastard right above me. I tried not to remember Nick's fluffy tabby cat. One time, I'd tickled his pale furry belly. That had been a trap. As Nick's mum washed off the blood in the kitchen sink and found some sticking plasters, she explained how cats in the wild hold their prey down with their mouth and front paws and rake with their hind legs to disembowel them.

If Billy the Cat did that to me now, I was well and truly fucked. Unless I could choke him senseless. Could I get my hands up to grab his neck? Should I go for his eyes? I suddenly had another idea. I lay limp, as if I'd surrendered. I turned my palm upwards beside my hip and flung my hand up. As soon as I felt silky fur, I grabbed hold of a loose fold of skin. I dug my fingernails in deep. I gripped as hard as I could and twisted even harder.

The cat's yowl deafened me. His muzzle smacked into the bridge of my nose so hard I saw a flash of yellow light. As he hissed with pain and fury, I felt drool trickle onto my cheek. I threw my head from side to side as if that could stop the bastard biting my face off. At least I didn't have to see it coming. I screwed my eyes tight shut.

I didn't die. Instead, I felt a cool night breeze brush across my face and a hell of a pain in my right wrist, as the cat smacked my hand with one massive paw to make me loosen my grip. When I let go, he sprang away, crashing through the undergrowth. I scrambled to my feet, breathing hard as I assessed the damage to my wrist. It was badly bruised, but not broken. That was some relief, as I looked in all directions, planting my feet as solidly as I could. I still had no idea how I was going to get out of this nightmare. Billy the Cat had every advantage on his side.

Then I realised a dark-haired, clean-shaven bloke was crouching in the undergrowth. He was rubbing his side. He stood up and walked towards me. He wore battered hiking boots with thick socks, and long hiking shorts above very hairy shins. His old-style rugger shirt with a collar made me think he should be playing fly-half.

Chapter Twenty-Five

'You keep your wits about you,' the unknown shapeshifter said, rueful. He was maybe a few years younger than me, with a Scottish accent I hadn't heard before.

'Who the fuck are you?'

'My name's Peter and I see no call for foul language,' he said mildly.

'I'm Dan.' And I wasn't going to apologise for swearing given the day I'd had. 'Where's Billy the Cat?'

The stranger pursed his lips. 'What's he done to bring you all this way?'

'That's between me and him.' Now I'd realised the biggest mistake we had made. When the wise women had said Billy Smith must have learned to shift into cat form, we should have asked ourselves who the hell had taught him.

'No, it's not, I'm afraid.' This new cat man did sound genuinely apologetic. 'We need to know how he's offended you before we can go any further.'

'Where is he?' I demanded.

'He's gone to ground just now. That's no great surprise. He knows he'll have to answer for bringing trouble down on the rest of us.' Peter smiled, friendly enough. 'Perhaps you can help us. Perhaps we can help each other.'

'How many of you is "us" and "we"?' I asked.

'We'll get to that in good time.' He glanced around, frowning slightly before looking back to me. 'One good turn deserves another. What can we do to balance the books, if you help us bring Billy to heel?'

That was a no-brainer. 'Clear up the trouble he's made at Westerknowe Castle for the Pennants. Then I'll think about helping you.'

Peter shook his head again. 'Help us catch Billy and we'll gladly help you, but we have to catch him first. We have to know what bargains he's made at the castle if we're to undo them.'

Bugger. The Scotsman had a good point. Also, I would need his help if I was to stand any chance of catching Billy the Cat. Even if he only had one or two mates with him, that was more support than I had. There was no sign of Hazel. She must be hiding somewhere in her hare form, watching and listening. Or she might be racing back to the holiday cottage without looking back.

I nodded. 'I want your word on it. That you – that all of you – will make things right at Westerknowe, as soon as you've got hold of Billy Smith.'

'Agreed. My oath on it.'

I could tell Peter was completely sincere. That was a start.

'How do you think I can help you catch him?'

'It seems he wants to talk to you. So if he was to see you walking along the road alone—'

'You want me to be bait, you mean?' I rubbed my aching wrist.

'If you like.' He wasn't apologising. 'We'll get to him before he reaches you, don't fret about that. Then he can explain himself to the rest of us. We'll set up a meeting where you can tell your side, and we can discuss who needs to make amends.'

I wanted to say sod that for a game of soldiers. Unfortunately, I could see this was most likely the quickest way to catch Billy Smith. If these cunning men dealt with one of their own causing trouble by asking for both sides of the story, he wouldn't want me crossing paths with any other cats. He would want to kill me, so I couldn't challenge whatever bullshit yarn he was going to spin.

'Well?' Peter prompted. 'Do we have a deal?'

'Yes.' I looked at the blocked road and the menacing presence by the shattered rocks. I could still see the chilling gleam of its eyes in the darkness. 'What the hell is that thing?'

'Oh, we'll settle him down again, never you mind.' Peter pointed back across the stream, at the road leading to the castle. 'Let's head that way, shall we?'

'Okay.' I certainly didn't want to get any closer to the thing by the rockfall, and the sooner we were back at Westerknowe, the sooner we could solve the Pennants' problems. 'Is there a better place for me to cross the water?'

Peter shook his head. 'Not that I know of.'

Oh well. My socks and boots were already sodden. I found the stretch of bank where we'd forded the stream earlier. As I looked for a safer place to step down, where the dark, crumbly soil hadn't already given way, I glanced from side to side, hoping to see Hazel. Nothing. I realised I couldn't see Peter either.

Before I could think of running, a great black cat bounded out of the darkness. He cleared the stream in a single leap. Bastard. He didn't have to bother about getting his feet wet.

I got across the stream without falling in. When I was about halfway to the road on the other side, I pretended to kneel and retie a bootlace. I'd stopped beside the little birch tree I'd taken hold of before. This time, the dryad radar showed me more things than I could make sense of. Whatever had been roused to block the road with that rockfall was a massive, malevolent presence. More cunning men were clustered over there, keeping their distance from the fearsome thing. Others were scattered through the valley, but I had no way to know which one might be Billy Smith.

There were a lot more of them than I expected. Why was that such a surprise? I had allies I could rely on. People who could do things I can't. Why had I assumed Billy Smith was a loner? We knew he had access to multiple names and bank accounts. I should have put these pieces together a lot sooner. I should have realised how much trouble Hazel and I were driving into. We should have waited and planned this far more thoroughly. What was rushing into this going to cost us before it was over?

I forced myself to concentrate. I needed to focus on what was happening here and now. I sensed a lot of animals being disturbed by the night's upheavals, but I still couldn't find Hazel. I told myself that the wise woman hadn't survived this long by being stupid.

Seeing Peter was back on two feet and walking towards me, I let go of the little birch tree and stood up. I walked up to the road and checked the Land Rover. If we both got out of this in one piece, we would need that roadworthy to get home. Peter stood and watched me.

I glanced at him. 'You said something about amends? Someone owes me the price of two new tyres and the cost of replacing that window.'

He nodded. 'Duly noted.'

That wasn't a promise to pay me. I was about to challenge him on that when he vanished. I didn't see the flash of uncanny light that dazzles me when Fin shifts into her swan form. Peter seemed to be sucked into an eerie shadow. That was unnerving.

I breathed deep. There was no point in hanging around. I left my keys zipped in my pocket. Leaving the Landy's lights on would drain the battery, but if someone drove up this road, seeing the parked vehicle should slow them down. Hopefully they'd see the bridge wasn't there any more before they crashed into the river.

I started walking towards the castle, lengthening my stride like a man with somewhere important to go. I listened hard for any sound of something stalking me, for any hint of footsteps behind me on the road. I didn't hear anything, but Westerknowe's East Lodge had just come into view when the scars on my forearm burned like the touch of white-hot metal.

A big black cat raced towards me, murderous fangs bared in a snarl. I braced myself. The cat accelerated. Three more cats appeared behind him, chasing. So much for Peter's promises. They were too far away. Billy would reach me before they could catch him. I tensed, ready to throw myself off the road, one way or the other, as soon as he committed to his leap. I hoped I'd be fast enough. I hoped I'd go the right way to escape those claws. I couldn't fight back with only one useful hand.

He didn't get a chance to jump me. The road was completely empty, but he managed to trip over something. The cat stumbled and his front paw buckled. His shoulder hit the deck, but his back legs didn't get the memo in time to stop. He flipped over onto his back in a clumsy somersault.

The three cats chasing him leaped. They landed on him, snarling and wrestling. I saw claws flashing and long tails lashing, but I had no hope of working out who was who, or who might come out on top. I did see Hazel, or rather I saw a hare lollop into the middle of the road to watch the giant cats ripping into each other.

She looked at me and wiped her long ears with her paws before dashing back into cover. If that was some sort of message, I had no clue what she meant, but I was willing to bet any money that Hazel had somehow tripped Billy up. Just in time to save me.

The tangle of fighting cats suddenly resolved itself. The snarling stopped and I heard a single low growl. One cat lay sprawled on his back with another one standing over him. Since the other two stood watching, I guessed Billy the Cat had lost.

The winner pressed a forepaw down hard on his throat. He raised his other paw high, talons extended, and slowly bared his fangs in what might be a grin. This wasn't a friendly one. More like the Glaswegian calling me 'pal' when he had his knife on me in the Land Rover. If Billy so much as twitched the tip of his tail, he would regret it.

That strange, sucking shadow blurred what I saw. A moment later, Peter was standing in the road, looking down at Billy. He was in his human form again, still flat on his back with his arms and legs limp. The other two were still looking on as cats.

Peter said something and offered Billy his hand. Billy took it, and Peter pulled him to his feet. They hugged each other tight. I felt queasy. Had Billy somehow convinced the younger man that he was the one telling the truth?

Then Billy raised his hands. Whatever he might have said to Peter, he had surrendered. I watched Peter search his jacket inside and out. He took Billy's knife and stuck that in his own back pocket. He took his wallet and phone as well. They talked for a few minutes. I was too far away to hear clearly, and in any case, they weren't speaking English.

Billy's chin sank to his chest. His shoulders sagged and he looked defeated. He agreed to something with a sullen jerk of his head. Peter walked towards me, easing a shoulder as if he'd taken a hard tackle on the rugby pitch. Billy followed with the other two cats padding silently after him. Their long tails swept to and fro.

'We need him to do the alarm,' Peter said briefly.

'Fair enough.' I started walking.

No one spoke. When we reached the East Lodge, four great big cats sprang over the gates with ease. I called them all bastards under my breath as I climbed over with a lot more difficulty thanks to my aching wrist. Peter and Billy Smith were standing watching when I dropped down on the inside. I'd have liked to slap that smirk off his face, but that would have wasted time. I had no idea which side of midnight we were now, but I was utterly knackered. I wanted to get this done and go to bed. Any bed would do.

We walked through the deer park and past the collections of ornamental pines. The castle was as dark and as silent as it had been when Hazel and I had left. Peter looked at me with an obvious question, and I led the way around to the back turret door.

Peter gave Billy back his phone. I wondered how many houses got burgled when Will Hall was selling herbal teas at a local craft fair. Did William Halsbury fence stolen property as well as supplying unsuspecting and blameless herbalists? Would Billy Smith answer for that to his fellow cunning men?

He looked up from the phone screen and nodded to Peter. He looked at the two other cats. They crouched ready. Peter opened the door. The alarm didn't go off as the cats sprang down the stairs. Seconds later, boggarts' shrieks startled roosting jackdaws out of the closest trees.

'How far away is the gatehouse?' I had no idea what to say if Henry Pennant unexpectedly appeared.

'Plenty far,' Billy growled. Shooting me a resentful look, he handed his phone back to Peter.

Boggarts came hurtling out of the door. They shot off in all directions, screaming with terror and bleeding where they'd been clawed. The cats chased after them. One leaped and landed on a boggart, seizing the vermin in its jaws and shaking it like a rat. When the cat spat it out, I was amazed to see the boggart lurch away. I'd thought its neck would be broken.

The boggarts' shrieks faded as they reached the far side of the deer park. Peter went into the castle without a backward glance. Billy looked at me, narrow-eyed and calculating.

'After you.' I gestured towards the door. There was no way I was letting that bastard follow me down those steps.

Peter had gone upstairs, using his phone as a torch. I drew the door almost closed behind us, and I really hoped Henry Pennant didn't turn up outside. He was bound to see the little light moving from one tower window up to the next.

At least we didn't have to go all the way to the top. Both of the hobs appeared by the door to the first floor. After a brief conversation with Peter, they turned and walked through the wooden panel. Peter opened the door to go through it like a normal person, and Billy and I followed.

The female hob did most of the talking. She was dressed in the same weave as her mate and looked near enough identical. I still couldn't understand a word she said, but I could see she wasn't happy. While she and Peter talked in short, forthright sentences, I saw the other hob looking more and more embarrassed. He started glaring at Billy. He was blaming him for something. The Glaswegian stared back, defiant, until Peter said something sharply critical to him. Billy looked down at the carpet tiles instead.

Now Peter and the hob were trying to outdo each other with politeness, as far as I could tell. Both hobs waved apologetic hands. I didn't see a flicker of remorse in Billy Smith's eyes. He sneaked venomous glances at me behind Peter's back. I stared back, expressionless. I really hoped Peter or whoever was in charge of these cunning men was going to be able to keep the bastard away from me and Fin. If not, we were really going to have a problem.

Suddenly the conversation was over and the hobs both bowed low. Peter returned the courtesy and snapped his fingers at Billy, who did the same, looking even more pissed off. No one was looking at me. Before I could work out what I was supposed to do, the hobs disappeared, walking into the dark panelling as if the solid wood was no more than a curtain.

Even in this dim light, I saw Peter's contempt as he looked at Billy. 'Right, that's done. You go on downstairs.'

'What did he promise them?' I asked.

'Nothing.' Peter sighed as he went down the stairs. 'They were trying to get rid of the guests because they thought the boggarts would leave if there was no food for them to steal. They thought that would help the Pennants. They've nothing against the Americans themselves.'

'That's good news, isn't it?'

'I suppose—' Peter nearly walked straight into Billy Smith's back. The Glaswegian had stopped dead on the stone threshold of the castle's back door.

'Out the road,' Peter protested.

Unwilling, Billy stepped onto the gravel. Taking a quick sideways step, he pressed his back against the white castle wall. Peter did the same. Now I could see why. The Green Man and the Hunter were standing on the edge of the grass. The Hunter's golden eyes shone bright with warning. The Green Man's eyes glowed ominous emerald green. In the next breath, they were both gone. Billy said something impenetrably Glaswegian under his breath. Peter looked at me as if he was seeing me for the first time.

'Are we done here?' I had to fight to stop a jaw-breaking yawn.

'I think so.' Peter handed Billy his phone. 'Lock it up.'

Before he was finished, the other two cats walked up. The stink of the boggarts was fading fast. By the morning, there'd be no sign they had ever been here. Billy handed his phone back to Peter and the two cats led him away over the grass towards the west. I tried to think what lay out in that direction apart from the sea.

'Let's get you back to where you're staying.' Peter walked off in the other direction.

I followed him back to the East Lodge. He didn't say anything and neither did I. What was there to say? When we arrived, I saw a Toyota 4X4 parked outside on the road. This time Peter climbed over the gate the same as me. The Toyota wasn't locked and the keys were in the ignition. Peter drove me away, going back the way we had come.

'What about the bridge?'

'Don't worry about that.'

Sure enough, once he had edged the Toyota safely past the Landy, I saw the crossing was intact. You'd never know anything had happened. I glanced at Peter, but decided against asking him about it. He was thinking seriously about something, and it wasn't the massive proto-giant or whatever that terrifying thing squatting by the road might be. That had gone back to wherever it had come from, though there were some signs of disturbance. Loose rocks were piled up beside the tarmac. I wondered who would notice this help-fully tidy landslide and wonder what was going on. That didn't seem very cunning to me.

We reached a junction. 'Where to?' Peter asked curtly.

I gave him directions and we soon arrived back at the holiday cottage. At least I had the keys, though there was still no sign of Hazel. I went in and Peter drove away. I drank a litre of apple juice without pausing for breath while the microwave nuked a lasagne. Hazel still hadn't turned up by the time I'd eaten. I'd even given it time to cool so I didn't burn my mouth.

Where the hell was she? Should I go back out to look for her? That seemed like a bad idea. For a start, I was so tired I could barely think. Now I'd had some food, I just wanted to sleep. I went to bed. I left the door unlocked. After the day I'd had, that didn't seem like much of a risk.

I didn't fall asleep though, not for a long time. I couldn't stop reliving those moments when I'd been pinned down by that big black cat. Reliving what I had done. I hadn't been debating the rights or wrongs of what I might do. I'd been driven by instinct, no more and no less. If I'd had a knife, I'd have used it, no question, but not because I wanted to kill the cat. The only thought in my head had been staying alive. Now I knew I would have done whatever that took. I wasn't sure how I felt about that.

Chapter Twenty–Six

Broad daylight woke me up. I hadn't remembered to draw the curtains before falling into bed. My first thought was my wrist was sore and stiff. My next thought was I was desperate for a pee.

I listened for any sounds from the living room. Nothing. Did that mean Hazel had got safely back and was asleep on the sofa bed? If she was still missing, I had to work out how I was going to find her, stranded without a vehicle in the back of beyond. Either way, I needed the loo. If she was asleep, I'd be as quiet as I could. I got out of the creaking bed and reached for my underpants.

'Dan? Are you awake? Tea's in the pot.'

I would have been more relieved to hear Hazel's voice if standing up hadn't made going for a piss even more urgent.

'Give me a minute.' I wrapped a towel around my waist, grabbed my wash-kit and headed to the bathroom for a swift shower. Hot water helped ease my hand. That pot of tea had barely had time to cool, so I brought a mugful back to the bedroom, snatching gulps while I dressed. When I went into the living room, Hazel was showering, so I stacked her bedding on a dining chair and folded up the sofa bed.

Hazel was nearly as quick as I'd been, coming out of the bathroom fully dressed. 'Brunch?'

I stared at her, then looked for a clock. 'We were supposed to see the Pennants first thing.'

'Don't worry.' Hazel took eggs, bacon and sausages out of the fridge. 'I sent them an email last night when I got in.

I said we had new leads to follow up and we'd be in touch later.'

'Okay.' If Katie and Henry weren't happy, there wasn't much they could do. Hopefully they should be ready to forgive anything once they realised their problems were over.

'Take a look outside,' Hazel suggested. 'That's what woke me up.'

I went to the front window. My Land Rover was parked outside. I shoved my feet into my boots and went out to check it over from bumper to bumper and from wheels to roof-rack. The broken window had been replaced and so had both punctured tyres.

That was a bloody good trick, considering I had the only set of keys this side of the Scottish border in my trouser pocket. One of those cunning men must be as good at breaking into cars as Billy Smith was at burgling houses. That made me wonder what other skills they might have between them, and where they did their recruiting. Had Peter spent time in prison? If the wise women knew his surname, what would they find out?

There was a folded piece of A4 paper on the driver's seat. I unlocked the door and read the neatly printed words and a mobile phone number.

Please ask Mistress Hare to call to speak to Iain.

I took that into the cottage along with the Landy's first aid kit. Hazel was taking nicely browned sausages out from under the grill. I showed her the message as she cracked eggs into a hot frying pan.

'Last night, the cunning men promised me a meeting.' I wondered why they wanted to talk to Hazel. Was that Peter's phone number or someone else's? I recalled how many unknown presences the dryad radar had shown me.

She nodded. 'We'll ring that number once we've sorted out the Pennants. Butter the toast, and tell me what happened after that cat jumped you.'

I went through everything while we were eating. 'Where did you get to?' I asked as I pushed my plate away.

Hazel spread marmalade on the last of her toast. 'Once I was fairly certain you weren't going to get eaten, I was mostly keeping out of the way of those cats. Thankfully, they soon decided persuading that rock spirit to back down was more important than chasing a stray hare's scent. I really would like to know more about whatever that was.'

Before I could say anything, she reached for her phone. 'I know. That's something for later. Let's get over to the castle.'

She was already calling Katie Pennant. I waited for her to finish that conversation and then held up my bruised hand. 'Can you strap this up for me?'

'Of course.' Hazel reached for the first aid box.

That felt a lot better. I laced up my boots, grabbed my keys, and we set off. It felt very odd driving back along the road where so much weird shit had happened last night. The valley and the bridge looked exactly the same, but everything was somehow more vivid. Yesterday's overcast sky had broken up into what the weather forecasters call sunshine and scattered clouds, but it wasn't just that.

Katie Pennant looked different too. She was waiting by the open East Lodge gate, ready to put the chain back on after we drove though. When I parked in front of the old building and Hazel opened her door, she walked up to us, smiling and relaxed. I tugged the sleeve of my sweatshirt down to hide the strapping on my wrist and avoid any awkward questions.

'Isn't this a nice day for the time of year? A bit of sun makes everything so much better, don't you think? Henry said you were following up a lead. How did you get on?'

'Very well.' Hazel got out. 'Shall I tell you now, or you and Henry together, when we get to the castle?

'Oh, yes, sure. He's waiting for us there.' Katie waited for me to lock up the Landy. 'Thank you for everything. For just being on our side. Honestly, I had no idea that would make such a difference. I slept right through until the children got up this morning.'

'That's good to know,' Hazel said warmly. 'And it's lovely to see this place in the daylight.'

'It's great, isn't it?' As we walked along the track to the castle, Katie literally had a spring in her step as she told us about assorted interesting trees.

I wondered what I might learn if I tried the dryad radar on one of those specimen pines. Was a slinking black cat out there watching us? I decided it didn't matter if there was. We had nothing to hide about what we were doing here today. We had that mobile number to call, and we'd do it in our own good time. If whoever was waiting for Hazel to ring was getting impatient, that was too bad.

Then something far more serious occurred to me, now I was thinking about the cunning men. What had those stupid fake monitors recorded when I'd been inside the castle last night with Billy and David? The cameras wouldn't have picked up the boggarts, but what about the cats that had chased them out of the basement? Shit. The sooner I got those bloody things back, the better. I only hoped Henry Pennant hadn't got curious this morning and taken a look for himself.

When we reached the castle, I breathed a little easier. Henry was waiting outside the front door with his phone in his hand. He didn't look like a man ready to accuse us of conspiring to let strangers into his property. In fact, as we got closer, he looked ten years younger than he had last night. That wasn't only thanks to some sunlight and a decent night's sleep.

'Hi there.'

He was alert and determined. That cut both ways. This morning I could see a man used to analysing and solving problems. A man who had made enough money to buy an actual castle using his skills and wits. I really had to keep him away from those fake monitors. I unfolded the black canvas holdall.

'Any news?' he asked Hazel as we reached him.

She nodded, serious. When she spoke to the Pennants, every word she said had the ring of truth. 'A colleague has been looking into Liam McGowan. He isn't any sort of psychic. That's not even his real name, as far as we can establish. He's certainly spent time in prison. You'll be well advised to throw his letter in the bin.'

'We will.' Though Katie's cheerfulness faltered. 'Does that mean he can't have been behind the trouble we've had here?'

'If he wasn't, what has been going on?' Henry wanted answers, and he was going to get them, one way or another.

'Let's check the monitors and see what's happened overnight,' Hazel suggested.

Shit. That was the last thing I wanted her to do. I should have thought this through earlier while we were still in the Land Rover. Then I could have said something to Hazel.

'Okay.' Henry's face was impossible to read as he accessed the security system's app on his phone. He paused and frowned at the screen. My heart pounded. Had Billy Smith screwed up? Then Henry shrugged and went up the steps to open the door.

'I'll check the monitors in the basement.' I hurried past him. I was able to get the first black box off the shelf before the others arrived. Henry was the first to reach the bottom of the spiral stair. I heard his surprise as I went through to the rear cellar to get the other monitor.

'Nothing broken. Not a thing.'

'The smell's gone. Could the drains have unclogged themselves?' Katie didn't dare believe what she was saying.

'Let's take a look.' Henry opened the door.

I was already heading up the spiral stair at the back of the castle, moving fast to collect the rest of the monitors. I soon found the ones Hazel had put in the corridors. She hadn't even switched them on. That was one way to make sure nothing inconvenient got recorded. I wished she'd mentioned that to me. Never mind. Up on the top floor, I shoved the last one in my holdall and waited for a moment to see if the hobs showed themselves. They didn't, so I went back down to the entrance hall, where I could hear voices.

Henry looked at me, expectant, as I came through the turret door. 'What did your equipment pick up?'

'Nothing,' Hazel answered before I could speak. 'That's right, isn't it, Dan?'

I had no idea what she was going to say, so I just nodded.

The Pennants were confused. Henry looked at me. 'You smelled that stink last night. You've read those posts online. If you think our guests were lying – that we're lying—'

'Oh, everyone's been telling the truth. We don't doubt that for a moment,' Hazel assured him. 'You've absolutely had a serious problem, but it's had nothing to do with ghosts. There aren't any ghosts in this castle, for a start. It wasn't fakery though. Nothing that a bunch of pesky kids could sort out. That's what our monitors would have picked up. This is genuinely one of those cases – those very, very rare cases – where something impossible to explain rationally has been happening. I know the right people to ask when I come across a situation like this. There's been – well, a temporary blight is one way to put it.'

Hazel was still telling the truth, even if this was nowhere near the whole truth. The Pennants looked at her, open-mouthed, trying to make some sense of what she was saying.

'Blight?' Katie didn't like the sound of that.

'Temporary?' Henry focused on what was most important to him.

Hazel nodded. 'It's already passing off. You've seen for yourselves that there's nothing broken today, and that foul smell has gone.'

'But everything that happened before now, that was real, right?' Katie was unwilling to doubt the evidence of her own eyes.

'Is there any way this could happen again?' Henry had already moved on. His priorities were clear. 'Is there any way to prevent that?'

Hazel looked at him, wholly serious. 'Give me your permission and I'll cleanse and defend this place with an appropriate ritual.'

'A ritual? Burning sage or whatever?' He tried to hide his scepticism and more than a little disappointment. 'How much will that cost?'

Hazel grinned. 'No burning herbs and no charge. It won't take me long, and then we'll be on our way. Though no one who's not in this room right now will take anything I'm telling you seriously. We'll keep this to ourselves, you have our word on that, and I recommend you stick to your story about bad drains as far as the rest of the world is concerned. You need to put this behind you, for your own sakes and for your business. The sooner the better.'

'No argument from me.' Henry shook his head, half smiling despite himself.

'So, this ritual...?' Katie looked at her husband, caught between hope and doubt.

Henry raised his hands. 'Go ahead. You have my permission.'

'And mine. And thank you,' Katie added.

Hazel walked to the middle of the entrance hall. She paused and shifted her feet, and I realised she was aligning herself with the cardinal points of the compass. As she closed her eyes for a moment, we heard her slow and measured breathing in the silence. Calm and unhurried, she pointed to her forehead, to her feet, then her right shoulder, her left shoulder and finally at her heart. The wise woman said something quietly as she made each gesture. I didn't catch everything, but one word sounded like 'Malkuth', and I recognised the last one easily enough. Amen.

'Amen.' Katie echoed with American emphasis. She blushed bright red when she realised what she had done. Henry took her hand with a fond smile.

I don't know if Hazel heard her. The wise woman was totally focused on what she was doing. She pointed east before sweeping her hand around to the south, west and north. At first I thought she was marking out the compass, until I saw her hand pause in five places. Her lips were moving, but whatever she was saying was so quiet even I couldn't hear her.

Then she did turn to the four points of the compass. This time I heard what she said loud and clear. Raphael. Gabriel. Michael. Uriel. I knew those names, even if I had no idea what Hazel was doing.

She paused for a moment and then turned to the Pennants. 'All done.'

'We have guardian angels now?' Wide-eyed, Katie really wanted to believe everything would be fine. Equally, she didn't want to risk being let down.

Hazel smiled. 'You won't have any more trouble.'

'Thanks, I guess.' Henry was still having trouble reconciling today's absence of foul smells and inexplicable damage with a lifetime's rejection of anything he couldn't verify for himself.

She grinned at him. 'Money-back guarantee.'

Henry was startled into a laugh. 'Can't say fairer than that.'

'Can I offer you some coffee? Some tea?' Not knowing what else to do, Katie opted for trying to be a good hostess.

'Thanks, but no. We're fine, honestly.' Hazel had left her coat on a window seat. She went over and picked it up. 'We'll let you get on. You should start letting people know the drains have been sorted out.'

'We could hold a folk music evening.' Henry had already been thinking how to get the news out. 'An open house. No charge.'

'Good luck with everything.' I hadn't been wearing a coat over my sweatshirt, so I was ready to leave.

'Right. Sure. Thanks.' Henry offered me his hand. 'Sorry you didn't find your ghosts.'

He wasn't sorry at all. In fact, he wanted us out of here so he could forget this had ever happened. I couldn't blame him for that.

'Not a problem,' I assured him as I swapped the holdall to my other hand and returned his handshake. 'I'm just glad it's sorted out.'

'Are you sure I can't offer you anything before you go?' Katie followed us to the door. 'Let me walk with you to the lodge—'

'There's really no need. We know the way and we'll lock the gate behind us,' Hazel assured her. 'You have work to do here, and we need to get on the road while there's still a decent amount of daylight.'

'Oh, right.' The thought that she might inconvenience us was enough for Katie to let us go. 'Well, you know where we are. Any time you're up this way, do stop by. Any time. And have a happy Halloween.'

That caught Hazel by surprise. She forced a smile as she opened the door. 'Yes, indeed. Thanks.'

I pulled the door closed behind us and followed Hazel down the steps. She was walking quickly across the gravel to the track leading to the east gate. 'Right. That's done. Now we can get on.'

'There's something I want to check before we leave.' I walked faster, reaching the Land Rover ahead of her. I slung the holdall in the back and went around behind the old lodge.

Hazel arrived as I was squatting down to examine the tyre marks where I had parked on our first visit here. 'What are you looking for?'

'This.' I held up a shiny new 70-mil nail.

'We could have had more punctures?' Hazel queried.

I shook my head. 'Two was enough, but I've been wondering how Billy the Cat made sure of that. Driving a nail into one of those tyres wouldn't be easy, or quick. I think they let the Landy do the work.'

I set the nail on the ground, with the head down and the point angled upwards. 'Put one of these on each side of the wheel with the tip wedged in the tread, and the weight of the vehicle would do the rest, whether I went forward or reversed. That would be quick and easy to set up without being noticed. And there's the other one.' I picked the glint of metal out of the earth and pine needles. I wondered if anyone was out there watching me.

'So you've satisfied your curiosity. And?' Hazel could see I had more to say.

310

I stood up and rattled the nails in my hand. 'We know Billy the Cat was a criminal before he was a cunning man. We know at least one of the others can break into cars without leaving a trace. We need to be careful.'

'We do,' Hazel agreed. 'You watch my back and I'll watch yours.'

'Right.' I wasn't sure how much good that would do if we were as badly outnumbered as we had been last night.

Chapter Twenty-Seven

I drove the Land Rover out through the castle gate and pulled up. Hazel snapped the padlock onto the chain. She had the sheet of paper with that phone number on it in her hand as she got into the passenger seat. She took out her phone and made the call. She put it on speaker before it rang.

Somebody answered so fast they must have been sitting waiting and watching their phone. 'Thank you for calling me.'

Hazel glanced at me with raised eyebrows. I shook my head. That wasn't Peter. This voice was older – a lot older – as well as hoarser and darker, though their accents were definitely similar.

'Thank you for letting me have your number,' she said politely. 'I take it I'm speaking to Iain?'

'You are indeed. And what shall I call you?'

'I'm Hazel.' If she wasn't getting the old cunning man's surname, he wasn't getting hers.

'Is young Daniel with you?'

Hazel raised a finger to stop me answering. 'He is.'

I looked out of the Landy's windows, wondering if anyone was watching us have this conversation.

'I believe we have things to discuss,' Iain observed. 'Best discussed in person, don't you agree?'

'Indeed. Where shall we meet?'

'Young Daniel has a satnav in his Land Rover. Check your messages.' The gravelly voice ended the call.

Hazel checked her call log first. 'Private number. What a surprise.'

Her phone pinged with a text notification. She showed me the postcode she'd just been sent, and I entered that into the satnav. I zoomed out on the map to get a better idea where we would be going.

'That's right on the coast. Out in the arse end of nowhere.' I glanced at her. 'Do we want to do this without any back-up?'

'I'll let a few people know where we're going.' Hazel quickly sent some sort of message on her phone. 'If you're okay to drive that far.' She gestured at my strapped wrist.

'I'll be fine.' I'd take some painkillers if I really needed them.

She fastened her seatbelt. 'Then let's get going. With luck, we'll still have some daylight when it's time to leave.'

That was optimistic, given how short the days were getting with autumn turning towards winter. I hoped she was right. Right about getting this done before dusk. Right that we'd be allowed to leave when we wanted. It was all very well making sure someone knew where to start looking if we disappeared. They could tell the police, and that would make a whole lot of trouble for the cunning men, but it wouldn't be much use to me or Hazel if we had already been eaten. I decided the sooner this meeting was over, the better, for a whole lot of reasons. Best get it started as soon as possible.

I drove as fast as I dared. When we hit a broader, recently resurfaced stretch, I put my foot down, and not only to get this meeting over. If any big black cats had been lurking in the trees at the castle, good luck to them trying to keep up.

'Ah,' Hazel remarked a few miles later. 'That explains it.'

'What explains what?' I was keeping my eyes on the road.

'That sign we just passed. This road's been improved to benefit the Scottish forestry industry. Supporting timber on the move.'

That made me grin. 'Sounds like Ents to me.'

'Or Birnam Wood coming to Dunsinane,' Hazel said lightly.

'Right.' Remembering that bit in Macbeth made me wonder what might be lurking in Scottish forests besides dryads. Wood woses for a start. Meantime, I watched out in case log lorries suddenly appeared swinging out wide, as I drove around a series of blind corners. Now I was even more glad we weren't in Hazel's Fiesta. An HGV loaded with timber could turn that into a roller-skate.

We turned off the good road sooner than I'd have liked. The satnav led us down yet more narrow lanes. These gorse-dotted rocky pastures were grazed by sheep which would probably fall over with shock if someone ever put them in a flat field. This landscape was as uneven as a rumpled blanket. The road constantly swerved and alternated between unexpected dips and unnerving blind summits.

I didn't need to stop in a passing place to let anyone going the other way go past, but that was no consolation. I didn't see any other vehicles behind us in my mirrors either. It wasn't even as if the satnav software was doing something stupid like ignoring a better route for the sake of saving five metres on the journey. I could see from the screen there were no other roads to take. We really were out here on our own.

At least it wasn't too long before I saw we'd nearly reached our destination. As well as the satnav showing me a little chequered flag, there wasn't much more road before we'd drive into the sea. I steered around one last hairpin bend where the road skirted a looming grey crag and pulled up to assess what lay ahead.

If this village had a name, someone had removed any signs welcoming careful drivers. Someone had planned this place though, back when it had been built. That had been a good many decades ago, maybe even a couple of centuries. Hazel and I were looking at the white-painted gable ends of four terraces of single-storey, slate-roofed cottages with squat chimney stacks. Two terraces faced each other on the right-hand side of this stretch of level ground. The other two terraces faced each other on the left. A narrow alleyway separated the back gates of the inner terrace on the right from the walled back yards of the houses that mirrored them.

'Where are we supposed to park?' Double yellow lines on both sides of the narrow lanes between each set of terraces struck me as a waste of paint. Surely anyone with half a brain could see a vehicle pulling up anywhere would stop anyone else getting through. But some people need things spelling out.

'Shall we see what's by the water?' Hazel suggested.

'Okay.' I put the Landy into gear. Yellow lines had to mean traffic passed through here at least sometimes. With no dead end or no-entry signs to indicate a one-way system, I drove slowly between the terraces that faced each other on the left.

'I can't see any lights,' Hazel commented, 'but these houses look well maintained.'

I had noticed that. Each frontage had wooden sash windows on either side of a solid wooden front door. Doors and windows alike were set right back in the thick stone walls so the sills were on the outside. That told me brutal winds must come off the sea in the winter. None of the dark paintwork was faded or flaking though. Someone made sure these houses were ready to face those storms.

I drove on. The terraces were longer than I expected, and the outermost lines of cottages were longer than the inside ones. The buildings at the far end of those outer terraces weren't houses, even though their roofs and walls followed the same lines as the rest. They framed a small square with a war memorial in the centre. Seeing faded white lines on the cobbles, I pulled up in a parking space and looked from side to side. The pattern of windows and doors on the building away to the right looked like a school to me. The one on this side was clearly a pub, though its sign was too faded to read. Those windows glowed with the only sign of life we had seen. I still couldn't see any other vehicles.

'I guess that's where we're expected.' Hazel unclipped her seatbelt and opened her door.

I got out and locked the Landy. If the cunning men wanted to see if I had brought anything unexpected with me, I could make them work for it. I looked out towards the sea beyond this little square. The levelled ground gave way to a sloping beach covered with sizeable grey boulders. Anyone wanting to reach the water without clambering over those would use the short wooden jetty. Its timbers were black with whatever protected them from cold winds, the rain and the sea.

A boat was tied up at the far end. Short and wide, it had a red-painted hull and an upcurved prow. A little foredeck and a squat square cabin with a red roof took up the front half. Anyone standing in the open well at the rear would have to take whatever the weather and waves threw at them. Three similar boats were tied to buoys a little further out. Given the local roads, travelling by water made a lot of sense around here. It also guaranteed there was no way we could follow the cunning men when they left. I wondered where the boats had come from, as well as how many cunning men had travelled here in each one.

Several long low islands lay not far offshore. They would give this village a fair amount of shelter from the Atlantic winds. Though the closest island would have been a much better barrier before half its high ground had been quarried away. I assessed that crag we had just passed. From this side I could see it had been quarried for stone as well. Though not any time recently. The exposed rock face was as weathered as the untouched flank. Well-established plants flourished in its crevices.

This village must have been where the quarry workers lived. I wondered who lived here now as I followed Hazel towards the pub. She opened the door. No one was talking inside. That wasn't a surprise. They would have heard the Land Rover pull up. They would have been waiting.

I counted eleven men, no women, sitting on stools around small tables or on wooden seats that ran along the walls behind bigger tables. Billy Smith sat between two others behind a table on the far side of the room. He was staring at his hands, resting clasped together on the table. He didn't look up. The fireplace in the end wall was burning what I realised after a moment's thought must be peat. The golden light came from oil lamps on the bigger tables. Real oil lamps, not fake flickering bulbs for olde-worlde ambience. I couldn't see modern light fittings or electric sockets anywhere.

This might be a pub but there wasn't a bar. A solidly built man came through an inner door with a jug in one hand, holding two pottery tankards by their handles in the other. He set the tankards on a table and poured beer from the jug. Neither man sitting there made any move to pay him. They were too busy staring at me and Hazel. The man with the jug headed for the back room without a glance our way.

A white-haired man with a mild, deeply lined face and bristling eyebrows sat alone at the table closest to the door. He was tucked into the corner where the bench seat along the side wall met the one underneath the front window. He offered his gnarled hand to Hazel. 'Good day to you. Thank you for coming. Will you sit and have a drink with me?'

We recognised his voice from the phone call. Hazel smiled as she shook his hand. 'It's good to meet you, Iain. A cup of tea would be welcome, or coffee. Whichever's not too much bother. It's a bit early for beer for me, and Daniel's driving.'

She slipped off her coat and draped it over the closest stool on the other side of the table. That had been put there so she had to sit with her back to the other men. Hazel settled herself comfortably, still smiling, still looking at the old man. The rest of the room could have been empty as far as she was concerned.

After a moment, Iain glanced at one of his minions and jerked his head towards the inner door. The minion went into the kitchen or whatever was through there. I wondered how long it took to boil a kettle on a peat fire. I ignored the second empty stool beside Hazel and took a seat on the other end of the bench under the window. This way, I could keep watch on these bastards. I took a good look at everyone in the room, each of them in turn. I made sure that they knew I was getting their measure. So they knew I would be on my feet as soon as any of them made a move. I was closest to the door, and I would grab Hazel and drag her out of there before the closest of them could reach us.

Of course, that wouldn't necessarily get us out of trouble. I had no way to lock the pub door after I slammed it, and it was anyone's guess if we could reach the Landy before we were caught. Then I'd still only have one and a half good hands for a fist fight.

One of the cunning men at a table in the middle of the room had noticed my bandaged wrist. He looked up from my hand and met my gaze with a sneer that was as good as a challenge. Peter was sitting beside him and nudged him in the ribs with an elbow. The first man scowled, saying something in what I guessed was Gaelic. He didn't care that I could hear him. More than that, he looked at me to make sure that I knew he knew I didn't understand a word he said.

I stared back, keeping my face as expressionless as I had on the day when I'd dealt with an arsehole who thought he was entitled to take up two spaces in the Blithehurst car park, to make sure no one would carelessly put a dent in his precious Mercedes.

'So what can I do for you?' A sweep of Iain's hand invited Hazel to commit herself first.

I saw a few of the cunning men smirk with approval at his tactics. I wondered how long we'd be sitting here while the wise woman and the old man tried to get the upper hand, before one of them would actually get to the point. It could be midnight before we got out of here. On the other hand, I couldn't feel any warning itch from the scars on my forearm.

But Hazel nodded, satisfied, as if old Iain had just done her a favour. 'Tell your man over there to stop killing people and leaving us to clean up his mess. Tell him not to recruit boggarts to ruin innocent people's businesses until they pay him a ransom to solve their problems.'

I saw what Billy had been up to was news to more than half the men here. Some were a lot more startled about the boggarts than they were about the deaths. I wondered how many of these cunning men did a little vigilante work themselves.

Old Iain was shocked, though not at what Billy had been doing. He knew all about that. He hadn't been expecting Hazel to be so blunt. He recovered fast, or at least, he thought he did. 'You misunderstand my role. We agreed to meet you out of courtesy, but each man here is his own master. We follow our own path to make a living. Cats who walk by ourselves, as you might say. I have no authority—'

'Oh, I'm sorry. We won't take up any more of your time.' Hazel stood up.

'But I can always advise,' Iain said quickly, 'and as an elder, my advice is generally heeded.'

Hazel sat down again. 'Then take my advice and tell your man to stop taking these risks. When he picks on the wrong person and he's caught, that will cause no end of trouble for us all.'

'You say when, not if.' Iain's face hardened. 'You have more faith in the police than I do. Who's to say he'll be caught? Besides, he's putting an end to trouble that nobody else cares to stop. The laws and the men who are supposed to defend the weak do nothing to help. Instead they use and abuse those laws to send men to prison for crimes they havnae done.'

Billy Smith looked up when Iain said that. Even in this dim light I saw the grievance burning in the Glaswegian's eyes. Had he been locked up for a burglary he hadn't actually been part of? It looked like that to me. Perhaps he'd been fitted up because the cops couldn't get him convicted for things he had genuinely done. Seeing at least half the men nodding surly agreement, it looked as if Billy Smith wasn't the only one who'd done time for someone else's crime.

Iain's level gaze challenged Hazel. 'The men who made those laws were as quick to send your people to the stake as they were to burn us alive, back in the day. We haven't recognised their authority over us since. Why should we heed them now? Why should we heed you?'

'We didn't go to ground, cowering and debating until somebody grabbed us to wring our necks,' a voice said somewhere over by the fireplace.

'Too afraid to fight back,' someone else spat from the shadows. 'Too feeble. Sitting bletherin' and greetin' like bairns.'

'Trying to save your own necks by pointing the finger at us,' the man beside him growled.

Hazel didn't turn a hair, looking steadily at Iain. 'It must have been easier for cunning men to run away and hide when few of them had ties to families and friends. Such choices weren't as simple for wise women who could name every one of the sick and the old who would suffer without their help. They had known the young wives carrying babies in their bellies since those girls had been children themselves. They knew mothers and infants could be at risk if they weren't there when their skills were needed. They stayed, willing to risk their own lives.'

The sneering man didn't like that. Nor did the others who had spoken up. A man at a different table got to his feet, scowling. 'An sgudal seo a-rithist.'

Whatever that meant wasn't polite. Though plenty of the others didn't like this row any more than I did. I tried to catch Peter's eye, but he was looking across the room, exchanging glances with someone else who was equally concerned.

Every head turned as the door to the back room opened. The thickset man came through carrying a round metal tray holding a teapot, a jug and two mugs, all made from the same glazed earthenware as the tankards and beer jug. If that was lucky timing, he should be out buying lottery tickets. If he had been waiting and listening on the other side of that door and he'd decided this was the time for a distraction, I'd like to buy him a drink.

He came over to our table and set the tray down without a word. Iain glanced past Hazel. I saw the old man's eyebrows bristle as he frowned. The men who'd stood up sat down again. They didn't look any less hostile.

'Aye, well.' Iain took a swallow from his tankard. 'There were hard choices to be made all round, right enough. Those were bad times and we all suffered losses.'

Hazel poured milk into both mugs and carefully swirled the pot around before pouring us each some tea. She handed mine over before taking a sip of her own. 'All the more reason to be careful now, and to work together to keep ourselves safe. All of us. We're not the only ones at risk these days.'

Iain nodded. 'Billy told us about yon swan maidens.'

I saw a lot of the cunning men wanted to know more about them. I wasn't at all sure I was happy about that. I'd really like to know what the hell Billy had said about Fin and Blanche. I drank some tea, hoping nothing in my face gave my anger away.

Iain put down his tankard. 'I'm sure Billy will be more careful. We'll all be more careful. We know what's at stake.'

Hazel shook her head. 'We need to know where you are and what you're doing, in general terms at least. We may even be able to work together—'

'No.' Iain's certainty did at least silence the outraged murmur her words had provoked.

Hazel wasn't about to back down. 'You know we can find you. We found Billy Smith—'

'And what?' the man by the fireplace demanded. 'You'll tell the polis where to find us if we don't do as you say?'

I heard a growl somewhere in the shadows. A real growl. Someone responded curtly, 'Èist rì Iain!'

I wished I knew what that meant. I'd really like to have some idea of who might be on our side.

'You won't find him again,' Iain assured Hazel. 'I can promise you that.'

'You're sure?' Now she challenged him. 'We'll be watching for the next time he uses the skills you've taught him to blackmail someone to line his own pockets. You'll want our help then, if the police catch up with him first.'

Old Iain scowled. 'Maybe he wouldnae have been so desperate if you had let him be. You chased him—'

'You're saying this is our fault? That we made him do it?' Hazel shook her head. 'The excuse of the abuser through the ages.'

Angry voices shouted her down. To be honest, I didn't blame them. That wasn't just uncalled for. It was a stupid thing to say.

'It's time for you to leave.' The bearded man who'd stood up earlier was on his feet again. 'You've had your say.'

'I haven't.' I drank the rest of my tea, thinking fast while everyone was still caught by surprise. They thought I was just her driver. I stood up to put the mug on the table. It couldn't hurt to show them I was taller than anyone else in this room. I didn't sit down again as I looked around.

'Your friend Billy hasn't only pissed off these wise women. He isn't only putting you and all the rest of us at risk if he screws up badly enough and the cops nick him for murder. He's got on the wrong side of some powerful spirits in the woods and the waters by dumping these bodies. Believe me, these are not enemies you want to make.'

It was good to know I wouldn't have to explain or justify what I said. The cunning men could hear I was telling the truth. That didn't mean they had to like it. Billy the Cat got some filthy looks, but so did I.

'Who are you to speak for them?' Iain demanded curtly. 'And I'm surprised that you put your trust in the so-called justice system, Daniel Mackmain, when you were dragged into court and convicted for doing no more than defending your own.' His narrowed eyes cut sideways to Hazel. 'You're not the only folk who can find things out.'

'We have powerful friends too,' the bearded man challenged me, belligerent. 'Spirits of moor and mountain. You've seen that for yourself.'

He sounded like a kid in the playground saying his dad could beat up my dad. I thought about telling him the Green Man and the Hunter had sent me. No, I wouldn't do that. For a start, my dad had taught me not to waste time getting into pissing contests with wankers. Besides, Peter already knew the Green Man and the Hunter were taking an interest. They would show themselves again when they were good and ready. I only hoped I was there to see Pussy Boy's face when they did.

'I'm someone they can trust,' I said calmly. 'Since my mother's a dryad.'

That got more of a reaction than I expected. Even Iain looked surprised. So Billy the Cat hadn't told anyone that bit of news, not even the old man. I guessed he hadn't mentioned the black shuck either. That would have meant explanations he didn't want to get into.

Hazel smiled at the old man, as if me speaking after her had been our plan all along. I wished it had been. Then I might know what I was going to say next, before she opened her mouth and said something else even more insulting. I thought fast. I wouldn't mention the shuck, or the hamadryads, come to that. Not until I knew exactly what story Billy had told.

For now, I'd stick with the things the cunning men knew Billy had done. Since we didn't want him washing up dead on the beach at Darley Combe, I could warn him to stay away from there. That would let the other cunning men know they had better make sure he did.

'There's a mermaid down in Devon who's ready to drown your friend over there if she ever sees him again.'

That caused a hell of a stir. Billy shrank down in his seat. Half a dozen men were on their feet, shouting at him in Gaelic.

'Suidh sìos agus bi sàmhach!' Iain slammed his empty tankard down on the table so hard I was surprised it didn't break. Even so, he had to shout a few harsh words before the uproar subsided into sullen silence.

At least that had given me a bit more time to think, even if I had no idea what had just happened. I spoke quickly, before Hazel or anyone else. 'I'm not so different to any of you. I have to live alongside the people who can't see what we know is out there. I have to work a job to pay my bills.'

Their beer might come in tankards like the ones artisan potters sell at craft fairs, and some of them wore sweaters knitted from hand-spun wool dyed every shade of lentil, but most of these men wore ordinary clothes bought from ordinary shops. This village might not be on the electricity grid, but it had a postcode and a mobile phone signal. That boat out there tied to the jetty needed diesel for its engine.

These cunning men were part of the everyday world, whether they liked it or not. They might like to think they were cats who walked by themselves, but my dad had read me that story when I was a little kid. If I remembered it right, the cat had seen the sense in sleeping by a warm fire in a place where regular meals turned up.

'I want to be left alone by the tossers who would make my life a nightmare if they ever suspected I can see the things they can't. You know the ones I mean. The ones desperate to prove their favourite legends are real. The ones who won't take no for an answer. That's why I'm here. If the Internet ever finds out what your mate over there can do, that's far more of a threat to me and mine than any cops could be.' I jerked my head at Billy. I swear, he'd have slid down under the table to disappear completely if he could.

Peter sprang to his feet, passionate as he spoke to the gathering. 'Tha ciall aig man an craobhean.'

From his tone and his gestures as he went on speaking, I guessed he was supporting me, but that was all I could tell. I saw Hazel looking down, apparently inspecting her finger-nails. That way she didn't have to see Iain glowering at her. Peter turned around and appealed to the old man. Hazel looked up and spoke before Iain could answer.

'I apologise. This situation makes me afraid, and fear makes me angry. I insulted you and I'm sorry.' She turned around on the stool. 'I apologise to you all.'

That shut them up. Iain seized the chance to clap his leathery hands. Hazel still had her back to him and the loud noise caught her by surprise. She stiffened, startled. Several men saw and laughed, mocking her. We still had a long way to go before she made any friends here. I didn't sit down, leaning against the entrance door. Anyone making a move would have to go through me.

The inner door opened and the thickset man stuck his head into the room. Iain said something to him, and the man disappeared. A moment later, he came in with a tray carrying an unlabelled green glass bottle and three glasses. Two younger men followed, taking glasses and bottles to the other tables. Given the family resemblance, they had to be the thickset man's sons.

Iain poured three generous measures of amber liquid. He offered one to Hazel as she turned around on her stool to face him. 'There have been over-hasty words on both sides. Shall we share a dram and start again, mistress? Mr Mack-main?' He offered the other drink to me.

'Gladly. Thank you.' Hazel took the glass from him and so did I. This was about more than a sip of whisky. For a start, these short-stemmed, flower-shaped glasses were antique lead crystal. I'd worked at Blithehurst long enough to know that.

Iain raised his glass to Hazel and then to me, saying something in Gaelic before he drank.

She returned the gesture. 'Your very good health.' She took a sip and nodded, approving.

'Cheers, and thank you.' I drank about half of mine. I don't often drink spirits and I'm not a fan of peaty whisky. I decided if I had to drink one, this would be it. Not that I'd find it in the shops, I was sure of that.

I saw everyone else drinking too, though they had been given everyday mass-market glassware. Even Billy threw back his shot, with a grimace as if he was swallowing unwanted but essential medicine.

'Shall we agree to respect each other, mistress?' old Iain asked Hazel. 'To set aside the mistakes of the past? As for trust, that can be earned. For my part, I can promise you my good faith. We have many interests in common, and we face the same threats nowadays. You have my phone number, and I have yours. Shall we agree to keep in touch if we think our people's paths might cross, to prevent any future misunderstandings?'

From the expressions around the room, I could see this was as far as the old man was willing to go. There were at least two factions here, maybe more, and not all the cunning men were here. I'd sensed far more in the valley last night. If he pushed too hard, Iain risked losing his influence.

Hazel nodded. 'By all means, and thank you, for my own sake and on behalf of my people. That seems the best way ahead.'

I hid my relief by drinking the rest of my whisky. I nearly swallowed the last drop the wrong way when Iain turned to me.

'Will you let me have your phone number, Mr Mackmain? So we can keep in touch as well?'

'Yes, sure. No problem. And please, call me Dan.'

'Daniel it is. Please excuse me, mistress.'

He edged along the bench. Hazel stood up to let him get out from behind the table. I didn't realise what was happening until Peter came up and gestured towards the door latch.

'We can all be on our way now.'

'Oh, right.' I stepped aside.

'After you, mistress.' Old Iain courteously waved Hazel towards the door.

'Thank you.' She put down her glass and put on her coat. She couldn't really do anything else.

I followed her out. I shivered in the cold autumn evening air. A sweatshirt had been enough earlier in the day, but coming out of that warm, lamplit room was a shock. I unlocked the Landy and we got in.

We watched the cunning men walk along the jetty to the waiting boat. They got on board and we heard the engine start. They crossed the short distance to one of the tethered boats and half the men climbed aboard that one.

'What's he doing?' Hazel wondered.

One of the thickset man's sons was running along the jetty. I expected him to slow down, to stop and wave when he got to the end, telling someone they'd forgotten their wallet or a coat. He didn't. He ran faster, and took a dive right off the end. I saw a shimmer like an unexpected sunbeam striking the water. Before he hit the sea, he was a seal. A moment later, someone leaned over the stern of the second boat, presumably talking to him down in the water.

'Selkies.' Hazel shook her head. 'I should have expected that.'

I looked back at the pub. The door stood open. The older man who had served us the whisky was leaning against the post and watching us. Given what we had just seen, he must surely be a selkie as well. The oil lamps glowed behind him.

I wondered if this alliance was why the cunning men didn't want to piss off the powerful beings who live in the sea. I started the engine and we drove away.

Chapter Twenty-Eight

We needed some dinner. We stopped at the first de-
cent-looking restaurant we saw. It wasn't cheap, but
my baked sea bass was excellent and Hazel said her salmon
was the best she'd had in ages. It wasn't as if we had much
choice. High-end hotels with a wealthy clientele were doing
fine around here, but businesses lower down the food chain
were being hard hit as their customer base got squeezed by
the rising cost of living. We'd passed several boarded-up
premises on our journey from Glasgow that must have been
going concerns until the last year or so.

We got back to the holiday let without any more excitement. After a good night's sleep, I woke up to hear Hazel on
the phone to someone. I grabbed a towel and my wash-kit
and headed for the shower. She acknowledged me with a
wave as she carried on talking, not letting whoever was on
the other end get a word in.

'No, the cottage is lovely. It's just that something's come
up. A family matter. Nothing dreadful, just tedious and
inconvenient. Obviously, we don't expect a refund. It's one
of those things that can't be helped.' She finally paused for a
moment. 'Of course. That's fine. Thank you very much, and
cheerio.'

She ended the call and looked at me. 'I take it you don't
want to stay here for the rest of the week?'

'No.' I carried on to the bathroom. Unstrapping my wrist,
I was relieved to find that felt a lot better. The bruising was
spectacular though.

By the time I was dressed, Hazel was eating toast and marmalade with one hand and hitting keys on her laptop with the other.

I opened the fridge. 'Okay if I have the rest of the bacon?'

'Fine.' Hazel looked up. 'Did you know there are quite a few islands off the west coast of Scotland where the communities gave up the struggle to make a living over the last hundred years? Places like St Kilda.'

The name rang a faint bell, though I wouldn't know where to look for it on a map. 'And?' I switched on the heat under the frying pan.

'I reckon at least one of those abandoned islands isn't anywhere near as deserted as it's supposed to be.' Hazel closed her laptop. 'We'll see what we can find out.'

'And then?' I looked at her. 'What will you wise women do?'

'Sit around endlessly discussing what we should do next, at least for a couple of months.' She grimaced as she reached for her coffee and realised the mug was empty. 'The cunning men had a point, much as I hate to admit it. Ever heard the expression "paralysis by analysis"?'

I hadn't, but that didn't matter. 'Right.'

Hazel came over and switched on the kettle. 'Tea for you? And shall I strap that wrist?'

'Yes, thanks.'

Our journey back to Blithehurst was long but straightforward, even if my bruised hand was aching like a son of a bitch by the time we got there. Hazel accepted Eleanor's offer of a guest bedroom for the night before she headed back to Exeter. The three of us sat around Eleanor's laptop and told Fin and Blanche what had happened.

Zan was nowhere to be seen at their end, and Blanche didn't mention the sylph. I thought about asking them not to pass on this latest news. I decided there was no point. Zan already knew most of what was going on, so they were bound to ask questions. It wasn't fair to expect Fin or Blanche not to answer.

For a start, when Zan realised the two of them were keeping something secret, there was every chance the sylph would go looking for explanations on their own. I hated to think how much trouble that could cause for us. Add to that, once we had some idea where the cunning men might be hiding, having a sylph on our side could come in useful.

Hazel set off for home the following morning as soon as it was getting light. I went with her as far as the back gate and locked it behind the Fiesta. I'd walk back and check up on the estate's woodlands. After everything that had happened over the past eight months, I wanted to get back to some sort of normality. Doing my usual job seemed a good place to start.

'Well?' Frai appeared.

'Is there news?' Asca was on my other side.

I told them everything that had happened. They listened, but neither of them spoke until we reached a fork in the road through the woods.

'We will make sure that none of these cunning men set foot on Beauchene land.'

Frai was looking at Asca rather than me as she spoke. The other dryad nodded, and they vanished.

I had been about to say I was pretty sure we could rely on the shuck for that, but, whatever.

Aled came over for the first of the Christmas craft fairs. That was a long, busy and thankfully profitable day. When everything was packed up and cleared away, I cooked dinner for us both in my cottage out in the woods.

Once we'd eaten, I fetched two glasses and the bottle of whisky that had arrived for me by special delivery the day before. There wasn't a note and I didn't need one. The bottle was unlabelled, and I recognised the aroma as soon as I uncorked it. So the cunning men knew where I lived. That was no great surprise.

'I'll take some water with mine, thanks.' Aled was stacking the plates and cutlery next to the sink. 'Got a jug?'

I opened a cupboard and passed him a Pyrex measuring jug. 'You can leave the washing-up. Come and sit down.'

I told him about the trip to Scotland, as well as explaining everything else that had happened. That took long enough for us both to drink a couple of glasses of whisky. I decided I preferred the cunning men's malt with some water.

Aled didn't say anything for a while after I stopped talking. His face was thoughtful. 'Have you told them anything about me, about old Annis or the Cŵn Annwn?'

'Nothing.' I shook my head. 'I've had no reason to.'

He nodded. 'I trust you, Dan, but until you have some really good reason, and you know, life or death, or risking life and limb, I'd rather you didn't mention me. Not until we know more about them and about these spirits of moor and mountain. Better safe than sorry.'

'Understood.' I did. Aled knew how dangerous getting on the wrong side of unknown forces could be. He literally had the scars to prove it, and I still felt that was my fault. I was relieved to see the marks on his face were fading, but I'd always know they were there.

He leaned forward to top up his glass from the bottle and the jug of water on the low table. 'Still, we know one thing about them. They make damn good whisky.'

I went to see my parents on the day before the winter solstice. Taking time off was no problem. After the last craft fair the weekend before, everyone at Blithehurst was on holiday until the third of January.

When I got back to the cottage, Fin's Toyota was already parked outside. I went in to find her chatting to Eleanor over coffee in the kitchen.

'I'm going over to the Dower House on Christmas Day. My brother Ben is coming up from London and Sophie and David are staying there until New Year,' Eleanor was saying. 'I'm pretty sure Sophie's going to tell everyone she's pregnant.'

I glanced over my shoulder to see if the dryads had heard that. Since there was no sign of them appearing to demand every detail, I shut the door with my foot. I was carrying an oak sapling in an earthenware pot in both hands. I wasn't about to leave that outside overnight and find Frai and Asca asking awkward questions in the morning.

'I'll leave you to it.' Eleanor put her mug in the sink. 'Do let me know how you get on. And please wish your family a happy New Year from me,' she added to Fin as she left.

'Will do.' Fin came over to slide her arms around my waist and hug me. 'What time do you want to get on the road in the morning?'

'As early as possible.' There was no knowing how bad the holiday traffic might be, even with a few days to go before Christmas Eve.

Setting off early was definitely the right call. We got to Nether Cullen before lunchtime. The Buck in the Dale was bright with coloured lights and I saw a Christmas tree in the window as we got close. I'd only managed to book us a room for the night because Anne had had a last-minute cancellation. Thankfully someone was pulling out of the packed car park as we rounded the corner.

I slotted the Land Rover into the empty space. 'I never realised how many people like to go somewhere else for Christmas.'

'So someone else can do the cooking and washing-up.' Fin shrugged.

I looked at her. 'Dad and I will do all that.' Once we were done here, we'd be taking the Yorkshire dryad's tree to my mum's wood, making a quick stop at Blithehurst to collect Fin's car. We'd spend a couple of days with my dad, and leave the Land Rover there, since we didn't need to take a small tree with us when we went over to the Fens to see in the New Year.

I looked at the time. 'We're too early to check in, but we could get a coffee if you like?'

Fin leaned forward to look up at the sky. 'How about we go and see this dryad while the weather's still good?'

I wasn't about to argue. I wanted to hand over the oak sapling as soon as I could. It was a bitterly cold day, but it was dry, so the walk should be easy enough. 'Suits me.'

Fin swapped her trainers for her work boots. We both had decent coats and hats and gloves. Fin had kept her backpack with her on the journey, with water and fruit and biscuits in case we found ourselves stuck in a tailback. She slung that on her shoulders while I carefully got my mum's gift to the local dryad out of the back of the Landy.

If anyone in the village saw me carrying the small tree across the road to the waymarked footpath, they weren't curious enough to ask, or they didn't think it was any of their business. No one was out and about enjoying a bracing country walk either. Maybe the cold was putting them off. The grass was still white with frost where the stone walls still cast a shadow even this close to noon.

We hadn't seen anyone by the time we approached the MOD fence with those unmissable warning signs. There was nothing posted there to say we couldn't go any further. I had already checked the website. It seemed the army didn't schedule exercises to get squaddies tired, cold and wet in the week before Christmas. Once we were out of sight of the kissing gate, I stopped for a breather. Even a little sapling gets bloody heavy when you have to carry it that sort of distance.

Fin was looking around. 'Are you going to let her know we're here?'

I flexed my hand and told myself there was no reason to expect the same sort of shock if I tried to use the dryad radar. I was here by invitation this time.

'I'm glad to see you are a man of your word, Dan.' The dryad appeared, looking the same as she had when I'd met her before. 'May I know your name, Mistress Swan?'

'Finele, but everyone calls me Fin.' She offered her hand.

To my surprise, the dryad shook it. 'You may call me Eika. Both of you.'

I nodded. 'Thank you.'

Eika startled me with a sudden smile. Sinking into a crouch, she studied the little tree my mother had sent her. She ran her fingertips over each furled brown leaf and every centimetre of bark. I told myself it couldn't possibly have died while I'd been looking after it for barely more than twenty-four hours.

Eika stood up. 'Let us see her settled.'

JULIET E. MCKENNA

Before I realised what she was doing, she took one of my hands as well as Fin's. The bare winter trees around us shivered and blurred. A moment later, we were in a completely different part of the wood surrounded by a host of oak saplings. The dryad was on her knees, digging a hole with her bare hands. I couldn't have put a dent in this frozen earth if I'd had a pickaxe.

'Can we help?' Fin offered.

'No.' Eika wasn't being rude. She was simply completely focused on what she was doing.

Fin and I stood and waited while she transferred the little tree from its pot to the hole. She passed her hand over the soil and stood up. No one would ever have known that the ground had been disturbed. The dryad wasn't finished. She moved over to the particular seedling she had clearly chosen to send to my mother. She scooped it out of the ground together with plenty of soil. The ground closed up without leaving a mark. As Eika dropped her sapling into the empty earthenware pot, the earth flowed around the root ball as the little tree settled itself for its journey.

'Will that be okay if I leave it overnight in a vehicle?' I couldn't help being nervous. I knew how eagerly Mum was waiting for this to arrive. I didn't understand why and neither did Dad, and she wouldn't explain. 'We're not going back to my mother's wood until tomorrow.'

Eika wasn't concerned. 'All will be well.'

And then she vanished.

'Oh, that's just great.' Managing not to swear, I raised my voice. 'We need to get back to the footpath without standing on a grenade. We don't know the way.'

Vatne appeared. 'I'll show you. Once you tell me what has become of this cat.'

That was an offer we couldn't refuse. Not that I wanted to. Fin and I found a fallen tree to sit on and I brought the Yorkshire naiad fully up to date.

'Tell Kalei, if you see her.' Then I wouldn't have to go through everything yet again.

'Very well.' Vatne nodded, looking thoughtful. 'This way.'

She didn't say another word as she led us through the trees to the path. That suited me. I was concentrating on carrying the pot with the sapling safely. Fin was looking around at the sleeping woodland. Thankfully the official footpath wasn't too far away. We reached it without anyone getting a foot accidentally blown off.

Fin turned to the naiad. 'Why does Eika want to swap these young trees?'

It wouldn't have occurred to me to ask her.

Vatne laughed. 'You mean you don't know?'

She pointed back up the hill. I saw a dryad. Not Eika. A young dryad. The youngest I had ever seen, though no one would mistake her for a child. As soon as she realised we had seen her, she vanished.

'What the fuck?' I stared at Vatne. 'Why would my mum send her here? When she's been alone for so long—' I couldn't go on.

Vatne shook her head, reproving. 'Mothers and daughters, Daniel. You know how it is. Or if you don't, I'm sure Fin can tell you.'

She dissolved into mist that flowed away to join the river. I was ready to curse naiads and dryads alike. I looked at Fin instead. I couldn't work out what to say. I didn't know what to feel. I saw she was equally at a loss.

We started walking. What else was there to do? By the time we were approaching Nether Cullen, I was at least thinking sufficiently straight to concentrate on not being seen. The last thing I needed was some local asking what I was doing with an illegally uprooted tree. I put the little sapling in the back of the Landy and locked the door.

I looked at Fin. 'Lunch?'

She wasn't thinking about food. 'I'm sure your mum will explain everything when we see her. Try not to let it get to you. And you know, Dan, I've realised something. When I was listening to you go through everything that's happened this year, when you told Vatne about the cunning men... You haven't only sorted out what could have been a massive problem for so many of us. You're the only one who could have possibly done it.' She smiled. 'I'm so proud of you.'

I managed to smile back. 'Let's celebrate with some wine with our meal.'

Fin kissed me. 'That sounds like a plan.'

We went into the bar and found a table. I opted for the Christmas menu while Fin had something meat-free. To be honest, I wasn't paying much attention. While we ate, Fin tried to explain what she thought 'someone' might have meant when Vatne had said 'you know how it is with mothers and daughters'. And with sisters, come to that.

I did my best to listen, but I couldn't help thinking about what she had said in the car park. Fin was right. I had sorted out the problem that had brought me to Yorkshire in the first place, all those months ago when last winter was turning to spring. I hadn't done it alone though, and that was what I had missed.

The crucial point was I couldn't have done it alone. There was absolutely no way. I'd had all sorts of help from all sorts of folk. Folk who didn't know each other or didn't necessarily trust each other. I was the person they had in common. The mortal with a foot in both worlds who they owed some favour, or who could do something for them in return.

I wasn't about to claim any credit for that. I'd spent the past few years doing the Green Man's bidding, nothing more. Now though, I started to wonder if he'd had something like this in mind all along. Him and the Hunter, who was clearly getting involved as well.

The winter solstice marks the longest night of the year. I wondered what the returning sun was going to show me in the year to come.

Translations

For those who are curious, the Gaelic in this story translates as follows:

Dè tha sibh ag iarraidh sassenachs? – What do you want, English speakers?

Suidh sìos agus bi sàmhach – Sit down and be quiet

Èist rì Iain! – Listen to Iain!

An sgudal seo a-rithist – This rubbish again

Tha ciall aig man an craobhean – The son of trees speaks sense

Acknowledgements

My thanks, as always, go first to those who have been essential in bringing Dan and his adventures into print and pixels from the start. Cheryl Morgan and Wizard's Tower Press continue to be utterly splendid partners in this ongoing venture. As editor, Toby Selwyn is committed to keeping my writing up to the highest standards. Ben Baldwin has met the challenge of this book's cover with his customary brilliance.

For this particular story, a few decades of reading Tartan Noir crime novels could only take me so far. I am sincerely grateful to Shona Kinsella for her invaluable input as Scottish cultural consultant, and for the Gaelic that baffles Dan. Liz Williams answered my questions and supplied invaluable detail on protective ritual practice, for which she has my thanks. As always, any errors or inaccuracies are my responsibility alone.

I very much appreciate the invitation from Cymera 2023 to participate in their highly regarded Festival of Science Fiction, Fantasy and Horror Writing in Edinburgh, as I was able to combine that visit with a research trip/holiday in Argyll. I can recommend the west of Scotland as a vacation destination, while the Cymera festival is an excellent weekend of SFFH panel discussions, readings and a great deal more. Do go!

As social media fragments, and folk head in different directions, it's reassuring to find this series has keen readers on the various sites I'm now using. Thank you to everyone whose personal recommendations for these books brings new readers to the series from far and wide. As with so many other titles from small presses, we could not keep going without you.

JULIET E. MCKENNA

The SF community of readers, writers, booksellers, convention committees and other fan event organisers continues to sustain me with friendship, support and encouragement. Thank you, everyone.

About the Author

Juliet E McKenna is a British fantasy author living in the Cotswolds, UK. Loving history, myth and other worlds since she first learned to read, she has written fifteen epic fantasy novels so far. Her debut, *The Thief's Gamble*, began The Tales of Einarinn in 1999, followed by The Aldabreshin Compass sequence, The Chronicles of the Lescari Revolution, and The Hadrumal Crisis trilogy. *The Green Man's Heir* was her first modern fantasy inspired by British folklore, followed by *The Green Man's Foe, The Green Man's Silence, The Green Man's Challenge* and *The Green Man's Gift*.

Her 2023 novel *The Cleaving* is a female-centred retelling of the story of King Arthur, while her shorter stories include forays into dark fantasy, steampunk and science fiction. She promotes SF&Fantasy by reviewing, by blogging on book trade issues, attending conventions and teaching creative writing. As J M Alvey, she has also written historical murder mysteries set in ancient Greece.

For more, visit www.julietemckenna.com

The Tales of Einarinn

1. The Thief's Gamble (1999)
2. The Swordsman's Oath (1999)
3. The Gambler's Fortune (2000)
4. The Warrior's Bond (2001)
5. The Assassin's Edge (2002)

JULIET E. MCKENNA

The Aldabreshin Compass

    1. The Southern Fire (2003)

    2. Northern Storm (2004)

    3. Western Shore (2005)

    4. Eastern Tide (2006)

Turns & Chances (2004)

The Chronicles of the Lescari Revolution

    1. Irons in the Fire (2009)

    2. Blood in the Water (2010)

    3. Banners in The Wind (2010)

The Wizard's Coming (2011)

The Hadrumal Crisis

    1. Dangerous Waters (2011)

    2. Darkening Skies (2012)

    3. Defiant Peaks (2012)

A Few Further Tales of Einarinn (2012) (ebook from Wizards Tower Press)

Challoner, Murray & Balfour: Monster Hunters at Law (2014) (ebook from Wizards Tower Press)

Shadow Histories of the River Kingdom (2016)   (Wizards Tower Press)

The Green Man (Wizards Tower Press)

    1. The Green Mans Heir (2018)

    2. The Green Man's Foe (2019)

    3. The Green Man's Silence (2020)

    4. The Green Man's Challenge (2021)

    5. The Green Man's Gift (2022)

The Philocles series (as J M Alvey)

    1. Shadows of Athens (2019)

    2. Scorpions in Corinth (2019)

    3. Justice for Athena (2020)

    4. Silver for Silence (a dyslexia-friendly quick read, 2022)

The Cleaving (2023)

Printed in the USA
CPSIA information can be obtained
at www.ICGtesting.com
CBHW022358141223
2665CB00005B/333

9 781913 892647